THE SECRET HEALER SERIES

The
MASTER
of MEDICINE

ALSO BY ELLIN CARSTA

The Secret Healer

The Draper's Daughter

THE SECRET HEALER SERIES

The

*M*ASTER

of MEDICI*N*E

ELLIN CARSTA

TRANSLATED BY TERRY LASTER

amazoncrossing

Text copyright © 2016 Ellin Carsta

Translation copyright © 2017 Terry Laster
All rights reserved.

Previously published as *Die heimliche Heilerin und der Medicus* by Amazon Publishing in Germany in 2016. Translated from German by Terry Laster. First published in English by AmazonCrossing in 2017.

Published by AmazonCrossing, Seattle

www.apub.com

Amazon, the Amazon logo, and AmazonCrossing are trademarks of Amazon.com, Inc., or its affiliates.

ISBN-13: 9781503943988
ISBN-10: 1503943984

Cover design by Faceout Studio

Printed in the United States of America

I dedicate this book to Lianne Kolf, to whom I give my heartfelt thanks and a great big hug.

Prologue

Everything had to change . . . and he would make sure it did. Of course, there would be casualties. It was unfortunate but unavoidable. The time had come to do what was required. But still one thing bothered him: he wasn't sure whom to trust or who might betray him. He turned the vial between his fingers. He had to be absolutely certain before using it as the poison would take effect quickly. Brooding, he gazed at the small glass vessel. He heard a knock on the door.

"I'm coming," he called out. He hid the vial in his desk's secret compartment, undetectable unless one knew exactly where to look. He stood up and then leaned heavily on the table, weighed down by the responsibility of the decisions he'd had to make. A hard road ahead, but once it was all over, he'd lead the life that Almighty God had preordained for him. He felt it with every fiber of his being. Together, he and his Creator would restore the natural God-given order. After straightening his spine, he shuffled slowly toward the front door, squared his shoulders, and pulled it open. He was ready.

Chapter One

Cologne, 1395

"Mother, I'm going to be a barber-surgeon—the head of my guild!" Veit jutted out his chin proudly.

Madlen smiled as she tenderly patted her son's dark, curly locks. "Is that so? And here I'd thought you'd be a lawyer like your father."

The six-year-old shook his head resolutely. "No."

"So you want to learn the healing arts?" She felt a sense of pride that her son seemed to share her passion for healing.

He shook his head again, this time even harder. "No, I don't want to heal people. I want to cut hair."

"You want to do what?"

He held up a finger. "I'm very talented." He ran over to the staircase. "Come down, Cecilia."

Madlen looked up to see her daughter, almost five years old now, standing on the staircase landing. "Oh, my heavens!" She picked up her skirts and ran upstairs. "What happened to you?" Madlen squatted in front of her little girl and touched the dark stubble that only a few hours ago had been long, lush curls.

Cecilia shrugged. "Veit said I look much prettier now, much more grown-up."

"You don't like it?" Veit had stepped behind Madlen and now gazed at his mother with disappointment. "You never like anything I do."

"You can't cut your sister's hair!"

"But I worked so hard on it," Veit moaned.

Madlen sighed, then looked in bewilderment at the few pathetic strands hanging listlessly from her daughter's freshly shorn head. "Really, Veit, look at this!" She gave her son a withering look, her blue eyes burning with rage. "I can't take Cecilia anywhere now. This is simply horrible."

"You're mean."

"I don't want to hear one more word from you. How could you do this to your sister? Go to your bedchamber." Madlen's tone of voice was harsher than she'd intended.

"I look ugly now," Cecilia whined. As Veit stomped away, she broke out in tears.

Madlen took a deep, calming breath, then forced herself to smile. "Not at all. What are you talking about? You have such a beautiful face, you couldn't be ugly if you tried." She lightly touched the stubble on her daughter's head again, trying her best to disguise her despair. "We'll have to sew up a nice little bonnet for you to wear for a while."

"I want my curls back!" Cecilia's whole body shook as she sobbed.

Madlen put her arm around her daughter and pulled her close. "I know, little one." She stroked her daughter's back. "Promise me one thing: if your brother comes up with another one of his foolish ideas, do not let him do it. Do you hear me?"

"Yes, Mother." Cecilia continued to sniffle. "I still have the hair. Can't we just sew it back on like we do when we make clothes?"

3

Madlen shook her head. "Unfortunately, we won't be able to do that, little one." She got up. "Come on, let's look for some nice fabric that we can use for a bonnet. What do you say?"

Cecilia frowned but wiped away her tears and grabbed her mother's hand as they headed to the sewing room. Madlen stopped in front of Veit's bedchamber. "Please wait a moment."

She opened the door and saw Veit standing in front of the window, kicking at the wall.

"Come here, please."

Veit looked at his mother, then reluctantly obeyed her command.

"Do you understand why I'm so angry with you?"

He shook his head.

She knelt in front of him, looking at his face. "Really?" she asked softly.

He sighed.

"What?"

He looked at her teary-eyed but remained stubbornly mute.

"You have to ask me before you can use the scissors."

"But you wouldn't have let me."

"If you knew that, then you also knew very well what you did was wrong."

Veit felt cornered. "But I wanted to show everybody how well I can cut hair."

"And now, because of how she looks, people will talk about her behind her back and other children will laugh at her, which will humiliate your sister to no end."

"I'll punch whoever laughs at her."

"You'll do no such thing."

Veit sighed once again. He felt miserable. It was better when his mother had scolded him. But now, as she talked to him in a friendly and loving tone, guilt washed over him. "But I think she looks lovely."

"You do?"

He shrugged.

Madlen rose and offered him her hand. "Come on. Let's look for some pretty fabric so I can sew a nice bonnet for Cecilia."

At first he hesitated, but then he took her hand and trotted along next to his mother, well aware that he'd done wrong. When they joined Cecilia, someone knocked loudly on the front door. Madlen walked over to the balustrade to see Gerald opening it. She instantly recognized the visitor. "Agathe," she gasped. "Gerald, let her in."

The guard stepped aside to let the woman enter.

The visitor looked up, smiling broadly. "My Madlen!"

Madlen lavished kisses on Veit, then Cecilia, then ran downstairs as quickly as she could manage with her skirts. The women fell into each other's arms, their embrace lingering for several minutes. When they finally let go, they gazed at each other as Agathe stroked her niece's cheek tenderly. "It is wonderful to see you."

"I'm delighted to see you, too! But why didn't you send word that you were coming?"

"I've come to bring you some news," Agathe announced rather ominously. Before Madlen could inquire further, Agathe noticed the children who'd followed their mother downstairs.

"That can't possibly be Veit and Cecilia. They're so big!" Then Agathe paused, and Madlen noticed the perplexed look on her aunt's face. "What happened to her hair?" Agathe whispered.

"Later," Madlen whispered back, shaking her head and gesturing at the children now at her side.

Agathe crouched down. "Do you two remember me?"

Veit nodded eagerly, but Cecilia shyly hid behind her mother's full skirts.

"Veit, you're almost all grown. What a big boy! I hardly recognize you." Agathe tried to catch Cecilia's eye. "I'm your mother's aunt. It's been a while since we've seen each other. You don't remember me at all?"

Cecilia took in the visitor's face. She had only the vaguest memory of her, but because of her mother's obvious joy over the unexpected guest, she managed a smile. "Oh, I remember you now," Cecilia said, although she wasn't sure of it at all.

"Gerald, tell Ursel that we need her help," Madlen said as she led Agathe and the children into the large dining room, furnished with a long wooden table and ten chairs, common to most large houses in Cologne. The walls were decorated with tapestries; two silver candle-holders rested on the table.

"Much has changed since I was here last." Agathe looked around as they sat down at the table. "The time and effort you put into decorating your home is quite evident."

"Thank you. We feel so comfortable here. We use this room mainly to entertain guests or when Johannes needs a place to conduct business."

Ursel, the housekeeper, appeared and placed a tray on the table. She nodded at the visitor as she set a goblet in front of her, then handed the children two smaller ones. Finally, she set down a large wooden board piled high with ham and fresh bread.

"Thank you, Ursel." Madlen gave the housekeeper a warm smile. The maid smiled back, then vanished as quietly as she'd appeared.

"I can't tell you how happy I am that you've come. And I'm sure Johannes will feel the same way."

"Unfortunately, I've brought bad news," Agathe said.

Madlen glanced at her children. "You two, let me have a moment alone with Agathe. We haven't seen each other for a long time and have some grown-up things to discuss."

"But we were going to choose some fabric for my bonnet," Cecilia complained.

"We'll take care of that later." Madlen paused, mulling over her options. "Or better yet—tell Ursel to show you the fabrics in the sewing room."

"It's all right, Mother." Cecilia slid off her chair, a look of disappointment on her face. Madlen felt sorry for her daughter, but she had a strong suspicion the news couldn't wait.

Veit grabbed his sister by the hand. "Come, Cecilia. We're going to find some really beautiful fabric for you."

Madlen waited until the door closed behind them before looking at Agathe, who picked up her goblet and took a big gulp.

"What's happened?"

Agathe lowered her goblet. "I wish I had better news. You know that your mother-in-law and I have become very close over the last several years, and she sought me out to deliver this message. It's about Johannes's father."

"What's the matter with Peter?"

Agathe reached across the table and took Madlen's hand. "He's sick, my love, very sick."

A shiver ran down Madlen's spine. "What kind of illness does he have?"

"His eyesight . . . it's getting worse and worse with each passing day. It won't be long before he's completely blind."

Madlen put her free hand over her mouth, then dropped it to her lap. "That's horrible. Has he seen a doctor?"

"Yes, of course. Elsbeth said he told her that there's nothing he can do. Soon Peter won't be able to see anything at all, not even light."

Madlen's thoughts whirled around in her brain. Her father-in-law, with whom she'd never had a close relationship, was anything but delighted when Johannes chose her, of all people, to be his wife. Johannes had defied all convention to marry her. Unlike Elsbeth, Peter had never respected Johannes's decision but over time had begrudgingly accepted the fact that his son was marrying for love, not to improve his social standing, as was the custom of the day. Her father-in-law's attitude toward her hurt Madlen deeply. Despite his faults, he'd always taken care of his own. As far as Madlen knew, he had always been independent, a good provider, and careful to protect his family's reputation.

Her stomach felt like it was tied up in knots when she realized that things would be quite different from now on. "What did Elsbeth want you to tell us?"

Agathe looked down and sighed, then looked Madlen directly in the eyes. "Exactly what you've probably already guessed. Peter is in no condition to manage the office. Johannes will have to take over from here on out."

Madlen gasped, then pressed her lips together. Her blood ran cold at the thought of moving to Worms. She felt her throat constrict and her breathing become labored as bolts of fear shot through her. Agathe squeezed her hand sympathetically. "I know this must be hard for you. Your life is here in Cologne."

"We feel so at home here, you know?" Madlen said, her voice quivering.

"I understand that very well, but it is a son's duty to take over his father's business when he's unable to take care of it himself."

Madlen nodded. "We always knew this day would come. I'm so sorry that I—"

"Hush now," Agathe said. "I know how you feel. You don't need to apologize."

Madlen smiled gratefully. From the very beginning, Agathe had been there for her. Madlen had been forced to flee her hometown of Heidelberg because a vile man had accused her of a murder she didn't commit. Without hesitation, Agathe had taken her in when she had materialized at her doorstep in Worms, scared, starving, and penniless. Knowingly harboring a fugitive had put her warmhearted aunt in grave danger. And now here she sat, bringing her niece bad news with every bit of sympathy and understanding she could muster. When Madlen compared her own reaction to her aunt's unflinching expressions of kindness, she felt ashamed.

"I'll speak with Johannes as soon as he comes home. We'll make all the necessary arrangements."

Agathe nodded. "You're doing the right thing. Who knows why the Lord imposes these burdens upon us? But I'm quite certain there's always a reason."

As much as she loved her aunt, Madlen couldn't fathom a deeper meaning behind her father-in-law's illness. "Everything's going to be all right," she said after a pause. "Despite the terrible news, I'm always so happy to have you here." She stood. "Come. Let's go see what the children are up to. They finally have an opportunity to get to know you better. Where are your things?"

Agathe stood, too. "I just brought a small bundle. I have to go back to Worms tomorrow."

Madlen was disappointed. "I don't think we will be able to prepare so quickly for an extended stay in Worms. If we ever do get to return here." She straightened up as she tried to push away her feelings of dread. "Wouldn't it be better to wait so that we can travel together?"

Agathe looked doubtful. "I don't rightly know. I have to take care of my own obligations."

Madlen grasped her aunt's hands. "Oh, please. It would do me so much good. Just a couple of days, Agathe. I've missed you so."

Her aunt smiled. "With such a heartfelt request from my darling niece, I can't very well say no." The women embraced, and Madlen's anxiousness lessened considerably.

"Thank you so much. Come on, let's go see the children. Who knows what they're up to?" Madlen shook her head. "You've seen Cecilia's hair."

"Yes. What in the world happened?"

"Veit decided that he wants to be a barber-surgeon. The leader of his guild!" she said, dismay clearly evident in her voice. "He wanted to show off his talent by cutting Cecilia's hair."

9

"I see," Agathe said. She couldn't help but grin. "Now, in my opinion, he would do much better to follow in his father's footsteps or take over his grandfather's office. I would definitely advise against the profession of haircutting."

The women burst out laughing, and the tension eased a bit. After spending a little time with the children, Madlen's heart felt lighter, and she wasted no more time thinking about the move to Cologne or Peter's unfortunate illness. She was just happy to be with her aunt again.

Chapter Two

Madlen knew her husband was a master organizer, but she was still surprised at how quickly they prepared for their trip to Worms. Within a day, he'd made all the necessary arrangements for their departure, which would be less than two days after Agathe had arrived in Cologne.

It was hard on Johannes. As the archbishopric's only lawyer, he worked on official business for Friedrich III, the archbishop of Cologne, virtually nonstop. These were uncertain times, and Friedrich had a habit of offending high-ranking nobles. Rumors of a conspiracy against him abounded, though Johannes hadn't discovered anything concrete. Of course, the peace treaty with the House of von der Marck had been adhered to for three years now. But it was well known that many influential people accused the count from Cleves of making too many concessions.

Friedrich III, who'd held the office of the archbishop of Cologne for a quarter of a century, had worked for years to offset the huge deficits incurred by the mismanagement and plundering of the archbishopric by his predecessors Adolf and Engelbert. He succeeded with the support of his great-uncle Kuno, who tendered generous loans and helped to raise taxes to protect the archbishopric. On one hand, this had endeared him to the emperor, Karl IV, but it had also inspired ire in most of the nobility. For a short while after Karl's death in 1378, unrest had reared its ugly head. But Friedrich was wise enough to put a stop to it before things got out of hand. Nonetheless, the voices of those who opposed the archbishop had become impossible to silence.

Accordingly, Johannes's concern was not only for his official duties; he also took an interest in the archbishop's personal welfare. He frequently and painstakingly assessed the mood of the commoners in town as well as that of the nobles. Now, because of a private matter, he was forced to turn his back on Cologne and on his employer. And on top of that, he had no idea when or if he would ever return to the city. But he had no other choice.

Veit protested when his mother told him he had to ride with his father. "I'm big enough and grown-up enough to ride on a horse all by myself," he announced, but Madlen was too tense to entertain a discussion.

"You will ride with your father, and Cecilia will ride with me. And I don't want to hear another word about it," she said before Johannes had a chance to reprimand the boy. They helped their children onto the horses, then climbed up on their respective mounts and rode off, followed by Agathe, Gerald the guard, Ansgar the servant, and Ursel the housekeeper. In the convoy, three additional horses were loaded down with personal items and clothing. Hans, the other servant, stayed behind to maintain and protect the house. Madlen's heart raced as she imagined never seeing their home in Cologne again.

◆ ◆ ◆

They rode in silence for most of the first part of the trip. From time to time, Johannes attempted to break the silence. But even he got caught up in his own thoughts, worrying about what awaited them in Worms and how he should proceed. It was a heavy burden for him to bear.

After the long winter, plants had begun to timidly poke their little heads out of the still-cold ground. Madlen began to point out various animals and wild herbs to her daughter. She patiently explained the properties of each herb and how to use them to cure various ailments.

It warmed Agathe's heart to see her niece engaging Cecilia with her simple but detailed explanations. How she had wished for her own children over the years! But it was not to be. After her marriage to Reinhard, she'd all but forgotten the horrors of her past, willing herself to leave bad memories behind. But when, after more than a year of marriage, she was unable to get pregnant, the memories came back to haunt her. She'd finally admitted to herself that she'd been fooling herself and her husband, that that fateful night so long ago had destroyed too much, had robbed her of the life she'd always dreamed of. After realizing the sad truth, she'd been tempted to confide in her husband. But although she believed he was a good man, Agathe listened to a little voice inside her head that advised her against sharing the horrid details of her past with her spouse.

She recognized the wisdom of this decision when Reinhard came home one day and told her about a dispute between his good friend Klaus and his wife. Klaus was a fisherman just like Reinhard, and he had recently discovered that years ago his wife had been taken by a man, apparently against her will. Oh, the profanities Klaus had used! And Reinhard did the same, cursing Klaus's wife, calling her a worthless whore. For a short time, Agathe had dared to question him. She'd asked her husband if Klaus had wondered about the truth of his wife's tragic story, or if he'd simply dismissed it as a falsehood. Reinhard's scornful laugh was answer enough. In his opinion, most women were only too glad to give men what they wanted and then later claim to have been forced.

It was during this conversation that Agathe understood that she could never entrust her husband with the gory details of her past. Knowing that their future would be childless, she decided to convince him that the fault lay with him, yet she did not reproach him for it. For some reason, Reinhard believed her. At first, Agathe wrestled with her guilt about this lie, which invalidated her husband's virility as well as his fertility. But the weight on her conscience didn't last for very long. She came to despise the way Reinhard spoke about women who had been violated through no fault of their own. Soon it no longer bothered her that she had convinced him it was his fault her womb bore no fruit. She'd kept the secret until his dying day.

Still, the fact that she could not have children hurt her every day. Even now, as she observed Madlen and Cecilia chatting and giggling together, she was reminded of what she'd wanted most in life. Just thinking about it put a knot in her chest.

"Isn't that right, Agathe?"

She'd been so deep in thought, Agathe hadn't noticed that Madlen had been speaking to her. "Forgive me. What did you say?"

"That there was a time when those plants over there"—she pointed at a green-and-yellow clump of vegetation—"were used to cure many Worms residents of a terrible cough." Madlen studied her aunt for a moment. "Are you feeling ill?"

"Oh, I'm fine," Agathe responded, a little too quickly. She noticed Cecilia's bonnet had slipped back a bit, allowing a bit of her freshly shorn head to show. She said to the little girl, "I was just thinking about when your mother lived with me in Worms. Those were frightening yet extraordinary days. She helped so many people. To this day, the whole city talks about her, even though she hasn't lived there in well over seven years."

"We both helped," Madlen corrected, "but you are right, in many ways it was a stressful time. But living and working together at your house was simply wonderful." She lovingly squeezed her daughter's shoulder. "It was then that I met your father."

"I can't hear you very well," Veit complained, turning around in his saddle and leaning past his father to look back at them.

"Agathe and I were just talking about the wonderful time we spent together in Worms before you and Cecilia were born," Madlen called out.

Veit shrugged and turned back around. Evidently, he'd thought he was missing out on a more exciting story.

"Certainly there will be a lot of work for you once we arrive," Agathe said, as her and Madlen's horses trotted side by side. "If you like, I will gladly take care of the children. I could show them the city."

"Oh, yes, Mother," Cecilia said. "That would be lovely. Please say yes."

Madlen kissed the back of her daughter's head. Cecilia cuddled up closer to her. "It's so sweet of you to offer, Agathe. You two don't need to persuade me at all. I would have asked you anyway."

Agathe smiled. "I am just glad we can find a silver lining in these difficult circumstances."

"What's so difficult?" Cecilia asked.

"As I already explained to you," Madlen said, "your grandfather is very sick. That's the reason we're going to Worms. Your father must take over your grandfather's merchant business."

"Oh! Well, it doesn't matter to me whether we live in Cologne or in Worms." Cecilia hesitated. "Mother?"

"Yes, little one."

"I don't remember Grandfather at all, just Grandmother. Is that bad?"

"No, my beloved. You'll get to know your grandfather in due time." Madlen tried to sound cheerful. It was no wonder that her daughter could barely remember him. In the years since Cecilia's birth, her grandparents had visited only once, and only because Peter was developing a business relationship with a nobleman who lived in Cologne and Elsbeth had insisted on accompanying him. Madlen knew Peter had been in Cologne other times on business but had never visited his son's family. And, to be honest, that didn't bother her one bit. Because Madlen's children were so young, it hadn't been practical for her to undertake the long journey to Worms, so she was grateful when Elsbeth found time to visit without her husband or made the effort to keep in contact by post.

"How much longer before we're in Worms?"

Johannes heard his daughter's question and turned around in the saddle to answer. "We just started riding. We'll take a short rest when we get close to Siegburg, and then we'll ride on to Uckerath. From there we'll make our way to Altenkirchen, where we'll spend the night."

"That sounds terribly far away," Cecilia said.

"So then will we reach Worms tomorrow?" Veit asked.

"No, not yet. Altogether, this trip will take four days," Johannes stated.

Cecilia had already fallen asleep in her mother's embrace by the time they reached Altenkirchen, just before the city gates closed. They had remained on the wide trade route, encountering several small groups of travelers along the way. Only after they'd ridden into the safety of the city limits did Madlen feel the strain she'd endured all day begin to melt away.

They found simple accommodations in an inn. The children stayed with Johannes and Madlen in their room. Agathe offered to share her room with Ursel, who thanked her for her friendliness and generosity. Ansgar and Gerald bedded down in the stables.

They all rode out before dawn. Veit could barely keep his eyes open. When Johannes mounted their horse, Veit leaned back and instantly went back to sleep. But Cecilia was wide awake and chatted amiably with her mother and Agathe.

They rode past Hachenburg and through Höchstenbach and Freilingen. They stopped to rest when they reached Wallmerod.

"How much longer must we ride?" Cecilia asked, starting to show signs of exhaustion. "I can barely sit one moment longer."

"It won't be long until we're in Malmeneich, and after that we'll be in Elz. Then it's only a short way to Limburg, where there's a cathedral and a castle," Johannes said in an attempt to lift his daughter's sagging spirits. "You will be so amazed!"

"But I don't want to see a castle," Cecilia said, pouting.

"I do," Veit said. "Are we going to sleep in the castle?"

"No, my son. It's reserved for the counts. But we'll find a good inn and eat so much our bellies will get this fat." Johannes stretched his arms in a semicircle out in front of him.

"So we will reach Worms tomorrow?" Cecilia persisted.

"The day after tomorrow," Johannes said.

Cecilia rolled her eyes. "I'd rather go back to Cologne."

"Believe me, we'll be in Worms before you know it."

When they mounted their horses again after a short rest, Cecilia leaned against her mother, closed her eyes, and fell asleep. When Madlen woke her up, they had reached Limburg.

During the third day of their journey, they made slow progress because the children frequently insisted on dismounting. At the foot of Kirberg Castle they rested and ate, then started in the direction of Wiesbaden. They were able to cross the Rhine in Mainz-Kastel that same day. Upon their arrival on the other side, they bedded down in a decent inn and fell fast asleep. They reached Worms the next day.

Shortly after they passed through the city gates, Agathe said good-bye and rode on to her own house. Madlen promised to follow her as soon as they greeted Elsbeth and Peter and assessed the situation.

A strange feeling crept over Madlen as they walked their horses up to her in-laws' house. Johannes rode beside his wife, worry written in the lines on his face. He looked at her and tried to smile before halting his horse in front of his parents' house. Ansgar dismounted his own horse and hurried over. He held his arms up. "Come on, Veit. Come on down to me."

Johannes lifted his son and deposited him into Ansgar's waiting arms. Then he swung himself off his saddle and stepped over to Madlen and Cecilia's horse to help his daughter down. After he helped his wife dismount, they both paused for a moment. Madlen stroked her husband's cheek. "We've overcome so much together over the years. Together we'll overcome this, too." He kissed her softly. Then Madlen took their children's hands and climbed the steps to the house, Johannes behind them. Ursel, Gerald, and Ansgar stayed below with the horses. Before Madlen could knock, the door swung open.

"Madlen! Johannes! Thank the Lord!" Elsbeth stepped outside and embraced Madlen, then Johannes and the children.

"It's so wonderful to see you, Elsbeth."

"Come in, come in!" Elsbeth noticed the small group standing with the horses at the foot of the steps.

"Wendel, show the Cologners where the stalls and the servants' quarters are."

"Yes, my lady." The servant, who'd been standing behind Elsbeth in the hall, walked past her and went down the stairs as Johannes, Madlen, and the children entered the house.

Madlen looked at her mother-in-law. "You look pale."

Elsbeth embraced her daughter-in-law again. She could no longer hold back her tears. "I'm so happy you're here." She released Madlen, then pointed upstairs. "Peter is lying in his bedchamber. He doesn't want to see anybody. I'm at the end of my rope."

"I'll take care of everything, Mother," Johannes said firmly. Only Madlen knew him well enough to hear the slight tremor in his voice.

Elsbeth continued to sob. "I'm so sorry. I've tried everything, and I've held on as long as I could."

"It was good that you sent Agathe," Johannes declared. "Now we're here, and we will make everything right."

"Thank you." Elsbeth looked at the floor; she seemed ashamed that she had to rely upon her son so much.

"And here are two little ones who want to tell you everything that's happened since they saw you last," said Madlen, nudging Cecilia and Veit forward.

After wiping away her tears, Elsbeth scrutinized her grandchildren. "What in the world happened to your hair?" she asked Cecilia.

"As you can see, a lot has happened," Madlen said, satisfied that she'd distracted her mother-in-law from her woes, at least momentarily. "The fact that your grandson would like to become a famous barbersurgeon is one of the many exciting things you can catch up on with the children." She winked at Elsbeth and was relieved when a smile spread across her mother-in-law's face.

◆ ◆ ◆

"Father?" Johannes entered the dark bedchamber, weakly lit by a small tallow candle on a chair near the bed. The room reeked of alcohol and human sweat, the odor stronger and more sour the nearer Johannes drew to the bed.

The room was silent except for the barely perceptible sound of low moaning.

"Father?" he repeated.

"Johannes?"

"Yes, Father. It's me."

Peter huffed. "It's about time."

Johannes sat down carefully on the edge of the mattress. "How are you, Father?"

"How should I be?" Peter spit out. "The Lord is taking away my eyesight, every day a little more. He's punishing me and I don't know why. I'm lying here and slowly rotting away. That's how I'm doing."

The stench of alcohol hit Johannes with even greater force as his father spoke. The younger man could certainly understand his father's bitterness, but the drinking made the situation worse for his mother, and that infuriated him.

"I'm here to help now," Johannes said.

"Now, yes!" Peter railed. "Where were you before now? With your archbishop, the oh-so-important Friedrich. And what about me? I am your father. You are my flesh and blood. It was your duty to stand by me when there was something to stand by. Now business has ground to a halt, and who knows how long before we have to sell off everything we own to the first scoundrel that comes along."

"We came as soon as we got the news."

"Pah! Your place should have always been here, in Worms. You should have managed my office like every other son does for his father. But you just had to be something bigger and better—a lawyer for the archbishop, no less! On top of that, you just had to marry a woman who could not be any lower in social standing. What kind of son does that?"

Johannes stood. "I'm glad to see you again, too, Father. Now, I must devote myself to the many tasks at hand."

"I need some more schnapps. Tell your mother to bring me some more schnapps."

Without another word, Johannes stepped away from the bed.

"Did you hear me, you good-for-nothing? I need some more schnapps!" Peter flung the empty bottle at his son, but with his poor eyesight he missed his intended target. Johannes stood perfectly still, burning with rage but forcing himself to stay calm. He bent down, picked up the empty bottle, and left the room, closing the door behind him.

Outside the room, he leaned against the wall for a moment and took long, deep breaths. He'd never had an especially good relationship with his father, and he knew that would never change. He was suddenly filled with anxiety. His father had once been a rich man. Was it true that the business was failing? With the considerable investments his family had made during its most prosperous times, it would take more than one short stretch of inactivity to lose everything, wouldn't it? Johannes decided to check the books at the first opportunity, to see how things really stood.

He also needed to think about the possibility of returning to his real job in Cologne. He knew that he needed to give the archbishop a definitive time frame. Though His Excellency Friedrich III had been sympathetic to his situation, Johannes knew the archbishop's kindness had its limits. The archbishop needed a lawyer he could rely on, and if Johannes was gone too long, His Grace would undoubtedly find somebody to take his place. And all this trouble because of a business Johannes didn't want to begin with, which, to add insult to injury, evidently stood at the brink of bankruptcy. He might even be forced to invest his own hard-earned money to make it financially viable again.

Johannes pushed off the wall and went downstairs. The cheerful voices of his children filtered out from the dining room; upon entering, he immediately noticed the beseeching look on his mother's face. "Well?"

He held up the empty bottle. "He wants more schnapps."

"All right." Elsbeth sprang up.

"Sit down, Mother. He can drink water or watered-down spiced wine."

"He'll be beside himself!"

Johannes smiled, but he was anything but happy. "Then I'll go back upstairs and calm him down." His eyes fell upon Veit and Cecilia, who had evidently noted the cheerful mood was shifting. "What are you two playing with there?" Johannes asked, warmth returning to his voice.

"Grandmother gave us these figurines to play with. We get to keep them."

"You don't say!" Johannes teased, putting his hands on his hips.

"Why not? You liked to play with them when you were a child. That's what Grandmother told us."

"Exactly right. Those are mine. And I'm not sharing."

Madlen suppressed a grin.

"Oh, please, Father. Please, please!" Cecilia went over to her father, who bent down on one knee so he could look directly into her eyes.

"You wouldn't even play with them anyway," Veit said.

"But what if we gave you a great big hug?" Cecilia suggested. "One so tight that you couldn't even breathe? Then could we keep the figurines?"

Johannes shrugged. "Who knows? I would think it over, at the very least."

Before he'd even finished the sentence, Cecilia had put her arms around her father and hugged him as tightly as she could. Veit marched over and did the same. Johannes embraced them both, then released them and stood up. "You win. I accept my defeat and declare you both the new owners of the figurines."

The children raised their arms in triumph. Madlen smiled, and Johannes looked at her and winked. Every day with him was a good one. She knew there was nothing and no one who could come between them and their happiness, no matter what trials and tribulations life presented.

"It's so wonderful to have you here," Elsbeth said. "This house felt so dreary, but now, because of you all, it is coming back to life."

"I will take care of everything, Mother. First thing I need to do is go to the office and take a look at the books."

"Helene will be serving our evening meal soon," Elsbeth said.

"Let me know when it's ready. I'm famished."

"We will."

"Good." Johannes started to walk in the direction of the office. He could hear his father hollering for more schnapps from upstairs. "I'll go tell Father that he'll be getting diluted spiced wine from now on."

"He won't like that, believe me," Elsbeth warned.

"I don't like everything that's going on here, either," Johannes responded. "He wants me to take on all of this responsibility, to become the man of this house. This is what I'm trying to do—whether he likes *how* I do it is of little concern to me."

With that, he climbed the stairs, taking his own sweet time despite Peter's increasingly loud screaming and swearing. Madlen and Elsbeth followed him, stopping at the bottom of the stairs and looking anxiously after him. He'd hardly entered the bedchamber when Peter's furious bellowing ceased. The women waited expectantly until Johannes appeared at the top of the stairway.

"What did you do?" Elsbeth asked, her voice trembling.

Johannes came down with a spring in his step. "I told him I expected him to behave in a manner befitting his honorable status."

Elsbeth raised her eyebrows. "That's it? That's what calmed him down so quickly?"

Johannes jumped off the last step and strolled over to the two women. "Exactly. I told him that if he didn't pull himself together immediately, then he wouldn't get one more sip of anything except water. That seemed to motivate him." Johannes pointed upstairs. "Do you hear? He's waiting patiently—and quietly—for his watered-down spiced wine. Would you ask Helene to bring it up to him?"

Elsbeth didn't know whether to be relieved or dismayed. She knew her son; he could be quite persuasive and often sharp-tongued. She wasn't sure she liked how he put his own father in his place. On the other hand, she hoped that he could get Peter to listen to reason.

Johannes seemed to read her mind. "I wasn't rude, Mother, just adamant. He's not himself at the moment, and I had to make him see that. We just have to wait a couple of days until his head clears. By that time, I'll have a better idea of how to proceed."

Madlen patted Elsbeth's arm. "We know this isn't easy for you, but you must trust your son. He'll set things right."

"You two are a gift from heaven!" Elsbeth exclaimed. "I'll tell Helene to bring Peter some diluted wine." She paused. "Actually, on second thought, it would be better if I go myself. It's time for the two of us to confront the reality of this situation."

Johannes laughed. "I expected nothing less from you, Mother." He kissed her on the forehead, then headed down the hall to the office and closed the door behind him.

◆ ◆ ◆

After Helene set the meal on the dining room table, Elsbeth got up to fetch her son. She knocked on the office door, then stepped in. She found Johannes bent over the books, a serious expression on his face. "Dinner is served."

He lifted his head with a start, as if he hadn't heard her coming in. "What did you say?" He shook his head. "Dinner, yes. Please, forgive me. Would it be too much to ask to be excused? I have quite a bit of work here, and I won't be finished for a while."

"Is it that bad?"

Johannes rubbed his eyes. "I'm not going to lie to you, Mother. Father's business wasn't in good shape, even before his illness."

"It wasn't?" Elsbeth stepped closer and took a seat on one of the two chairs placed in front of the desk. "But before your father became ill, he was traveling constantly on business, more than he'd ever done. And he told me he was making substantial profits."

Johannes could see from the books that Peter had actually closed a lot of business deals. It also seemed that he'd been spending money hand over fist. Johannes couldn't prove it, but he surmised that much of the money had been spent at taverns or brothels.

"It looks as though some of his business contracts didn't pan out as well as he'd wished. He didn't tell you, so as not to upset you," Johannes said, purposely being vague. "The fact is that we hardly have enough money to get through the next few weeks if we don't stir up some business and quickly."

Elsbeth covered her mouth with her hand. "My Lord, that's terrible. Then let's stir up some business immediately."

"I'll do my best, but it's not going to be so easy."

"Why not?"

"The counting house and the warehouse are both as good as empty. We have no money, no spices, no cloth, and no other goods to sell."

"What?" she shrieked.

"I'm sorry, Mother. I wish I had better news."

"What are we going to do now?"

Johannes leaned back in his chair and took a deep breath. "I don't know." He immediately regretted his words when he saw the look of desperation on his mother's face. "Not yet anyway," he added, then stood up. "You know, I changed my mind. I will join you and the others for dinner. It will be a nice distraction, which almost always brings me closer to a viable solution; I also think better on a full stomach."

He walked around the desk, took his mother's arm, and gently helped her up. They left the office to join the others.

◆ ◆ ◆

Johannes told Madlen everything that evening once they were in their bedchamber. They'd plopped down on the bed, Madlen cuddling up close to her husband and laying her head on his chest.

"What are you going to do now?" she said.

"At first I thought of riding back to Cologne and cashing in our savings so that we can buy some merchandise and get my father's trade going again. But when I reexamined the numbers, I realized even that would not suffice, even if we invested every penny we ever saved over the years." He sighed. "I think we're going to have to take out a loan."

"And from whom would we borrow these funds?"

"As you know, my father has a seat on the city council. I'll make his friends there aware of the situation."

"You would be in debt to the city?"

"I don't think we have any other choice."

"And you believe that you'll be able to do all that? I mean, it's been a long time since you've worked in the merchant trade."

"A lawyer understands enough about business to run a merchant trade."

"You sound so cavalier." Madlen gave him a friendly poke on the shoulder.

"Unfortunately, I don't feel so cavalier. I'm just trying to keep my chin up."

"And if things don't work out, will you close the office and take your parents with us to Cologne instead? You can go back to your real job rather than managing this failing business that you never wanted in the first place. We would all be able to live off what you earn from the archbishop."

"Good idea. I've thought about that, too. But that would kill my father and break my mother's heart." Johannes sighed.

"So, you would give up your own life so that your parents could continue theirs and save their reputation?"

"Yes, I probably would."

"I was afraid you'd say that." Madlen paused for a moment. "Would you mind if I asked for Agathe's help? She has good contacts in Worms and knows a lot about the merchant trade."

"Thank you. That's just the kind of help I need right now." Johannes pulled his wife closer and kissed her, soft and tenderly at first and then with growing passion. Soon he began to untie the ribbons at the neck of her nightgown.

"Hold on a minute! I thought your head was filled with worry."

"All the more reason to . . ."

Madlen smiled at him seductively. "In that case, I will do my part, whatever the cost." She laughed.

"A truly courageous wife," Johannes said, pulling her closer and putting his lips to her neck.

Chapter Three

First thing the next morning, Johannes went to the courthouse to ask for an emergency meeting with the city councilmen. After the message was relayed by the mayor's messengers, sixteen councilmen agreed to meet him.

Johannes was stunned by the reaction of the councilmen when he introduced himself and made his request. It appeared that the high lords and his father's supposed friends were not, in fact, sympathetic to him at all. Johannes soon learned that Peter had accumulated a considerable amount of debt. Most of the councilmen had lost patience with him long ago, after they'd repeatedly insisted on repayment to no avail.

Johannes's revelation that his father was going blind did not evoke the least bit of empathy from the high lords. Even worse, several of them did not mince words as they launched into a tirade, calling Peter Goldmann an infamous womanizer who had ruined his reputation long ago with his propensity for alcohol. Johannes was horrified. This scandalous version of his father was so completely different from what he had believed about him all these years.

When he walked out of the meeting room, Johannes felt more miserable than ever. Nobody in the city would lend Peter Goldmann one red cent, there was no doubt about that. And more alarming still,

Johannes's own honor had been tarnished. As he left the town hall, he overheard some of the lords talking about him, saying that the archbishop of Cologne had somehow developed a deft hand with money, which clearly explained why he'd chosen Peter Goldmann's son as his lawyer and confidant.

Johannes stumbled through the streets of Worms in a daze. Since he was his father's son, they took him for a swindler, a liar, and a witless windbag. What humiliation! He had no desire to spend another second in this city.

Johannes angrily slammed the door to his parents' home when he entered. He felt like a beaten-down dog.

"What happened?" Madlen had been chatting with Helene in the dining room; she hurried over to her husband when she heard the door slam.

"Where is my mother?"

"She's taken the children to Agathe's. Oh, my heavens, Johannes, you're scaring me. What happened? Please tell me!"

"We're going back to Cologne today. Inform the servants."

"What? But we can't just simply—"

"We can and we will," Johannes interrupted. "I will not stay one more day in a city where it's a disgrace to be Peter Goldmann's son!"

Madlen stepped closer and took her husband's hands. "Johannes, I'm begging you to tell me what happened," she said, despair in her voice.

Willing himself to slow his breathing, Johannes let his shoulders drop. "It was an absolute nightmare, Madlen."

"What happened?"

"Let's go into the office. I have to sit down."

The couple walked into the office, then plopped down on the chairs in front of the desk. Madlen held Johannes's hands as he told her what had played out at the courthouse. She nodded time and again, trying to maintain control over her own mounting fear.

"If the archbishop of Cologne ever gets wind of this, our family will be ruined. And all because my father has gone from being a successful businessman to a whore-mongering drunkard," he said finally.

Madlen took a moment to sort out her thoughts. "How can we stop Friedrich from finding out? If we return to Cologne and you take up your duties again, it will only be a matter of time before somebody tells him what your father's done."

"I'm sure I'll figure it out somehow."

Madlen shook her head. "The Wormsers most certainly have a record of your father's debts. And one of his creditors will tell Friedrich that you stood before the council to ask for help. Then he will ask you why you didn't tell him yourself."

Johannes was silent, at a loss for words.

"There's only one solution: ride back to Cologne and speak with the archbishop. Ask for his help. He's rich and he trusts you. If he hears about the situation from your own lips, he will take it as a sign of good faith and stand by you. He won't blame you—your appearance in front of the Worms city council proves that you knew nothing about your father's debts or disgraceful behavior."

Johannes thought it over for a moment. "You're right," he said. "I must go back to Cologne to speak with Friedrich."

Madlen nodded. "There's no other way, if you don't want the family to be destroyed."

"Whose family would be destroyed?" Elsbeth stepped into the doorway.

Johannes stood up and went over to her. "Mother, please sit down for a moment. We must speak with you."

Elsbeth nervously pressed her lips together and followed her son to the chair he'd just gotten up from.

"Listen to me carefully, Mother. We have no time to lose," Johannes said, leaning against the desk.

Johannes explained what had occurred, and he told her that he had to leave for Cologne as soon as possible to prevent something even worse from happening. Elsbeth seemed unusually calm, nodding pensively several times. She finally reached for Madlen's hand. "What about you and the children?"

"We'll stay here and await Johannes's return. He'll be able to cut his travel time in half by not dragging us along."

"What can we expect from the creditors when you're gone?" Elsbeth asked her son.

"Frankly, I don't know. My appearance before the council confirmed what they already knew anyway: that they might never get their money back. It's possible, even probable, that they will pay you a visit here in the next few days."

"I'll speak with the servants. Henceforth, Gerald will keep watch at the door," Madlen said. "We'll let the children stay with Agathe for the time being." She looked at her mother-in-law. "It would probably be prudent for you to stay at Agathe's house, too. You'll be safer there."

Elsbeth patted Madlen's hand. She looked between her daughter-in-law and her son and back again. "Please believe me. I had no idea about any of this."

"We believe you," Madlen said.

"We have no time to lose." Johannes stood and left the office. "Ansgar, saddle up my horse!" he yelled.

"Yes, my lord!" the servant's voice called back from the other end of the house.

Madlen stood and followed after her husband to the foyer. "At least take Ansgar with you so you won't be completely unprotected."

Johannes pulled her into his arms. "He'll only slow me down. I'll be much faster if I go it alone."

"But—"

Johannes silenced her with a kiss.

"You'll have to manage my parents' house until I get back. Promise me that if the creditors come to the door, you'll tell them that I am getting their money and will be back in a few days. That should calm them down."

"Yes, I promise."

"I'll just throw on a coat and go. If Helene could prepare me some food, I won't have to stop."

"I'll take care of it," Elsbeth said. She'd been following their conversation; now she stepped past them and rushed over to the kitchen.

"I'm worried, Johannes."

"I know." He kissed his wife again, tenderly. "I'll be back as quickly as possible."

Madlen held him close; a minute longer, and she wouldn't have been able to hold back her tears. Johannes gently eased out of the embrace. "I'll get my coat now." He looked upstairs. "But maybe first I'll go up to that drunkard's bedchamber and punch him in the face."

Madlen wasn't sure whether this was a real threat. She watched her husband nervously as he tromped upstairs. She was quite relieved when, moments later, he hurried back downstairs, his coat slung over his arm.

"Your horse is ready, my lord." Ansgar had stepped inside the hall adjacent to the inner courtyard.

"My thanks."

"And here are your provisions for the journey." Elsbeth came out from the kitchen and handed her son a bundle.

"Thank you. I'm certain that Helene prepared something delicious as usual." He tried to smile but couldn't quite bring himself to do it. He embraced and kissed Madlen again. "Take good care of the children! I'll be back before you know it. And then everything will be as it should."

"I know." Madlen tried to exude confidence. "I'll tell the children you said good-bye and that you'll be back soon."

Johannes bade farewell to his mother, then started to walk down the hall. He stopped and turned around. "One more thing." He pointed upstairs. "He'll be drinking nothing but water, no matter how much he screams and shouts and fusses and fights. If you must, lock the door to his bedchamber. He gets water, nothing more. Wine and schnapps have brought enough shame on this family."

"So be it," his mother said. She took Madlen's hand as if to steady herself.

It seemed as if Johannes had something more to say, but instead he simply waved good-bye. Madlen stared at the empty hallway for a few moments. He had gone. Just like that. She was possessed by an overwhelming fear that this might be the last time she'd ever see her husband.

"Come on," Elsbeth said, pulling her out of her thoughts of doom and gloom. "We must get out of this house. Otherwise I'll go insane. Let's go to Agathe's." She gripped Madlen's shoulders and pushed her toward the door. Too stunned to resist, the younger woman started to move. But the ominous feeling she had about her husband's departure remained.

◆　◆　◆

"Please, Agathe, you have to tell me the truth. Did you know about this?" Elsbeth looked at her pleadingly.

Madlen's aunt shifted in her seat. This line of questioning made her feel quite uncomfortable. What could she say without provoking criticism or offending? "I heard gossip now and then," she admitted. "But there's always gossip; that's just what people do."

"What are people saying?" Elsbeth persisted, her expression cold.

"Why do you want to torment yourself like this? The truth has already come out, and that's bad enough. Why do you want to do this to—"

"What are people saying?"

"They say that Peter is a skirt-chaser and that he paid well for it, if he had to. He also procured the necessary herbs and potions if a girl became pregnant by him." Agathe sighed.

Elsbeth closed her eyes, obviously choking back her tears. Madlen glared at her aunt.

"She insisted on hearing what was said! Don't look at me like that. I don't deserve anybody's reproach."

Elsbeth opened her eyes. "I'm not reproaching you. It's just that I'm dismayed that you never told me, despite the deep friendship we've developed over the years."

Agathe bowed her head. "I came close to telling you many times. But then I thought it was none of my business, and I didn't want to hurt you. Besides, I had no idea how you'd take it." She reached for Elsbeth's hand. "I do not want to lose your friendship."

"I understand," Elsbeth said. "And I probably would have done the same thing in your position."

"What are you going to do now?"

"I can't do anything. Everything is in Johannes's and the archbishop's hands now. Let's pray that Friedrich doesn't blame Johannes for what his father did."

"I know Friedrich," Madlen said. "He's an intelligent and sensible man. He has succeeded where so many others have failed: he freed the diocese of its debts. If anybody knows about indebtedness, it's him."

Suddenly there was a racket at the front door. "Roswitha must be back with the children," Agathe said. "I promised I'd take them to the harbor later. Do you want to come along?"

"We might as well, since we can't really do anything while we're waiting for Johannes to return. The question is whether we can leave Peter alone for so long," Madlen said.

"I'm too outraged to waste another thought on my husband!" Elsbeth blurted out. "And I'm not ready to go home to creditors waiting at my door."

"Then stay here," Agathe said. "Helene will take care of Peter. He doesn't deserve any more care than that after what he's done to you. You'll have some peace and quiet here and, most importantly, the children will not be exposed to any of this foolishness."

As if on cue, Cecilia and Veit barged in. "Mother! We went to the market with Roswitha. Look, she bought us some candied fruit."

"Candied fruit?" Madlen threw Agathe a look.

"Yes, I gave her permission to do so," the aunt confessed. "So what? I see them both so rarely that I can't help but spoil them a bit."

"Your mouth is smeared with sweets." Madlen took out a handkerchief and handed it to Veit.

Veit wiped his face. The stickiest parts stubbornly remained.

"Are we going to the harbor soon, Aunt Agathe? Please?" Cecilia crawled up onto her great-aunt's lap. Agathe pulled the little girl close.

"Of course. I promised you both we would." She looked at Madlen uncertainly.

"And Grandmother and I will come, too," Madlen declared.

"Really?" Cecilia said excitedly.

"But first you have to go wash your face."

"Come on, Veit," Cecilia said as she loosened herself from Agathe's embrace and slipped off her lap. Her brother followed without objection.

"Your children are simply amazing." Agathe watched them as they raced toward the washroom.

"So true," Elsbeth agreed. "They've brought the house back to life." She wrung her hands. "I only regret the terrible circumstances that brought them here."

"Don't even think about that," Madlen told her. "I have no doubt that Johannes will convince Friedrich. And then everything will be all right again."

Elsbeth gratefully regarded her daughter-in-law. "Let's go to the harbor with the children. A little fresh air will do all of us good."

◆ ◆ ◆

"So you see that fisherman's boat there?" Agathe pointed. Cecilia and Veit followed her outstretched arm with their eyes, then nodded eagerly. "That used to belong to us."

"You had a boat?" Veit was impressed.

"Yes, that's right. My late husband was a fisherman."

"So why are you a seamstress now?"

Agathe smiled good-naturedly. "Because the Good Lord gave me a special talent for trade, and the guild allowed me to practice. I am a fortunate woman."

"What's a guild, Agathe?" Cecilia asked.

"Well, it's a kind of union of men that ensures that the merchant trade and skilled craftsmen flourish and prosper in our beautiful city."

"That's really nice of those men to take care of things like that," Cecilia said.

Agathe smiled. "Yes, little one, I couldn't agree more. That's really nice of them."

"Madlen?"

Everyone turned in the direction of the voice. A woman rushed toward them.

"It's really you! My Lord, it's really you!"

"Otilia!" Madlen exclaimed.

The two women embraced. "I had no idea you were in Worms. What a pleasant surprise!"

"It's wonderful to see you, Otilia. How are you?"

"Excellent. And my daughter, Reni, too." Otilia greeted Elsbeth and Agathe, then looked at the children.

Madlen followed her gaze. "Otilia, this is my son, Veit, and my daughter, Cecilia."

Veit tried to remember how to behave toward a stranger, especially one that was so fancy and well dressed. He finally decided to bow, and his little sister curtsied. Madlen looked on, nearly bursting with pride.

"The last time I saw you, you were just a young maiden. And now you're a mother! How time flies. You look happy, Madlen. And there is no one in the world who deserves happiness more than you." Otilia leaned down to address the children. "Do you know that your mother is a great woman? Years ago, she saved my daughter Reni's life. And today my Reni is a mother herself! She has given me the most charming grandson."

Cecilia looked up at her mother. "What did you do, Mother?"

"Do you remember the herbs I pointed out on the way here? They helped cure Reni from a terrible cough."

"That's really nice of the herbs," Cecilia said.

Veit shuffled his feet impatiently. "Can we go now, Mother?"

"Yes, Veit. Soon."

"What a coincidence that you're in the city at the exact same time as another healer!" Otilia exclaimed.

"What do you mean?" Madlen looked at her uncertainly.

"You haven't heard? He's passing through on his way to Heidelberg. He'll be teaching at the university there. Can you imagine? He studied in the Orient, and he's bringing his knowledge here!"

"Really?" Madlen's eyes lit up. "In the Orient? The most gifted scholars of our time are from there. And he's on his way to Heidelberg?" A look passed between her and her aunt. Agathe knew all about her niece's unquenchable thirst for the practice of the healing arts.

"How often I've longed to be a man so that I could study medicine!" Madlen said.

"But if you were a man, you wouldn't have been able to give birth to us," Veit said, furrowing his brow indignantly.

"That's true, my love." She smiled as she stroked his cheek.

"Would you like to be introduced to him?" Otilia asked. "He's our houseguest. My husband is a good friend of his father's."

Madlen looked back and forth between Agathe and Elsbeth, then at her children.

"Don't worry," Elsbeth said. "We can take care of them."

"Really? Are you sure it's not an imposition?"

"Of course not," Agathe said. "Why would it be? Elsbeth and I will finally have the children all to ourselves. It's no bother at all."

Madlen hesitated, then made her decision. "It would be an enormous pleasure to meet your guest, Otilia."

"Wonderful. Then come with me. I've already told him so much about you. He will doubtless be just as glad to meet you, too."

Madlen kissed Veit and Cecilia on their foreheads and hugged Agathe and Elsbeth. She could hardly wait to get to Otilia's house.

❖ ❖ ❖

"Franz, may I introduce you to Madlen? She's the woman I told you about, the one who healed Reni. She's renowned as the secret healer throughout Worms. Madlen, our guest, Dr. Franz von Beyenburg."

"She honors me more than I deserve," Madlen said, then stepped toward the honored guest. "May God bless you!"

"And may He bless my lady with health and happiness," Franz said politely.

"It's such a pleasure to meet you, sir."

"Same here. I've heard so much about you already."

"Really? I'm certain that Otilia has praised me too much, out of gratitude for Reni's recovery. Nonetheless I was happy to help."

"Let's sit down and enjoy a bit of spiced wine," Otilia offered, motioning toward an adjoining room.

Madlen furtively studied Franz as they strolled into the room. She was surprised to find that he wasn't her father's age. In fact, he didn't seem any older than Johannes. He was about as tall as her husband, but in contrast to Johannes's blondness, his hair was almost black, with wild curls cascading down the nape of his neck.

"Please, sit down. Oh, how glad I am to be present at this gathering!" Otilia clapped her hands together excitedly. "I just need to tell the maid that we are ready to be served. I'll be back in a moment."

Madlen smiled at her as she left the room. She felt a bit uncomfortable being left alone with a man who was little more than a stranger. It was such an unusual situation that she almost regretted accepting the invitation.

"Otilia said that you heal with medicinal herbs?" Franz said, breaking the silence.

"Well, in truth it's been a very long time since I've practiced the healing arts."

Franz smiled. "Once the knowledge of the healing arts is acquired, one never forgets it. What made you give it up?"

Madlen searched for the right words. "Actually, I never really made that decision. I started out assisting a midwife in my hometown of Heidelberg. She treated female conditions of all sorts. She taught me a lot about medicinal herbs and their effects. For a while I secretly hoped to become a midwife, or at least to be allowed to heal people whenever I could." She looked down at her hands. "But the Lord chose another path for me."

"Which was?"

The memory of when she'd been accused of killing a baby and its mother still held a terrible power over Madlen. Suddenly she felt as though a thick rope was tied around her chest. She swallowed hard.

"It's a long story," she said evasively. She was glad when Otilia returned, followed by the maid.

"A little refreshment will be just the thing," Otilia declared. She took two goblets off the maid's tray and handed them to her guests. The maid poured such generous servings of spiced wine that Madlen was tempted to refuse her drink. But she didn't want to be rude and so she allowed herself to be served. Otilia sat and looked expectantly from Franz to Madlen and back again.

"And? Have you two been talking about the wonders of the healing arts?"

"Madlen . . . Oh, excuse me. May I call you Madlen?"

"Yes, of course."

"Good. Call me Franz. Madlen was just saying that early in her career she had been attracted to the treatment of women's conditions."

"That's true. I know my herbs. But I know that has little to do with the true healing arts."

"I must respectfully disagree. The correct and very careful application of herbal remedies often brings about a more successful cure than traditional medical intervention, which has a rather low success rate."

Madlen cocked her head to the side and watched Franz closely. She liked the way he talked and, even more, what he said. He had such a pleasant way about him. When he returned her stare, she felt embarrassed and quickly looked away.

"I hear you studied in the Orient. Please, tell me all about it!"

Franz laughed. "In the Orient? Me? Who told you that? No, I studied at the Schola Medica Salernitana, the medical school in Salerno. And that is well known to be in Italy," he joked.

"Oh, not in the Orient? Didn't you say you had teachers from the Orient?" Otilia said in surprise.

"Yes, that's correct. The curriculum does include the medical knowledge of the old Orient. Does the name Constantinus Africanus mean anything to you?"

"No, unfortunately not," Madlen said, a bit ashamed of her ignorance.

"He was a famous herbalist. People say he originally came to Salerno as a North African trader. He had extensive experience in the medicine of the Middle East and eventually converted to Christianity. Africanus also translated important Arab and Greek medical documents as well as the teachings of Hippocrates."

Madlen's heart started racing. Hippocrates! She had studied whatever she could about this great man. To her, he was more than just a Greek scholar; her admiration for him was so all encompassing that sometimes she had to remind herself not to equate the great physician with God.

"Yes, I've heard a lot about the teachings of Hippocrates," she said.

"I admire this man and what he accomplished beyond all measure. I heard many stories about him as a child. From that time on, there hasn't been a single day that I didn't want to be just like him." Franz chuckled. "Well, despite my best efforts, the light of day shows me all too clearly that that was only a dream."

"Don't say that," Otilia said. "You've acquired an outstanding reputation."

Franz accepted the words of praise with a nod, then turned to Madlen again. "You still haven't told me why you gave up the healing arts."

"Well, I'm just a woman."

"Yes, I see that. But that doesn't answer my question."

Madlen wasn't sure what to say. She shrugged. "I got married and had children." She looked at Otilia and then added, "And if I can be quite frank with you, I was often forced to hide my activities—and myself."

"And what forced you to do this?"

"I'm not a real doctor, and it's common knowledge that only a real doctor can heal. All others will"—she lowered her voice—"very quickly be seen as working with the devil."

Franz laughed. "Yes, people are quick to condemn that which they do not understand. You've got that right. But that's not what I meant. When you said just now that long ago you hoped to become a midwife or healer, your eyes lit up. So, I wonder, why did you give up your gift for the herbal healing arts? Have you never wished to become a physician? Don't you believe that the Lord might have intended this for you? Marriage and children needn't prevent you from following your innermost desires."

"With all due respect, Franz, I do believe you aren't taking me seriously."

"Please forgive me if I've said something offensive. I haven't been back from Salerno for very long, and evidently I need to refamiliarize myself with the customs of this land." He observed Madlen for a moment. "Now I suspect where my mistake lies. Are women here still not permitted to go to university or to become physicians?"

"Franz, I ask you, what are you talking about?" Otilia said indignantly.

Franz lifted his hands in defense. "Please, let me explain. It's just that the more enlightened traditions of other countries have become so second nature to me that I take them for granted."

Madlen's heart beat wildly. Was this man out of his mind, or did she understand the implications of what she'd just heard, something she'd never thought possible?

"Let me tell you a story," Franz continued. "More than three hundred years ago, there was a woman named Trotula von Salerno. She was certified in the healing arts and in medicine, and she was a member of the Schola Medica Salernitana. That was a long time ago." He took a sip of his wine. "Women are still able to study at the Schola Medica Salernitana to this day, though there are not as many women as men at the school. Believe me. I've seen it with my own eyes. And so, should you ever want to explore the vocation of the healing arts, as soon as your children no longer need your support, you could."

Madlen was speechless, her mouth hanging open. Even Otilia, who always seemed to know what to say, sat mute.

"Please, forgive me. It was not my intention to be didactic," Franz said. "Nevertheless, if I may speak from personal experience, the burning desire to help and heal people is such that it can consume those who try to suppress it."

Madlen felt sick, as if she had to vomit. She stared at her glass of wine. Then she jumped up. "Please excuse me," she blurted out, dashing out of the room.

She fled from the house. After just a couple of steps, she was forced to stop in the street to throw up. When she was done, she straightened her skirt and walked on, but she was forced to stop again as nausea threatened to overcome her once more. She panted, the world spinning dizzily. She shut her eyes briefly, then ran on. Her legs seemed to take over, carrying her to the harbor, then to Agathe's house. She was completely out of breath by the time she reached the front door. She knocked as hard as she could. Roswitha opened it, but before she could say anything, Madlen had stumbled in and collapsed onto the floor.

"My Lord, what has happened to you?" Roswitha shut and locked the door and knelt in front of her. "You're as white as a ghost. What should I do? Should I send for the doctor? Can you stay here by yourself? Your aunt isn't back yet. Please, Madlen, say something."

Madlen continued to pant. "Just give me a moment."

"Don't you want me to fetch somebody?"

Madlen held out her hand to Roswitha. "It's all right. I'm already better." The maid helped her to her feet. "I'll just lie down until Agathe and Elsbeth come back with the children."

"I'll prepare a brew," Roswitha offered. "And if you'd like to tell me what happened, all you have to do is say so."

"I don't even know myself. All of a sudden everything felt . . . strange." With that, she walked up the stairs and into her bedchamber, closing the door behind her.

Chapter Four

Johannes changed his horse three times and took only one short rest, during which he hastily choked down some bread and a bit of jerky and gulped down all the water in his flask. Even in the dark of night he kept his horse at a gallop. He reached Cologne the evening of the next day.

Hans, the servant who'd remained behind to tend to the large house, was surprised to see his employer again after so short a time.

"Is everything all right, my lord?" Hans asked. "Nothing happened to your family, I hope."

Johannes laid his hand on the servant's shoulder. "No, Hans. Everything's all right. My wife and the children are well. They are safe at my parents' house in Worms."

"Thank God." Hans saw that the horse was exhausted and soaked with sweat, but he didn't dare ask about it. "Then allow me to take care of the horse." He whispered soothingly to the animal as he led him into a stall in the back courtyard.

Johannes considered going to the archbishop right away but rejected the thought. It was already much too late, and he wanted his employer to be in a good mood when he went before him.

In the kitchen, Johannes sliced off a piece of ham and filled a mug with beer, which he immediately gulped down, then filled his mug again. When Hans came in, Johannes didn't have to think twice before pouring his servant a large mug of beer, too.

"I'm tired, hungry, and thirsty. And we're the only ones here. Sit down with me and keep me company, Hans." Johannes lifted his mug and took a gulp. "And if I fall asleep right here in the kitchen, then do me a favor and drag me to my bedchamber."

"I will do that, my lord." Hans held up his mug and drank. After that, they drank four more rounds.

◆　◆　◆

The next morning, every single bone in Johannes's body hurt. His head felt so heavy that he could barely lift it, the pain showing on his face as he pushed himself out of bed. He regretted not stopping after the second mug.

Still feeling light-headed, he staggered to the washbowl and was pleased to find that Hans had filled it with fresh water the evening before. He dipped both hands in the water and splashed his face. He noticed some soap shavings lying on the narrow wooden shelf. Madlen loved to use this luxury item from time to time; she'd rub it between her fingers, savoring its wonderful smell. This normally didn't appeal to him, but now he bent over and breathed it in. The scent reminded him of his wife, and a smile lit up his face. Oh, how he loved her. He dipped his fingers in the cool water one more time and splashed his face again. Then he picked up a towel and dried himself off. Though he always paid attention to how he dressed, today it seemed more important than ever, and so he chose his clothes carefully. When he finished dressing, he combed his hair then stepped out of his bedchamber.

"Hans," he called as he closed the door behind him.

"Yes, my lord?" the servant called from below.

"I would like to eat something before I see the archbishop."

"Yes, my lord."

"And I intend to start my journey back to Worms today. Can you pick out the strongest and fastest horse for me?"

"Yes, my lord. Certainly you won't be able to use the same horse as yesterday. I was just in the stable. He has not fully recovered yet."

"I cannot blame him. I haven't recovered, either."

Johannes took his time getting to the archbishop's office. From his work as a lawyer, he knew that one's presentation was infinitely more important than the substance of one's arguments. So it was of the utmost import to appear composed and confident upon his arrival, two qualities he did not feel in the least at the moment.

Johannes's horse trotted to the archbishop's house, where the clergyman lived when he stayed in Cologne. Two guards he knew well stood before the door; one of them stepped forward and dropped to a knee.

"God be with you, Counselor."

"The Lord be with you," Johannes said. "I would like to see the archbishop."

"He's not here, my lord. He's in the great hall."

"The great hall?" Friedrich seldom frequented the archbishop's palace, as it was popularly referred to because of its magnificent architecture; its grand halls were more than two stories high and it was normally reserved for court days, celebrations, and receptions. But as far as Johannes knew, there wasn't anything like that scheduled at present.

"Yes, my lord."

"Good. Thank you. God protect you." With that, he started in the opposite direction, toward the cathedral and past the market, until he finally reached the palace.

No guard blocked his way when he sought admittance at the north gate. He walked through the expansive corridors until he reached the archbishop's office in the east wing.

Surprisingly, he'd encountered only a few other employees along his route; normally the place was abuzz with activity. None of the staff, who had known Johannes for years and had been informed about his departure, seemed surprised to see him back so soon.

Only Friedrich was surprised when his servant announced Johannes's arrival. "Enter, my friend. You're back much earlier than I had dared hope."

"I wasn't expecting to be back so soon, either," Johannes said. "Nevertheless, it's a relief to find you well and to see that you survived my absence these last few days."

"Sit down. Your impression deceives you. It's never been more important to have you here than it is today."

"What has happened?"

"Bartholomäus is dead."

Johannes looked at his employer incredulously. Bartholomäus was Friedrich's vicar. He tended the affairs of the diocese and had been in the archbishop's service for many years. Johannes knew how much Friedrich counted on and trusted this man. "What? When did he die?"

"The day after you left."

"But he wasn't old. He was younger than I am!" Johannes wrinkled his brow.

"The doctor said that he was probably poisoned. He had cramps, then he vomited, and, finally, he died in excruciating pain."

"Poisoned?"

"Yes. His servant heard him screaming, and when he saw the state his employer was in, he immediately fetched the doctor. But by that point it was too late. The good doctor was the one who suggested the possibility of poisoning."

"Damn!" Johannes balled up his fist. "Do you have any idea who could have done this?"

"If I did, believe me, that fellow would already be dangling from the highest gallows. But I can't understand it." The archbishop got up and paced back and forth, hands behind his back. "We live in peace. Even the counts of Cleves keep their agreements. The people are happy." He stopped and looked at Johannes. "If it's true that Bartholomäus was poisoned, then his death was intended to weaken me. And by God, it has all but succeeded. But my anger will fortify me as I seek to bring the culprit to justice!"

"We must find out who's responsible for this."

"I'm leaving for Rome tomorrow. This trip has been planned for a long time, and my duties and contracts require that I go. Therefore, I transfer the task of solving this cowardly murder to you. You are a quick thinker with the ability to see through people's words to their true intentions. We have no time to lose."

"Isn't it the sheriff's job to find the murderer? If I get involved, he might end up feeling that his authority has been undermined."

"I don't care about the sheriff's feelings," Friedrich said indignantly. "Yes, he'll sulk. But I need a man I can trust. And you're it."

Johannes rubbed his eyes.

"What's the matter?" Friedrich asked.

"I rode back here so quickly because I'm in the middle of my own difficulties."

"What kind of difficulties?" Friedrich walked over to his chair, sat down, and looked at Johannes in anticipation.

"It's because of my father," Johannes began.

"He's ill, you already told me that. But that's something for a physician to handle, not an attorney."

"Not in this instance."

"What's happened?"

Johannes's expression darkened. "My father is buried in debt, and my family's reputation is ruined. There's no merchandise left, the counting house is empty, and his creditors are demanding repayment."

"And do you have this money?"

"Part of it, but far from all of it. I wouldn't be able to come up with it even if I sold my house and all my possessions."

The archbishop shook his head. "It's not wise to sell things in desperation." He pointed a finger at his employee in warning. "Besides, you can't sell your house because I need you here in Cologne, and you, as legal counsel for the archbishop, need to have accommodations worthy of your stature."

"But I can't stay. I only came here to report the situation to you. I must make my way back to Worms today."

"I can't let you do that. I need you here."

"And my family needs me there."

Friedrich leaned forward and glared at Johannes. "I need you here," he repeated slowly, maintaining eye contact as he spoke. "And when your archbishop gives you an order, you must obey."

"Yes, Your Grace," Johannes whispered as he lowered his head.

"Good. Today I will send a messenger to Eckard von Dersch, the bishop of Worms, and advise him to pay off all your father's debts in full there, after which I will reimburse him for his troubles."

"You'll do what?" Johannes said, eyes wide with astonishment. "I thank you, my lord. But what will we do with my father's business? It must be rebuilt. Otherwise, I won't be able to pay back my debt to you and soon we'll be in the same situation as my father and his creditors are in today."

Friedrich mulled it over briefly then called his servant, who instantly appeared at the door. "Inform Leopold that he needs to come here right now. And bring a pen and some parchment, too."

"Yes, my lord." The servant bowed and left the office.

"Leopold is a talented merchant who knows business like no other. For years he's managed everything here, frequently amazing me with his acumen. He'll take care of your father's books so that the business will flourish once again, and your family can enjoy its usual prosperity. As soon as your father's business shows a profit, it will be up to you to employ someone to administer its affairs. But you must agree to remain in Cologne and bring Bartholomäus's murderer to justice. I want to see that swine strapped to the wheel."

"Yes, my lord. I thank you."

Friedrich waved his hand as if shooing away a fly. "Twenty-five years ago, when I took over the office of the archbishop, it was drowning in debt. It was my great-uncle who helped me by using his enormous fortune to satisfy the debt, and what once had been an arid desert blossomed into a lush green field. And we'll do the same for your father's business."

There was a knock on the door.

"Enter," said the archbishop. A young man entered. "Ah, Leopold, my good friend. I have a proposition that will most certainly appeal to you." He explained to his subordinate what was expected of him. Leopold listened attentively, acknowledging the archbishop by nodding his head.

Johannes observed the man. He was a good head and a half shorter than Johannes was and alert, with a full head of dark hair. His body was slender, his face pale. Evidently, he'd never done a single day of physical labor his entire life.

"I'll need three men whom I can send to the market and on merchant trips to buy and sell goods not available locally," Leopold said. "I'll also need four sacks of gold coins so that I can purchase a large inventory of wares."

"Whatever you need, Leopold. And give me that." Friedrich pointed at the quill in Leopold's hand. "I will write a letter to the bishop of Worms to tell him to collect enough money to discharge these debts and also to support you and your undertakings without reservation."

Leopold nodded. "Thank you, Your Holiness, for your trust and goodwill."

Friedrich nodded. "Now go and prepare everything. We certainly don't want our attorney to worry and thereby be distracted from properly executing his tasks here."

"Yes, Your Grace." Leopold bowed deeply, nodded at Johannes, and left the room.

Johannes thought he must be dreaming. With virtually no hesitation and little consideration, the archbishop had miraculously disencumbered him from the burden of his family's financial woes. "I don't know how to thank you, Your Grace."

"I do. Find Bartholomäus's murderer. And find out how the vicar was poisoned. I can almost hear my enemies scurrying down the hallways and creeping around the palace, like diseased rats. Bring them to justice, Johannes. Find out who is behind this, and then use an iron fist to crush whoever so dared to declare war on me like this. I want to hear every single bone in their bodies breaking on the wheel—each and every one." He banged his hand on the desk so hard that Johannes flinched.

"I'll take care of it, Your Grace." With that, he stood up, bowed, and went to the door. "I thank you for everything. I will find this fiend, and when I do, I will gladly break every bone in his body myself. I promise you that."

Friedrich nodded, satisfied, as his attorney left the room.

"Just a word, Counselor," Leopold said, approaching Johannes, who'd just shut the door behind him.

He tilted his head toward the guards. "Let's go over there." Leopold followed him into a niche under arched windows.

Before the other man could speak, Johannes said, "I must explain to you, sir, how my father came to be in this position."

Leopold waved his hand dismissively. "I don't have to know any-thing. The archbishop gave me a job to do, and I intend to accomplish it to the utmost of my abilities."

"Then you don't want to know what happened?"

"No. I can't change what's already happened. What's coming my way is what piques my interest. I want to know what awaits me in Worms."

Johannes took a deep breath. "I see that you are an honorable man and a man of action. When you arrive at my parents' house, you will see everything for yourself very quickly. My father was once a well-known, successful merchant, an extremely wealthy man. Now he lies in bed, almost completely blind and owing a fortune to half of Worms."

"Was it this illness that ruined his business?"

Johannes hesitated. How much truth would be enough for Leopold to assess his task? "The illness was a part of it. The other part was schnapps."

"I understand," Leopold said dispassionately. "So tell me, then, how angry are his creditors, and is there anyone I should keep an eye on in particular? Who is your father's most bitter adversary, the one most likely to take advantage of his misfortune?"

Johannes thought about it briefly. "I'm sorry, but I don't know. There used to be this old Bengalese merchant who always seemed to enjoy upstaging my father, but he has been dead for a long time, and as far as I know nobody else covets my father's business. Quite the con-trary. My father's creditors' only hope of getting their money back is if his business becomes successful again."

"That's even worse than I feared. A man who has no enemies or adversaries, who doesn't even have a rival, won't be taken seriously." Leopold scratched his chin. "Well, we'll change all that." He patted Johannes's arm amiably. "I'll take care of everything. By the time we speak again, either here or in Worms, your father and your family will have enemies again. Leave it to me." He seemed quite satisfied with this statement.

"Thank you." Johannes paused, asking himself why he'd just expressed his gratitude to this man. Why would he want to have enemies?

"So your wife is currently in Worms? Can I rely on her cooperation?"

"Of course. Please send my greetings to Madlen. I'll write a note for you to give to her, if that's all right. That way I can explain everything."

"That would certainly make my job easier."

"Good. When will you be departing?"

"In an hour."

"So soon?"

"I've been given an order from the archbishop. And I've known the man well enough to know that he expects his orders to be followed straightaway. I'll need to find a man to send to Dortmund, a man to send to Bonn, and a man to send to Dusseldorf. I myself will proceed to the harbor to order the necessary supplies. I don't want to arrive in Worms empty-handed."

Johannes admired Leopold's meticulousness and authoritativeness, how he'd devised a clear, comprehensive plan in such a short time. Friedrich couldn't have chosen a better person to undertake this formidable task.

"I shall be forever in your debt."

"No," Leopold said. "I'm not doing this for you or your family. I'm doing this out of allegiance to the archbishop. I will handle everything to his utmost satisfaction." He stepped back and nodded at Johannes. "And now, if you will excuse me, I'm in a bit of a hurry. Write your message. I'll personally deliver it to your wife. I will set out as soon as all the preparations are made. God be with you, Counselor."

"And with you, too," Johannes said, but Leopold had already turned around and left without looking back.

Chapter Five

"Someone wishes to speak with you, my lady."

Madlen propped herself up in bed. After Elsbeth had left the house with the children, Madlen had gone to her bedchamber to lie down. She felt exhausted and miserable after what had happened the day before at Otilia's house. "Who is it, Helene?"

"He says his name is Franz von Beyenburg and that you would know him."

The feeling of heaviness gave way to nausea. What could she say so that she wouldn't have to receive him? "I'm truly not feeling well. Please tell him I'm indisposed at the moment, Helene."

"Yes, my lady." The maid closed the door carefully behind her.

Shortly afterward, somebody knocked on the door again. Madlen had stood up and gone to the window to observe the street below. Was she mistaken or had the guest not left yet? Another knock on the door. Before she could answer it, the door opened a crack.

"But you can't do this, my lord," Helene was saying.

"I'm a physician, and thus, if your mistress isn't feeling well, I'm the right man in the right place." Franz von Beyenburg pushed past the maid and entered the room.

Helene followed him in, then shrugged helplessly at Madlen.

"It's all right, Helene. Take him to the dining room. I'll speak with my visitor there." She would have preferred to avoid him entirely, but at the very least she would not have the meeting here in her bedchamber.

Franz smiled at her. "I accept your invitation," he said politely but firmly, then turned toward the door. He paused. "You are coming, aren't you?" He had no intention of going any farther until he was certain she would be joining him.

"Yes." There was something about this man that gave Madlen pause. She didn't know whether she found his outrageous boldness delightful or irritating. But there was no time to think about that now, for fear that he'd turn around and linger in her bedchamber. So she gathered up her skirts and hurried after him.

"Did you eat something that upset your stomach?" Franz asked as she stepped through the doorway.

"Possibly."

"Should I prepare you a medicinal brew? I have a remedy in my quarters, which I could fetch immediately."

"Let's just see how it goes."

They walked down the stairs, one after the other. Madlen was glad to be behind him so she didn't have to feel his eyes on her. "I must apologize for my behavior yesterday. I felt ill all of a sudden and, well, I just couldn't stay."

"I understand. You probably ate something that upset your stomach."

"That's probably what it was."

They reached the dining room, and Madlen offered the visitor a place to sit.

"A splendid house you have here. I like it very much."

"It belongs to my in-laws. We're guests, visiting for only a short time."

Helene entered and put two glasses of spiced wine and some pastries on the table.

"Are you sure that you should drink spiced wine?" Franz asked.

Madlen didn't know whether the question was sincere or if Franz was teasing her. But he must have suspected that her stomach was just fine. "Thank you, Helene."

The maid curtsied and hurried out of the dining room.

"Would you be kind enough to leave the door open?" Madlen asked. "Then I can hear when Elsbeth comes back with the children."

"Your eyes light up when you talk about your children. Did you know that?"

"Why are you here?" Madlen refused to let their conversation stretch on longer than necessary.

"I was wondering . . . Please, if you would be frank with me. What was the real reason that you ran away so hastily yesterday?"

"My stomach . . ."

He shook his head. "No, that wasn't the reason." He seemed genuinely concerned. "You can trust me, Madlen. Perhaps you were frightened?"

"Why in the world would I be frightened?" She refused to expose the emotional turmoil raging inside her.

"Because I told you something you never in your wildest dreams thought could be possible. For you, a woman studying medicine and becoming a physician has always been a completely absurd notion. And now to discover through me that it is indeed possible overwhelmed you. Isn't that right?"

Madlen crossed her arms as she searched for an appropriate response. Helene knocked on the dining room door then walked in. She looked as though she'd been crying.

"Please excuse the interruption, my lady." She tried to suppress her sobbing.

"Helene, my God, what's happened?"

"It's just that . . . please excuse me," she stammered. "The master . . . he wanted schnapps, and I, I didn't want to . . . because the mistress told me not to . . . But then . . . he hit me! I don't know how he knew where I was since he can't see me." She put a palm to her reddened cheek. "He hit me really hard. He's never done that before. Sometimes he would . . . when he was drunk . . . but he never hit me." A steady stream of tears flowed down her face.

Madlen stood, went over to her, touched her on the shoulder, and then pulled her close. "I'm so sorry, Helene."

The physician stood.

"I'm so very sorry you've been exposed to this unpleasantness," Madlen said. "My husband's father, Peter, is not usually like this. The disease causes him to be angry." She examined the maid's cheek. "It will hurt a bit for a few days, but it is nothing serious. Go and pour yourself a strong drink. It will make you feel better."

Helene brushed her tears away with the back of her hand, curtsied, and then left the room without another word.

Madlen gestured toward the chair. "Please take a seat, my lord, if it so pleases you. A sip or two of wine would do us some good as well."

They could hear Peter all the way from his bedchamber upstairs, bellowing at the top of his lungs. Helene returned and pointed upstairs. "Should I tend to him?"

"No," Madlen said unwaveringly. "Let him scream himself hoarse."

"I thank you, my lady." With that, Helene disappeared through the doorway yet again.

Franz sat and pensively turned the wineglass in his hands. Madlen sat, too.

"My father-in-law's eyesight has been worsening each day, and now he can't see anything at all. Since he can no longer run his mercantile business, he lies in bed all day, demanding schnapps. And when he gets it, he pours it down his throat at once." She picked up her glass and took a sip. "I hope and pray that my husband returns soon to straighten out the situation. Above all for Elsbeth, my mother-in-law, who is understandably at the end of her rope."

"Disease can grind people down like a stone," Franz said. "Why is he going blind?"

"The doctor who examined him could not give us a diagnosis. No matter what he did, Peter's condition worsened. And now he's blind." She shrugged. "The doctor said there was no cure. And, as far as I know, there's no herbal remedy that can cure Peter, either."

"I agree that an herbal remedy won't help. But if it is what I think it is, then I might be able to remedy the situation."

Madlen stared at him wide-eyed. "You can help him?"

Franz nodded. "If I might be allowed to examine him, I could say so with more certainty."

Madlen felt uneasy about letting the doctor see her father-in-law. This was a decision best left to Elsbeth, Johannes, or even Peter himself, if he were in his right mind. But only her father-in-law was present, and after what Helene had just reported, the sick man was undoubtedly in no condition to make such a decision. So, she pulled herself together. "Agreed."

"Good."

"Please give me a moment to go up first and talk to him. I'll call for you when he is ready."

"I'll be waiting here."

Madlen stood up and turned to go but then turned around. "This is a rather uncomfortable situation for me, and I feel compelled to be completely honest. Until my husband returns, I do not have the funds with which to pay you for your medical services."

"Don't worry about that."

Madlen smiled gratefully. "Then I will be right back."

"I'll wait here," he said again.

Madlen made her way upstairs. "Peter? It's me, Madlen," she said, pushing open the door to his bedchamber. The stench of excrement hit her nostrils. Although light was streaming in through the window, it seemed to Madlen as though the room was darker than the rest of the house.

"Did you bring me some schnapps?"

"No, Peter."

"Then get the hell out of here, you goddamned harlot!"

Madlen straightened her spine and walked to his bedside. Peter lifted his head, evidently trying to ascertain where she was.

"There is a man downstairs, a doctor, who wants to examine your eyes."

"A shark who only wants to extract silver from my pocket!" Peter braced himself, then spat toward where he guessed Madlen was standing. She stepped back, although she'd been standing too far away for him to have hit his target.

"You don't have to pay him."

"Oh, no? So what does he want instead? I guess the fact that you are pleasing to God is payment enough?" He laughed hoarsely. The insult implied in this remark sickened Madlen.

"I'll fetch him to examine you."

"I'll let him have it when he gets close enough."

"No," Madlen said firmly. "You will not."

"Who do you think you are, you harlot?"

"What have you become?" Madlen went to the window and looked out. "The first time I met you, when Johannes introduced me to you and Elsbeth, I was nervous but also full of admiration for you and your accomplishments. But look at you now—a drunkard, drowning his wretchedness in alcohol and driving his family to ruin. Now Johannes has to come up with a miracle to make things right!"

"How dare you to talk to me like that!"

"Yes, I dare indeed. And I'm not finished yet. I'm not asking you to allow yourself to be examined. I'm demanding it. And I expect you to accept the help that this doctor offers you. And then you will rise from this bed and, little by little, become the man you used to be."

"I'm blind!" Peter bellowed.

"Yes, but you're not dead. Maybe the doctor is capable of helping you, I don't know. Even if he can't, that doesn't entitle you to lie here day and night, yelling for schnapps."

"Get the hell out of here!"

Madlen knew she wasn't getting anywhere. "Now I'm going to get the doctor. And if you behave yourself, I will bring you some schnapps afterward."

Peter seemed to think it over. "How much schnapps?"

"One glass."

"A large bottle."

"I will give you a bottle two-inches full, but only if you behave in nothing less than an exemplary fashion."

Peter hesitated, then blurted out, "Send that goddamned quack in."

"I'll go get him now." Madlen gathered up her skirts, left the room, and walked over to the landing. "Doctor," she called out, "would you be so good as to come up?"

"I'm coming," he called back.

Before the doctor went into Peter's bedchamber, Madlen held him back by his arm. "I hope he doesn't kill you altogether. I can't promise he won't try."

"People who are very sick can be difficult. This kind of behavior is not foreign to me. Don't worry." With that, he went in.

"Peter, this is Dr. Franz von Beyenburg. Franz, this is my father-in-law, Peter Goldmann."

"May God bless you," Franz said as he stepped closer to the old man's bed. "Excuse me, Madlen. Is it possible to get more light in here? I need as much illumination as possible."

"I'll ask Helene." She looked at Peter, who lay there completely silent. She didn't trust him, and she wondered what he'd do in her absence. She left the room with a feeling of dread and hurried downstairs to find Helene.

When Madlen returned to the bedchamber, the doctor and Peter were conversing quietly and calmly.

"We have been talking about the process by which Mr. Goldmann's eyesight has worsened," Franz said, looking up. "I need a closer look, but something tells me he has cataracts."

"Cataracts?" Madlen sighed. "That's what we were afraid of. There's no cure for that."

Helene came in with four lanterns, put them down, and left again without a word. Franz asked Peter to sit on the edge of the bed, then positioned two of the lanterns so they lit up the old man's face. He asked Madlen to hold up one of the lanterns, then held up the other with his left hand.

"Please, sit up tall, lift your chin, and look straight ahead."

Without resistance, Peter obeyed the doctor's orders.

Franz squatted down in front of him as he continued to hold up the lantern. He signaled to Madlen to hold up her lantern as near to Peter's face as possible. Madlen complied, observing what Franz was doing. She was becoming more and more fascinated by the second. She could learn so much from this man.

Franz swayed the lantern in front of Peter's eyes. "Yes," he declared after a while, "cataracts."

With that, Madlen's hopes were dashed. She sighed.

"I already knew that," Peter said. "There's no cure. I'll rot right here in this bed, and there's nothing I can do about it."

"I have operated on cataracts many times," Franz said. "There's always some danger of complications, but so far none of my patients have complained. Trust me. I will restore your eyesight."

Franz turned to Madlen. "I have everything I need in my room at Otilia's house. We can start the procedure whenever you are ready."

"And you won't poke my eyes out?" Peter asked.

"I can assure you, Peter, that the doctor knows what he's doing. You can trust him." She tried to sound confident, even though she secretly believed that what the doctor was planning was quite impossible. But she didn't want her father-in-law to sense her skepticism.

"You will see again," Franz said confidently. "Of that you can be sure."

Chapter Six

Usually, before coming home to a hearty welcome from his family, Johannes enjoyed the peace of the ride. But now Johannes was feeling melancholy, knowing full well that he would be returning to a silent house, that nobody awaited him there. Veit and Cecilia's cheerful laughter and occasional screeching would be absent. He missed his wife and children more than he could say.

Things had been different before Madlen had walked into his life, when he had nothing but his work to focus on. He was content to be alone, as he'd always been a somewhat solitary person. Johannes had often felt that cultivating social connections was more trouble than it was worth; he took no pleasure in it like other men his age seemed to. After his marriage to Madlen, after they'd moved from Worms to Cologne so that he could fulfill his obligations to the archbishop, he'd realized how lonely he'd felt his whole life. Now he'd become the person he'd always wanted to be through his love for Madlen and the children. Being without them now hurt him deeply, almost physically.

He wondered whether he shouldn't have tried to convince the archbishop to at least allow him to return to Worms to see his family.

It would have done him good to speak with Madlen. But he knew Friedrich. It was senseless to attempt to get his employer to approve such a plan. The archbishop was a determined man who seldom compromised. It was how he'd succeeded in staying in the archbishop's chair for a quarter century. When he'd taken office, he'd not only cleared the diocese's debt but also extended his sphere of influence and forced men who had been far superior in wealth to their knees. Friedrich never really wanted to be a clergyman. He wanted power, and he'd seized it when the opportunity presented itself. A man like that wasn't easily swayed.

When Johannes arrived home, he yelled, "I'm home!" out of habit, but of course nobody was there to respond. He went into the kitchen, cut off a slice of ham, and sat down. Hans was nowhere to be seen. It didn't take long before there was a knock at the front door. Johannes stood up, crossed the hall, and pulled the door open.

"May God bless you. I'm the doctor who examined the archbishop's colleague. He asked me to come see you."

"Please, come in." Johannes opened the door wider. "Let's go over there." He pointed to his office. "You must excuse me, our housekeeper and the other servants are in Worms, which is where I should be, too. But never mind. Can I offer you some refreshment?"

The doctor held up his hand. "Thank you, but I don't have much time. How can I help you, Counselor?"

"I have a question regarding the vicar's death. Was Bartholomäus still alive when you were called to see him?"

"Yes, my lord, but not for long, and he was in great pain. He had cramps, terrible cramps."

"Cramps, you say? Were there any other symptoms?"

"Yes, his skin was cold and clammy. He was vomiting continuously and could hardly breathe."

"How long did this last?"

"Well, he expired not long after my arrival. But I can't say exactly how long he was ill before I was called in."

"And you believe it was poison?"

"I suppose. Years ago, when I was young and first practicing medicine, I examined a child with the same symptoms."

"A child?"

"Yes. The boy had been playing with other children along the riverbank, where he found an unusual plant."

"And this plant was the cause of the boy's death?"

"Precisely. The plant is called monkshood, and it unfolds itself with barely a touch. The other children only touched the plant and got away with severe nausea. But that boy put the plant's flowers in his mouth and chewed. His death was excruciating."

"And Bartholomäus? Let's say that it was this plant, as you suppose, this monkshood . . ." Johannes thought of Madlen, who said that, with a carefully prescribed dose, most plants can be used to heal. How he wished she were here right now so that he could call upon her extensive knowledge.

"Yes?"

"Is it possible that this plant was used to cure the vicar of some ailment?"

"You mean, is it possible that he might have taken too much by accident?"

"Exactly."

The doctor shook his head. "No, my lord. Monkshood kills when ingested and nothing less. And everybody familiar with this plant knows it."

"I understand. So tell me, please—after you examined the vicar and determined that poison was likely the cause of his demise, did you speak to his guards?"

"Yes, my lord, but not right away. I was primarily focused on caring for the dying man. However, I wasn't able to prevent his death or alleviate his suffering."

Johannes thought it over. "When you were telling me about the boy, you said that even though the other children only touched the plant they became sick."

"Correct."

"If Bartholomäus was administered this poison, wouldn't his murderer have come in contact with the plant?"

"Not necessarily. If he ground the petals carefully with a mortar and pestle or something similar, or gave the deceased a drink with the poison in it, he could very well have avoided touching it."

"Hmm." Johannes stroked his chin thoughtfully. "When do you think he might have been given the poison?"

"It depends on the amount administered to him. I would estimate, depending on how much he consumed, it could have been one to three hours before his death."

Johannes considered this information carefully. If what the doctor said was true, Bartholomäus had to have been poisoned in the very early morning hours.

"Do you have any more questions for me?"

"Excuse me? What did you say?" Johannes, deep in thought, hadn't heard the doctor.

"Do you have any more questions for me? I'm in a bit of a rush and would like to be on my way, if you have no more questions."

"Oh, of course. Please forgive me." Johannes stood. "You've been very helpful."

"It was my pleasure. But now I must devote myself to those I can still help."

The two men walked over to the door. "I have one more question," Johannes said.

"Yes?"

"Who would know about this plant, this monkshood?"

The doctor paused to consider Johannes's question. "Well, herb merchants, women trained in the use of herbal remedies, those type of people but not exclusively. The truth is, you don't really need a formal education; much of the knowledge about plants and herbs is passed down from generation to generation. When it comes down to it, the murderer could have been anybody."

"I understand. Thank you. I appreciate your help."

The doctor nodded, said good-bye, then left. Johannes hung back, lost in thought. In spite of the late hour, he decided to go to Bartholomäus's house in the hopes of tracking down one of the deceased's servants for questioning.

❖ ❖ ❖

Johannes knocked on the door and called out many times, but nobody answered. He couldn't help but think that somebody inside must have heard him. He waited a moment, then knocked on the door once again. Nothing. It was dark inside, with no light coming through the crown glass windows. But had there been a flicker of light when he had approached the house? He briefly considered his options. Was someone there but choosing not to answer the door? And why would that be? He knocked one more time to no avail. Then he turned and walked away, a strange feeling running up and down his spine.

❖ ❖ ❖

After breakfast the next morning, Johannes returned to the late vicar's house, but again nobody answered the door. After waiting for some time, he knocked again. A well-dressed stranger stopped in the street. "God be with you. The vicar isn't there and he's not coming back."

"The Lord be with you," Johannes said to the man. "I know about the vicar's death. I wanted to speak with his servant. I was here yesterday and nobody answered the door."

"You want to speak with Christopeit? He was there yesterday," the stranger said. "I saw him myself. He got picked up late last evening, and he was carrying a big bundle with him. If you ask me, he's not coming back."

"Who picked him up?"

The stranger shrugged. "I didn't recognize the men. I live right over there. I've often seen people coming in and out of the vicar's home. But I've never seen," he said, shaking his head, "the people who were here yesterday."

"And did you get the impression that the vicar's servant, this Christopeit, went with these strangers freely?"

The man thought it over. "Yes, I think so. The only thing I found unusual was the hour that the men set out. But I wouldn't say that Christopeit was forced to go with them."

"Thank you for your time." Johannes nodded. "May I ask your name?"

"Dietrich Tillich."

"Lord Tillich, can you tell me whether you would recognize the men if you saw them again?"

The man tilted his head as if weighing his answer. "The one man, in any case. He was very tall, like you. And his hair was almost as blond as yours. The others . . . no, I think most likely not."

"And you live right over there?" Johannes confirmed.

"That's correct, right there." Lord Tillich pointed to one of the neighboring houses. "If there is something I can do, feel free to come over."

"Thank you. I'll probably stop by at some point."

"Fare thee well," the neighbor said and nodded to Johannes as he walked on.

"The Lord be with you," Johannes returned as he headed in the opposite direction, toward the archbishop's residence.

◆ ◆ ◆

"What do you mean he was taken away by two men?"

"It's just like I said. One of the neighbors told me. He said that one of the men was unusually tall and had blond hair like me. Do you know anyone like that?"

The archbishop thought about it. "No, not as far as I know." He plopped down hard on the chair. "And what do you hope to find out from Bartholomäus's servant?"

"Who had the opportunity to administer poison to Bartholomäus. I spoke with the doctor. He said it was unlikely more than three hours would have passed between the time the vicar took the poison and the moment of his death."

The archbishop exhaled noisily. "Is it possible that Bartholomäus took it by mistake? A medicine that might cure someone in small quantities can kill in larger doses."

Johannes shook his head. "I asked the doctor that exact question. He said that this plant is extremely poisonous, and one touch can make a person quite ill. Whoever administered it to Bartholomäus wanted him dead."

A knock at the door. "Yes?" Friedrich grumbled impatiently.

"Your Grace, everything's ready for your journey."

"I'm consulting with my legal counsel. Send me the scribe!"

"Yes, my lord." The servant bowed and walked out.

"The vicar always took care of my administrative duties during my absences. So now I won't be staying away for as long as I had originally planned. I can't stop thinking about the motive for Bartholomäus's murder. What do you suppose it could be?"

Johannes thought for a moment, then shrugged. "I really don't know, my lord. So far as I can ascertain, there was no reason to kill Bartholomäus. Of course, it might weaken your administration for a couple of hours or maybe a couple of days. But I can't imagine that it would affect the balance of power in the long run."

Someone knocked on the door, and Friedrich granted permission to enter. The scribe stepped in, bowed, and looked at the archbishop expectantly.

"I need a document," Friedrich informed him, "that states that in my absence, Johannes Goldmann is empowered to preside over my administration. Additionally, I proclaim that I support the attorney's directives, which are to be obeyed as if they came from my own mouth. I would like three copies of this proclamation, which I will sign. One goes to my attorney here, one will be locked up in the scribe's study, and I'll take one myself as proof that this was decided today, should the document be challenged. Do you understand?"

"Yes, Your Grace."

"Good. Then get to work forthwith and bring me the document as soon as you've finished."

"Yes, Your Grace." The scribe bowed and departed.

Johannes stood there, looking at his employer. "Your confidence in me might very well be excessive, Your Grace."

"I doubt it. These are uncertain times; Bartholomäus's death proves it. I need someone strong and utterly trustworthy." As was his habit when deep in thought, he stood up, went over to the window, and looked out. "I can't explain Bartholomäus's death. But one thing I do know: you need to stay alert, Johannes. If Bartholomäus was killed because of the competence he demonstrated in his position, and now you hold the same position, you could end up suffering the same fate."

"I'll be careful, my lord. Tell me, please, where are you traveling to?"

"To Rome to visit Pope Bonifatius IX. It can't be postponed."

"Should I send you a message there as soon as I've discovered who's behind this heinous crime?"

Friedrich turned around to look at him. "I'll send you couriers at regular intervals to whom you can report. They'll know where to find me."

"Yes, Your Grace."

Another knock on the door. "It's impossible for the scribe to have finished so quickly," Friedrich said. "Come in!"

The servant appeared at the door, then bowed even deeper than before. "My lord . . . I, I have . . . some news."

"What are you talking about, Hugo?"

Hugo shifted from one foot to the other. "Your travel companion, my lord . . . His servant just hurried over here . . . He's dead, my lord. Lord Bernhard von Harvehorst is dead."

Friedrich took a couple of quick steps toward him, and the servant winced. "How? How did he die?"

"It's terrible, a sinful death, my lord. He hanged himself. He put a rope around his neck and ended his life."

"Never!" Friedrich roared. "I know Bernhard. He is . . . he was," he corrected himself, "a tough old dog. More than any of us. He would never have ended his own life, especially in this way!"

Johannes turned to the servant. "Where is the deceased now?"

"Still in his house, I imagine."

"Good. I need someone who can show me the way."

"I'll come with you," Friedrich said.

"That's probably not such a good idea. Evidently somebody is trying to prevent you from taking your trip by eliminating your closest associates. I doubt that von Harvehorst hanged himself, just as surely as Bartholomäus didn't poison himself. Someone's trying to hurt you, and I don't know why or wherefore. Let me go and find out what happened."

"Even though my journey is urgent, perhaps I should wait to go to Rome until after these crimes are resolved."

"No, that is just what the culprit wants," Johannes said. "Tell me, Your Grace, what meetings have you arranged on this trip and what was to be decided? It seems likely that someone wants to prevent you from accomplishing something."

Friedrich thought it over. "That can't be it. There are no special meetings or important decisions to make. No arguments or disputes to resolve. At least nothing that would be of any great importance. This trip is strictly a formality."

"Who knows about the trip?"

"Everyone here, from the lowliest maid to the auxiliary bishop."

Johannes realized this line of questioning wasn't going anywhere.

The scribe entered through the open door, where the servant still stood. "Your documents, my lord."

"Bring them to me," Friedrich ordered. "I will sign and seal them in front of these witnesses." He took the parchment and went to his desk. When he was finished, he handed one copy to the scribe, one to Johannes, and placed the third one on his desk. "I will keep this one for myself. And now I will take my leave. What you've concluded, Johannes, seems logical. After I arrive in Rome, I will send you a courier riding on our fastest steed with the expectation that you'll be able to identify the person behind these murders soon."

The scribe took the parchment entrusted to him, respectfully said good-bye to the archbishop, and walked out.

"I will tell your messenger everything I discover," Johannes said. "And now, I will make my way to von Harvehorst's residence."

"Go with God," Friedrich said.

"God be with you. Return home safely."

The archbishop nodded and looked contemplatively at Johannes for a moment. Then he indicated with a wave of his hand that Johannes could leave. As he walked out the door, Johannes wondered if he'd ever see his employer again.

Chapter Seven

Madlen was extremely tense as she waited in the dining room. It wouldn't be too long before the doctor came to perform the procedure. She'd promised to assist him, but in the meantime she'd become unsure about whether she could go through with it. Finally, after so many years, she was resuming her lifelong passion for healing people. But this was something entirely different. It was one thing to give people medicinal herbs to alleviate their afflictions. But to operate on somebody's cataracts? Wasn't this the kind of thing that only charlatans and traveling surgeons did to make money off of the desperate? After the quack had all but vanished into thin air, the poor people would take off their bandages and discover no improvement whatsoever. How could she be sure she could trust Dr. Franz? She wrung her hands nervously until Cecilia came over and cuddled up to her.

"Are you really going to help the doctor?" The little girl sounded worried.

Madlen pulled her daughter onto her lap. "Yes, sweetheart, I am."

Cecilia began to cry.

"What's the matter, little one?"

"You're going to help him poke out Grandfather's eyes?"

"What? How did you come to that ridiculous conclusion?"

"Veit told me." She nodded her head knowingly. "The doctor is going to stick a big fat needle into Grandfather's eyes and leave behind two big black holes."

"Oh, for heaven's sake!" Madlen closed her eyes for a moment to gather herself. It took all her might to suppress the profanity on the tip of her tongue. Sometimes her son really was impossible. "Why do you listen to Veit? You know very well that he loves to make up stories to frighten you."

"But this time it's true. The doctor is coming and bringing a big fat needle, isn't he? I overheard you and Grandmother talking about it."

"Yes, the doctor's coming, that's true. Not to poke out your grandfather's eyes, but to make him see again. He's going to heal him, not hurt him." She stroked Cecilia's arm tenderly.

"And then will Grandfather really be able to see? Are you sure?"

"Yes, I am." Madlen reassured her daughter, although she had considerable doubts about the whole thing herself. "The doctor studied in a foreign land and knows everything about healing all kinds of ailments."

Cecilia didn't seem convinced.

"And do you want to hear something else? In Salerno, where he came from a short time ago, he learned how to treat cataracts, which is what your grandfather has. He's returned the gift of sight to hundreds, perhaps thousands, of people. For him it's as easy as it is for you to tie the laces on your dress. First, one has to study hard to learn how. But as time goes by and with a little bit of practice, it becomes second nature."

Astounded, Cecilia looked at her mother. "And so that's what it'll be like for the doctor to make Grandfather see again?"

"Exactly right." Madlen felt guilty for oversimplifying this intricate procedure. But she wanted to allay the little girl's fear, not scare her to death with cold, hard medical facts.

"Then I'm going to tell Veit that what he told me was silly." She pulled away from her mother's embrace, then slid off her lap.

"You do that. And tell him for me that I forbid him to upset you or anybody else with any more nonsense." She gave her daughter a kiss on the forehead.

"I will." Cecilia stomped away resolutely. At the door she almost collided with Elsbeth, who patted the colorful bonnet that still covered her granddaughter's almost bald head.

"Shouldn't the doctor be here shortly?" Elsbeth asked Madlen.

"He'll be here soon." Madlen tried to exude confidence, though she herself was a bundle of nerves.

Elsbeth rubbed her hands together. "I'm freezing. Why is it so cold in this house?" She went to the table and sat down across from Madlen. There was obvious tension in Elsbeth's face, and her prominent cheekbones seemed to jut out more than ever. Elsbeth had once been a beautiful woman, but recent difficulties, along with the constant marital turmoil she'd put up with for years, had taken their toll. Now she was pale and thin.

"Maybe you should lie down for a little while," Madlen suggested, leaning over the table to put her hands on Elsbeth's. "Your hands are ice-cold."

"I would, but I can't seem to relax no matter what I do. Oh, I can't wait for this to be over."

"It won't be much longer till we've ridden out this storm," Madlen said, trying her best to give her mother-in-law an encouraging smile.

"And do you really believe the operation will be successful?"

"Yes, I do. You need to trust the doctor."

"When Peter can see again then everything will be all right. He used to be different, you know? He's probably been dealing with this affliction for much longer than I was aware of."

"Elsbeth, I know my words might seem harsh, but even if the procedure is unsuccessful and Peter can never see again, his condition could not be worse than it is now. So any change will be an improvement. And as far as Peter's business, Johannes will be back in a few days and he'll have good news for us, I just know it. One way or the other, the current situation will be resolved. You must have faith, Elsbeth. That's the most important thing."

"I'm afraid that I've lost a good part of my faith over the years."

"That's quite understandable. But we're here now, and we'll stand by you and make life good again. Believe me."

"I do believe you." Elsbeth squeezed her daughter-in-law's hand. They jumped in surprise at the knock at the front door.

"That's the doctor, no doubt," Madlen said as Elsbeth stood.

"Helene, Helene!" the older woman called. "Where is that girl? Please open the door! How long does it take to open a door?"

The maid, who had already reached the door, winced at her mistress's harsh tone. Madlen rose from her chair, and she and her mother-in-law went into the foyer to greet the doctor.

Madlen introduced Franz and Elsbeth to each other. The doctor was as calm as ever.

"Are we ready then?" he said, turning to face Madlen.

"Could you please be so kind as to watch over the children?" she asked her mother-in-law.

"In my current state, Helene would probably do a better job of that than I. I don't have the strength . . ."

"But I want you to do it," Madlen insisted, certain that a distraction would do Elsbeth good.

"All right. I'll take care of them."

"Thank you." She turned to Franz. "Please, let's go upstairs. Everything is ready. We've brought in all the lighting we could find and laid out clean towels and strips of linen."

"Say, might you have some time to talk when we're finished here?"

"It would be my pleasure," Madlen said politely, although she feared a conversation about her studying medicine almost more than she feared assisting with the cataract surgery.

Upstairs, she tapped softly on the door, then entered the bedchamber. "Peter? The doctor is here."

"I've been waiting for you," Peter said. He sounded cheerful, if not enthusiastic. "Please come in and give me back my eyesight."

"That's what I intend to do." Franz stepped over to the bed confidently; Madlen followed him more hesitantly.

"We need a chair," Franz declared. "We'll need to spread the lanterns around in a circle so that I can see better. Madlen, you will get behind your father-in-law and hold his head. Here, I'll show you." He moved a nearby chair into the center of the room, helped Peter to his feet, led him over to the chair, and helped him sit. Then the doctor stood behind the chair. "You'll take his head like this and press it against your chest. You'll hold his forehead with both hands so he doesn't move. And you, Peter, you must try with all your might not to move even a little bit. One little twinge and your eyes could be destroyed forever."

"I'll stay as still as I possibly can," Peter assured him.

"Good." The doctor stepped around to the front of the chair. "Please, help me arrange the lanterns." He moved two other chairs, one for himself, which he set directly in front of the patient, and the other, on which he placed two lanterns, off to the side. The other lanterns he and Madlen arranged in a semicircle around Peter.

"I think I can see well enough now. Please step behind your father-in-law."

Madlen took her place.

The doctor picked up a leather case wrapped in cloth and opened it. Inside lay an assortment of needles and scalpels, which gleamed in the flickering light. Then he picked up the towels and linen strips and arranged them neatly side by side.

Madlen noted how clean and well maintained his instruments were. She felt a surge of confidence that he wasn't simply making empty promises. Perhaps this procedure could really make a difference.

Franz took out a big bronze needle then laid the leather case on the bed and sat down on the chair in front of Peter.

"Maybe I should drink a little schnapps before we start to calm myself?" Peter's voice was trembling.

"No, that won't be necessary. All you need to do is simply lean your head back onto your daughter-in-law and make sure not to move. And don't speak any more, otherwise your head will move."

"Yes, Doctor," Peter said meekly.

Madlen held onto Peter's forehead and pulled his head gently back, onto her chest.

"Now open your eyes. I'm not going to hurt you. You won't feel any pain." The doctor moved the needle toward one of Peter's eyes, then looked up at Madlen. "I will explain each step so that you'll know what I'm doing. This is the only way to learn."

"Thank you," Madlen said, although it seemed strange that he would do such a thing.

"I'm sticking the needle into the corneal limbus, right here on the outer edge of the iris. I am moving the tip through the pupil." He spoke so calmly and with such concentration that it seemed as though he weren't executing the operation himself but simply observing.

"Now, I'm cutting through the zonular fiber, and now I will press the lens down, like so." He glanced at Madlen, who watched in fascination as he deftly wielded his surgical instruments.

"And that's it. I'll hold it for a moment so the lens doesn't rise back into its former position," he explained, holding the needle. Madlen was rapt, so much so that she could barely breathe. Peter seemed completely calm, neither moving nor speaking, simply leaning his head against Madlen's torso.

"That's enough," the doctor said as he carefully pulled out the needle, having verified that the lens had indeed stayed in the intended position. He seemed satisfied. "Peter, you can move your head if you want before we proceed with the other side."

"That was it?"

"On one side, yes. I'll wrap a bandage over your eyes as soon as we're done with both sides. Close your eye until then. I'll tackle the other one now."

Peter shook his head briefly, then obediently leaned it back again. Madlen held his forehead. Just like before, Dr. Franz described each step of the procedure. When he was done, he picked up the towels and the strips of linen he'd laid to one side and prepared a bandage.

"So. That's it. Your suffering is over. I'm confident that when we remove your bandages in a few days, you'll be able to see the smiling faces of your grandchildren."

"I dare not hope for that."

"Have hope. And now that everything is done, please fetch some schnapps for my patient and me," Franz said, grinning at Madlen.

She took a couple of steps toward the door. "I don't know how I can ever thank you." Without waiting for acknowledgment, she raced out of the bedchamber. As she hurried down the stairs, Elsbeth stepped into the hall.

"And?"

Madlen embraced her mother-in-law. "It went perfectly. The doctor said that in a few days Peter will be able to see again."

Elsbeth was white as a sheet, though tears of relief had begun to run down her face. "I can hardly believe it."

"Believe it, Elsbeth. And believe that everything will be all right!" Madlen broke away from the embrace.

"Where are you going now?"

"I'm getting some schnapps for the doctor and also for Peter—he's earned it."

"Bring one for me, too," Elsbeth said as she walked unsteadily toward a chair.

As Madlen went into the kitchen, Elsbeth collapsed onto the chair. Cecilia and Veit walked over and hugged their grandmother, who laughed as tears of joy continued to run down her face.

When Madlen returned, Cecilia asked, "Is it true that Grandfather will be able to see again?"

"Yes, my beloved." Madlen knelt in front of her daughter, a bottle in her left hand and two glasses in her right. "He will."

Cecilia turned to Veit and gave him a triumphant look. Then she looked at her mother again. "And will everything be all right now?"

"Yes, my little one. Everything's going to be good again." She pressed a kiss onto Cecilia's cheek, rose, and went upstairs with the glasses and the bottle. When she got to the bedchamber, Peter was lying in bed, and the doctor was sitting on its edge. The two men were speaking softly.

"Oh, you're back. We were just talking about you."

"Oh?" Madlen handed the doctor the glasses. He held them so she could fill them up.

"Yes. I've been having a stimulating conversation with your father-in-law about whether, in his opinion, women should be allowed to become doctors or not." Franz put one of the glasses into Peter's hand. "Your father-in-law is a very open-minded man."

"I can't thank you enough if this procedure is a success," Peter said. "I'll repay you as soon as I am able."

"Don't give it another thought. But there is something that you can do for me."

"Me? What can a blind old man like me do for you?"

"Help me convince your daughter-in-law to join me in Heidelberg and sit in on my medical lectures. Just as a guest, of course."

"And what would be the purpose of that?"

Franz turned to Madlen and held her gaze as he answered Peter. "I recognize passion when I see it. And your daughter-in-law's eyes burn with a passion for healing." He turned toward the patient again. "Besides, I know all about what happened here some years ago. Otilia told me how Madlen saved many lives despite her fear of being discovered. One recognizes a true doctor not by his or her gender, but by his or her passion for the vocation, and by his or her deeds." He turned to Madlen again. "And you are called to heal. To deny that would be a sin."

Madlen was speechless. Why was the doctor being so persistent?

"Even if I wanted to, I couldn't go," she said. "Not yet anyway. I'm awaiting my husband's return. He's going to revive Peter's business, and he'll need my full support. And of course, there are the children."

"Certainly not an easy situation," the doctor acknowledged. "And if you were to come later?"

"I don't know. What good would it do? I'll never be allowed to be a doctor . . . in this country anyway."

"Probably not. But you could find out if your passion for healing burns as bright as I think it does. And should that be the case, Salerno is not too far away."

"And what about my husband and children?"

"I will help you find a way to make it happen. And if this isn't the right time, then at a later date. But don't give up on your dream—if you do, you will live to regret it."

"Why do you say that?"

"Because I know." He sighed. "My sister was a healer, just like you. But she felt her dreams were unattainable, so she abandoned the medical training that would have led her to a fulfilling life. Afterward, it was as though a dark cloud followed her everywhere; she no longer laughed, she was utterly joyless. On the morning before her arranged marriage to an older businessman, she was found lying on her bed as though sleeping peacefully. But she did not wake up—she had poisoned herself." Franz choked back his grief. "A mortal sin, I know. But I can understand her desperation. You could take away all my earthly goods and I would survive. But if I were prevented from healing others, it would kill me." He pressed his lips together. "Now you know why I've been so insistent. I don't want you to go down that same terrible path."

"You must go, Madlen," Peter said, and Madlen couldn't have been more surprised. "I know what it's like to be followed by a dark cloud. I would never want that to happen to you."

Madlen was overcome with emotion. "I need to go . . . to go see my children and Elsbeth."

"Think about it," Franz said as she left the room.

"I will. I promise."

Chapter Eight

The body of Bernhard von Harvehorst hung like a wet sack from the end of the rope, his face swollen, his tongue hanging grotesquely from the side of his mouth. Urine had puddled below him, and a chair lay tipped over on the floor.

"Why haven't you cut him down?" Johannes asked indignantly.

"I can answer for that." The same doctor to whom Johannes had spoken about Bartholomäus's death stepped forward from the back of the room. "When I arrived, it was obvious that he could no longer be helped. I knew he was in the archbishop's circle of close associates, so I thought you should have a look at him first. That's why I sent for you."

Johannes was surprised. "You sent for me? I knew nothing about that. I happened to be with the archbishop when he got the message. That's how I found out."

The doctor shrugged. "Then the messenger I sent is probably still standing in front of your house."

"What can you tell me about the deceased?" Johannes said, getting back to the topic at hand.

"First of all, it was unnecessary to call me since he'd already been dead for several hours."

Johannes stepped closer to the body. He took the man's right hand and inspected it. "His knuckles are bloody, as if he'd been fighting somebody before he died."

The doctor stepped closer and inspected the wrist, too. "You are correct. And I noticed something else." He picked up the corpse's left hand. "Do you see the abrasions on both wrists? It looks as though his hands were tied with a coarse rope."

"There was a struggle, and Bernhard von Harvehorst must have fought back. After succumbing, his wrists were tied before he was hanged. Then when he could no longer fight back, or perhaps after he was already dead, someone removed the ropes from his wrists to make it look like suicide."

"That would be my conclusion, too," the doctor said.

"The deceased was a very big man—it would have taken at least two strong men to overpower him. Where are his servants? Somebody must have witnessed or at least overheard something."

"The maid is sitting downstairs in the parlor. She's the one who found him here."

"I must speak to her."

"Can we now cut down the deceased from this shameful position?"

"I would be grateful if you could take care of it."

The doctor nodded and waved over one of the guards. The doctor stepped onto a chair and reached up with a knife to cut the rope while the guard held the body so that it wouldn't flop onto the floor. Once the rope was cut, the guard laid von Harvehorst down carefully.

Johannes left the room and went downstairs. A woman sat there; he estimated her to be in her midforties. She cut a robust figure; evidently things hadn't gone too badly for her in the last few years. She held a handkerchief to her face as she cried, shaking uncontrollably.

"Are you the housekeeper?" Johannes asked.

She nodded.

"What is your name?"

"Duretta, my lord."

"My condolences, Duretta."

"If only I had been there! Then this never would have happened. His grief must have got the better of him. It's just so terrible." She pressed the handkerchief to her face again.

"Grief? Over what?"

"You don't know? His wife died recently. Not even six months ago. And now him, too . . . What will become of me?"

"No, I didn't know that. But I can tell you that you are not to blame for your employer's demise. He did not hang himself."

"He didn't?" She looked at Johannes with surprise.

"No. And if you had been here, you probably would be dead, too. Tell me, where were you last night?"

"My sister was ill," she said through her tears. "I took care of her children so she could sleep through the night. She has five children and the youngest ones—they're twins—are just two months old. My sister is rather frail, and she urgently needed some rest. God didn't give me any children of my own, or a husband. So, I take care of hers when my master allows it."

"I understand." Johannes stroked his chin pensively. "When did you leave here yesterday?"

"Before it got dark, my lord. I prepared my master his meal, and then he said that I could be on my way. So, I went."

"And then you came back here first thing in the morning?"

"That's correct. It was very quiet, so I thought my master might not be home. I didn't go out again right away to the market, but then later I finally did. When I came back, I found him." She began to cry again. "From now on, whenever I close my eyes I'll see that image of him hanging there. I just know I will."

Johannes considered the housekeeper. Something didn't seem quite right about her account, but he couldn't put his finger on it. He looked around. Everything seemed clean and orderly; there seemed to be no trace of a struggle down here. Either the murderers had tidied everything up after the attack, or the deceased had known them well enough to let them into his bedchamber without reservation. Suddenly Johannes realized what was bothering him.

"Your master was going to take a long trip today with the archbishop. But I see he hadn't packed. And upstairs there's no luggage, not even one bag. Why is that?"

From the perplexed look on her face, the housekeeper obviously didn't understand. "But, my lord, that's not true. My master didn't intend to go on that trip." She looked down at the floor.

"But I know with certainty that Bernhard von Harvehorst was supposed to accompany the archbishop on his trip to Rome."

"No, my lord. I don't mean to contradict you, but my master had changed his plans. The quarrel was even worse than it seemed at first."

"What quarrel?"

She kneaded the handkerchief in her hands. "I would prefer not to talk about it, my lord."

"I have no patience for your preferences. I order you to tell me immediately!"

She looked at him pleadingly. "But I don't want to be the one who gets punished."

"Nobody will punish you if your conscience is clean. So tell me right now!"

She cried for another moment, then looked up. "Who gives you the right to ask me these questions?" Her expression had completely changed. A minute ago she had seemed frightened and timid, now she seemed leery.

"I'm investigating the death of your master in the name of Friedrich III, the archbishop of Cologne."

She shrugged, then her eyes widened and she shook her head.

"Didn't you hear me? You must answer me!"

"But if you are acting on behalf of the archbishop, I mean, if you're working for him . . . then you must know . . ."

"No, I don't know. Speak right now, or the punishment you so fear shall come to pass."

"The argument with the archbishop," she said, her voice trembling.

Johannes guessed that he'd learn more from the housekeeper if he used a gentler approach. He pulled up a chair and sat down directly in front of her. "My good woman, you can speak openly. I must clear up the death of your master, and to do that, I must have accurate information. You won't be punished. Whatever you reveal will be for my ears only. I give you my word about that."

She lifted her head and gazed at him through red-rimmed eyes. "Swear to it on the life of your children."

"All right, I swear to it on the life of my children."

She looked at him dubiously. "You do have children, don't you?"

"A boy and a girl, yes." Johannes smiled.

"All right, then. I want to believe you." She exhaled loudly. "You know that I'm just a simple woman and don't really understand such things, but I do know that the argument was because of the archbishop's actions in operating the newly acquired fiefdom. As I understand it, an injustice occurred when the archbishop didn't keep his promises."

"An injustice? What kind of injustice?"

"I don't really know, my lord. But my master told me that the archbishop had taken what he wanted without thinking of those who had stood beside him during a difficult vote. Those were his words."

Johannes considered what this complaint could be referring to. He himself had led some negotiations about the surrender of a fief, but those proceedings were mutually agreed upon, always honoring the provisions as set by law. "By chance, do you know where this fief was?"

"No, my lord. Unfortunately, I don't know that."

"Can you tell me when your master decided not to accompany the archbishop? And how the archbishop reacted to this announcement?"

She shrugged. "My master didn't talk to me about that."

"I understand." Johannes got up. "I may return if I need to ask more questions."

She began to cry again. "I don't know if I'll be here then. There's nobody here to run a household for. Where am I going to go now?"

"I'll ask the archbishop if he knows anyone who needs a steadfast and loyal housekeeper such as yourself. Provided there are no heirs, nobody will object to you staying at the house in the meantime."

"Thank you, my lord."

"I'll send you a message as soon as I speak with the archbishop. Stay here until then."

"Yes, my lord."

"Good. May God be with you."

"And with you, my lord."

Johannes went upstairs again. The doctor and the guard had laid Bernhard von Harvehorst on some sheets, and the doctor promised he would ensure that the body would be picked up by the mortuary chapel in a timely fashion. They all left the house together, bade each other farewell, and went in different directions.

Johannes hurried to reach Friedrich before he left on his trip. As he got closer to the archbishop's palace, a very bad feeling came over him. How would he tell Friedrich that Bernhard von Harvehorst had no intention of accompanying him on his trip? Or was Friedrich already aware of this? Should he keep this knowledge to himself?

He crossed the marketplace, taking long, quick strides as he went. On the outskirts of the marketplace, he came upon two merchants quarreling about space for their respective stalls. He kept going, finally reaching the archbishop's residence.

The guards greeted him, and for the second time that day let him pass. He'd barely stepped into the building when Friedrich's personal servant met him.

"Is you master still here?" Johannes asked.

"Yes, but not for much longer. The horses have been prepared."

"I'll be brief." With great determination, Johannes walked toward the archbishop's study, which was flanked by guards, and stepped up to the door.

"I'm bringing the archbishop a report about the death of Bernhard von Harvehorst," he stated. One of the guards knocked and announced his arrival.

"He can enter but he needs to make haste," the archbishop said from within. Johannes stepped into the study.

"Your Grace, I've just come from Bernhard von Harvehorst's house. He was murdered, my lord."

"Murdered? That's what I suspected." Friedrich balled up his hand into a fist. "How?"

"He was beaten, tied up, and then hanged."

"The dirty pigs! Bring me the person who did this!"

"There's nothing I'd rather do." Johannes hesitated, then decided to ask the question. "I know you're in a great hurry, my lord, but if I am to sort out the murders of Vicar Bartholomäus and Bernhard von Harvehorst, I must collect as much information as possible."

"Yes. What are you getting at?"

"Well, it's strange indeed. Bernhard von Harvehorst's housekeeper didn't think her master was going with you on a trip today. On the contrary. She stated that von Harvehorst had no intention of accompanying you. From what I could gather, it's because of some sort of dispute."

The archbishop looked at Johannes quizzically, then suddenly became enraged. "What are you implying?"

"In your opinion, why would the housekeeper make such a statement? I told her that I was questioning her on your behalf, and after that she claimed that her master hadn't planned on going on the trip, that he'd told her quite clearly that he was staying in Cologne. I saw firsthand that he hadn't packed any bags. I can't explain it myself, and I'm asking you to help me." Johannes exhaled. He had formulated the question in the most innocuous way possible, trying to avoid making Friedrich feel threatened.

"I would gladly help you," the archbishop said, now somewhat calmer, "but I'm as confused as you are. I'm positive that Bernhard von Harvehorst wanted to accompany me on this trip."

"Was there a dispute as the housekeeper maintained, or did she lie in this respect?"

"No, it's true. We argued about a variety of things. Most recently, we disagreed about the interpretation of a promise concerning some fiefs. But this conflict was resolved weeks ago."

"Did he end up sharing your views?"

The archbishop's face relaxed completely now. "No, not at all. And that's just as well because von Harvehorst was correct. After our fight, if that's what you want to call it, I took the documents in dispute and examined them again. I'm a man who keeps his word, and von Harvehorst served me well by drawing my attention to the points we'd argued about. Finally, I ended up agreeing with him."

"So, he convinced you?"

"Yes, he did. You know, archbishop or not, if I can't trust my closest colleagues or advisers to come to me with an honest opinion, I might as well be talking to a wall. I don't need advisers who just say what they think I want to hear. My predecessors made that mistake, and we know what that meant for the diocese. No, Counselor. Bernhard von Harvehorst always pointed out my shortcomings and lapses in judgments directly and without circumlocutions. He was a brave man who could humble and teach many a nobleman a thing or two. That he was murdered in such a cowardly manner breaks my heart." He rubbed his eyes. "If you ask me, you should go back to the housekeeper and ask her when she found out about this so-called dispute that supposedly made von Harvehorst change his mind about the trip. She must have had a reason to lie. That he decided not to accompany me at the last minute is completely ridiculous."

"I'm sorry," Johannes said.

"For what? Because you had some doubts? Because you were brave and confronted me, with the greatest respect, with your questions? I thought I made myself clear. My grandfather used to say that a man's thoughts must find their way to his tongue, or else he will never get the answers he seeks."

"Your grandfather was a wise man."

"He was."

"Well, then, Your Grace, I wish you a pleasant journey. I will fulfill the tasks bestowed upon me with the greatest of care."

"I know you will."

Johannes bent to one knee, and Friedrich stretched out his hand so that the lawyer could kiss his ring. Then Johannes straightened up and looked his employer directly in the eyes. "It fills me with great pride to have your trust. May God be with you and protect you during your journey."

"Find this fiend! May God be with you!"

As Johannes walked away, he felt the weight of the great challenges he would have to face. The first thing he needed to do was to interrogate the housekeeper again about what she'd said, in light of what the archbishop had told him.

◆ ◆ ◆

At von Harvehorst's house, Johannes knocked several times but nobody came to the door. The situation reminded him of when he had tried to gain entry to Bartholomäus's house. Had the housekeeper simply disappeared like Bartholomäus's servant had? That just couldn't be. He'd told her quite explicitly that she needed to stay put. He knocked again, this time even harder. When no one answered, he rammed his shoulder against the door with all his might until the lock finally gave way. The door swung open, slamming against the wall behind it. Johannes paused and looked down the street to see if anyone had noticed him breaking into the house. But nobody seemed to be paying him the least bit of attention.

Johannes looked around the silent entryway. It seemed that no one was coming.

"Is anybody here?"

No answer. He walked through the house, opening every door to verify that nobody was home. The place was empty. Johannes climbed the stairs and looked into the bedchamber where Bernhard von Harvehorst had lost his life. It looked the same as before, but Johannes's feeling had changed. Now he was more curious than ever as to what had happened. Where had the housekeeper gone? Did she go voluntarily, or had someone kidnapped her? And what about Bartholomäus's servant, Christopeit? Johannes still hadn't been able to discern his whereabouts. He'd even asked two of the archbishop's guards to keep their ears and eyes open for information about Christopeit's disappearance when they patronized the local pubs. But nobody seemed to know anything. And now the housekeeper had vanished as well. She was the only witness, the only one who might have been able to help him discover Bernhard von Harvehorst's real intentions regarding the journey with the archbishop.

Johannes was growing more suspicious; perhaps something more sinister was afoot than he'd first imagined. It made him both nervous and furious, as well as determined. He would figure out who was behind all this. But first, he had to find the housekeeper.

Chapter Nine

"We've come on behalf of Eckard von Dersch, the bishop of Worms. Please come with us."

"Why?" Madlen looked perplexedly at the two men standing before her outside the front door.

"We don't know ourselves. Please, come with us."

Madlen wondered what the bishop of Worms could want from her. Was it about Peter's debts? But then why would they require her presence? She had nothing at all to do with it—she was, after all, only his son's wife. Why hadn't the bishop asked for Elsbeth? It had to be about something else. A shiver ran down Madlen's spine. Was it something to do with the cataract operation? She'd only held Peter's head, and the man who had operated on him was a real physician. Her throat constricted at the thought that history could not only repeat itself but come crashing down upon her. The slander, the constant worry she'd be discovered, the fear of death. Silently, she implored God to deliver her.

The guard cleared his throat. "Are you coming, my lady?"

Elsbeth had stepped behind Madlen. "No. I will not allow my daughter-in-law to leave this house as long as we do not know what the bishop wants from her."

"But we have our orders."

"That is your problem."

"But you just can't—"

"Don't tell us what we can or cannot do," Elsbeth said. "I've put up with enough unpleasantness lately. My daughter-in-law has stood by me, through thick and thin. As long as we are in the dark about the bishop's intentions, I cannot allow her to go with you."

The guards fell silent, dumbfounded.

"Well, then," Elsbeth said, "there's nothing more to say. Please send the bishop our warmest regards and ask him if he would send a messenger to disclose the reason for his request. May God bestow upon you a safe return." With that, she closed the door and locked it.

Madlen looked at her with terror in her eyes. "You've angered the bishop's men."

"Whether they're angry or not is debatable, but I am tired of being pushed around." She put her hands on Madlen's shoulders. "You know, since you've been here, I've started to regain my former vigor. You have my endless thanks for everything you've done for Peter and me. Now it's time to use my strength to make you stronger, too. Trust me."

"That's what Johannes always says." Madlen smiled.

"Well, of course. He's my son after all," Elsbeth said as she winked at her daughter-in-law.

"Who was that, Mother?" Veit came out of the kitchen, followed by Cecilia.

"Just two of the bishop's men. He wanted to send us his regards."

"That's very nice of the bishop," Cecilia said.

Madlen stroked her daughter's head, still covered by the bonnet. "Yes, little one. That is very nice of him." Madlen threw a look at Elsbeth, then couldn't help but laugh. "And I think the men will come again soon to send the bishop's further regards."

"For some reason, I do believe you are correct," Elsbeth said, laughing along with Madlen. The sudden outbreak of good cheer was interrupted by a knock at the door.

"I'll get it," Elsbeth said, grabbing the door handle. She took a deep breath and opened the door. She was surprised to see Franz von Beyenburg standing there.

"Doctor, how wonderful to see you," she said, stepping aside to let him in.

Franz couldn't disguise his own surprise. "God bless you! Have you all been waiting at the door for me?" He looked from Elsbeth to Madlen then to both the children.

"Of course!" Madlen said. "Because we're so grateful for your treatment of Peter."

"All right," Franz said skeptically. "Now, then. Today the bandages come off. So we'll just see how grateful you should be."

"I'm absolutely confident." Elsbeth closed the door behind him.

"Doctor, please go right on up. Should I follow you?" Madlen asked.

"Of course. Bring some fresh water. We will use it to moisten the bandages before we remove them—that will make the process easier."

"I will," Madlen promised, then waited a moment until the doctor was out of earshot. She whispered into Elsbeth's ear, "I doubt that the bishop's men will leave us alone. What should we do if they come back?"

"Be strong," came the prompt answer. "Something I haven't been for far too long—I was so afraid of what could happen. But that's all over now. It's as if I have lived in a fog all my life. But no more." Elsbeth raised her chin proudly. "Go on up and help the doctor. I'll make sure that he gets the water." She pulled Madlen close. "In difficult times, it's we women who must set everything straight. And so it will be again."

◆ ◆ ◆

"Please keep your eyes closed," the doctor said as he carefully pulled away the moistened linen bandages.

Peter kept perfectly still; he didn't move a muscle. It looked as though he were holding his breath. Madlen stood next to the doctor, who was sitting at the edge of Peter's bed. She watched his every move with great interest.

"So." He laid the last bandage onto a small table. "I've removed them all. Madlen, please dip a fresh piece of linen in the water."

She dutifully dunked the cloth in the water, then started to hand it to the doctor.

Franz shook his head. "You do it."

She hesitated briefly, then bent over toward Peter. Franz stood, freeing up his seat. Madlen sat down and got closer to Peter's right eye with the cloth. "I'm going to touch your eyelid now," she said and dabbed at it carefully. Then she did the same thing to the other eye. "Tell me if this feels uncomfortable in any way."

"It's fine," Peter whispered.

Madlen bent over the bowl of water, rinsed out the cloth, and repeated the procedure.

"You do that very well," Franz said.

Madlen felt better than she'd felt in a long time. How she relished helping people. A sense of strength and joy swept through her.

"I think that's enough." Franz's voice was warm, almost tender.

Madlen let the cloth slide back into the bowl. She picked up a dry one and dabbed at the remaining water underneath Peter's eyes.

"Now we're going to snuff out all the lights," Franz explained, "so that when you open your eyes, the brightness won't be too much for you."

"Thank you."

Madlen's heart was beating in her throat as Franz put out three of the lanterns. Now the room's only illumination came through the crown glass window and from one flickering lamp. Franz sat down on the other side of the bed so that they flanked Peter on both sides.

"Now, open your eyes slowly."

Peter kept his eyes closed at first as he breathed deeply. His eyelids fluttered. He waited a moment, then pressed his lips together, opened his eyes, closed them, and blinked. Then he opened his eyes wide, closed them again, and opened them. He looked straight ahead. Madlen didn't know if he could see and didn't dare ask. She looked right into his eyes, trying to detect any emotion. A tear ran down Peter's cheek. Madlen didn't know what to think. She looked at the doctor, who had a broad smile plastered across his face.

"Was it a success?" Madlen asked Franz nervously.

"You've fixed your hair differently," Peter remarked as he regarded Madlen. "It looks charming."

Madlen touched her hair, grasping the implication of what Peter had said.

"You see my hair," she whispered. "You see my hair!" she called out, tears of joy streaming down her face. Without a thought she bent over to put her head onto Peter's chest and embrace him.

"Yes, I can see. Everything's going to be all right now, you have my word." He looked at Franz. "There is no way I can ever repay you. Regardless of how much money I give you, I will be forever in your debt."

Madlen let go of Peter and stood up.

"Healing changes lives," the doctor said, gazing at Madlen. She returned his look. "Don't ever forget what healing has done for your father-in-law and what it means for your entire family." He cleared his throat. "And never forget what this moment means to you."

"I'll never forget," she promised.

"Good. I will be staying at Otilia's house here in Worms for four more days. Then I will leave for Heidelberg. Please come over soon and share your decision with me. And if you wonder for even a split second whether medicine could be your destiny, then accept my invitation to come hear my lectures for a few days. I would be delighted to accompany you to Heidelberg."

"I will think about it. I promise you."

"That's all I can ask." The doctor turned to Peter. "You should rest. You certainly can't expect to take to your work again. You may be overwhelmed by many different sensations. Give yourself some time to get up, and get up only when you think you're ready."

Peter reached out to take Madlen's and the doctor's hands. "You both have my eternal thanks. You are good people, better than I could ever hope to be. As God is my witness, I vow that from this day forward, I will be a righteous man, a man of integrity." Then he let go of their hands.

Madlen choked back her tears and stood up. "I'll go tell Elsbeth that you are doing well and are able to see again."

"Can you ask her to come see me? There are many things that I must ask her forgiveness for."

"I'll tell her."

The doctor stood up as well. "I wish you a good recovery. I believe that God took away your eyesight for a reason. And now he's given it back to you. May God be with you."

"And with you, Doctor. May God protect you."

Madlen said farewell to the doctor and told Elsbeth the good news. Before they removed the bandages, Madlen had sent the children to the market with Helene, who promised to bring Veit and Cecilia to Agathe's house afterward.

Madlen went into Peter's study, plopped down on the comfortable chair behind his desk, and propped her legs up on a small stool. She was starting to doze off when Elsbeth came downstairs. Madlen sat up immediately. She could see that her mother-in-law had been crying. "Well?"

Elsbeth sank down on one of the visitor chairs, covered her face with her hands, and dissolved into tears. Madlen got up and walked around the desk. She set her hands on Elsbeth's shoulders, then pulled her close. "Shh, shh, everything's going to be all right," Madlen whispered.

"I know," Elsbeth finally said. Then she looked up at her daughter-in-law.

"What's the matter?"

"It's as though, after so many years, God gave me back the man to whom I gave my heart." She laughed, cried, then laughed again. "It's truly a miracle!"

Madlen pulled up the other visitor chair, sat down in front of Elsbeth, and took her hands. "The doctor said that God sometimes afflicts people so He can teach them something. Then He gives them their health back when they've learned the lesson. Do you think this might have happened to Peter?"

Elsbeth looked at Madlen thoughtfully. "Yes, I believe that's what happened. Peter had lost his way, and our Lord, in all His wisdom and benevolence, took away his eyesight. And He was all the more benevolent to let him regain his vision."

As Madlen started to respond, someone knocked on the front door. "I'll get it." She stood.

"I'll come with you," Elsbeth said. "I think we know who's at the door."

They went to the door, holding hands. Madlen opened it and Elsbeth stepped forward. "What can I do for you? Did you bring the information from the bishop that we requested?" Elsbeth asked.

The guard stared at her. "We have a message from the bishop stating that he wishes to speak to Johannes Goldmann's wife."

"And what would be the reason?"

"It's confidential. We're only supposed to say that he is with an envoy from Cologne who wishes to speak with the lawyer's wife about a certain matter."

"Johannes is back from Cologne?" Madlen said. "Is my husband with the bishop?"

"No, not your husband. Just an envoy."

Madlen's body temperature went from hot to ice-cold. Of course it wasn't Johannes. He would have come to her first and taken care of business matters later. Even so, this didn't explain what the bishop of Worms wanted with her. "Did something happen to my husband?"

"I do not know."

"I'll come with you."

"I will, too," Elsbeth said. "Wait a moment. I just need to inform my husband."

"Good. But please hurry. The bishop is rather annoyed that we didn't succeed in bringing you earlier."

Elsbeth gathered up her skirts, then ran upstairs. A few minutes later she ran back down the stairs so quickly that Madlen was afraid she might fall. The women exchanged a look, then followed the guards.

Madlen stumbled more than she walked, her thoughts fixated on Johannes and his welfare. She kept telling herself that nothing had happened to him. But why would he have sent an envoy if he was coming back to Worms anyway? Or had someone else sent the envoy? As she contemplated the situation, the guards stopped. Madlen looked up and saw that they were already standing in front of the bishop's estate. Two guards flanked the entrance.

"Please wait here."

The women nodded mutely as the guard took his leave.

"The bishop will receive you now," said the guard when he returned. "Follow me."

Madlen and Elsbeth trailed after him. The building's interior more than made up for what it lacked on the outside. It was glorious. Madlen looked around. The foyer was at least twice as big as the foyer of her house in Cologne. The walls were handsomely decorated, and small tables with silver candlesticks helped to light the room.

"This way," the guard said. He knocked once, then opened the door.

"There you are." The bishop came out from behind a massive desk to greet the women. A man Madlen had never seen before sat in the visitor's chair. He arose and stood there calmly.

"Please, take a seat," the bishop said. "Because this is about business matters, I've chosen this room for our discussion." He motioned toward the chairs. "Please sit down. I assume you know my guest?"

"No, unfortunately not," Madlen answered.

"My name is Leopold Baumhauer. I'm in the service of the archbishop of Cologne. I bring a message from your husband," the man said as he dropped to his knee.

"Is Johannes all right? Has something happened to him?"

"The last time I saw him he was doing quite well. On account of his duties, he's currently not at liberty to leave Cologne to resolve the issues that await him here."

The bishop walked behind his desk and took a seat. He waited until his visitors sat down, too, before speaking. "I do believe it would be best if you would more thoroughly explain to the attorney's wife why we have summoned her here today."

Leopold pulled out a rolled parchment. "This will undoubtedly explain a lot to you."

"Can the reading of the scroll wait until after our discussion?" the bishop asked, a bit impatiently. "This affair has already taken up more time than necessary, so let us discuss only what concerns me."

"Gladly," Madlen agreed. "But it's still not at all clear why my mother-in-law and I are here."

"It is because she is Johannes Goldmann's mother and you are his wife that we are gathered here," Leopold said.

Madlen was as confused as ever.

The bishop waved his hand as if shooing away an annoying insect. "With all due respect, you can clear up that matter later. Briefly: we are here because our revered archbishop relayed a document through this envoy instructing me to pay off Peter Goldmann's debts. The entirety of the funds will be reimbursed to me by the archbishop, plus some compensation for my efforts."

Madlen and Elsbeth looked at each other, their mouths open in astonishment.

"You're paying off my husband's debts?" Elsbeth asked.

"So it seems. The archbishop had no idea what the exact sum would be, which is why he asked me to resolve the unfortunate matter in his stead. This will also help to restore your husband's reputation. The document didn't exactly say that part, but sometimes it's best to read between the lines." He raised his eyebrows. "Be that as it may, it's the archbishop's wish that I follow his instructions to the letter. First thing tomorrow I will announce that your husband's creditors, upon presenting the relevant documents, will be paid back in full, at which time Peter Goldmann will be relieved from his debts and, I imagine, from the greatest of his worries."

"What do we have to do in return?" Madlen asked suspiciously.

"In return? My good woman, I am only complying with the archbishop's wishes. And the archbishop will be compensating me with a few coins for my help."

"Ten percent of what you spend to repay these debts, to be exact," Leopold confirmed. "Which is substantially more than a few coins."

"Whether ten percent or just a piece of silver, it makes no difference to me. I am simply doing this to engender the goodwill of the archbishop."

"Of course," Leopold said. "And as he wrote, the archbishop owes you, shall we say, a personal favor, should you ever face difficulties while in office."

"This is the way allies build their alliances," the bishop said affably.

"Perhaps," Leopold said, then turned to address Madlen. "It was important to your husband that this matter be agreed upon not only by the archbishop, the bishop, and myself. He wanted you to be made aware of it as well. That's why I've insisted on your presence here today."

"I understand. This is typical of how my husband would deal with such a matter."

"Well, as far as I'm concerned, then, the matter is resolved." The bishop rose. "If you would excuse me, my office brings with it many responsibilities."

"Of course," Leopold said, standing. Madlen and Elsbeth got up, too, not having fully processed all that had just taken place.

The three politely took their leave, then walked out together.

"You said your name is Leopold Baumhauer, correct?" Madlen asked.

"Yes, that is correct."

"Lord Baumhauer, have you already found accommodations? You're not riding back to Cologne today, are you?"

"No, certainly not. I'm planning to remain in Worms for quite a while."

"Oh?"

"Indeed. This is the second part of the archbishop's mission assigned to me."

"And what is this mission?" Madlen asked.

"I've been authorized to revive the Goldmann family business, to help it to flourish once again," he explained cheerfully. "Tomorrow or the next day, we'll be bringing the necessary funds to the counting house in order to restock the warehouse."

"But, but, we can't just—" Elsbeth started to argue. Leopold raised his hand to silence her.

"My mission is clear. And I will fulfill it, come what may."

"But my husband can do this now, since his cataract operation was a success. He can see again, and therefore he is quite capable of taking care of the business by himself!"

"That, my good woman, will not be possible." He was friendly but firm. "The archbishop is paying off your debts, and it is with his money that I will purchase the merchandise to stock the warehouse. The business will be run in the Goldmann family name, but that is only a front. Whether you like it or not, henceforth the archbishop has the final say in your house and in your business until every last penny is paid back to him. I have been assigned to make this happen. So, be happy and let me do my job."

Elsbeth and Madlen were speechless.

"So, would you be so kind as to show me the house where I will be living and working during this time? I'm practically dying of hunger."

Elsbeth was the first to shake off her dismay. "Certainly," she said. "Please, come this way." She took Madlen's arm and pulled her along. Peter had just regained his health, and Elsbeth couldn't imagine how he would react to the news that they no longer had a say in their own house or business. In a split second, her recently acquired resolve had blown away like so much dust in the wind. The archbishop's envoy looked quite satisfied as he walked next to her, whistling a little ditty. Elsbeth felt she was in an absurd dream from which she hoped to wake up.

Chapter Ten

"I've bidden you here today to fulfill an important mission for Friedrich, our archbishop." Johannes stood before twelve guards seated at the long dining table. Johannes had found it necessary to receive them in his own home. First of all, to make clear that henceforth all reports were to be made directly to him. Secondly, he could offer them a sip or two of spiced wine, something he certainly couldn't offer at the archbishop's residence. He hoped his hospitality would inspire their loyalty. Friendliness combined with the right amount of discipline had always worked for him, and he hoped to continue to succeed with this approach. He held up a parchment.

"You will see in this document that the archbishop has transferred his full authority to me during his absence. Therefore, I stand before you as your direct employer." Johannes handed the document to the first guard and instructed him to read it before passing it on to the next man, though he doubted that even half of those assembled were literate. "A copy of this same document can be found in the scribe's office at the archbishop's residence, in case anyone doubts its authenticity."

The guards exchanged looks all around. They had no reason to distrust him, but Johannes waited until the document had made the rounds before continuing. "You are all good men! Of course, the archbishop holds this opinion as well. We have his wholehearted trust. Therefore, I'm going to need every single one of you in order to help solve the two murders that occurred within the last few days."

The men shifted nervously in their seats. "Are you certain the vicar was murdered?" the man who sat directly in front of Johannes asked. "I heard that it could have been his heart."

"Your name is Anderlin, right?"

"Yes, my lord."

"Good. Please bear with me as I learn your names. Well, Anderlin, whoever told you that Bartholomäus died because of his heart was misinformed. He was poisoned, and his death was excruciating." Johannes let his words sink in. "And two nights ago, the archbishop's vassal, Bernhard von Harvehorst, was attacked, beaten, bound, then hanged from his neck."

"Von Harvehorst is dead, too?" one of the guards asked.

"Yes. And what is your name?"

"Linhardt, my lord."

"Yes, Linhardt, he is dead."

"I'm Georg," the man next to Linhardt said. "I heard about von Harvehorst's death and that he'd hanged himself. And that it was probably because of his wife."

"I heard that claim as well. But it is incorrect—the doctor and I saw the man ourselves. He did not hang himself."

"Who do you think is responsible?" Linhardt asked.

"I have no idea. And that's why I need all of you. It is the archbishop's wish that these crimes be solved immediately. After Bartholomäus's death, his servant, Christopeit, disappeared. Apparently he was escorted away by two men. I've already asked in various inns around town, and nobody seems to have seen Christopeit since then."

"Do you suppose there is a link between the two deaths?" Georg asked.

"Yes. But then we can't call them simply 'deaths,' can we? They were murders! Two cowardly, cold-blooded murders. It's up to us, the men in this room, to bring the killer or killers to justice." He let his gaze fall upon each man in turn. "I don't know much yet, but the murders seem to have been an indirect attack on the archbishop. Somebody is trying to hurt him. Everyone here has thus far successfully protected Friedrich, and we must ensure that this murderer does not come near our employer. He who protects the welfare of the archbishop also protects the welfare of the entirety of Cologne."

"I heard that Bernhard von Harvehorst and the archbishop were at odds," Linhardt said. Some of the other men murmured in agreement.

"I heard that, too," Georg said.

"Where did you hear that from?" Johannes said.

"I think all of us heard that," Anderlin said, looking around. "Isn't that true?"

Everyone nodded.

"This gives me all the more reason to believe there is a conspiracy," Johannes concluded. "That quarrel was settled several weeks ago. The archbishop even had the wisdom to finally take Bernhard von Harvehorst's point of view."

This was evidently news to the guards.

"Tell me, how did you learn of this rumor of a quarrel between the two men?" Johannes asked.

Finally, Georg spoke. "I heard it firsthand, my lord, as I was on guard duty in the study that day. Wolfker and Niclaus were there as well as another guard, whose name I do not know."

"That's true. I'm Wolfker, my lord, and even though we weren't trying to eavesdrop, they were yelling so loudly that everyone in the building must have heard them." Wolfker gestured to the man next to him. "And later when we talked about it, we were amazed at how fierce the quarrel was." The guard next to him nodded.

"I understand. What happened next?"

"Bernhard von Harvehorst stormed out in a rage," Georg answered.

"When was that?"

"About two weeks ago, my lord."

"Did Bernhard von Harvehorst ever return to the archbishop's residence after that?"

"Yes. Exactly three days ago I saw him there," another guard said.

"Your name?"

"Wilhelm, my lord."

"Good, Wilhelm. What did you observe?"

"Bernhard von Harvehorst arrived, and I informed the archbishop. He received the visitor immediately."

"And what was your impression of this meeting?"

"It wasn't anything unusual, my lord."

"Did they fight?"

"No, my lord, they didn't fight. At least, I didn't hear anything. And when von Harvehorst left, he seemed quite satisfied."

"This confirms what the archbishop told me, namely that the dispute was settled weeks ago. Now there is the important matter of von Harvehorst's housekeeper, Duretta. Frankly, I'm afraid that she and Christopeit could be in on it."

"Why?" Anderlin asked.

"Well, yesterday I returned to von Harvehorst's house and it was completely empty, though I explicitly told the housekeeper to stay there."

"What can we do, my lord?" Linhardt asked.

"We must find the people who saw the deceased last, namely Duretta and Christopeit. Take to the streets of Cologne. Ask around, and listen to what people are saying at the market, at the inns, and in the pubs." Johannes thought for second. "And announce to all that there is a reward of twenty pieces of silver for anyone who brings me one or both of them."

The men traded looks. "Does that go for us, too, my lord? Or just for the citizens of Cologne?"

"For everyone. Bring them to me here, at my house. And if anything happens that seems unusual to you, inform me immediately. Do you understand?"

The guards nodded.

"Good. Now go and do your duty."

The men set off. Johannes closed the door behind them, then leaned against it. The tasks ahead would undoubtedly prove to be quite challenging, and he wanted to finish them as quickly as possible. He walked into the kitchen, picked up a mug, and filled it with beer. He plopped onto the bench and took a big slug.

Hans walked in. "Are they gone?"

"Yes, Hans, they are. There are some mugs left over in the dining room."

"I'll take care of it, my lord. I'll be the maid today." He laughed as he scrutinized his master. "You're worried, my lord."

"You're right about that," Johannes agreed. "I have to solve two murders, and I don't have the slightest idea who did it or why."

"May I?" Hans pointed to the beer.

"Help yourself."

Hans took a mug, filled it, and placed it on the table. Then he sat on the bench across from his employer.

"I'm only a simple servant," Hans said. "You're a lawyer, a well-educated man." He took a sip. "Certainly I can't be of much help to you. But I can say with confidence that if there's one thing I know, it's people. If someone kills a vicar and a nobleman, he must have a very good reason."

"And what might that be?"

Hans shrugged. "That I don't know. But certainly someone with such a good reason wouldn't commit the murders himself."

"Why not?"

"Because the killer would most likely be a high lord whose face people would recognize."

Johannes scratched his chin, like he always did when deep in thought. "Go on."

"What did the vicar and von Harvehorst have in common?"

"I'd only had a few meetings with von Harvehorst, and our conversations were always focused on contracts, agreements, and negotiations. I knew the vicar better. He was different than the archbishop. He wasn't a world leader, just a simple clergyman. His religious beliefs guided his actions. The archbishop's power was unimportant to him. Indeed, the vicar made every effort to fight for Friedrich's spiritual salvation, to stand by him and counsel him so that the archbishop could devote himself to his official duties."

"So both men were, in their own ways, very important to the archbishop," Hans deduced.

"That's correct."

The two sat in silence for a moment.

"The vicar also wanted to accompany the archbishop on his journey to Rome," Johannes continued. "Friedrich counted on their opinions." Suddenly he sat straight up.

"What just occurred to you, my lord?"

"Since both of them are no longer with us, the archbishop will have to replace them. The question is, with whom? Who would travel with the archbishop in their stead?"

Hans held up his mug. "It was a pleasure to help you figure things out, sir." He took a big slurp.

"You may be a servant, but you sure don't act like one, Hans."

"Everything I know I learned from you, my lord."

"First thing tomorrow morning, I'll find out who is riding with the archbishop."

"And what will you do, my lord, if you recognize this person?"

"I don't know yet. I need to sleep on it. Tomorrow I'll have an answer." He smiled confidently. "Yes, then I'll know the answer."

They both drank a second beer together before Johannes decided that was quite enough and proceeded to his bedchamber. Thoughts whirled about in his head. At first he pondered the crimes, but then he began to think about Madlen. Normally he would discuss these kinds of things with her, not with Hans. Johannes and Madlen's conversation would be much longer, more in depth and intense, the type of conversation that made him look deep into his soul. Madlen always helped him to think things through in a logical way. He needed her. He missed her with every breath he took.

He hoped that Leopold had delivered the letter to his wife in which he tried to explain why he couldn't leave Cologne—not yet anyway. If he solved the murders, there would be no reason to remain in Cologne any longer. He inhaled deeply then exhaled. Then he could be with Madlen again. He wondered whether she'd be cross with him. Would she feel betrayed because Leopold had been dispatched to revive the family business? A feeling of despair swept over him at the thought of Madlen being upset without him. He rolled onto his side.

But the thoughts didn't cease their whirling. How was his mother? Did she have the strength to get through all of this? She'd looked terribly wan when he'd seen her last. Guilt and anxiety weighed heavily upon his very soul. Had he behaved properly when he'd submitted to the archbishop's wishes? Or should he have insisted on staying with his family in Worms? If he had done so, the archbishop would have undoubtedly refused to rescue his family from the financial situation his father had created, despite the fact that Johannes had been the longest-serving legal counselor the archbishop had ever had. No. He had this one opportunity to make things right. Though he tried to calm himself with this thought, it was several hours before he fell into a fitful, dreamless sleep.

◆ ◆ ◆

Johannes had just finished eating breakfast when someone knocked on the front door. He opened it to find Linhardt standing there.

"God bless you, my lord. The housekeeper has been found. But no one will be able to claim the reward."

"What happened?"

"Please, my lord, come with me and see for yourself. They've just pulled her in from the river. It must have been one of the cargo ships that had been sailing close to shore."

"What are you talking about?"

"Her hands and feet were bound. One of the ships must have pushed against the corpse and torn the rope which had been tied around a rock to keep her body submerged. It's not a pretty sight, my lord."

"I'm coming." Johannes didn't stop to put on his coat. The days were getting warmer, always a reason to rejoice. Warm weather meant there would be crops growing in the fields, bringing about new life. But this was evidently not the case in Cologne. People seemed to be dying faster here than they could be buried.

With a grim expression on his face, Johannes walked down to the harbor with Linhardt. A throng of people had formed, and Johannes's bad mood got even worse.

"Let us through," he demanded irritably as he and Linhardt made their way through the crowd. When they reached the corpse, Johannes only glanced at it briefly.

"Who found her?"

A man walked over to him. "That would be us, my lord," he said, gesturing to the man standing next to him. "The trading vessel there in front and another boat got too close to each other. They narrowly avoided a collision, which is why the cargo ship was sailing closer to the shore. The captain thought he felt a slight impact on the ship's hull, but when he looked he didn't see anything."

"Where's the captain now?"

"On his ship." The man nodded his head in the ship's direction. "He boarded again after we recovered the corpse. It seems he doesn't have much of a stomach for this kind of thing."

That was easy for Johannes to understand, since the swollen corpse with its bound arms and legs was anything but a pretty sight.

"What happened after the ships almost collided? Did the captain tell you he thought he heard something bump against his hull?"

"No, my lord. That wasn't necessary. The ship hadn't moored yet when we saw the corpse floating on the surface. We rowed over in our fishing boat and pulled her out."

Suddenly a terrible scream cut through the air. "Duretta!"

Johannes turned toward a distraught woman as she fell to the ground next to the deceased. She screamed once more, then bent over the corpse and began to wail.

Everybody took a step back.

"Wait here. I would like to speak with you again," Johannes said to the fisherman. He walked over to the woman. She was still on the ground, crying inconsolably.

"Come on." He stretched out his hand to her, but she didn't react. He bent down and took a hold of her shoulders so that he could pull her up. As he did so, he got a closer look at the deceased. He hesitated.

Johannes let go of the woman's shoulders and squatted down to get a better look at the corpse's face. "But—" He broke off. "Come on," he ordered in a sterner tone. "Stand up." He rose and pulled the woman up with him. "Who are you, my lady?"

The woman wiped her tearstained cheeks with the back of her hand. "My name is Margret, my lord. Duretta was my sister."

"Duretta? You're saying the deceased here is Duretta?"

"Yes, my lord." The woman looked at him in a daze.

"And who did your sister serve?"

"She was Bernhard von Harvehorst's housekeeper, my lord."

Johannes looked at the people around him. "Which one of you fine citizens knows this woman?"

A few people hesitantly raised their hands. Johannes pointed to a woman standing in front, whose clothing had seen better days. "You there! Step forward. Which of these women do you know by name?"

"Both of them, my lord," she said as she stepped forward.

"From where?"

"Margret doesn't live very far from our house. She works for some spice merchants. Her son and mine worked together as carpenter apprentices." She looked at the deceased. "And I know Duretta, too." She paused. "I don't know from where, but I recognize her nevertheless."

Johannes nodded and motioned for her to step back. "You there!" He pointed at a tall, lanky man. "Do you know her?"

"I know Duretta because my lord and Bernhard von Harvehorst worked together. I ate some meals in the servants' quarters with her, while I awaited my master."

More people stepped forward to be questioned, but their answers were always the same. Some knew one sister, others knew them both. All of them agreed that the dead woman on the ground was Duretta, Bernhard von Harvehorst's longtime housekeeper.

"You there. Bring the body to the morgue and make sure that this woman gets a proper burial."

"Who should we say will pay for this?" asked the man.

"Tell him that the attorney Johannes Goldmann will ensure that he gets his money."

"Yes, my lord."

Johannes turned to Margret. "Tell me, when was the last time you saw your sister?"

"I believe it was seven, no, about eight days ago. My youngest are twins. They were sick. I was barely able to do my work. Usually we'd see each other at the market, but because I had to stay home, Duretta and I hadn't seen each other much lately."

"Didn't your sister watch your children just the other night?"

"Watch my children? Of course not. How could she have done that?"

"All right. Thank you." He took one last glance at the deceased's face and her battered body. Her hands and feet were still bound, and another rope hung loosely from her ankle.

"Thank you for taking on the cost of my sister's burial," Margret said, pulling him out of his thoughts.

He nodded. "Go, take care of your children. And try to forget this image of your sister before it burns forever in your mind."

"It's too late for that," she responded bitterly. She took one last look at her sister then walked away.

Johannes waved over the fisherman he'd spoken with earlier.

"Should I retrieve the captain so he can confirm what I said?"

"Later, if it becomes necessary." Johannes turned around. He pointed toward the boats. "Is one of those yours?"

"Yes, my lord. That one in front."

"Bring me to the place where you found the body."

"Yes, my lord." The fisherman turned without another word and Johannes followed him. As they climbed into the boat, from the corner of his eye Johannes saw several men wrap the body in a sheet, lift it, and carry it away. He tried to stay standing but eventually sat down when the fisherman picked up the oars and started rowing with strong sweeping movements. The boat glided smoothly through the water. Johannes tried to calm his nerves. What was he expecting to find?

"How much farther?"

"Not much farther, my lord." The man pointed. "Right there, where the Rhine widens." He took a couple more strokes, then pulled the oars out of the water and let the boat drift. "It's around here somewhere."

Johannes stared down into the dark water. "How deep is it here?"

"Not so deep as in the middle. A loaded ship wouldn't normally sail here."

"So whoever sunk the corpse wouldn't have been in a ship with a deep draft."

"I would agree with that, yes."

"And it's far enough from the harbor that tugboats wouldn't be able to come here, either?"

"Yes, my lord, that is correct."

"The murderer could have been pretty sure that the corpse wouldn't resurface. He must be quite familiar with the Rhine."

"I hope I'm not leading you astray by saying this, but if I wanted to get rid of a corpse, I would dump it here."

Johannes took another look around. "Me, too." He thought of something. "Give me one oar and you take the other. Let's put them in the water and see whether we bump into anything."

"But—"

"Just do it." He looked over at the dock where some people were standing. "You there!" he called out. "We need more boats here." Johannes waved to get their attention. "There's a reward!"

Only then did the people seem to take notice. Immediately several men jumped in a boat and rowed over.

"What kind of reward, my lord?"

"That depends on what we find. If it is what I think it is, the archbishop will no doubt be quite generous."

The fisherman needed only a second to respond to Johannes's offer. He began to pull his oar deeply through the water.

"Nothing here. Let's try farther out," the fisherman said as he noticed other boats heading toward them.

"You know the Rhine better than I do," Johannes said, returning his oar.

The fisherman rowed a bit farther, then handed one of the oars back to Johannes. Together they searched the water. When the other men reached them, Johannes explained what they needed to do. At first they stayed close together, but soon they spread out in a large circle.

Johannes couldn't say for how many hours they searched. He was just about to give up when somebody cried out.

"Found something!" A man waved his arm around excitedly.

"Row me over there," Johannes ordered the fisherman, who looked somewhat disappointed.

"Here, my lord." The other man pulled the oar through the water until he met resistance.

"Let me see." Johannes climbed into the other boat and took the oar, then tried it himself. Slowly and smoothly, he pulled the paddle through the water until it bumped into something solid. "Somebody's got to go down and see what that is."

"For how much?" came the succinct question.

"Thirty silver coins."

"Thirty silver coins even if it's only an anchor?"

"Thirty silver coins no matter what it is."

Without hesitation, the man plunged into the water, then emerged near the boat, took a deep breath, and dove down. After a moment, he came up again. "I need a knife."

One of the other fishermen pulled one out and handed it to him. Without saying what he'd discovered, the man dove down again. Everyone stared at the water in fascination. Air bubbles surfaced, and soon they could make out some movement.

"Help me," the man gasped after emerging. He pulled something toward the boat.

A brief look was enough for Johannes to recognize a human corpse.

Two men in the boat bent over and lifted the corpse. Then they helped their friend out of the water.

"He was tied to a stone down there," the man said.

"Everyone gets thirty silver coins, and you get sixty," Johannes declared. The men cheered.

Johannes grabbed the waterlogged coat and turned the body over. "Just as I guessed," he murmured.

"You know this man?"

"Indeed. I would bet my life this is Christopeit, Vicar Bartholomäus's personal servant."

"How did you know we'd find him here?"

"I didn't. But the housekeeper's body was here, and I suspected Christopeit might have met the same fate. Now, take us back to shore."

As the fishermen moored their boats, Johannes saw Linhardt, who had been waiting on shore for his return.

"What did you find?" the guard said.

"I believe we found Christopeit. He was dumped in the Rhine, exactly like the real housekeeper."

"The *real* housekeeper?" Linhardt asked. "What do you mean by that?"

"The woman we found earlier, who many identified as Bernhard von Harvehorst's housekeeper, Duretta, was not the woman I spoke to after von Harvehorst's death."

"What? I don't understand."

"I met an impostor claiming to be Duretta."

"Why would somebody do a thing like that?"

"That I don't know," Johannes responded. "Not yet, anyway. But that state of affairs is about to change."

Chapter Eleven

"Absolutely not!" Peter yelled, his face scarlet. "Nobody runs my businesses for me! Nobody gives me orders in my own house and in my own office, envoy of the archbishop or not!" This was the first time in months he'd gone into his office, only to discover that he was no longer authorized to be there.

"But, Peter, we have no choice," Elsbeth pleaded.

Leopold looked from one spouse to the other, glanced briefly at Madlen, and looked at Peter again.

"What was Johannes thinking by sending this lackey, who now considers himself the administrator of my business?"

"If I may be permitted to speak—your son did not make this decision. It was entirely the archbishop's doing," Leopold said pleasantly.

"It seems as though you take great joy in seeing me in this position!" Peter glowered at the younger man.

"What position?" Leopold shrugged. "Correct me if I'm mistaken, but until the archbishop's intervention, you had a huge debt, an empty warehouse, and no way to care for your family. Now Eckard von Dersch—the bishop of Worms himself!—has taken responsibility for the full payment of your debts, and I have taken on the responsibility of making your businesses flourish again. So I don't understand why you are angry."

Peter made a fist.

"He's right," Elsbeth said quickly, before her husband could resume his ranting and raving. "No matter how you look at it, he is right." She turned to Leopold. "Can I assume that when there's enough money to pay back the archbishop's loan, your job here will be done?"

"Exactly. As soon as the business is thriving and all debts are paid, I will send a message to the archbishop to request my return to Cologne." Leopold smiled amiably again.

"But I don't want people to tell me what I can and cannot do in my own business," Peter whined. "I'm an experienced businessman and not used to taking orders."

"Nobody will tell you what to do," Leopold Baumhauer stated simply. "Why would they? You'll have nothing to do with it at all."

"What do you mean?"

"My mission is to manage the business in your name. You are in no position to quarrel about or contest any of these commercial activities. The archbishop trusts me, and you can trust me as well."

"I have a reputation to protect!"

Leopold looked over at Elsbeth. "I had hoped that I wouldn't have to be so brutally honest, but you give me no choice. You once had an unassailable reputation as an honest businessman, whose word carried weight and who fulfilled his obligations. But at this point, your reputation is ruined."

Peter started to protest, but Leopold held up his hand to silence him.

"I'm not judging you. I don't even want to know how it got to this point. That's not important to me. My task is to make amends and leave behind a thriving business." He looked Peter directly in the eyes. "You know better than anyone what led to this terrible situation. But have you thought about the repercussions for your son and his family? He is the attorney for the archbishop of Cologne, one of the most powerful men of our time. To retain his position, your son's reputation must be beyond reproach."

Peter's expression changed. Though still irritated, he seemed to become more contemplative. He sat down slowly onto a chair. "By God, I didn't think about that." He looked over at Madlen. "I'm sorry, my child. I was only thinking of myself. It was never my intention to harm you, Johannes, or the children."

"Nobody is angry with you," Madlen assured him "You heard it from the envoy's own mouth: it's not important how this all came about."

Peter nodded, then looked at Elsbeth. "I'm sorry. You don't deserve any of this."

"We can speak about that some other time," she said, blushing. "Now the only thing that matters is getting back on our feet. We must stick together and help Lord Baumhauer however we can."

"Thank you." Leopold bowed.

Peter sighed. "Good. What can I do? Show you the books?"

"That won't be necessary. Why look at the books when there are no assets?" He grabbed his leather case and pulled out a folder. "Today we begin anew," he declared. "Everything else is behind us."

"I thank you," Peter said, only a hint of resentment left in his voice.

"I take great pleasure in helping others. I'm excited about the job ahead. Where can I freshen up? A well-groomed exterior is almost as important as the merchandise we peddle."

A remark was on the tip of Peter's tongue, but he suppressed it. "So be it." He looked at his daughter-in-law. "Madlen, can you show Lord Baumhauer the house? And tell Helene to prepare a bedchamber for him."

"Of course." She motioned for Leopold to follow her.

"Elsbeth, stay, please," Peter said. "I would like to discuss something with you."

"Of course."

Ellin Carsta

Madlen stopped and for a moment watched her in-laws. She had a feeling that Peter might come up with a plan to circumvent Leopold Baumhauer's authority. She decided to speak privately with her mother-in-law later. "Let's go," she finally said to Leopold. They left the office together.

"Helene," she called out. "Helene, are you there?"

"Here, my lady." Helene walked into the hall from the kitchen, drying her hands on a towel.

"I would like to introduce you to our guest or, to be more exact, our new administrator. This is Lord Baumhauer. He's come from Cologne to help us revive the business."

Helene curtsied. "God be with you, my lord."

"God be with you, maid." Leopold cocked his head to the side, a slight smile forming on his lips as he studied her. When Helene noted his expression, she blushed and bowed her head.

"Could you be so kind as to prepare a bedchamber for our administrator, Helene?"

"Yes, my lady."

"Oh, and tell me: What did Agathe say? Is she bringing the children here, or should I go fetch them?"

"I've been wondering about that. I've been waiting for them a long while. Would you like me to go to your aunt's house and pick them up?"

"No. Take care of the bedchamber. I'll show Lord Baumhauer the rest of the house. If Agathe doesn't get here soon, I'll go myself."

"Yes, my lady." Helene nodded to Leopold then disappeared into the kitchen again.

"Please, follow me upstairs."

"My pleasure." They climbed the stairs together. "May I ask you something?" Leopold said.

"Of course."

"Would it be too much of an imposition to ask you to call me by my first name? I would like your in-laws to do the same. It's better if we appear casual."

"Why is that?"

"It builds confidence. Whoever does business with us should get the impression that the administrator is not an outsider but a person who knows the Goldmann family well, and who has the trust of the archbishop. That will make things easier for me."

"But how will people know that the archbishop sent you?"

Leopold smiled. "How fast do you think word will get out that the archbishop of Cologne, His Excellency himself, is paying off Peter Goldmann's debts, and that an administrator working in his service will be putting the family's business affairs in order?"

They reached the upper floor and Madlen stopped.

"I suppose it won't take long. From now on, I will address you as Leopold, just like a close friend or family member would." She took a couple of steps and opened the first door on the right. "Helene will prepare this bedchamber for you. I hope it is to your liking."

Leopold entered the room. "I don't need much." He looked around. "This is very nice, actually. When I travel with the archbishop, it is a completely different story."

Now a question that had been haunting Madlen since visiting the bishop of Worms came to mind. "May I ask you a question, Leopold, and trust that you will give me an honest answer?"

"If it doesn't concern confidential matters, of course."

"Why is the archbishop doing all this? I mean, who knows whether this entire enterprise will be successful or whether the business will recover or even if he'll get his money back? Plus, doesn't he need you by his side in Cologne? Why is he being so generous?"

"I'll give you the honest answer you've requested," Leopold said. "Money doesn't matter to Friedrich. He has enough of it, more than enough. At one time, he needed his great-uncle to unburden the diocese

123

from its debts. Since then, the archbishop has accumulated a veritable fortune. Even if he paid Peter Goldmann's debts ten times over, it wouldn't put a dent in his reserves."

"Nevertheless, he doesn't have to do this."

"No, of course not. But he wants to. And that's why I'm here. He holds your husband in great esteem, and he knows just how valuable Johannes's legal counsel is. He can do without the money but not without your husband's expertise. The archbishop is a power seeker, a true imperial monarch. He's been holding the office of the archbishop for over a quarter century. How many before him have been able to do this? I predict he will remain in power even longer, assuming that he doesn't fall prey to an attack on his life."

"Why do you say that?"

"What did your husband tell you about why he is staying in Cologne?"

"I haven't had time to read his message."

"Well, I'm assuming that he told you the truth. Besides, almost everybody in Cologne already knows about it anyway. It must practically be common knowledge by now." He exhaled noisily. "There's been a murder. The archbishop's vicar, Bartholomäus, was poisoned. And something tells me that there's more to it than just this one wicked deed. I took little pleasure in departing from Cologne because, to be honest, I am deeply concerned about the archbishop's welfare, even though he left for Rome shortly after my own departure and is a good distance from Cologne. Something is afoot. I just know it." He looked at Madlen. "I talk too much." He smiled. "You husband is a wise man. The archbishop trusts him. He will solve Bartholomäus's murder. He was the right choice for this task."

Madlen could hardly wait to open the scroll and read her husband's message. "Thank you for your honesty."

Helene had come to the doorway, and she now cleared her throat. "May I prepare the room now?"

"Yes, Helene. Thank you. Come now, Leopold. I'll show you the rest of the house."

He followed her readily, but not before throwing Helene a certain look as she started to prepare the bed. She didn't look up, concentrating completely on her work. But Leopold was sure that she'd noted it. With a smile on his lips, he left the bedchamber.

"We were planning to get underway just now," Agathe said after greeting her niece at the front door.

"Mother!" Cecilia embraced Madlen while Veit let her pat him on the head.

"I was getting worried."

"We were delayed," Agathe raised an eyebrow and inclined her head toward Veit.

"What has he done this time?"

Veit looked pleadingly at Agathe. "Nothing much," she finally said. "But tell us: What's happened to you? The whole city is talking about it."

"What?"

"People are saying that the archbishop of Cologne sent one of his men to pay off Peter Goldmann's creditors. But that's just idle gossip, right?"

"No, Agathe, it's true."

"But how?"

"Johannes," Madlen said proudly. "Johannes is important to the archbishop, so that's why he's arranged all this."

"Did Johannes return, too?"

"No, he is unable to come for the time being. He must remain in Cologne because of certain recent events."

"So Father hasn't come back?" Cecilia said.

"No, my little one, unfortunately not."

Cecilia was disappointed, but smiled bravely anyway. "When is he coming?"

"I don't know." Madlen hugged her daughter close. "But say, did you tell Aunt Agathe that your grandfather can see again?"

"Oh, yes," Agathe answered. "She told me right off. It's almost a miracle."

"No," Madlen said. "It's the knowledge of healing."

Agathe scrutinized her niece. "No, Madlen."

"What do you mean?"

"I see it. In your eyes I can see the fire of an old passion that almost cost you your life. Fight it. Fight it with all your might."

"Supposing there was a chance?"

"I don't understand." Agathe looked at the children briefly. "Do you want to stay for a bit? I can ask Roswitha if she can watch the children."

"Yes!" Cecilia said.

"Well, good. Let us talk about this." Agathe stepped aside to let Madlen in and closed the door behind her. "Roswitha," she called out. "We're not leaving yet."

The housekeeper came over. "I was wondering how long you were going to stand in the doorway."

"I would like to speak with my niece." She pointed to Cecilia and Veit. "Do you have time to—" She didn't have to finish her sentence. The maid held out her hands to the children. "Come on, you two. I'm always happy to have you here a little while longer."

The siblings ran to her, and together the three of them walked toward the kitchen. Agathe knew that Roswitha meant every word she'd said—it was no secret how much the maid wanted children. During the last few years, Agathe often thought about whether Roswitha would not be able to have children because of what her young faithful servant had done in the past. Was God angry at her? Agathe believed it was wrong for Madlen to have helped Roswitha terminate her pregnancy. Later, Roswitha had married Sander, and everything had gone well for them.

Roswitha had become pregnant several times, but she always miscarried around the fifth or sixth month. It was as if she'd been cursed. Agathe knew the probable cause of her troubles but said nothing. Roswitha was a simple, honest woman who had her heart in the right place. She had made a mistake, but Agathe didn't think that a person should be punished her whole life for it. She'd often prayed that the Lord would give her maid a healthy baby. Roswitha was still young and Sander was a strong man. One of these days everything would work out. Agathe wished the couple all the best.

"Come sit down," Agathe said as she and Madlen entered the sewing room. When Madlen had lived with her aunt years ago, they'd sewn beautiful dresses together in this room. They'd spent some lovely hours here, and there were times when Agathe missed that harmonious companionship so much that the memory of it almost took her breath away.

"Well? Are you going to tell me what Veit did?"

Agathe waved her hand dismissively. "It wasn't so bad. We were walking along the Rhine, and he tried to climb down an embankment over some slippery grass. I told him that he shouldn't do it. That's when it happened."

"He fell into the water?"

"Yes, but don't worry, he wasn't in any real danger. He fell near the edge. But his clothes got so soaked that we had to hang them up to dry. That's why we got back so late."

"Why can't that child simply behave?" Madlen said despairingly.

"Come now. He's a boy with a mind of his own. There's nothing wrong with that."

"Sometimes I wish that he didn't have such a mind of his own. Then I wouldn't be so worried all the time."

"Speaking of having a mind of one's own, let's talk about healing," Agathe said, changing the subject.

Madlen cleared her throat. "I know what you're going to say," she said. "But things have changed."

"Oh? How?"

"The doctor—Franz von Beyenburg is his name—told me about a school in Salerno where women can study medicine."

"The man is feeding you a load of rubbish," Agathe scoffed.

"No, really. It's true. In a few days he's going to Heidelberg to teach at the university there." Madlen swallowed nervously. "And he offered to let me be a guest student there for a few days." The truth was out! She looked uneasily, even fearfully, at her aunt.

"To what end?" Agathe asked calmly.

"What do you mean?"

"Well, you are a mother of two and the wife of an attorney in the service of the archbishop. Besides that, you were planning to help take care of your in-laws. Why, I ask you, would you want to waste your time learning about the glorious wonders of medicine if you'll never ever be able to use this knowledge?"

Madlen opened her mouth, then closed it again, at a loss for words.

"There's no denying the fact," Agathe continued, "that there's no good reason for you to do this."

Madlen looked at the floor. "But I want it so much."

"I also longed for a lot of things in my life, but I had to leave those longings behind."

Madlen pressed her lips together. She loved her aunt with all her heart, like the mother she'd never known. The woman who had given life to Madlen had lost her own life during childbirth. But in this moment, she was quite perturbed by Agathe's harsh tone, a tone that invalidated Madlen's feelings and lifelong yearnings. "Oh?" Madlen heard herself asking. "Wasn't it your wish after Reinhard's death to escape from the life of a fisherman's wife? Didn't you risk everything to become a seamstress?" Madlen gestured to the fabrics strewn around the room. "Isn't this exactly what you wanted? And you got it."

"Yes," Agathe admitted. "It's true. I didn't know if my sewing and business skills were good enough, or if I'd have any customers to buy my dresses. But I had only myself. I didn't have a husband or children to take care of, which made things much easier for me."

"Please forgive me," Madlen said. "I shouldn't have said those things."

"Oh, Madlen." Agathe took her hand. "I understand, really I do. But we aren't in Salerno. Around here, nobody would trust a female doctor, not to mention that, with your current responsibilities, you have little or no time for such things. God has blessed you, and his blessing is one Roswitha and I would be only too thrilled to have. Be satisfied! To have everything and yet still want more will only ruin what you treasure most. Please, believe me."

Tears ran down Madlen's cheeks. "You're probably right," she conceded. "It was just a fantasy, a silly dream that can never become a reality. Tomorrow morning, I'll thank the doctor for his generous offer. And then I'll return to my in-laws' house and take care of my children."

"I'm relieved to hear you say that."

Madlen got up. "Thank you, Agathe. Please forgive me for my selfishness."

Agathe embraced her niece. "Of course." They walked into the hall, and Madlen called her children. In short order, the siblings ran up, followed by Roswitha, who could hardly keep pace with them.

"Come on. We're going home."

"Have you been crying, Mother?" Cecilia asked.

"Me? No! Why would I be crying? I have the two most wonderful treasures in the whole world, so I have no reason to cry."

"That's true," Cecilia said. She embraced Agathe and Roswitha then took Madlen's hand. Veit had already opened the door and was standing there waiting. They said their farewells, then Madlen set off with the children. She breathed in the fresh air. There was nobody around, and Madlen enjoyed watching her children playfully scamper down the street.

Elsbeth had evidently been expecting them when they finally reached the Goldmanns' house, because Madlen had barely knocked before her mother-in-law opened the door.

"You're finally here. We were getting worried."

"Forgive me. I had to discuss something with Agathe."

Elsbeth embraced her grandchildren and led Madlen into the house. "And Peter and I have something to discuss with you," she said jubilantly.

"Oh?" Madlen was surprised. What could it be? It must be good news, because Elsbeth looked so happy.

"Peter told me everything. Even the promise that you made to the doctor to think about his offer." She took Madlen by the shoulders and looked into her eyes. "Lord Baumhauer, ah, I mean Leopold, told us that there isn't anything for us to do here right now, so we are free to ride with the doctor to Heidelberg. While you listen to his lectures on the miracles of medicine, Peter and I will take care of the children." Elsbeth embraced Madlen, who was utterly stunned. "Tell me, now, isn't that exciting?"

Chapter Twelve

"Do you remember me?"

"Of course. You're the man who was asking about Christopeit."
Dietrich Tillich opened the door a bit wider. "Please, come in."

Johannes thanked him and entered the house, which was very dark
despite the sunny morning. While the vicar's house only a few yards
away was spacious and beautifully decorated, this man's home was furnished with dusty, mismatched furniture, making it seem cramped and
oppressive.

Dietrich offered Johannes a seat at the somewhat rickety dining
room table.

"Some spiced wine, my lord?"

Johannes held up his hand. "I've already eaten breakfast. Thank you
for your hospitality."

"What can I do for you?" His host sat down in a chair on the other
side of the table.

"We found Christopeit." Johannes got right to the point. "He was
murdered."

"Murdered?" The man's eyes opened wide. "Why?"

"Probably because he knew or thought he knew who was behind the vicar's murder."

"That's terrible! How can I be of help to you?"

"You said that you saw the men who took Christopeit away."

"Correct, my lord."

"Would you be able to recognize them if you saw them again?"

The man shook his head slowly. "There was the one with the light-blond hair. He was a rather young fellow and very tall, without a doubt. I can only remember the approximate height and weight of the others. I'm sorry. If I'd known that something was amiss, I would certainly have paid more attention."

"It's not your fault," Johannes said. "Tell me, had you ever seen any of these men before? Possibly as guards or as visitors to the vicar's home?"

He thought about it. "No, I don't think so. Or maybe once. As guards." He knitted his brows together. "Yes, I think the tall blond man was there as an escort once."

"Escorting whom?" Johannes's heart started to beat quickly.

"If I could tell you, I would. But I really don't know."

"Perhaps it was a high lord?"

"Yes, certainly. But I don't know which one. There were a lot of high-ranking people going in and out over there."

"You've been a great help, Lord Tillich." Johannes stood up. "I may call on you again, if I find someone who fits your description of the tall blond man."

Dietrich stood up, too. "You know where to find me."

"My thanks."

◆ ◆ ◆

The attorney walked back to his house, thoughts dancing in his head. If Madlen were here, she would undoubtedly help him make sense of things. His wife's face emerged in his mind's eye. Her light-blue eyes, her soft skin, her delicate, beautiful face, the mole on her upper lip. Her smile whenever she saw him. If she were in Cologne, she would stand by him during these difficult moments! He shook his head to keep these thoughts from overwhelming him. She was in Worms taking care of his parents, and that was all to the good. He knew she'd be needed there even when Leopold Baumhauer's help was no longer necessary. Knowing that she was supporting Elsbeth and helping to care for his blind father made being away from Madlen somewhat more bearable.

When Johannes returned to his house, a strange feeling told him to proceed with caution. He looked around. Was he being watched? Two women were walking down the street, and a small boy was playing with a dog. Other than that, there seemed to be no one else out and about. He looked around one more time but saw nothing unusual. Yet he sensed a looming threat, and a feeling of being watched clung icily to the nape of his neck.

After a moment's pause, Johannes decided not to enter his house and instead began to walk toward the archbishop's residence, taking a route through the market. Were the murderers tailing him? He stopped abruptly, frightening a woman who had been walking behind him; they just barely avoided a collision. He spun around, taking in his surroundings. The people at the market seemed to be minding their own business. Or were they? Had he just seen someone watching him from the alleyway? Johannes rushed to the spot but found no one. He was becoming more and more certain that somebody was watching him. Whoever it was, he was getting too close for comfort. "I'll get you, you scoundrel," Johannes called out into the alley. Then he turned around and proceeded to the archbishop's palace.

"God protect you," the guard said by way of greeting as Johannes reached the door.

"And may God be with you," Johannes replied. "Say, are Anderlin, Georg, Linhardt, Niclaus, Wolfker, and Wilhelm here?" Johannes was determined to rally a group of guards he could trust. He knew Anderlin, Georg, and Linhardt had been in the service of the archbishop for several years now. He wasn't so sure about the other three, but they'd seemed dependable at their last and only meeting. He only hoped that he hadn't gotten the wrong impression.

"I've seen Anderlin and Niclaus. Wolfker, too," the guard said. "I'll have to ask about the others."

"Please do. Tell them that I will be expecting them at my house."

"Yes, Counselor. I'll take care of it."

"My thanks. I will—" he stopped short. He almost didn't believe his eyes. "Over there, by the colonnade, that man. Is he one of the guards?"

The guard craned his neck to look. "They're both guards, my lord."

"I mean the tall one with the light-blond hair. What's his name?"

"His name is Benedict, my lord. He hasn't been here long. He's currently in training."

"And the man next to him?"

"That's Dietz. He has a lot of experience."

"Who hired this Benedict?"

The guard glanced uncertainly at his colleagues, who were deep in conversation. Then he shrugged. "I don't know, my lord. It was probably Vicar Bartholomäus. He managed such affairs, until he died, of course. He even hired me."

"Me, too." Another guard stepped forward.

"Hmm." It struck Johannes that he knew way too little about the administrative duties of vicars, deacons, and deans. He wondered if he should speak to Benedict right away, but then it occurred to him that this might not be wise. He had to be cautious so as not to raise suspicions.

"That will be all. Don't forget to send me those guards I requested."

"Yes, my lord."

Johannes turned and walked toward the marketplace once more. Was someone following him? He wasn't sure but suspected that it was the same fellow as before.

As soon as Johannes loped up his front steps, Hans opened the door.

"Thank God you're here, my lord."

"Did something happen, Hans?"

"A woman was here. She wished to speak to you about an urgent matter. I suggested that she wait for you but she declined. I got the distinct impression that she was in a hurry." Hans paused. "Or she was frightened."

"Frightened? What about?"

"She didn't tell me. She wanted to speak with you and you alone."

"Did you get her name?"

"She told me to tell you she's the other Duretta. She said you would know what that means."

"The other Duretta? She was here? And you let her go?"

"But I . . . I didn't know . . . ," Hans stammered.

"When did she leave?"

"I don't know exactly, but it's been a good while."

"Did she say where I could find her?"

"No, my lord. She told me she would return as soon as possible."

Johannes exhaled noisily. "Then we have to pray she keeps her promise." Johannes looked down the street, hoping to see her. Though he looked far and wide, he didn't recognize a soul. If only he'd gone right back to his house, he wouldn't have missed her. He might be closer to solving the murders, at least the murder of Bernhard von Harvehorst. He sighed as he walked into the house and closed the door behind him. Johannes felt exhausted, drained. He wondered whether the task the archbishop had bestowed upon him was simply too big to take on alone.

It was almost noon when the guards arrived. The woman who claimed to be the other Duretta had yet to return.

"I imagine you all know what we discovered in the harbor yesterday."

"Christopeit?" Georg said.

"Correct. Christopeit and Duretta, Bernhard von Harvehorst's housekeeper."

The guards looked at him expectantly. Johannes was hesitant to tell them about the woman who had claimed to be Duretta appearing at his house that morning. He didn't know if he could trust them all.

"We have at least four murders to deal with," Johannes continued. "We have to assume that Christopeit and Duretta were murdered because they knew who killed their employers."

"Then why weren't they murdered immediately?" Linhardt said. "I mean, why go to all the trouble? First the vicar, and one day later his servant. And the same for von Harvehorst and his housekeeper."

"A good question. I can't say for certain, but I would guess that Christopeit didn't fully realize who was responsible for his employer's death. More than likely, he revealed his suspicions to the wrong people."

"And the housekeeper?" Niclaus asked.

"I believe she was probably killed on the same day as her master."

"Why do you think that?" Georg asked.

"Because the woman I interrogated that day introduced herself as Duretta, but she was lying. The real Duretta was probably already dead, just like her employer. Her body had most likely been dumped in the Rhine by that time."

"Why bother? The killer could have simply left her in von Harvehorst's house. Then there wouldn't have been the danger of being caught while dragging her body away," Linhardt said.

"Because he wanted us to believe that Bernhard von Harvehorst had committed suicide. The impostor admonished herself for leaving him alone, but of course her tears were nothing but a clever ruse. Believe me, when we find this false Duretta, she'll have a lot to account for."

"Are you absolutely certain that the body pulled out of the Rhine was not the same person you talked to previously?" Wolfker asked.

"How did you know that the deceased was really von Harvehorst's housekeeper and not some other maid?"

"Her sister Margret identified the deceased. And there were several people who confirmed that we had the right woman."

"I understand," Wolfker said.

"Now that we've cleared that up, I would like to ask you something. Which one of you knows a guard by the name of Benedict?"

The men exchanged glances. "We all know him, my lord," Linhardt answered. "He's one of the younger guards."

"What do you think of him?"

Linhardt shrugged. "He's one of us. What are you suggesting?"

The lawyer considered whether to reveal what he knew. He finally decided that he had no other choice if he wanted to make any headway.

"He fits the description of one of the men who took the vicar's servant away. Maybe Christopeit returned to Bartholomäus's house after that—we don't know. But at this point, Benedict could very well be one of the murderers."

"Who gave you this description?"

"A man named Dietrich Tillich who lives near Bartholomäus's house."

"Is he trustworthy?"

"He has no reason to lie. He described the man to me two separate times: the day after the vicar's death, when I went to speak with the servant, and then again yesterday."

"And he was completely sure?"

"I would like to say so. When I saw Benedict at the palace, I thought of the neighbor's description immediately." Johannes paused. "Here's the plan: One of you will go to the palace and tell Benedict I have a task for him at the vicar's house. Then you'll accompany him there. The rest of us will bring the witness. If he recognizes Benedict, we'll make an arrest."

"I'll do it," Georg offered. "I know Benedict and often stand guard with him. He trusts me."

"Good. Then we have only one more issue to discuss before we go. Does anyone know who is riding with the archbishop instead of the vicar and Bernhard von Harvehorst?"

The men exchanged looks again. This time it was Niclaus who answered. "Lord Domkeppler Godart Keyserswerde, Secretary Heinrich, and the vicar general."

Johannes knew these men. He mulled over which of these lords was most likely to be a traitor but couldn't come to any definitive conclusion. "Why are three men traveling with the archbishop when only two needed to be replaced?"

The guards shrugged and shook their heads.

"Which one of them would be most likely to betray the archbishop?" Johannes asked point-blank.

"Do you believe the archbishop is in danger?" Wilhelm jumped up. "Why are we just sitting around then? We must go after them!"

"Sit down," Johannes said. "We don't know who the traitor is or what his intentions are. The guards riding with Friedrich will protect him. I highly doubt the traitor would be so stupid as to try to kill the archbishop en route. He could have done that just as well in Cologne." Johannes scratched his chin. "No. Something else is going on. Perhaps the traitor plans to interfere with a negotiation or prevent a treaty from being signed."

Wilhelm sat down, still snorting with rage.

"The best way to help the archbishop is to find out who's behind the murders. After that, the motive will reveal itself. Georg, retrieve Benedict. We will meet you at the vicar's house with the witness."

"Yes, my lord."

All rose. Georg left first; the other men waited while Johannes consulted with his servant. He found Hans in the inner courtyard and stood close so that nobody could hear what they were saying. "If this impostor, this false Duretta, comes back, don't let her out of your sight. I won't be gone long. Tie her to a chair if need be."

"But, my lord, I can't—"

"She is involved in Bernhard von Harvehorst's murder conspiracy. You can and you will hold her here, do you understand?"

"Yes, my lord." Hans lowered his head, obviously uneasy about what he was being asked to do.

◆ ◆ ◆

"We'll wait up here. Stay perfectly still," Johannes said to the witness as they came to the top floor of the vicar's house. It had been relatively easy to break in, but Johannes wondered if it had been necessary to ram Bartholomäus's front doorframe so violently.

"I don't feel especially comfortable about this," Dietrich Tillich said. "What if he sees me and then decides to make me his next victim?"

Johannes gestured to the guards. "Five of the archbishop's guards surround you. What are you worried about? That the tall blond fellow will take down all of them and then attack you?" Johannes smiled good-naturedly. "No, my good man. Do not worry. Nothing will happen to you."

"If you say so, my lord." The doubt in his voice was unmistakable.

"Quiet," Anderlin hissed. "They're coming." The seven men ducked down.

"What are we supposed to pick up here?" Johannes heard somebody saying. He leaned over the balustrade to get a glimpse of the speaker.

Georg entered the house with the tall blond man. "We need to get some parchments. The archbishop's attorney doesn't want anything confidential to be removed." Georg glanced up, signaling to the other men that he knew they were there and wished for them to stay hidden.

"Wait here. I'll go check the study," Georg said, leaving Benedict in the hall.

Johannes touched the witness's shoulder and motioned for him to take a look. Tillich warily moved toward the railing then leaned over it. He pressed his lips together as he scrutinized the guard below. Then he leaned back again. "That's him," he whispered.

Benedict looked up.

"Get him!" Johannes hissed and, in the blink of an eye, the guards jumped up and rushed down the stairway. Benedict pulled out his sword and took up a fighting stance but faltered when he recognized his colleagues.

"You?" he said. They grabbed him and threw him to the floor; Benedict dropped his sword.

"Have you all gone mad?" he roared. "What is the meaning of this?"

One of the guards kicked the sword away, and it slid across the floor with a metallic clang. The guards pulled Benedict to his feet.

"What is the meaning of this?" he roared again.

"I'm arresting you on behalf of Friedrich III, the archbishop of Cologne," Johannes called down from above.

"Why?" Benedict said, watching Johannes as he made his way downstairs.

"For high treason against our employer," he said when he reached the bottom. "And for murder."

The blond guard's jaw fell open. "Treason? Murder? Me?"

"Take him to the dungeon. Do not let him speak to anyone. Two of you will guard him. Say nothing if your colleagues ask you what's going on. Trust no one. Do you understand?"

"Yes, my lord," Linhardt said. "I'll take the first watch."

"I will join you," Georg said.

"Good. I have to return to my house. Then I will come to the dungeon and speak to this fellow." Johannes looked at Benedict, frowning.

"And in the meantime, you should consider revealing everything you know."

"But I don't know anything!" Benedict shouted as Linhardt and Georg led him away. Tillich stepped forward from his hiding place. "Can I go now?" he asked nervously.

"Yes. And thank you. You have provided untold assistance to the archbishop."

The man nodded, walked down the steps, and left the house.

"What should we do now?" Niclaus asked.

"Go to the archbishop's palace and keep your eyes and ears open. I wouldn't be surprised if news of Benedict's arrest gets around and alerts his coconspirators."

The men bade farewell and left, uncomfortable with the idea that one of their own could be involved in this sordid affair.

Johannes went to his house. Once again, he had a feeling that he was being watched. But he didn't care. He would get them, every single one of them. He had just reached the door when a voice called out from behind him. "Please, Counselor, might I have a word with you?"

He instantly recognized the voice. "Duretta," he said, turning around. "Or . . . what should I call you? It was wise of you to come to me. The noose is slowly tightening."

"I'll tell you everything if you promise that nothing bad will happen to me. I thought I was leading you astray as a kind of a prank."

"A prank about the circumstances surrounding a murder?"

"I know that what I did was wrong. But I didn't kill anybody, I swear I didn't."

"Come into the house and explain yourself. And don't leave out a single thing."

The woman gathered her skirts and hurried up the steps to stand directly in front of him. "I'm so sorry. Please! You must believe me. I never saw one cent of that money and—" She froze, her eyes widened. Then she groaned.

"What is it?" From the corner of his eye, Johannes sensed movement at the opposite end of the alley. The woman started to collapse, and he grabbed her under her arms. "What happened?"

She leaned heavily against him. Then he saw it: an arrow sticking out of her back. "Hans!" he shouted at the top of his lungs as he desperately tried to keep the woman from collapsing even farther.

Hans threw open the door and immediately grasped the situation. He grabbed the woman and pulled her into the house.

"Get the doctor!" Johannes yelled, and Hans took off running. But before Hans reached the bottom of the steps, she'd taken her last breath.

Chapter Thirteen

God protect you, my beloved Madlen,
I am aggrieved to be sending you a message instead of hold-
ing you in my arms and speaking with you face-to-face.

Unfortunate events here in Cologne dictate my
choices. I don't wish to upset you, but I also don't want
to lie. There has been a death, a cold-blooded murder of
our revered Vicar Bartholomäus. Because of his official
duties as the archbishop, Friedrich could not cancel his
trip to Rome. And so, before his departure, he formally
authorized me to solve the murder.

Everything that will happen for the Goldmann fam-
ily will happen because of the archbishop's magnanimity.
It will be carried out by Leopold Baumhauer, the envoy
who delivered this scroll to you. I beg you, my dear, don't
be cross with me. There is nothing more I desire than to be
with you. As soon as I've concluded my tasks here, I will
leave for Worms, to be happily reunited with you and the
children. How I long for that moment!

Leopold plans to quit Cologne as soon as possible,
therefore I have only a moment to scribble these few lines.
I will send you other messages as soon as I am able.
Your loving husband,
Johannes

Madlen read her husband's message over and over until she cried herself to sleep. She woke up throughout the night, rolling from one side to the other and falling asleep again. But then she would wake with a start, until she finally couldn't take it anymore. She went downstairs, gathered up some fabric and sewing supplies, and started to work on a new bonnet for Cecilia. The diversion did her good, calming her considerably.

◆ ◆ ◆

At the break of dawn, Madlen snuck out. She knew that Agathe always got up before Roswitha to work on her dresses in the quiet of the early morning. Madlen felt compelled to speak with her, and so she made her way to her aunt's house.

It was a bit gloomy outside as she walked along the empty streets, so different from when there were people about, different from the hustle and bustle of everyday life.

In order not to wake Roswitha and her husband, Sander, who occupied one of the back rooms, Madlen tiptoed to the window of the sewing room and called out just loud enough for Agathe to hear her from inside. After a moment, Agathe opened the front door. "For heaven's sake, Madlen, you scared me half to death! Has something happened? Are the children all right?"

"Yes, the children are just fine." Madlen embraced her aunt. They then tiptoed down the hall to the sewing room.

"What are you doing up at such an early hour?"

When her niece told her to sit down, Agathe knew it couldn't be good news.

"Elsbeth and Peter have offered to accompany me to Heidelberg. They would take care of the children so that I could sit in on the medical lectures there." Madlen glanced nervously at her aunt. "After what you said yesterday, I had let go of any notion of studying medicine. But when I got home, Elsbeth surprised me with this offer."

"And now you would like to have my blessing?"

"I won't go if you are truly against it," Madlen said.

"No." Agathe's answer was decisive. "I will not let you manipulate me like this."

"What do you mean?"

"I am quite aware of your passion for the healing arts. You want my support, though you know that I feel what you're planning to do is wrong. It's not fair of you to pressure me to stand beside you on this issue."

Madlen bowed her head. "I didn't mean to pressure you," she said meekly.

"Explain it to me, then. How can listening to this doctor be more important than your children?"

Madlen grew furious. "That's not fair. I love you with all my heart, Agathe, but don't you dare say anything like that again."

A tiny smile crept onto Agathe's face. "Forgive me, please. It was a temporary lapse. I was angry, and I wasn't thinking clearly."

"Why? Why are you so angry?"

Agathe leaned back onto her chair. "To tell you the truth, I'm jealous."

"Of me? But why?"

"Because you have everything I ever wanted. You have a husband with whom you are truly in love, two wonderful children, and, on top of that, a passion for healing the sick. Is it any wonder that a simple woman like me envies you?"

"Oh, Agathe." Madlen embraced her aunt and then took a seat in the chair next to hers. "You're not really envious of me, are you?"

"No, my darling, I am incredibly proud of you. And I love you from the bottom of my heart. It's just that I'm afraid you could lose everything for a dream that can never be realized."

"I know that. Believe me, Agathe, I'm no simpleton. I know I could never become a real doctor. But I have this feeling"—she put her hand on her bosom—"deep inside of me. I want to heal. I say this because it's how I feel—that God is with me when I'm given the opportunity to heal the sick. And to be able to listen and learn would fulfill me like almost nothing else."

"Your eyes light up when you talk about healing."

"I feel quite content as a wife and a mother. But is it really so wrong to want to listen to the words of this great doctor?"

"No," Agathe said. "No, it's not. I was wrong to judge you and to try to talk you out of it." She took Madlen's hand. "When will you be leaving for your journey?"

"Tomorrow. But only if you're not angry with me."

"Tomorrow? Well, all right, then. *We* will leave for Heidelberg tomorrow."

"We?"

"Of course. You don't think I'm going to stay here, do you?" She stroked Madlen's cheek. "In the years since you came into my life, you've been like a daughter to me. And even though you live far away, you are always in my heart. So, I will accompany you to Heidelberg as my way of supporting your decision. I'm here for you, my darling girl. You can count on me."

Madlen gave her aunt such an enthusiastic embrace that the older woman almost fell off her chair.

"With one condition! That I'm the first person you heal." The women burst into laughter. Roswitha appeared at the door, rubbing the sleep from her eyes. "Is everything all right?"

"Yes," Agathe said. "Everything is all right. Madlen is going to Heidelberg tomorrow morning, and I'll be going with her."

Roswitha was so surprised that for a moment she didn't say anything. "Then I'd better prepare a good breakfast first thing tomorrow morning," she finally said, then left the room shaking her head.

Agathe and Madlen began to giggle. "Just give her some time to wake up," Agathe joked. "Being up so early is just a bit too much for her."

◆ ◆ ◆

Madlen, Agathe, Elsbeth, Peter, Gerald, Ursel, Ansgar, the children, and the doctor left for Heidelberg the next morning. Elsbeth decided that Helene would stay at the house to care for Leopold, and Madlen had contracted a messenger to deliver a letter explaining the situation to Johannes in Cologne. The administrator was happy to support Madlen's ambitions, so when Elsbeth and Peter asked if they should stay to help him, he told them that he worked best alone and preferred no interference from them.

The doctor was thrilled that Madlen had accepted his invitation.

"What was it that ultimately convinced you?" he asked, his horse trotting next to Madlen's mare.

"My in-laws," Madlen said without hesitation. "They took me by surprise."

"It was probably the only way they could have persuaded you."

"You might be right." She smiled. "I'll admit that I had my doubts . . . and my Aunt Agathe did, too." She pointed her chin toward her aunt, who was riding with Cecilia. Veit was riding with his grandfather, and the boy seemed to be enjoying the old man's tales of long ago.

"Why?" the doctor asked.

"Probably because I have more than most women do, and therefore am more fortunate than I probably have a right to be."

"But your good fortune doesn't preclude you from learning."

"Yes, I agree. Can you tell me what I'll be learning from you when we're in Heidelberg?"

"Well, I'll be speaking about the human body, what keeps it in balance and what poisons it. And how to treat the illnesses we run into most frequently. There are so many kinds of injuries and illnesses that at first glance seem incurable. But they are often not all that difficult to treat. Take your father-in-law's condition, for example. The cataract procedure changed everything for him, and for many others." He pointed at Peter. "Look at him now, riding and chatting with your son. As if it has always been that way." Franz looked straight ahead again. "People take their health for granted until a disease takes hold. Before that moment, they are focused on other things, be it financial success or finding a nice person to marry. But when they become ill, they can think of nothing but becoming healthy again, to regain what they'd taken for granted."

"You are completely right. I've seen a lot of sick people. They all have that same doleful look."

"I know what you mean. Please, tell me how you became interested in the healing arts."

"What should I say? As a young girl, I helped a very good friend, a midwife. She had a wonderful way with women. I was about thirteen when I assisted with my first delivery." She cleared her throat. It wasn't easy for her to talk about it. "You know, my mother lost her life when she gave me mine. For as long as I can remember, I've wondered whether she might have lived if she'd had the right kind of care."

"It's impossible to say," the doctor said. "Each delivery is different. If I could be so bold as to give you my advice: Try not to let such ruminations overtake you. They are useless and introverting, and they make you sad and rob you of your vitality."

"Of course you are right. But sometimes it's impossible not to think of these things."

"Then I advise you not to fight it. Think it over, while at the same time asking yourself how you can spare another from the same horrible fate. But don't think any more about the past. It's a waste of time."

"Thank you for the advice. I'll try my best to follow it."

"What are you expecting from your time at the university?" Franz asked.

"I don't know exactly. But someone once told me if I don't take advantage of this opportunity, I'll regret it for the rest of my life."

"You are wise to listen." He smiled at her. "Follow your heart, Madlen."

"I will," she promised. And with these words, she felt happier than she had in a very long time.

◆ ◆ ◆

Around noon, they arrived in Wallstadt. They stopped to rest, and Cecilia asked whether this trip would be as long as the one from Cologne to Worms. The little girl breathed a sigh of relief when Madlen said no.

Right before they reached Viernheim, they took another rest, then rode on until they reached the large bridge that crossed over the Neckar. Madlen halted her horse and gazed across the river to the opposite shore. It had been years since she'd last been here. Her brother, Kilian, and a young woman named Irma had helped her escape Heidelberg when she'd been falsely accused of killing a baby and its mother. About a year after Madlen's court battle ended, Kilian took Irma as his wife. From letters that Irma and Kilian had dictated to a scribe, Madlen knew that they'd been blessed with a daughter. Like so many women, and despite Irma's hopes, after the first baby she'd been pregnant several times but had always miscarried in the first trimester. Madlen didn't know what effect this had had on her and regretted not being able to be there to stand by her sister-in-law. She'd only been able to offer her condolences and encouragements through her letters. So it made Madlen all the more excited to be returning to the city she'd grown up in to see for herself how they were faring.

"What's the matter?" Agathe asked, noticing Madlen's hesitation at the bridge.

"Oh, nothing really. I'm just thinking about all that happened the last time I was here." She threw her a look. "You know what I mean."

"Of course I know what you mean," Agathe said loudly enough for everyone to overhear. "You're talking about the false accusations and the trial that ended with an acquittal."

"Otilia already told me all about it," the doctor called out cheerfully. "But thank you for including me in your conversation."

Agathe smiled. "Keeping secrets from you isn't easy."

"I should hope not."

Madlen was relieved. Even though she'd been exonerated and the real culprit had been arrested, she still felt ashamed just for having been accused. She nudged her horse's flanks and rode to the bridge's watchtower. The guards waved the little group across the bridge without hesitation. With every step her mare took, Madlen's excitement grew.

"Why haven't we ever come to Heidelberg to visit my uncle?" Cecilia asked.

"Because your father works for the archbishop and so is needed in Cologne, and your uncle Kilian, your aunt Irma, and your cousin Juliana live here. Just think how long the trip from Cologne to Worms is! And from there it takes at least one more day. Would you really want to travel such a long way so often?"

The little girl shook her head. "Veit," she called out, "in the future, we will live in the same city. I don't want you to be so far away from me."

Veit hadn't been following the conversation. "What do you want?" he said, annoyed.

Cecilia waved him off. "Oh, I'll tell you when you get married."

Veit shrugged and leaned back against Peter again.

When they reached the far riverbank, the group greeted the guards.

"Would you like to visit your brother and father first?" Elsbeth asked Madlen.

"Actually, I would rather look for accommodations first. My brother doesn't have enough room for all of us at his place, and I don't want to put him in an awkward position."

"So let's find a decent inn," Agathe said.

"Let me bid you all farewell for now and make my required appearance at the university. A bedchamber is awaiting me there, and I hope it's comfortable," Franz said, arching his back. "I'm not used to such a long ride, and I am looking forward to a nice bed." The doctor turned to Madlen. "May I suggest that you come to the university at noon tomorrow? I'll have sorted everything out for your arrival by then. Oh, and can you please tell me where the university is?"

"When I was here last, it was over there," Madlen said, pointing, "and I doubt its location has changed since then. Just keep going straight ahead."

"I'm certain I'll find it."

"I'll be there at noon tomorrow. Thanks so very much, Doctor. God protect you."

"And may the Good Lord hold each and every one of you in His hand!" He bowed ever so slightly then rode off.

Madlen led the rest of the group to an inn that once upon a time had been quite a respectable establishment. She sincerely hoped it hadn't changed since then.

"If it's more expedient for you, I'll go inside to inquire about the availability of their accommodations," Gerald offered.

"Yes, thank you," Madlen said.

"We'll be staying in an inn?" Ursel, the housekeeper, groaned. "In Worms there was hardly any work for me, because Helene, that little busy bee, always took care of everything. And now an innkeeper will be taking care of everything. Why couldn't I have simply remained in Cologne where I'm needed?"

"Don't worry. There will be work," Madlen assured her. "Be happy that you can rest in the meantime."

"How can people be happy without work?" Ursel shook her head in bewilderment. "Sometimes I simply don't understand you people."

Madlen smiled. She knew that Ursel wasn't trying to be rude when she complained about this or that. Never being satisfied was just her way. Most of the time, she complained about having too much work, what with the children and their big house in Cologne. Sometimes Madlen felt guilty about it. But now that she'd heard with her own ears the housekeeper complaining for the opposite reason, Madlen decided to make a mental note not to take her grumbling too seriously in the future.

Gerald came back outside. "They have four rooms available."

"Good, we'll take them all."

"Ursel and I can share a room," Agathe offered. "Then you can share a room with the children. Peter and Elsbeth can take the third room, and Gerald and Ansgar can share the fourth."

"We have no problem sleeping in the stall with the horses," Ansgar said.

"Nonsense. You've earned a comfortable room. Thank you, Agathe."

"Let's bring in our belongings right away. I'm famished, and I want to sit down on something besides the backside of this old nag."

The children played outside the inn before helping to carry the bags to the rooms. Although they were exhausted from riding all day, they seemed cheerful, almost giddy.

"It will take hours before they calm down," Madlen whispered to Elsbeth as they walked upstairs to their respective rooms.

Elsbeth looked at the children. "Just wait until they lie down on their beds and you rub their little heads. They'll fall fast asleep in no time."

"I really hope you're right."

◆ ◆ ◆

Late in the evening, when all had made their way to their bedchambers to get a good night's sleep, Madlen lay in her bed contemplating her situation. She held Cecilia on her right arm and Veit on her left. It was uncomfortable, but she didn't dare move, because the children were finally asleep. Her mother-in-law had been wrong about how things would go with them—the children wouldn't calm down and had given over to bouts of wild laughter, chitchat, and pranks late into the night.

Madlen felt guilty that she hadn't at least tried to go for a quick ride over to Kilian's place before dark. She asked herself whether she hadn't secretly settled in a little more slowly than necessary so that she wouldn't have to go over there right away. But why would she do that? Why was she reluctant to see him?

She gently pushed Cecilia's arm away when the little sleepyhead flung it across her face. Then she rolled over. She remembered how Kilian looked when he was that age. They both had the same light-blue eyes and dark hair. Anyone could immediately see the resemblance. As a little girl, Madlen had always admired her brother. When they were children, Kilian would hide the large stick their father used for beatings. She had no reason to fear seeing her only brother now, and she sincerely wanted them to have a happy reunion. With this thought, she fell asleep. She woke the next morning with both children still in her arms.

◆ ◆ ◆

With Cecilia and Veit flanking her, she knocked lightly on her brother and sister-in-law's door. For a moment, there was no response. Madlen knocked on the door again, this time louder.

"One moment." The door opened, and Irma stood there looking as if she'd been struck by lightning. "Madlen?"

153

"God bless you, Irma."

"Madlen!" she shrieked. She hugged her sister-in-law enthusiastically. Veit and Cecilia let go of their mother's hands so Madlen could return the warm embrace. With tears in their eyes, the women hugged tightly, pulled apart to look at each other, and then hugged again.

"It's so wonderful to see you," Irma said.

She looked down and noticed the children. "My goodness, you're practically a man! God bless you, Veit. And Cecilia, right? You're just as beautiful as your mother."

"Veit cut my hair even though he's not a real barber," Cecilia said. "Before that my hair was as long as Mother's."

Irma suppressed a smile. "God will let your hair grow again, and it will be even longer than it was before. And it will be even more beautiful."

"Really?" Cecilia's face lit up. "You have beautiful hair."

"At one time, my hair was just as short as yours." She pushed back the little girl's bonnet. "Yes, that's exactly what my hair looked like. But look at me now." Irma turned and touched the end of her hair, which flowed down her back almost to her hips.

"Did you hear that, Mother?"

"See there," Madlen confirmed. "A person gets thick, beautiful hair like that only if it has been cut quite short once."

"That's why I did it," Veit added with a haughty look, for which Madlen would have liked to scold him.

"Come on in. I am overjoyed you're here. And Kilian will be as well."

"How is my brother?" Madlen and the children each took a seat around the table. Kilian and Irma's cottage was small and simple, but Irma had succeeded in making it feel cozy despite its size.

Irma's expression changed. "It's hard for him," she said, tears welling up in her eyes. "You couldn't have known. Our Juliana was taken from us last winter."

"No." Madlen put her hand over her mouth. "Oh, please God, no."

Irma nodded. "Many people here in Heidelberg got sick, and many died. It was a terrible time. Few were spared a death in the family."

"But why did they die?"

"God alone knows. We thought for a time that we'd been spared. Then Juliana got a fever. The doctor couldn't do anything for her. She fought for her young life for nine days. Then the Lord saw fit to take her."

"I'm so sorry." Madlen grasped Irma's hand across the table.

"I pray that the Lord, in His infinite goodness and wisdom, will bestow another child upon us, one that will grow to adulthood."

"That's right. You shouldn't give up hope."

"I won't. But since the loss of Juliana, Kilian has changed drastically. He gets in fights, and he often comes home in the middle of the night. Yet I refuse to believe that I have lost him for good."

"Let me talk to him. Hopefully, I can help."

"I would be forever grateful."

"Where is he now?"

"In the woodshop. At least, I hope he is."

"And Jerg?"

"Your father is in his cottage, I think. He rarely works. I prepare meals and bring them over to him. But he doesn't have a kind word for me or anyone else."

"He's always been like that. It's not your fault, Irma."

"It's good to hear you say that. Now, tell me some good news. How is everybody in Cologne? You look so beautiful. What are you doing in Heidelberg?" She looked toward the door, as if expecting more visitors to drop in at any moment. "And where is Johannes? I hope nothing has happened to him."

"Oh, no. He's still in Cologne. It's a long story. I just came by to let you know that we're in Heidelberg. We rented some rooms at the Golden Rooster."

"How long can you stay?"

"I don't know exactly. It's so . . ." Madlen tried to think of the right words. "There's a reason we came here. Agathe and my in-laws came with us."

"What for?"

Madlen took a deep breath. "I've been given permission to listen to some medical lectures at the university." There. She'd said it. She anxiously awaited her sister-in-law's reaction.

"At the university?"

"Correct. Dr. Franz von Beyenburg, a very wise man who studied in Salerno, will be delivering lectures there."

Irma didn't seem to understand what Madlen was saying. She shook her head. "I don't want to be rude but . . . the university? I mean . . . why?"

"In order to determine whether I want to go to Salerno at some point to become a doctor." With that, Madlen had expressed something that, up until now, she'd hardly been able to admit to herself.

Irma looked at the children, who were quietly following their conversation. She didn't say anything more.

"I know it sounds strange. But it's true: women do study medicine there," Madlen said.

"Madlen, you know how much I love you. But it sounds to me as if you've lost your senses."

Madlen tried not to show her hurt feelings. "Don't misunderstand me, Irma. It would have been nice if you'd been happy for me, but I did not expect it. The decision to do this lies with me alone."

Irma shook her head. "God becomes angry with those who endlessly want more instead of being grateful for the gifts they've already been given."

"God has blessed me with a keen intellect and a gift for healing so that I may be of use."

"You make me nervous." Irma looked from Cecilia then to Veit and back again. "How could you?"

"What do you mean?"

"He will take them from you, Madlen. The Lord will take your children, I know it. I too wanted more than I had, and He took my Juliana away. I'm begging you, don't go to the university!"

This was just too much for Madlen. She was losing patience with her sister-in-law's stubbornness and ignorance. "We're going now," she said, standing up. "Please inform Kilian that I was here and that we're staying at the Golden Rooster. I would be thrilled to see him again."

Irma got up, too. Cecilia and Veit slid off their chairs. "I see that evil already surrounds you, sister-in-law. Why do you refuse to see the dark clouds enveloping you?"

"Irma, you're talking nonsense."

"Mother, I'm frightened," Cecilia said, looking furtively at Irma, who had a stony look on her face.

"We need to go now. Give our regards to Kilian. And may God protect you."

"And may God's wrath—which will surely be brought down upon you—be moderate."

The door slammed shut behind them.

Chapter Fourteen

"Who have you been working with? Who picked up your pal Christopeit? Tell me right now!" Johannes pounded his fist so hard against the wooden door that it clattered. "Otherwise, I swear to you, I will order the archbishop's guards to come in here, and then I will leave and lock the door behind me. When I return, I'll be able to wipe up what's left of you with a damp cloth."

"But, my lord . . ." Benedict sat on the filthy floor, pressing his hands against the sides of his head. "I already told you! I wasn't with this Christopeit, and I didn't pick him up!"

"You are willing to lose your life for a traitor," Johannes concluded. "Is the payment so great that you would deceive the archbishop and ally yourself with such treachery? Give me his name!"

Benedict ran his hands over his face. "I haven't done anything, and I don't know why you're accusing me. The archbishop is my employer. I have always been loyal to him."

"What about your family?"

Benedict sat upright with a jolt. He stared at Johannes. "My family?"

"As far as I know, you have two sisters who serve two good households. What do you think would happen to them if they were brought here by order of the archbishop, whom I represent, to be interrogated? I could have a nice little discussion with their masters about you being suspected of treason. What do you think their employers would do with them then?"

"You can't do this, my lord."

"Oh, indeed, I can. And I will if you don't confess immediately."

"But I can't confess," Benedict shouted at the top of his lungs, "because I haven't done anything!"

"You were seen, my dear fellow. You and your cronies. There's a witness."

Benedict looked up. His eyes were bloodshot. "Then the witness is wrong. Or he's lying. I don't know, my lord! Please keep my sisters out of it! They haven't done anything."

"Where did you go with Christopeit the night after Bartholomäus's murder? And who were your companions?" Johannes felt as though he'd already asked the same question a hundred times. It had become a sort of chant he could recite backward and forward.

"I wasn't at the vicar's house," Benedict answered exactly as he'd already done so many times.

"Then it seems that your sisters' fates are sealed." Johannes stood up.

"No, my lord, please. I beg you. I'll confess. I'll confess to whatever you want."

"What took you so long?" Johannes crossed his arms in front of him. "Who were your companions?"

"I don't know them, my lord."

The attorney raised his eyebrows. "And you expect me to believe that?" He sighed. "And who contracted you to do this?"

"A stranger. I don't know his name."

"What are you doing, boy?" Johannes shook his head. "You just said that you would confess."

Tears slid down Benedict's face. "What can I tell you? What do you want me to say? It was me and me alone. I thought everything up by myself and killed everybody. Tell me what to confess and I'll do it. You want a name? Tell me a name and I'll swear that he was involved. You want to tie me to the wheel and break every bone in my body? Do it. I won't resist."

Johannes paused for a minute to think. Did he understand Benedict correctly? Did the guard think that it was a matter of simply naming someone—anyone? "How old you are, boy?"

"Nineteen, my lord."

"And how is it that you're in the service of the archbishop?"

"Because I'm skilled in battle and weaponry, and the opportunity presented itself," Benedict said, baffled.

"The opportunity?"

"I know a guard named Gisbert. He helped me get an interview with the vicar, who then helped put me in the service of the archbishop. It was a blessing, my lord."

"A blessing in what way?"

Benedict didn't seem to understand the question. "Because I could henceforth be in the service of the archbishop." He shook his head. "This is the highest aspiration of any healthy young man of goodwill."

The way Benedict spoke about his service made Johannes stop short; the young man's eyes lit up when he talked about the archbishop.

"The witness described you and then identified you unequivocally. What reason would he have to make this claim if it wasn't the truth?"

"I don't know, my lord." The young man shook his head. "I've never done anything to anybody."

The young man slumped in a heap on the floor. Over the course of his legal career, many people had lied to Johannes. By now, he could sense a falsehood, and more often than not his intuition would be proven right. He believed what Benedict told him now was the truth. Maybe the witness really had been wrong.

The cell door opened. "Can I speak with you, my lord?" Linhardt said.

"Of course." Johannes stood up, went to the cell door, then turned around. "I'm coming right back."

Benedict nodded weakly but didn't say anything. The attorney left the cell then pulled the door shut behind him.

"I have something to report," Linhardt declared. "It's about the three men who were supposed to accompany the archbishop in place of the deceased."

"Yes?"

"The vicar general isn't traveling with him."

"No?"

"No. He's still in Cologne, my lord. His brother took his place."

"His brother? Why?"

"I haven't found that out yet, my lord. Should I make an appearance at the vicar general's?"

Johannes contemplated his options. "No. I'll do it myself." He glanced at the door of the cell. "Linhardt, stay here with Benedict and protect him with your life."

"Do you believe he's in danger?"

Johannes scratched his chin. "We have yet to solve this recent round of murders. The woman impersonating the housemaid Duretta came to me to divulge the name of the person who had pressured her to lie. And for that reason, she was killed. Benedict swears he wasn't with Christopeit or at the vicar's house. But the witness described him and later identified him. Nothing is how it seems, and I still have no idea who is behind all this. As long as I don't know what's going on, I can't trust anyone." He looked at Linhardt. "But I do trust you. Therefore, I'm putting Benedict under your protection."

"You can count on me, my lord."

Johannes placed his hand on Linhardt's shoulder. "I know. And now I'm going to see the vicar general."

◆ ◆ ◆

"Counselor! Please, come in." The vicar general gestured to Johannes to take a seat on one of the two chairs placed at a small table near the crown glass window.

"God be with you, Monsignor. I hope my unannounced visit isn't an inconvenience."

"Not at all. On the contrary. We seldom have the opportunity to talk beyond legal concerns. I am pleased that we're able to speak now that the archbishop is out of town."

"That is one of the reasons I wanted to talk to you. From what I heard, you were planning to accompany Friedrich in the late Vicar Bartholomäus's stead."

"That's true. But it wasn't possible."

"Why not?"

"You haven't heard? People always say the palace walls have ears," the clergyman joked. "I'm not feeling so well these days. It's probably something I ate."

"You haven't been poisoned, too?" Johannes anxiously scrutinized the vicar.

The vicar general waved his hand dismissively. "Oh, just a little malaise, nothing more."

"You should let a doctor examine you."

"Definitely not. I'm fine. And even if I had been poisoned, I'm stronger than the others. In fact, I've almost completely recovered."

"So, that was the reason you didn't ride with the archbishop?"

"Yes, it is. My brother offered to ride in my place, and Friedrich agreed. Why do you ask?"

Johannes didn't know how to express his fear that a traitor might be among those accompanying the archbishop, at least without making it sound like he was accusing the vicar general's brother.

The clergyman furrowed his brow. "Feel free to speak from your heart, Counselor. You seem to be rather preoccupied."

"That's correct. I'd like to discuss some recent unfortunate events." Johannes hesitated once again. "The murders, to be exact."

"Horrible, truly horrible. I've been told the archbishop assigned you to investigate those heinous crimes. You can be certain of my full cooperation."

"Thank you. Please, forgive me, but circumstances force me to be quite frank. I suspect that one of the three men accompanying the archbishop is behind the murders."

The vicar general looked at him thoughtfully. Then his expression changed to downright incredulity. "Without implicating anyone else, it simply can't be my brother. The only reason he's riding in my place is because of my recent health concerns." He paused, thinking. "And we can rule out the others, too. Lord Domkeppler Godart Keyserswerde has been in the service of the archbishop for so many years that he's undoubtedly proven himself beyond reproach. As long as he's out of town, I'm in charge of his jurisdiction. I assigned my brother to assist him during the journey so that he can better fulfill his duties. The third member of the group is Secretary Heinrich. Though he's not been in the service of the archbishop for as long as the others, he's a capable man who couldn't be more reliable. The responsibilities Vicar Bartholomäus would have taken over for the archbishop now rest with him." He looked at Johannes. "Are you sure it's one of them?"

"I have no other explanation." Johannes sighed. "The murders happened right before the archbishop's journey."

"That's true." The vicar general stood and positioned himself in front of the crown glass window, his back to Johannes. "You think it's my brother?"

"I don't know for sure. Please, forgive my candor."

The vicar general shrugged. "You're just doing your duty."

"Then please allow me to ask: Whose idea was it for your brother to take your place after the murders? His or yours?"

The vicar general seemed to deliberate; he knit his eyebrows and clenched his jaw. These movements made his cheekbones seem more prominent, and he looked thinner and more gaunt than usual.

"It was my brother," he decided. "But believe me, his loyalty to the archbishop is equal to mine."

"In your opinion, what reason might your brother have to accompany the archbishop? How would he profit from this series of despicable events? Which tasks would he assume in the service of the archbishop?"

"Well, he would be active only in an advisory capacity. As you know, my brother is an attorney, like you. There are a number of fiefs that need to be distributed; that is one of the reasons the archbishop had an argument with Bernhard von Harvehorst. Vicar Bartholomäus also disagreed with him over this topic, now that I think about it."

"But the quarrel was settled weeks ago," Johannes said.

The vicar general turned around, seemingly surprised. "Are you sure of that?"

"Yes, the archbishop himself told me."

The vicar general seemed pensive. "Well, then, so be it."

"Is there anything else I should know?" Johannes became wary—could Friedrich have downplayed the matter after Bernhard von Harvehorst's death?

"No," the clergyman answered quickly—too quickly, in Johannes's opinion.

"Well, then." Johannes stood. "I will take my leave now. Please send me a message if something else occurs to you or you get wind of something. Anything can be an important clue."

"Certainly, Counselor. May the hand of God protect you."

"And may God be by your side always." With that, Johannes left.

He went straight to the dungeon. Now he had more questions than ever, and he became even more anxious as he contemplated the spate of recent murders. Then there was the guard who, though he claimed innocence, had to be involved somehow. And there were the three honorable men accompanying the archbishop—honorable men who perhaps weren't so honorable after all. Then there was the archbishop, who'd stated that a quarrel had been settled—but maybe had not been.

Johannes didn't know whom to trust. The murderer or murderers must be nigh. The impostor Duretta had been murdered *after* the archbishop and his entourage had begun their journey. And even if Benedict was responsible for murdering Christopeit, he couldn't have killed the impostor because by then he'd already been arrested. The thoughts drumming against his temples gave Johannes a terrible headache. By the time he got to the dungeon, his skull felt as though it might explode. He entered the building and, squinting as the light grew dim, went down to the dark cell. He was relieved to see Linhardt standing at the door to Benedict's cell.

"Did anything happen while I was gone?" Johannes asked without ado.

The guard shook his head. "All is well. I just looked in on him. I believe he's fallen asleep."

"Open it!" Johannes ordered. Linhardt unlocked the door and Johannes entered the cell. Panic seized him when he saw Benedict lying on his side, his back to the door. Was he sleeping or was he . . . Johannes hurried over and shook the prisoner's shoulder.

Benedict awoke with a start. "Forgive me. I am just so exhausted."

"It's all right, young man." Johannes breathed a sigh of relief. He absolutely had to do something to calm his nerves.

Chapter Fifteen

"Somebody should slap that woman until she comes to her senses," Peter grumbled.

When Madlen returned to the Golden Rooster after her visit with Irma, she'd put the children under Ursel's care so that she could tell Agathe what had happened. Then they went to Peter and Elsbeth's quarters.

"Did you tell her about how medical knowledge benefited me?" Peter said, getting worked up.

"No, I didn't have the chance to get to that point." Madlen bowed her head. "I don't think it's about her doubting the efficacy of medicine. It has more to do with her inability to accept the fact that women can acquire this kind of knowledge just like men can."

"But she's a woman herself," Agathe protested. "Yes, I know. I, too, had my reservations. But for a completely different reason—I was concerned about you." She looked at Madlen's in-laws. "I was afraid that Madlen would endanger herself, that some backwoods doctor—and by that I don't mean Franz von Beyenburg—would be suspicious of her desire to heal the sick. I was worried that one of Franz's students or a Heidelberg doctor would make wild assertions about our Madlen out of envy, malice, or stupidity." She sat down next to Madlen and lightly stroked her back. "Unfortunately, most men take no pleasure in seeing women in occupations traditionally held by males. But the idea that a woman would carry on that way"—she shook her head—"is beyond me."

"Irma believes God will punish me," Madlen said, "because she thinks I take the blessings He's bestowed on me, meaning Veit and Cecilia, for granted."

"Such nonsense!" Elsbeth said. She was about to say something else, but Peter cut her short.

"Do you know who God really punishes? God punishes those who destroy, for no good reason, what they have been blessed with. He sends them terrible coughs or disfiguring blemishes or blindness. Oh, yes, I thought a lot about my transgressions and the wrath of God when I was lying there in darkness without any hope of improvement. Now I understand God's lesson, possibly more than any of you here in this room." He pounded his fist on the table. "Years ago, I was too stupid to recognize how dreadfully you'd been mistreated, Madlen. I didn't support you when some fiend accused you of murder and then brought you to trial. But here I am today, by your side. And I will not allow anybody, regardless of who they are, to talk you out of what the Almighty has in store for you."

"What are you talking about?" Elsbeth interjected. "Madlen's never said that she wanted to study medicine. She's just going to listen to a handful of lectures, that's all. And then we'll ride back to Worms."

"And soon thereafter, we'll ride on to Cologne," Madlen added, as if to reassure everyone that she hadn't forgotten about her husband.

"Yes, that's true," Agathe said. "But as long as we're with you, we'll make sure that nobody insults you or does you harm. Begrudging you a few hours at the university is a grave injustice." She pulled her niece into her arms. "Don't listen to anybody who says what you are doing is wrong. Listen to us. We believe in you. Other people speak only out of envy."

Someone knocked on the door. Madlen went to answer it, but Agathe held her back, then walked over to the door herself and cracked it open. When she recognized the face, she immediately opened the door wide.

"Kilian!" Madlen shouted, jumping up. She ran to her brother and fell into his arms. He held her close, then picked her up and whirled her around in a circle.

"I almost can't believe it. Is it really you?" He embraced her again. Finally, he released her and greeted his aunt and Madlen's in-laws.

Madlen was reluctant to include her brother in the discussion his sudden appearance had interrupted. However, Agathe was less reserved. She immediately informed Kilian about Madlen's invitation to be a guest at the university, and how his wife had reacted to it. Agathe made her annoyance and her indignation about Irma's statements quite clear. Kilian listened attentively. "And because of that ridiculous conversation, Madlen actually doubted whether she should go to those lectures, because she was worried that God would be angry with her and would make her children suffer," Agathe said in conclusion. Kilian looked at his sister, who returned his glance uneasily. Then he shook his head, smiled, chuckled, and broke into gales of laughter. "You're not really going to listen to the foolish rantings and ravings of a madwoman, are you?" To Madlen, her brother's laugh seemed a bit forced, exaggerated, almost sinister. She didn't say anything but waited patiently until he'd calmed himself. Had he lost his mind?

"I'm relieved that you see it that way as well," Agathe said.

Kilian gradually quieted. "Dear sister, when have we ever given credence to such nonsense?"

"She's your wife. What has happened to her?"

"You know about Juliana's death?"

"You named her after your mother," Agathe noted sadly.

"Yes, she had our mother's name," Kilian said. "And she was a wonderful girl, so full of life, so innocent."

"Irma told me what happened last winter."

"Yes. Many people died here in Heidelberg. Sometimes I ask myself if you could have helped had you been here."

Madlen wasn't sure whether her brother's words were meant as an admonishment. He seemed to have noticed her confusion because he quickly added, "Your life is in Cologne and you couldn't have prevented the epidemic anyway. Our despair was almost too much to bear."

"Do you know what kind of disease it was?"

Kilian shook his head. "Nobody knows, not even the doctor or the oh-so-acclaimed medical students. They were struck down just like the whores, farmers, and everybody else."

Elsbeth winced at his coarse language.

"And one day, when the danger was almost over and fewer people were dying, Juliana fell ill. Each day, life slowly faded from her body. It broke our hearts."

"I'm so sorry," Madlen whispered.

Kilian wiped away a tear. "After that, everything changed. My wife decided I was to blame for our daughter's death. Me!"

"She blamed you? Why?"

"A few days before Juliana became ill, Irma and I sat down together to talk. We'd just put wood on the fire because the nights were turning cold. I don't think we've ever had such a cold winter. That day, old Jaspar had paid his carpentry bill. God only knows where he got the money. Most likely he borrowed it to replace his tavern's tables and benches, which had been torn to pieces in a recent brawl. Anyhow, Irma and I were relieved because now we'd have enough money to put food on the table for several weeks. We were having a nice conversation when I said to Irma that I never would have thought I could be happy being a family man and a husband. Now I realize it was a mistake to admit that to her." He sighed.

"Why? Weren't you just telling her how happy you were at that moment?"

"Indeed. But then she asked me what I would have done with my life if I hadn't married her."

Knowing her brother, Madlen anticipated Kilian's answer. He would have tried to be honest with his wife. As a young boy, all he wanted was to board one of the big trading vessels and set off for distant lands. And he'd always loved to draw. But neither of these things would have been conducive to building a normal life. During Madlen's trial, Kilian and Irma had become close, but she'd been more interested in him than he was in her.

"I told her that when I was younger I wanted to go to sea and sail, far, far away, to the Orient."

"And she didn't like that," Peter guessed.

"No, she didn't. Not at all. She scolded me for being ungrateful and taking for granted what I had with her and Juliana. But that wasn't true."

"And a few days later, when Juliana became ill, your wife blamed you," Agathe concluded.

"Exactly. Since then, nothing's been the same."

Madlen put her hand on her brother's. "When I spoke to her, she said that *you* were the one who had changed. She insists that you hardly come home anymore, that you spend most of your free time at the pub."

"That's true," he admitted. "But only because she assails me with accusations as soon as I walk in the door. She even told me that she wouldn't sleep with me unless I swore to ban every thought about what I wanted to do before we married from my head. She was convinced she would become pregnant and, because of my bad thoughts, the child would be taken away from us again. I had to swear to it on her life." He laughed without mirth.

Agathe shook her head. "I'm afraid she is close to losing her mind."

"Or maybe she already has," Peter said.

"What can I do? That's how it is now. And I have given up all hope that it will ever change."

"You must have patience," Madlen said. "She is a mother grief-stricken over the loss of her child."

"And I"—he pounded his chest—"am a father who has also lost his child. My little girl, my beautiful little pearl." He couldn't hold back his tears.

Madlen stroked his back gently, trying to calm him. "Everything will be all right. Believe me. Everything will fall into place."

Kilian wiped away his tears, annoyed with himself. "Let's not talk about this anymore. I'm embarrassed about how much I've said already."

"It was good that you talked it out," Elsbeth said compassionately. "And Madlen is right. Everything will fall into place. Time heals all wounds."

The church bell rang and Agathe looked up. "Quickly, Madlen. You promised the doctor you'd be at the university at noon."

Madlen opened her eyes wide.

"I'll walk you there," Kilian said, standing up.

"But the children—"

"We'll take care of them. Now run!" Agathe ordered.

The siblings hurried down the steps of the inn. Madlen felt guilty because she hadn't had a chance to say good-bye to her children; she swore to herself that that would never happen again.

They ran down the city streets, as they'd often done as children. The only difference was that Kilian held her hand firmly now, which he never would have done when they were younger; he would have thought it made him look like a weakling. But now he was glad to have his sister back, if only for a short time.

They reached the university campus. Madlen was nervous, but she didn't have time to think about it. She quickly embraced Kilian and suggested that he return to the Golden Rooster that evening so they could enjoy a meal together. Kilian agreed. She briefly considered whether to invite her father. She hadn't spoken to Jerg yet. But because of her rush to get to the lecture, she put that worry aside. She brushed her brother's cheek with her lips and ran in.

She barely had time to admire the building's high stone walls, the intimidatingly opulent architecture. When she came upon the first few men, she slowed her pace. She didn't want to seem panicked, like a chicken with its head cut off. Several men scrutinized her in passing, but they didn't say anything. So, she nodded as she strode by, and they responded in kind. Once she'd passed, she started running again, until she reached the end of the hall. She had no idea whether to turn right or left but finally decided to turn right. She kept running. She went a bit farther and met six more men walking in the opposite direction. They were around her age and well dressed; a few might have even been a few years younger than she. She slowed her pace again, straightened her spine, and hoped with all her might that her bonnet hadn't slipped back. She summoned all her courage and addressed them as though they were all equals. "God bless you. I'm searching for Dr. Franz von Beyenburg."

"Oh?" one of them said. "Are you ill? Maybe I can help you." Madlen thought his tone was a bit forward and shyly bowed her head.

Another one pushed his way forward. "We're on our way to the doctor's medical lecture." His tone was friendly and Madlen looked up. "You may accompany us if you wish."

"That would be very nice. Thank you so much."

"Well? Let's get going," the man said as the group resumed their route. He dropped back to walk beside Madlen, who had fallen behind. "My name is Thomas, Thomas Winterberg."

"I'm Madlen Goldmann. Glad to meet you."

"What do you want from the doctor?"

Madlen hesitated then decided to answer his question. After all, she'd be sitting with these men and listening to Franz von Beyenburg's lecture in a few minutes anyway. "The good doctor invited me to be a guest at his lectures."

The first man stopped abruptly, and the others followed suit. "He did what?" They all turned to stare at her.

"Is something wrong with your ears?" Thomas said. "Let's go."

One of the men refused to budge. "But she's a woman."

"Well, that's just wonderful—at least your eyes are working," Thomas teased. "Are you going to go now, or are you going to let your feet take root here?"

The man still didn't move, but the others started walking, whereupon he started to move forward, too. The man made Madlen's skin crawl; she threw Thomas a furtive look.

"That charming gentleman ahead of us is Hubertus von something-or-other," he joked loudly enough for the others to hear. "I've forgotten the last part of his title. I must say the way he behaves sometimes is quite tiresome."

"Hubertus von Megenberg," the man called over his shoulder without turning around.

The man's attitude was haughty and intimidating. Madlen pressed her lips together.

"Where are you from, Madlen?"

"I'm from Cologne."

"Cologne? That's very far away. And you've come here because of the lectures?"

"Well, actually I just came from Worms. But that's kind of a long story."

"You can tell me some other time," Thomas said amiably. "Oh, look. We're here."

Madlen stopped in front of an imposing wooden door, trimmed with huge iron hinges and looming at least twelve feet high and just as wide. Upon entering, Madlen found long, sturdy wooden benches instead of the chairs she'd been expecting.

Dr. Franz von Beyenburg was sorting through some papers, his back to the students. Then he turned around, and a big smile spread across his face when he saw Madlen. She froze in her tracks while the others found their places on the benches.

"There you are. I was worried that you might have changed your mind."

Madlen smiled. "Of course not." She leaned toward him. "Although I must confess that I don't feel completely comfortable here."

The doctor understood exactly what she meant without further explanation. "Stand next to me. I want to introduce you so you'll feel a bit more at home."

"Thank you."

The doctor waited a few moments to make sure that everybody had a place to sit. Then he looked around the room and found his voice. "Greetings! My name is Franz von Beyenburg. My full title is Master of Medicine of the University of Salerno." He stepped behind Madlen and took her shoulders so that the students' attention would be directed on her. "Without studying at the Schola Medica Salernitana, this young woman already knows more about healing than most of you here in this room. That's why I've invited her to attend these lectures."

Hubertus von Megenberg immediately spoke up. "But she's a woman."

"I congratulate you on your impressive powers of observation," Franz von Beyenburg said with a grin. "And may I ask your name?"

"Hubertus von Megenberg. My father is a big donor to this university."

"Then pray pass along my eternal gratitude to the honorable patriarch of your family. Tell me, if you would, Hubertus von Megenberg, what do the words *consule naturam* and *natura est operatrix, medicus vero minister* mean?"

"'Let nature be thy counsel'; 'nature is the worker, the physician is but her minister,'" von Megenberg answered.

"Excellent. Those are the mottoes of the physicians of the Salerno School of Medicine. I will encourage you to embrace these precepts. Very wise, don't you agree?"

Hands clasped behind his back, the doctor took a few steps. "Would you like to be a part of that institution, Hubertus von Megenberg?"

"Yes, Doctor."

"Good. Then I will inform you that the Salerno School not only produces Masters of Medicine; it also accomplishes something else, something that will undoubtedly catch on here in this country sometime in the future. Women study medicine there. And not only that. They compose articles, many of which, in my opinion, are works of great importance. Incidentally, this has been occurring for the last two hundred years." He stopped and smiled. "Obviously, we are a bit behind the times here. But we shouldn't grieve over it. If we are wise, we'll follow in Salerno's footsteps, not only in the healing arts but in our general philosophy. Are we all agreed?"

Murmuring and nodding answered the question.

"Good. So I beseech you, Madlen, to take a seat like everyone else here in this room and listen to what I have to offer."

"There's a seat here," Thomas said, and Madlen thanked him with a smile. She walked over and sat down. As she did, Madlen worried Hubertus von Megenberg's look of scorn would burn a hole right through her.

❖ ❖ ❖

"That was incredible!" Madlen let herself fall back onto the bed, opening her arms wide to allow the children to throw themselves upon her.

"Mother! I missed you so!" Cecilia cuddled up to her.

Veit jumped up and down on the bed, making it creak and groan precariously.

"Stop it, Veit," Madlen ordered.

"Tell me everything," said Agathe, who had pulled up a chair. "Were there any difficulties?"

Madlen sat up and leaned against the wall, holding Cecilia in her arm. "There is a fellow, a Hubertus von Megenberg, who will undoubtedly not be my friend."

"Well, you're not there to make friends. Was it just like you imagined?"

"Better. Dr. Franz is a Master of Medicine. He talked about human anatomy and about how students in Salerno gain and improve upon their knowledge by dissecting animals."

"What?" Cecilia screeched. "Does that mean they cut up animals?"

"It sounds worse than it is," Madlen said, trying to wriggle her way out of an uncomfortable explanation. She silently noted to herself to exercise more caution in the future when talking about her experiences, especially if the children were around.

"How many days will you be allowed to sit in on the lectures?" Agathe asked, her words hitting Madlen right in the heart. An oppressive feeling had come over her when she'd asked herself this same question as she walked back from the university to the inn. She knew that this new, bright world of learning would be closed again to her all too soon.

"I don't know. Probably not many."

Agathe noticed the change in Madlen's spirits. "Well, today was your first day, and you still have plenty of time there," she said cheerfully. "It's the way life is. Enjoy it while it lasts."

"That's good advice. I will take it to heart."

"When do we get to go back to Cologne?" Veit asked.

"Why do you ask?" Madlen pulled him close. "Don't you like it here?"

"It's just not our home."

"True." Madlen pursed her lips. "It won't be long."

"Well, I think it's wonderful here," Cecilia said. "We can never sleep in your bed at home because Father's there . . . and we have Agathe, Grandmother, and Grandfather here, too."

"They were in Worms already," Veit said.

"But not in Cologne." Cecilia made a face. "When we go back home, we won't be able to see them like we can now!"

"Everything in life has its time," Madlen said, expanding on Agathe's comments. "We're here now, and we'll be in Worms again soon enough. And then we'll be back in Cologne. Let's make sure to appreciate every single moment."

"I agree," Agathe said. "It will be getting dark soon. Why don't we go to the market and have a look around?"

The children agreed immediately, but Madlen hesitated. "I haven't seen my father yet." She looked at Agathe. "Don't you want to see your brother after all these years?"

"I don't know Grandfather Jerg," Cecilia stated. "I would just as soon go to the market."

Veit agreed with her. The children never had any qualms about sharing their opinions on such things.

"Well, all right, then. I'll go visit him tomorrow, as soon as I return from the university," Madlen said, telling herself that she was simply giving in to the children's wishes. But the truth was she didn't mind postponing this visit for yet another day.

Chapter Sixteen

My beloved Johannes,
So much is happening, and I miss you more than words
can say.

I was horrified and deeply pained when I found out
about Bartholomäus's death. I know that you appreciated
the vicar's soft-spoken and sensible ways. The archbishop
was wise to assign you to solve this terrible crime. I pray
that you've already been able to convict the murderer
by the time you get this letter. Since you wrote to me of
this terrible death, another person got his life back. Your
father is cured. Peter can see again, Johannes! And there's
more good news. He's become more thoughtful and friend-
lier, and kinder than I've ever seen him in all these years.
He says he has a feeling that God sent him the illness so
that he would repent, and now that He has taken it away,
Peter has vowed to prove that he understands His lesson.
It is truly a miracle.

Your mother is infinitely grateful for his recovery, but more than that for the transformation of his character. She grows stronger every day. She smiles again and seems to enjoy every single moment she has with the children.

This is all because of the healing hands of a man who'd found accommodations at Otilia's house here in Worms. The man's name is Dr. Franz von Beyenburg. He studied Eastern medicine at the medical school in Salerno, and he will travel to Heidelberg to teach at the university there. He performed a cataract operation on your father. I was astonished by how simple it seemed to him. I assisted and almost couldn't believe it.

Before I met him, Otilia had told the doctor how I had helped her daughter, Reni, with the deadly cough. Because he himself had a sister who was proficient in the healing arts—hers is a story that doesn't have a happy ending—he offered me the chance to go to Heidelberg and sit in on his medical lectures for a few days. Did you know that women are allowed to study medicine as well as jurisprudence at the school in Salerno? I had no idea that was possible, but Dr. Franz said that it's completely accepted there and that it's been that way for more than two hundred years.

Don't worry, my beloved. I know my place and I know where I belong. Even your parents, perhaps out of gratitude for Peter's recovery, offered to travel with me to Heidelberg and take care of the children, so that I can go to the university. Agathe will also accompany us.

I almost forgot to mention that Leopold is already busy paying off debts and filling up the counting house and the warehouse. This Leopold is really a very amusing character in his own way. He seems happy to tackle his assigned tasks, and he explicitly told Elsbeth and Peter to accompany me to Heidelberg. I think he's glad that Peter won't be constantly looking over his shoulder.

By the time you receive this letter, we'll already be in Heidelberg. I'll write to you as soon as we leave from there, and I hope we'll see you again soon in Worms.

With eternal love,
Your Madlen

Johannes dropped the letter he had received from the messenger earlier that evening. He didn't know what to think. His father could see again? How was such a thing possible? Certainly, he'd heard about these kinds of operations, but he always assumed it was wishful thinking or exaggeration or outlandish fantasy from the minds of desperate people. He had to agree with his wife that this doctor had indeed performed a miracle. Yet something held him back from being too happy about it. First of all, he knew his father all too well. He might be able to resist the temptations of alcohol and women for a while, but would he be able to give up these vices for good? Johannes seriously doubted it. That wasn't the only thing that worried him. He was more concerned about his wife's enthusiasm, which was all too plain in her letters—enthusiasm about the doctor, to be exact. Johannes tried to calm down, reminding himself of Madlen's passion for healing. He knew she felt it with every fiber of her being. And he also knew that she'd never been able to completely abandon this passion, even though she'd sworn off the practice of healing years ago.

She was a faithful and good wife who'd always stood by his side. She'd always lent him a sympathetic ear for his every concern, and she listened patiently when he talked about a trial or problems with a pending lawsuit. She listened when he ridiculed those who had succumbed under pressure or given up too quickly. She didn't judge him even though his official duties sometimes required him to pressure witnesses or the accused. And she was a wonderful mother who educated both of their children well and loved them from the bottom of her heart. But there was one thing that neither Johannes nor the family could give her: the opportunity to practice healing. He knew that on occasion she must have longed for her former life, though those times were often wrought with dangerous, even life-threatening, hardships. But Madlen never complained. She led a good life, and Johannes did everything he could to make sure she was happy and fulfilled. But sometimes, when she was discussing ailments or injuries with him or other people, he noticed that Madlen couldn't help but recommend various medicinal herbs. She would withdraw from these conversations, leaving ill acquaintances or sometimes doctors to their own devices, only after Johannes gently prompted her to do so. He realized it was likely frustrating to have the knowledge to help others, only to be discouraged from sharing it.

Johannes sighed. He knew that he had to concentrate on the murders, but his mind kept wandering to his wife and that doctor. What did he look like? Was he an old man, a crazy old goat in his waning years, who simply wanted to convey the knowledge he'd acquired in the course of his long life to his young students? Yes, that's who he was. But what if he wasn't? Johannes was a few years older than his wife, but despite that they'd fallen hopelessly in love seven years ago. Their marriage was completely different from many others because their decision to marry had been a mutual one. Johannes was quite happy not to have entered into a halfhearted, loveless relationship. But what if the doctor wasn't much older, or only a little bit older than Madlen, like Johannes himself? The study of law and medicine took a long time. It was possible that this Franz von Beyenburg was the same age as Johannes. And he was a doctor, the kind of professional whom Madlen admired above all. Plus, he imagined this doctor was around her all day, while Johannes was forced to remain in Cologne.

He picked up the parchment and placed it on the table. He reached for the beer-filled mug and sat heavily upon a chair. He was so drained he could barely keep his eyes open. When he emptied the mug, he stood, refilled it, picked up the parchment, and dragged himself upstairs to his bedchamber. He kept drinking as he climbed the stairs, beer trickling from the corners of his mouth and down his neck. He pushed open the door to his bedchamber with such force that it slammed against the wall. Johannes waited to see whether Hans would call up to check that everything was all right. But he didn't hear a peep. He'd seen Hans for a moment earlier, but the servant had discovered a hole in the roof and was busy patching it.

Johannes removed his shoes and with the parchment and beer mug in hand walked over to the bed. He sat down on the edge, finished off the beer, and reread the letter. The beer had its expected effect, gradually numbing his senses. But the anxiety that his wife's letter had triggered remained. Finally, he let the parchment slip from his hand and glide to the floor. He slumped down onto the bed and fell fast asleep but awoke in the middle of the night, cold enveloping his stiffened limbs, to crawl under the blankets, where he fell back to sleep.

The next morning he couldn't remember exactly what he'd dreamed. As he woke, the image of Madlen contentedly cuddling a good-looking doctor emerged in his mind's eye.

Johannes got up, went to the washbowl, and dipped his hands in the cool water. He splashed some of it onto his face over and over again. He felt miserable. He'd made absolutely no headway in the murder investigation, and imagining his wife's activities was driving him to the edge of madness. What was it she'd written? Had Elsbeth and Peter really offered to accompany her to Heidelberg? Johannes didn't think of himself as completely old-fashioned, but wasn't Madlen attending lectures at the university without even discussing it with him first going just a bit too far? What had gotten into her?

He got dressed and went downstairs. "Hans? Hans?"

"Yes, my lord." Hans had evidently just come over from the servants' quarters.

"Prepare breakfast. I don't have a lot of time. And then find me a reliable messenger to take a letter to Heidelberg today."

"Yes, my lord." Hans disappeared as quickly as he'd come.

Johannes walked over to his study and sat down behind the desk. He took out a piece of parchment and a quill and began to write.

> *My dearest Madlen,*
>
> *There is so much I would like to write in response to your letter, but I have little time these days. There have been other murders, which I'm obliged to solve. I'm overjoyed to learn that my father has been cured. Now with Leopold's help, it will be possible to steer the business back to prosperity. My mother is a strong woman and will undoubtedly stand by him.*
>
> *I was surprised to read about your intentions with regards to the university. Even more astonishing is the news that my parents encouraged you and thereby neglected to do the right thing. Your place, my Madlen, is here. Here by my side.*
>
> *Now, because the difficult situation that initially brought us to Worms is being settled, I ask you, no, I demand that you and the children immediately return to Cologne. I'll send you money via a messenger so that you can hire two guards to accompany you, the children, and the servants.*
>
> *Please get underway forthwith as we have no time to lose.*
>
> *Your loving husband,*
> *Johannes*

When he read the letter through, Johannes wasn't comfortable with the demanding tone he'd used. He'd ordered her to come home right away. He'd never addressed Madlen in this way, never mind having written her such a letter. Had he gone too far? She was a young, passionate woman. Was it right to order her around like that? On the other hand, she was first and foremost his wife, and he was responsible for her. Even if it was true that women were able to study in Salerno, his opinion on the matter was clear. It didn't matter to him if other women studied there, but his own wife taking part in this absurdity was another matter. He and the children needed her. Yes, he was right. Women must capitulate to their husbands. However, as he studied what he'd written, his firm conviction began to melt away. He simply couldn't shake the feeling that he was making a mistake as he slid the scroll into its cylindrical leather case and sealed it shut.

◆ ◆ ◆

After breakfast, Johannes went to the dungeon to speak to Benedict again. Wilhelm had taken over the watch and stood in front of the prisoner's cell. The attorney had given strict instructions that only Anderlin, Georg, Linhardt, Niclaus, Wolfker, and Wilhelm were to be entrusted with guarding Benedict. He couldn't afford to trust anyone else right now. And even though he wasn't completely sure about these six men, he would at least know who was responsible if the prisoner escaped or was injured.

Johannes found Benedict safe and awake. But the prisoner still couldn't tell him any more than he could before. So Johannes instructed the guards to feed him and to keep their eyes open, while he did his part to solve the murders.

Johannes headed toward the archbishop's residence to speak to the guards who had recently been on duty with Benedict. He had to make sure that the witness was mistaken, and he needed to confirm Benedict's claim that he hadn't been with Christopeit that evening.

He strode calmly and confidently through the streets of Cologne. When he turned a corner, he collided with someone who had obviously been hiding behind the wall. The young man, whom Johannes guessed wasn't any older than sixteen—eighteen at most—opened his eyes wide in fright and cried out. Johannes grabbed his arm.

"I've got you now!" The attorney pinned the young man's arm behind his back, and he cried out in pain. "Scream as loud as you want. You're coming with me."

"Let me go. I haven't done anything. I haven't done anything!" He thrashed and writhed.

"I beg your pardon," said a merchant who had hurried over upon hearing the young man's cries. "What's going on here?" He recognized Johannes. "Oh, Counselor. Forgive me. I didn't see you at first."

"Can you help me bring this fellow to the dungeon?"

"Certainly," the merchant said. He grabbed the boy's other arm, making him cry out again.

"What has he done?"

"He's been following me to see if I am getting close to his boss."

"To his boss?"

"To the man who either committed several murders himself or contracted an assassin to do his dirty work."

The young prisoner thrashed, and the merchant retaliated by giving him a swift punch to the kidney. "Behave yourself. Otherwise you might not get to the dungeon in one piece."

The frightened young man obeyed, walking as well as he could considering his captors' tight grip on him. When they reached the dungeon, one of the two guards on watch came over to assist them. Johannes surrendered his new prisoner to the guard, then thanked the merchant for his help. As the attorney followed them to the cell, the young man started to put up a fight again.

"Take him down to Benedict's cell," Johannes ordered. The guard nodded and began to pull him down the stairs.

"Halt," Linhardt said when the guard and the prisoner reached him. "There's already someone in here—" He stopped midsentence when he saw Johannes walking behind them.

"It's all right, Linhardt," Johannes said, and Linhardt open the cell door. "I'm going in, too. Let's just see how happy these accomplices are to be reunited."

Benedict, who'd been lying on the ground with his head nestled in his arms, got to his feet.

"I've got somebody for you," Johannes announced as Linhardt shoved the new prisoner into the cell.

Benedict scrutinized the man then gazed at Johannes.

"Don't you have anything to say to your friend?"

Benedict had a blank look on his face.

"Greetings," he mumbled and then looked at Johannes as if checking if he'd done the right thing.

Johannes looked back and forth between the two of them. The new prisoner looked at the floor.

"Linhardt, take this one to a different cell."

"Yes, my lord." Linhardt grabbed the young man by the neck and upper arm and led him out. Benedict watched what was going on with great interest.

"I'll be back," Johannes announced and left the cell. Johannes looked through the peephole of the cell door and saw that Benedict had slumped back down onto the floor. The attorney could no longer ignore his doubts about this prisoner being a traitor and murderer.

"Where did you put the new prisoner?" he asked Linhardt when he returned.

"In the last cell way in the back. I thought that it might be better if those two didn't have the opportunity to speak to each other."

"A good idea. Is there another guard there?"

"No, my lord. I'm alone at present. Should I open the new prisoner's door for you?"

"Yes. Let's see why this young man was so eager to spy on me." Johannes looked around and then picked up one of the chairs positioned against a wall. "I'm going to take this."

"As you wish, my lord."

Linhardt led Johannes to the back and unlocked the cell door. "Shall I lock the door behind you?"

"Leave it open. Just let that peasant try to get past me," Johannes responded.

"Call me when you're ready."

"I will, Linhardt. My thanks." Johannes entered the cell. The young man was crouching on the ground next to a pile of dirty straw. The lawyer was immediately struck by the difference between this cell and the one Benedict was in. Evidently the guards still considered Benedict one of their own, because his cell was immaculate compared to this one, with its disgusting smell of excrement, harsh in Johannes's nostrils.

The boy looked up, and his eyes filled with tears. "My name is Wentzel, my lord."

"Wentzel." Johannes pushed the chair into place, then sat down. "Why have you been following me?"

"I wasn't following you."

The lawyer sighed. "You know, Wentzel, it's tiring, so very tiring, to be lied to over and over again. And do you know what happens when I'm tired? No? Then I'll tell you: when I'm tired, I lose my patience quite easily. And right now I feel absolutely exhausted, and it's getting worse by the minute. Do you follow me?"

Wentzel nodded but said nothing.

"Are you from Cologne, Wentzel?"

"Yes, my lord."

"And who is it you serve, Wentzel?"

The boy hesitated. "I serve no one, my lord."

"How do you get money if you don't work?" Johannes's voice was calm but threatening.

Wentzel didn't answer.

"I asked you a question."

"I, I . . . sometimes I help out around the harbor."

"Sometimes you help out around the harbor. And nothing else?"

"No, my lord."

"Do your parents live in Cologne? Do they give you something to eat every once in a while? Do you have a brother who cares for you? A sister?"

"No, my lord. Nobody."

"I see. So no one will come to mourn you when you're dangling from the gallows, gasping for your last breath?"

Wentzel looked up. His breathing accelerated. But then he lowered his head again. "No, my lord. Nobody would come."

"I see. So the prospect of an early end doesn't make any difference to you?"

Wentzel shook his head.

"Well, I don't believe you, even if you think it's true. I've seen many hangings, and in the end they all beg for their lives. What do you think you'll do, Wentzel?"

He shrugged.

"It's all the same to you?" Johannes cocked his head and scrutinized the boy. "So your life is worth nothing to you?" The attorney's tone was gentle. But then he could no longer contain his rage, and he lost his composure. "Tell me who you work for!"

Wentzel shook his head.

"Tell me right now! Why were you following me?"

"I wasn't. I was just walking down the street."

Johannes was on the verge of slapping the young man senseless. "Why did you follow me?" he repeated.

The boy shook his head again.

"Believe me, the guards will be happy to beat it out of you." He got up from his chair and walked toward Wentzel. "I'll find out what I want to know. It's up to you to decide how it goes."

Wentzel looked at him. "If I tell the truth—what's in it for me?"

Johannes was taken aback. "You actually believe you can negotiate with me?"

"I believe what I know is worth something to you."

"I'll see what I can do for you when you give me all the names."

"If I do, then I'll need to leave the city. I'll need money and a horse."

"Not so fast." Johannes was baffled by the young man's transformation. A few minutes ago, he'd been frightened and cowering, and now he was bold and assertive. "You could give me any old name. Therefore, I can't promise to let you go. Give me a name, and I'll give you my word that your sworn statement will be more important to me than your punishment."

"If I tell you, it must stay between us until I can get out of Cologne."

"Are you trying to wrest a promise from me without giving me anything in return?"

"I give you my word, even though you may think it's worthless. But as soon as I've told you the name, you'll understand why I have to leave Cologne."

Johannes scrutinized the young man again, shook his head, then sighed. "I give you my word. Now give me the name."

Wentzel got up. "And I'll need money to survive elsewhere for a while."

"How much?"

"Not a fortune. One hundred groschen."

"One hundred groschen? You can stay here until you rot."

"A hundred groschen. The name is worth that price."

"I'll give you fifty if the name is truly worth something. Then and only then."

"Fifty and a horse."

"Deal. But then you have to give your statement to a scribe in front of two other witnesses so that I can make the arrest and bring the case to court."

Wentzel laughed. "My good man, I wish you nothing less than the full support of God in that endeavor."

Johannes found his remark quite odd. He wanted to ask Wentzel what he meant by that but then decided against it. "The name."

"All right, then, I have your word as a man of honor. The name of the man is Friedrich von Saarwerden, archbishop of Cologne."

Chapter Seventeen

The next day, Madlen arrived at the lecture hall before the other students and even before Franz. The door to the hall was still closed, so she strolled through the commons to the garden to admire nature's blossoming. She recognized most of the plants at first sight, and she could discern others based on their distinctive aromas. In the distance, she saw the doctor walking toward the lecture hall. She abandoned her inspection of the plants and approached him.

"Madlen!" he said. "You're early."

"God bless you, Doctor. Or would you rather I address you as Master of Medicine?"

"Just call me Franz. God bless you. It's indeed a joy to see you. You're beaming like the sun."

"I feel it, too. I'm completely ecstatic about what I learned yesterday."

"Really? Then imagine how you'll feel when we really go into detail. What a pleasure it will be to teach you."

"Would you be so kind as to allow me to ask a bold question? What does the dean say about allowing a woman to be present at your lectures?"

"I want to be honest with you, Madlen. Matthäus von Krakau doesn't intend to be a dean forever. He'll soon be taking over the office of rector of the university. Rupert II, the count palatine of the Rhine, appointed him as his own personal counselor and father confessor, an esteemed and highly influential appointment. But he must constantly be on the alert to keep his position secure." They continued to stroll through the campus and entered the lecture hall building. "Dean von Krakau is actually vexed by your attendance at my lectures. But he hasn't opposed it publicly just yet. I made it clear to him that it would be only for a few days." They reached the lecture hall, and the doctor opened the huge door. "The dean hasn't said anything, but I believe he might even like making lectures available to women. It would prove his magnanimity and tolerance." The doctor winked.

"So, I can stay?"

"For a little while. And to answer your next question: it won't cost you a penny."

"That's exactly what I was going to ask you."

"Yes. I already know you quite well, Madlen." He gave her a look she didn't quite know how to interpret. He stood close to her, probably closer than would be considered seemly.

She cleared her throat. "Well, I'll take my place now," she said, walking past him and sitting down. She could feel her face flush and hoped that her blush would fade in short order.

The students gradually streamed in and took their places. She was pleased when Thomas entered the lecture hall and took a seat next to her. "Well? Did you process the lecture about dissecting animals?"

"Ages ago," Madlen answered self-confidently. She felt wonderful. This hall, the doctor, the students . . . the opportunity to focus on medicine and healing! Madlen could hardly wait for the doctor to begin his lecture so she could soak in every bit of knowledge she possibly could . . . while she had the chance.

"Agathe, what's the matter? He's your brother. You truly don't want to go with us?"

Agathe turned away so Madlen couldn't see her face. "We really don't have any kind of relationship, Madlen."

Madlen took Agathe by the shoulders and turned her so they were face-to-face. "Is everything all right?"

Agathe lifted her head. "Yes, my love, everything's fine. Please go without me."

"As you wish."

Cecilia and Veit had been quietly following the women's conversation.

"Come on, you two. Let's go."

They said good-bye to Agathe and set off. They ambled leisurely down the streets of Heidelberg, Madlen describing the buildings to the children as they went, her childhood recollections vivid in her consciousness. Some things seemed as if they'd happened only yesterday. Others seemed to have occurred millions of years ago. Her memories of the past weren't all good, and like always she shuddered at the thought of the time seven years ago when she'd been jailed after being unjustly accused of murder.

"Madlen?"

She stopped and turned around. She almost couldn't believe her eyes. "Sheriff!" she exclaimed, thrilled to see her old friend.

The man approached her with arms open wide then evidently decided to be more prudent and bowed politely instead. "The bravest woman I've ever met. It's wonderful to see you."

"God bless you, Sheriff!"

"And who do we have here? Don't tell me these are your children!"

"Yes. Veit and Cecilia." Madlen beamed with pride.

"I would have recognized those eyes anywhere," the sheriff said, looking at Cecilia. Then he turned to Madlen again. "I've thought of you quite often and wondered how you might be doing. I truly rue the day you left Heidelberg, but I can certainly understand the reasons for your departure, considering all that happened to you here."

Madlen glanced at the children and then looked again at the sheriff. He instantly understood that his candid references to those dark times weren't quite appropriate for the children's ears.

"Do you know, children, that your mother is greatly admired in this city? She taught many people here about justice and righteousness."

"Really? But our father is the attorney in our family," Veit said.

"That may very well be, my boy. Nevertheless, your mother is a very brave woman."

Veit had never thought about whether his mother was brave or not. She was just his mother. "I guess." He shrugged.

"Are you here to visit your brother and father?"

Madlen was unsure whether to tell the sheriff the real reason for her visit.

"Hey, wait a minute," he said before she had a chance to speak up. "But of course." He slapped his palm against his forehead. "I should have known! Oh, what am I saying, I must have known . . . You're the woman who's attending the lectures of that doctor, the Master of Medicine. Am I right?"

Madlen nodded. "As a matter of fact, what you heard is true. How did the news get around so fast?"

"Yesterday evening, some students at the inn were talking about it. Not everyone was in favor of what you are doing. But that would never dissuade you, right?" He laughed good-naturedly. "You haven't been in Heidelberg for years, but when you finally return you instantly become the talk of the town. Madlen, you haven't changed one bit."

"Is that bad?"

"Oh, no, come now, relax. How long will you be staying?"

"Not too long. Only a few days. Then we'll be traveling back."

"I do hope that we'll be able to meet one more time before you go. But while I have you here: I'm having such pains right here." He put his hand on his sternum. "I have a burning sensation, it's like fire. Even if I drink and drink, it doesn't improve."

"Go to the monastery gardens and ask them for some balm. Then prepare a brew with it. It will get better immediately."

"Is that right? I gave a traveling barber-surgeon two pieces of silver. That scoundrel told me to rub horse manure on my skin. I did it over and over again. I reeked so badly that no one would come near me. And now you're telling me that all I need to do is prepare a brew. Oh, Madlen, if only you lived here in Heidelberg!"

Veit began to hop from one foot to the other, obviously impatient.

"It was a pleasure to see you again, Sheriff. May God protect you."

"May the Lord bestow luck and happiness upon you."

A warm feeling enveloped Madlen as she walked away with the children. This had been her childhood home, and she was still remembered. It was comforting to know she had not been forgotten.

◆ ◆ ◆

Unfortunately, this glorious feeling left her when they reached her father's cottage. She gulped, summoning her courage. The truth was, Jerg wasn't a pleasant person. She knew from his stories that he'd been a far nicer person before Madlen's mother died. Apparently he'd been helpful, industrious, and friendly. But Madlen had never known *that* man. Though she tried with all her might, she couldn't remember him ever saying a kind word to her. And worse by far was when he'd get drunk and beat her or Kilian, though her brother had gotten more than his fair share of those beatings. But she didn't want to think about that now. She lifted her hand and knocked on the door. No response. She knocked on the door again, this time louder.

"Father? It's me, Madlen." She knocked again. She didn't dare open the door without permission, uncertain as she was of Jerg's condition. She could only hope it wasn't too awful. Up until now, she had done her best to introduce her children to friendly people who treated each other with respect.

"Father? Open up, please. It's me, Madlen."

She heard a sound from inside. Then the door popped open. Jerg stood there pantsless, wearing only a linen shirt. He reeked of alcohol and his hair stuck up wildly in all directions. The smell of human excrement nearly bowled Madlen over, making her sick to her stomach. Cecilia put her hand over her mouth and Veit pinched his nose shut.

"Madlen?" Jerg slurred. "Naturally. Who would have thought that a wench like you would turn up around here again?" He spat at Madlen's feet.

Madlen was at a loss. She didn't have the best memories of her father, but she hadn't expected this greeting.

"Mother, can we please go?" Cecilia pleaded and took several steps back.

"I've come with my children to visit you, Father. If you are indisposed at this time, we can come back later."

"If I'm indisposed," he mocked. "Oh, yes, the famous healer who married a lawyer. And what about me, huh? What do I get out of it? Who asked what I wanted?"

The stench was unbearable, but the words he hurled at her were even worse. "All right . . . Well, we're going now. If you want to, you can come visit us when you're in better shape. We're staying at the—"

"Better shape?" he roared. "You'll never see me in better shape." He stepped toward Madlen menacingly.

She pulled Veit back, took Cecilia's hand, and stepped away from the cottage. She scrutinized her father for a split second. What in the world had she been thinking by coming here? The man was pathetic, still blaming others for his woes, the way he'd done all his life. "It was a mistake for us to come here, and there's actually no reason for you to visit us. So, I can only say to you here and now, adieu. May God bestow happiness upon you."

"You filthy little whore! You nasty bitch. At least give me some money, you slut!" Jerg spit.

"Let's go, children."

"You're not going anywhere until you pay me for everything I gave you over all those years," Jerg called out.

Madlen kept a firm grip on her children's hands and didn't turn around. She knew that she'd never make the mistake of visiting her father again.

◆ ◆ ◆

When they got back to the hotel, Madlen summarized for Agathe what had happened. Her aunt gave her a hug and told her that she shouldn't think about it anymore. When they went downstairs for their evening meal with Peter and Elsbeth, Madlen didn't want to waste more than a few sentences explaining what kind of man Jerg had turned into.

"Can Ursel take us up to bed?" Cecilia asked, her eyelids drooping from exhaustion.

"Of course." Madlen motioned for Ursel, who had just finished eating, to accompany the children upstairs.

"Now that the children are gone, I can say this: I'm ashamed that not too long ago, I wasn't so far off from such behavior," Peter said. "Agathe, excuse my openness, but it seems to me that we are all close enough that I can touch upon this sensitive topic in your presence."

"I'm happy that you turned your life around and got back on the right path," Agathe responded. Peter acknowledged her with a look of gratitude.

"I don't understand how a person can behave like that," Madlen said. "I know I don't have the right to say anything since this is all my fault."

"Your fault? What are you talking about?" Agathe asked.

"He was different before my mother died. During childbirth, she gave me life but sacrificed hers."

Agathe sat up straight. "Yes, your mother died giving birth to you, but who told you that other nonsense?"

Madlen thought it over, but she couldn't remember who'd told her that story, just that Jerg claimed over and over again how happy he'd been when Juliana was alive, before Madlen was born. They'd had wonderful years together; they'd been each other's best friend. Madlen shrugged. "My father did."

"What utter rubbish! Jerg was—and still is—exactly like our own father: a rotten cur who thinks only of himself. Jerg was a good carpenter, but whatever he earned he squandered at the tavern. He was better for a very short time while he was courting your mother. But after they married, he went back to his old, despicable ways. Indeed, Juliana was forced to endure a great deal after she started sharing her life with that scoundrel. And he wasn't happy with her, because Jerg was never happy with anything or anyone. He only told you those outrageous lies to hurt you, because he enjoys hurting people. It's the only thing he has a real passion for."

Madlen gaped at Agathe.

"I'm sorry, my love, but somebody has to say it. I can only hope that your brother comes to his senses before he goes down the same path."

"Kilian isn't like that."

"Kilian drowns his sorrows in alcohol and stays away from home so he doesn't have to listen to his wife scold him for his despicable behavior. And you still say he isn't like that?"

Madlen's throat constricted, the thought of her brother turning into the same wretched person as her father making it difficult to swallow. Agathe was right. Kilian was becoming exactly like their father. But he would never admit it. "I'm going to speak to my brother."

"Yes, do that," Elsbeth said. "But I fear Agathe might be right, that it could soon be too late."

Madlen looked around then stood. "Please, excuse me. I'm tired and would like to go look in on the children."

"May the Lord watch over you, my child," Peter said. Madlen gave him a smile then climbed the stairs, her legs leaden. She felt miserable but at the same time liberated. For years, her father had blamed her for his misery after her mother died giving birth to Madlen. But he'd lied. If Madlen's mother were still alive, he'd have someone to curse and beat—or worse—whenever he wanted. With every step, she felt lighter, as though relieved of a heavy burden she'd carried all her life. She never wanted to see her father again.

❖ ❖ ❖

It was only her third day at the university, but Madlen felt at home there, as if she'd never done anything else. She strolled down the cobblestone streets, her spirits high as she enjoyed the warmth of the morning sun on her face. She felt freer than she had ever felt in her life. Again, she was early. When she got to the campus, she saw a man sitting on one of the huge boulders that dotted the grounds, but paid him no mind.

"Excuse me, but is your name Madlen Goldmann?" he said when she got closer.

Madlen stopped. "God be with you, my lord. Yes, it is. Do I know you?"

He stood up. "I wish that were so, but no, we have never met. My name is Hyronimus Auerbach."

"I've heard about you though we've never met. I believe your name was mentioned at my"—Madlen blushed, bowed her head—"trial seven years ago. You're a doctor, right?"

"That's correct. Would you be so kind as to give me a minute of your time?"

Madlen looked toward the lecture hall to estimate how much time she had. "Just for a moment," she said.

"This won't take long," he assured her. They walked until they reached a short wall. "Would this be a good place to sit down for a spell?" the physician asked.

"Yes, certainly." Madlen looked around. There wasn't a soul in sight. As soon as she saw someone coming, she'd end their conversation. "What can I do for you?"

"Well, probably nothing. I would like to understand your intentions."

"My intentions?" she repeated. "In regards to what?"

"Well, we've never had a woman attend the university here in Heidelberg. This is your birthplace, that much I know. I'd like to know whether you plan to use the knowledge you acquire as a physician or as a healer."

So that's what this was about—he was afraid she might steal away his patients. "Don't worry. I don't intend to remain in Heidelberg. I'll be returning to Cologne soon with my children."

"A pity."

"What do you mean by that?"

"Well, I'm in your debt, though you'd have no way of knowing that."

"I believe you must be mistaken. Nobody's in my debt, especially not someone I'm meeting for the very first time." Madlen craned her neck to see whether any other students had arrived. She didn't see anyone.

"Do you need to go?" the physician asked. He'd been following her gaze.

"When I see the other students arriving. Please forgive me, but I don't want to be late."

The doctor smiled. "You're quite impassioned."

At this moment, Hubertus von Megenberg walked onto the campus grounds and disappeared behind a wall as he followed the walkway into the lecture hall. Madlen became anxious. "Please, tell me what you want from me."

"This is something that cannot be discussed in haste. Tell me, would it be possible to talk to you later, when you aren't in such a hurry?"

Thomas came walking down the street. Madlen waved.

"If it's that important to you, then yes, of course," she agreed. "Please excuse me now." She stood up. "May the Lord protect you." Before he could reply, she hurried off. Thomas stopped and waited for Madlen. Before entering the lecture hall, she turned to look back at Hyronimus Auerbach; she felt guilty for running off. The physician waved amiably.

Madlen and Thomas headed in.

"Who was that?"

Madlen shrugged. "A doctor. His name is Hyronimus Auerbach."

"What did he want from you?"

"I don't really know. He was waiting for me when I got here. We're going to talk later."

Thomas chuckled. "You attract one doctor after another, like bees to honey."

Madlen laughed. "Come on, we need to be ready for the venerable Master of Medicine."

"You can hardly wait, right?"

"Right. These lectures are the most wonderful experiences of my life." She immediately regretted her remark. "After my children," she added hastily, "and my husband, of course."

"And so on and so forth." Thomas smiled, taking ahold of the doorknob. He didn't open the door immediately. "If I, a future doctor, can give you a bit of advice: stop feeling guilty. It's good that you're here. It's good that you want to learn. It doesn't make you a bad wife or mother."

Madlen looked at him gratefully and took a deep breath. "Your advice does me good, Doctor," she joked, but both felt the truth of her words.

◆ ◆ ◆

"Have you been waiting here the whole time?" Madlen gave Hyronimus Auerbach a look of surprise. She'd just exited the building and was preparing to head back to the Golden Rooster.

"Of course not. I just returned a little while ago. Do you have time to speak with me now?"

"Yes, if it's not going to take too long. My children are expecting me."

"Then I'll be sure not to keep you. If it's all right, we can talk on the way to your accommodations."

"Yes, that would be good."

They strolled at a leisurely pace. "I'm happy that you found your way back to Heidelberg. Although I'm sure Cologne has more to offer you."

"I like Cologne very much, but not because of the city itself. It's because we have our house, our family home, there. And the people are very friendly in Cologne, very welcoming to strangers."

"That's the spirit of a big city renowned for commerce," the doctor said. "May I ask how long you'll be staying here in Heidelberg?"

"Like I said before, just a few days."

"Do you have other commitments that would keep you from staying longer?"

Madlen glanced at him out of the corner of her eye. "What exactly do you want from me, Doctor?"

"It's about what I suggested before, Madlen. Oh, forgive me, may I call you Madlen?"

"Of course."

"You can call me Hyronimus."

The notion of calling someone so much older than her by his first name struck Madlen as rather odd.

"Madlen," Hyronimus went on, "do you remember Matthias Trauenstein?"

Just hearing his name startled her.

The doctor noticed. "Of course you remember him, what a silly question! The bastard wanted to hang you from the gallows." He took a deep breath. "For years, I served the nobles. Did you know that?"

"Yes. It was mentioned at the trial."

"Then did you also know that it was my duty to care for his victims time and time again?"

"Yes."

"Not an easy job, if I do say so myself. To see such injuries inflicted intentionally eats away at your very soul." He tapped his forehead. "Everything I've seen is in here and will haunt me for the rest of my life. I'm in your debt because you were the one responsible for bringing Matthias Trauenstein to trial and getting him convicted for those horrendous crimes. God forgive me, but I was quite relieved when I heard of his execution."

"It didn't look good for me for a long time," Madlen said. "I owe it all to the negotiation skills of my legal advocate at the time, Andreas von Balge. I'm a free woman today thanks to him."

"Yes, I remember him. He left a few years ago now. A man like that has undoubtedly found great success."

"He deserves nothing less. Unfortunately, I haven't heard from him in a long time."

"To get back to the reason I wanted to talk to you . . ." Hyronimus Auerbach paused for a moment, then continued. "There are many women here in Heidelberg and elsewhere in this land who are suffering horrors similar to what Adelhaid Trauenstein faced in her day. It's quite difficult for a man of the healing arts to endure—to see such suffering, to bind wounds, to search for words of comfort, only to be called again to tend to a patient a few days later."

"Why are you telling me this?"

"I heard from the sheriff that you were in the city. We've often spoken about the suffering of these poor women. The sheriff intervenes as much as he is able. He has personally beaten some of those so-called honorable husbands black and blue." A slight smile flitted across Hyronimus's face. "I didn't feel sorry for a single one of them."

"It's forbidden to beat your wife without cause."

"As it is also forbidden to inflict bodily harm disproportionate to a wife's real or imagined transgressions. But these men find a 'reason,' believe me. I've observed the recent increase of violence in the home. But inflicting bodily harm isn't the only problem. These men treat their wives worse than cattle. And if they get really drunk . . ." The doctor stopped, swallowed. "There was a woman, a beautiful and charming maiden from a good family, with a good education and a big dowry. Her father agreed to give her in marriage to an esteemed patrician—a councilman."

"Are you talking about Adelhaid Trauenstein?"

"No, though this story is very similar to hers. Well, this young woman wasn't just beautiful on the outside. No, she had an inner glow, an angelic light. She lit up any room she entered." His expression changed. He walked ahead. Madlen followed, guessing that he didn't want her to see that his eyes were welling up with tears.

"Not long after she married this repulsive villain, something happened."

"What?"

"At first she simply seemed more serious. Her exuberance, her cheerfulness, vanished into thin air. She hardly spoke. Then she claimed to have tripped and fallen down the stairs, but I didn't believe it for one second."

"Her husband beat her for no reason?"

Hyronimus Auerbach nodded. "I could see it in her eyes. It was as if her light had been extinguished."

"What became of her?"

"I would go to her residence, even though I hadn't been called, but she was always indisposed, unable to receive guests. I was sick with worry, so I spoke to her father and told him frankly what I thought was going on."

"Did he help her? Usually relatives have a right to intervene if the woman has committed no transgressions worthy of a beating."

He shook his head. "We had a falling-out. He upbraided me, called me a fool for asserting such things about this handsome and rich patrician. And so I left it at that."

"Until you were called to her again?"

"Exactly." The doctor stopped, looking up as if trying to remember. "What I saw took my breath away. He'd raped her so brutally that her insides were lacerated and torn apart. Heaven only knows what he used to inflict this kind of injury."

Madlen's stomach lurched; she covered her mouth with her hand.

"Her entire upper torso was beaten black and blue. I still don't know which of her injuries ultimately led to her death. But I couldn't save her."

Madlen caught up to Hyronimus and laid a hand on his arm. "I'm so sorry."

Tears again welled up in the physician's eyes. "She was my niece, Madlen, my brother's daughter. There wasn't anything I could do to help her. And my brother couldn't forgive himself for not listening to me." He did his best to suppress a sob. "They found him two days later. My brother committed a mortal sin—he took a rope, went to the woods, and hanged himself."

Madlen was so shaken that she couldn't speak.

"Nobody should have to experience that kind of thing. But times are hard, and many local businesses are failing. To drown their sorrows, some merchants go to taverns and get drunk. When they get home, many of them hit their wives and take them by force." He shook his head. "I can't bear it any longer. I can't bear to see one more broken woman."

Madlen was deeply touched. "Thank you for your trust, Doctor. I understand why you told me this. I must carefully consider whether I want to pursue this vocation, if I can endure seeing the pain and suffering that you've run up against."

"No." He stopped abruptly. "On the contrary, I believe you are strong enough to handle it."

"So then why are you telling me this?"

"Because I hope to get you on my side. On my side and the sheriff's side. The sheriff has advised women to call out for help if they're being beaten or raped so as to have enough proof to press charges against their husbands, but not one woman thus far has dared to do so."

"Out of fear," Madlen said.

"Yes, out of fear. But primarily because they don't believe they have the right, although our Germanic law book, the Saxon Mirror, explicitly lists wife beating as a punishable offense. They think, 'I am just a woman.' But someone like you—a woman who goes her own way despite being subjected to false allegations and gross injustices—can change the way these women think. You, Madlen, have the gift to empower these women so they can resist."

"Well, oh, my . . . I can't, I mean . . . I don't know what to say."

"You wouldn't be doing it alone. I only ask that you come with me to visit one of these women. Nothing more. I fear for this woman's life. The sheriff does, too, but he can't do anything if she doesn't report her repulsive husband."

"I don't know." The thought of this terrible violence made Madlen's skin crawl.

"I'll understand if you refuse. But please, think about it."

"I will."

"Is it all right if I visit you again tomorrow for your answer?"

"Yes, do that," she agreed.

He bowed, expressing his deference to this woman he so admired. "You have my highest respect, Madlen. May God protect you."

"Thank you for your confidence. May God be with you."

Chapter Eighteen

Johannes didn't know what to believe anymore. He was so annoyed about that rogue Wentzel's assertions. The archbishop! What utter nonsense! So that's who'd sent the bastard to tail him? Friedrich wasn't even in Cologne.

"You can forget about any kind of compensation for such absurd lies."

"You may not like what I'm saying, but that doesn't make it any less true," Wentzel stated boldly. "And I demand that you keep your part of the agreement."

"You know what the punishment is for slandering the archbishop?"

"You wanted to hear what I know. And I told you."

"Tell me exactly what it is you did."

"I followed your every move so I could report where you'd been."

"Who hired you to do this?"

"I don't know his name or his face. When I have something to report to him, I go to St. Alban's Church and light a candle there."

"How does he know it's you?"

"The candle is a different color than the others."

"Then what happens?"

"I check the church every hour. When the candle disappears, I know he is waiting for me in the vestry. Then I go in and tell him what I've witnessed."

"You've seen his face?"

"No, my lord. He wears a monk's habit and covers his face and head with a hood."

"How tall is he?"

"Shorter than you."

"Have you noticed anything special about him?"

"No, my lord."

"What does his voice sound like?"

"It isn't especially distinctive."

"Would you be able to recognize it if you heard it again?"

"Yes, my lord."

"Good. So how did you come to the conclusion that this man is in the service of Friedrich?"

"Because he told me."

"And you believe him?"

"There doesn't seem to be any reason not to."

Johannes relaxed a little. It was not at all certain that this man had been hired by Friedrich. But whoever he was, he was bold enough to claim just that.

"What are you thinking?" Wentzel asked.

"If what you say is true, then we can arrest this man right away. I'll come with you. Two guards will accompany us, in case you try to escape."

"And what kind of message should I bring him?"

"Just make something up, it doesn't matter. The second you meet up with him, we'll barge in and arrest him."

"And what will happen to me?"

"As we discussed, you'll give your sworn statement to a scribe and two witnesses. Then you'll receive money and a horse so you can leave Cologne."

Wentzel nodded. "Agreed."

"Then let's pray to God that this wasn't some idiot prankster playing you for a fool." Johannes paused. "What have they paid you thus far?"

"Ten groschen, my lord. And three more if I report something of importance."

"And what was important to this man?"

"Well, I got more money when I reported that woman's visit to your house. And also when you went to the harbor."

"You need to know this: That woman is dead. Murdered. Or did you murder her yourself?"

Wentzel held up his hands defensively. "I didn't murder anybody, not now, not ever. But I did see who it was," he said, smirking.

"You saw who killed her? And you're just telling me this now?"

"You didn't ask."

Johannes scrutinized him. "If you really saw that, then tell me how the woman was murdered."

"With an arrow from a crossbow." He turned around and pointed at his back, at exactly the same spot where the woman had been pierced. "Right about there."

"That's right. All right now, out with it: Who killed this woman? Do you know him?"

"I got a good look at him and know where to find him."

"Then tell me right now!"

Wentzel cocked his head, grinning from ear to ear. "And for that information, I would need another fifty groschen. Agreed?"

"You're a real creep, aren't you?"

"Yes, that's probably true. But I'll soon be a rich creep."

"Fine. A hundred groschen and a horse. But I want to know who it is immediately."

"Then let's go see him."

"Describe him to me now. You'll stay here."

"Here? With Friedrich's guards? If you leave me here, they'll probably stab me with a dull knife as soon as you're gone." He shook his head. "No, Counselor. If you want my help, then you shouldn't leave my side, and vice versa."

Johannes thought it over. "Fine. Then come with me. First we're going to go light a candle."

"I'll have to get one from my bedchamber."

"Where is that?"

"In one of the rooms near the harbor."

Johannes nodded then signaled Wentzel with a movement of his head to follow him outside. When Linhardt saw them leave the cell, he hurried over. "You stay where you are," he growled at Wentzel.

Wentzel raised his eyebrows and looked at Johannes. "Tell him."

"We need him as a witness," Johannes said. "He's going with me. Keep an eye on Benedict."

"Wouldn't it be better to take a few guards with you?" Linhardt said, giving the young man a swift appraisal. "He's not strong, but I bet he's light on his feet."

"He knows very well that it's to his advantage to stay by my side." Johannes didn't want to broadcast the fact that he'd promised to give Wentzel money in exchange for his testimony.

"Well, then, as you wish, my lord." Linhardt went back to his place outside Benedict's cell and plopped down on his chair again. Johannes and Wentzel climbed the stairs. For a moment, Johannes wondered whether he was doing the right thing. Everything Wentzel told him could have been a lie to get the young man out of his cell so he could make his escape. But his intuition told him that Wentzel was sincere. His description of the man in a monk's robe seemed too outlandish to be a lie. And Wentzel had been able to describe exactly how and where the false Duretta had been hit by the arrow. No, this brash young man had seen it—Johannes was completely sure about that. And soon he would find the murderer, who might very well be responsible for the other deaths, too. He could hardly wait.

But first it was a matter of finding out who was so keen on knowing his day-to-day whereabouts. The thrill of the hunt seized Johannes. He was finally making some headway in solving this puzzle.

The guards at the jail's entrance seemed perplexed as Johannes and Wentzel walked out of the building. They asked the attorney if they could do anything for him. He assured them that everything was fine.

❖ ❖ ❖

The two walked side by side to the harbor, as though they were the best of friends. What Wentzel referred to as his room was in truth nothing but a run-down old shack, the wind blowing into it through every nook and cranny.

"Why haven't you looked for some sort of gainful employment?" Johannes asked.

"And what is your idea of gainful employment?"

The attorney shrugged. "Carpentry, barrel making, butchering, or brush making."

Wentzel shook his head. "The same old thing day in and day out just isn't for me. Most of the time, I don't stay very long in one place. Today I'm in Cologne, maybe tomorrow I'll be in Dortmund or Koblenz. Whichever way the wind blows." Together they went inside. The room was sparsely furnished with a simple cot. No chairs, no tables, just a cot.

"How did you meet the man who hired you to keep an eye on me?"

Wentzel turned to Johannes. "I was in a tavern, and a couple of men started a fight. I didn't have anything to do with it, but I got hit. And then more men joined in and finally everybody was hitting everybody else."

"And then?"

"The innkeeper sent for the police and insisted that we all had to pay for the broken benches. Suddenly this fellow put his hand on my shoulder and said he could get me out of it. He said he had a deal for me, but I had to decide quickly. Truthfully, I was too drunk to really understand his offer. I just wanted to get away so I wouldn't be thrown in jail. I've been in jail once—not here, but in Trier. I thought the rats would eat me alive. Jail is not for me. I didn't know what jail would be like here in Cologne, so I figured I could sleep it off, earn some money, and be free."

"The man in the tavern, is that the one you met with in the church?"

"No, my lord. The fellow at the tavern is somewhat taller."

"And he succeeded in getting you out of there in time?"

"Yes, my lord. We escaped down some alleys, until he stopped to explain to me what I had to do."

Wentzel walked to a corner of the room and picked up a candle from the floor. He signaled to Johannes that they could go.

"What exactly did he want you to do?" Johannes continued once they were outside.

"He took me to your house and said that I should follow every move the occupant made. Then he described what you looked like." Wentzel pointed to Johannes's light-blond hair. "It was easy to recognize you."

"Didn't you think about running away as soon as he left you alone?"

"Briefly. But he warned me before he left."

"What did he say?"

"Something like 'Everyone who watches someone else is also being watched,' and that even thinking about not fulfilling my contract would mean my certain death. Then he explained to me about the candle and St. Alban's Church and all that, and he left. I staggered back to my room and thought about what to do. The prospect of being paid a few groschen to follow you was quite attractive."

"So the next day you began to follow me?"

"Correct."

"When was that?"

Wentzel thought it over. "A few days ago. The first day you went to the bishop's palace and from there to Bernhard von Harvehorst's house. Yes, that was the first time I followed you." He seemed almost proud to have remembered it so clearly and to have fulfilled his contract.

"So that was the same day I'd gone to the archbishop's and found out about Bartholomäus's and von Harvehorst's deaths?"

Wentzel shrugged. "Maybe. I can't really say."

"Yes, it must have been." Johannes paused. "Why do you believe that the archbishop was the one who authorized your contract, when he could hardly have been the man at the tavern?"

"Because he told me."

"Who? The man in the tavern?"

"No. The man at the church. He said that he relied on my silence, and that I would be in the service of the archbishop of Cologne."

"A rather bold assertion," Johannes grumbled. "What about when the woman was shot with the arrow?"

"What do you mean?"

"Well, didn't it occur to you that perhaps it wasn't proper to keep your mouth shut about that? It is your duty to report a murder."

"First of all, I have to tell you, someone like me would not voluntarily go to the sheriff's office, file a report, and then, ultimately, get blamed for the crime. Secondly, they would no doubt have asked me what I was doing to have witnessed the crime so accurately."

"I understand. Do you know where we can find this man?"

"When I saw what he'd done, I disregarded our contract so that I could follow him and not you. I knew it wouldn't be difficult to find you again. After all, you usually only go from your house to the palace and back again. I was curious. And from what I saw of you, nothing seemed amiss." He rubbed his pointer and middle finger against his thumb as if there was coin between them. "You'll need to pay me good money for pointing him out to you."

Johannes was about to reply, but they'd already reached St. Alban's Church. While Johannes stood at the entrance, Wentzel went in, put the special candle in a candleholder to the right of another one, and lit them both. Then he came back out.

"What now?" Johannes asked.

"We can either wait here, or I can show you the house the archer disappeared into."

"The second option. Your boss would probably flee if he saw me here right out in the open."

They walked down the street to Johannes's house.

"I was hiding there," Wentzel said, pointing to a gap between two houses across the street.

"But I was over there." Johannes gestured with his outstretched arm. "I would have at least been aware of you or seen you when I climbed up the stairs."

"Correct. But I was already there. As I said, it wasn't especially difficult to follow you. After a day, I knew exactly which way you always go."

"I'm sorry that I wasn't a bigger challenge for you," Johannes said. Wentzel smiled.

"When I saw that you were heading home, I'd take a shortcut through the palace courtyard's narrow alleys then walk down some side streets to settle down here."

"Settle down?"

"Sure. I'd stay in front of your house until I was sure that you'd gone to bed. Then I'd go back to my room to get a bit of sleep and then come back here first thing in the morning to wait for you to come out again."

"You're not stupid, Wentzel. If I may give you some advice: Think about what you want to do with the rest of your life. Someone like you, who can think on his feet and quickly comprehend complicated situations, can undoubtedly take up a career that wouldn't constantly put him in danger of winding up in jail."

"So you want to recruit me?"

"I'm just trying to inform you," Johannes responded good-naturedly. "Let's continue. When did you see the shooter and where was he standing?"

"Come on." Wentzel walked over to stand in front of a nearby wall. "He stood right here. If you hadn't had your attention focused on the woman, you would have been able to see him."

"Damn! If only I'd paid more attention! And did you recognize his face from here?"

"No."

"No?"

"No. The first time I saw his face was when he was standing in front of an inn, looking around in all directions to make sure nobody was following him."

"He didn't see you?"

Wentzel held out his arms. "Please, my lord. Of course not. He had no idea that I knew who he was."

Johannes felt almost proud of the boy. "Very well. Now show me where he lives. It will be my pleasure to put him behind bars where he belongs."

"Better him than me," Wentzel said cheerfully. "We've got to go this way." He stopped abruptly.

"What is it?"

Wentzel looked around. "Did you hear that?"

"No. What do you mean?"

"Oh, it's nothing. Let's go." They reached the street corner. "I think it's just around—" Wentzel flinched, but it was too late. Johannes was hit hard on the head. Before he went down, he saw a man in a monk's robe hitting Wentzel with a heavy wooden cudgel. Then the attorney lost consciousness.

Chapter Nineteen

Madlen didn't know what to think and even less what to do. She felt weighed down by the responsibility that Hyronimus Auerbach had entrusted her with. Yes, she knew it was more than just a few men who abused their wives. And like any person who had a heart, she was haunted by the viciousness and cruelty of it all.

Long ago, Johannes had told her a story about a time before he was the archbishop's attorney. A man had asserted his legal rights after his wife was raped so viciously that afterward she was unable to bear children. The husband demanded to be awarded damages from the offender, a nobleman with deep pockets, who had committed the crime while drunk. To him, it wasn't about the humiliation or pain that had been inflicted upon his wife. It was just about money. Johannes had forced the perpetrator to formally apologize to the woman and her husband before the high court, after which the rapist paid the agreed-upon fine and then disappeared.

Now, Madlen's stomach was rebelling. She had told neither Agatha nor Elsbeth nor Peter about her conversation with Hyronimus Auerbach. She was too confused at the moment to take them into her confidence. First, she had to clarify her own thoughts on the matter.

She wasn't quite ready to hear their opinions about the proposal, not until she was at peace with it herself. How she wished that Johannes were by her side. He would know exactly what to do. What would he think about it? Would he dissuade her from getting involved? Would he tell her it was none of her business? After all, she didn't even know the woman's name or her social standing. Who was her husband? A high-ranking official or a simple craftsman? Madlen suspected the former. She pictured in her mind Matthias Trauenstein, the man who had accused her of causing the death of his unborn child and, later on, his wife. He was an important man, a highly respected patrician. But in Madlen's eyes, he was nothing but a cowardly swine who abused his authority just because he could. The thought of him made her shudder.

She pulled the blanket over her daughter; the little girl had kicked it off in her sleep. Veit was sleeping on Madlen's other side, cuddled close. She took great comfort in the sound of their light snoring.

But soon her thoughts returned to Hyronimus Auerbach. What was this man thinking by asking her to do this? What had he said? He was in her debt because she'd fought Matthias Trauenstein, while he had obediently cared for the brute's wife's wounds after she'd been raped and beaten. Suddenly the children felt too close; she felt as though she were suffocating. She carefully wriggled out of bed and stood up. Her heart beat so violently that she became dizzy. She had to lean against the wall to keep from collapsing.

In the far corner, she noticed a tallow candle glowing weakly on a small table. Madlen went over and sat down. Did memories of the past cause her to pick up the candle and let it continue to burn? Long ago, she'd noticed the calming effects the light of a flickering candle had on the infirm, especially when she swayed the candle from side to side and in so doing caught their eye, focusing their attention. A warm feeling came over her. She held the candle in front of her and began slowly swaying it side to side. She inhaled and exhaled as her eyes followed the light. She closed her eyes and opened them again, still swaying the candle back and forth. Madlen started to feel calmer, her heartbeat slowing as her anxiety subsided. Then she put the candle on the table again, leaned back in the chair, and looked at the light, her breathing calm and even. She was relieved to notice her mood improving.

Madlen closed her eyes again. She thought about Johannes, about Cologne, about her house where they lived together so happily. Was her husband doing well? Maybe he had already solved Bartholomäus's murder and was on his way to Heidelberg. In a few days, he would undoubtedly be standing downstairs in the tavern asking for her. She saw herself standing at the banister. She would see him, hurry down the steps, and let herself fall into his arms. A soft sigh escaped from her lips. How lucky she was to have a husband like him! He was exceptionally kind and honest. Johannes treated the servants fairly and was respectful to even the most downtrodden. In contrast to other parents, he never acted like the children were stupid or didn't know about life. Yes, she was fortunate to have him. And she knew that he needed her as much as she did him. He often said that he was well aware of the good his family did him. This was the most time they'd ever spent apart. And why? So Madlen could attend Franz von Beyenburg's lectures. In Worms, Agathe had told her that listening to the doctor's lectures would be a waste of time since she'd never become a doctor anyway. Was her aunt right? Had she done the right thing by coming here instead of returning to Cologne once her in-laws' problems were resolved? Madlen's uneasiness grew. Shouldn't she be by her husband's side, supporting his work, especially now as he investigated the murder of an important man? Madlen rubbed her tired eyes. Did she really have the right to be here in Heidelberg just to chase a dream that could never truly be fulfilled? Why couldn't she just be satisfied with what she already had? She looked over at her children soundly sleeping and then again to the flickering candlelight. Her thoughts whirled in her head.

Why, she asked herself, did she want to practice the art of healing? To prove to everybody that a woman could be a doctor? To be showered with honors and accolades? The candlelight flickered as Madlen's eyelids started to close again. Why did she want to heal? Though barely able to keep her eyes open, she asked herself the same question over and over again. Finally, she blew out the candle, dragged herself over to bed, and crawled under the blanket with the children.

The question continued to echo in her mind as she fell asleep. Suddenly, the answer came to her in a moment of clarity as if a voice had whispered it softly in her ear. She wanted to help! She simply wanted to help. And she was determined to do so.

◆ ◆ ◆

"I would like to speak to all of you," Madlen announced as Agathe, Elsbeth, Peter, and the children sat down for breakfast. Ansgar had eaten and was probably tending to the horses now. Ursel and Gerald had devoured their meal earlier, hurrying as if they had a whole mountain of work to do like they did at home in Cologne. Madlen didn't know how those two passed the time, but she didn't want to delve into it. There were more important things to deal with right now.

"What is it?" Peter asked, shoveling a spoonful of porridge into his mouth.

The children looked at Madlen with great interest. She regretted having to discuss important matters in their presence, but there was hardly a minute in the day—except for her time at the university—when they weren't nearby. And it wasn't possible to speak with her in-laws or Agathe there at the university.

"Yesterday, I spoke with Hyronimus Auerbach. He's a doctor here in Heidelberg."

"Hyronimus is a funny name," Cecilia said.

"Shouldn't make any difference to you. It's not your name, after all," Veit argued.

"Because I'm not a boy."

"Even if you were, you wouldn't be called that because our parents wouldn't have named you that."

"You don't know anything."

"I do so. I'm a boy and my name isn't Hyronimus."

"Yours isn't and neither is mine." Cecilia glared at her brother, who looked at her uncertainly, apparently unable to follow his sister's illogical train of thought.

"Anyway," Madlen said, sparing Veit from having to respond to his sister, "this doctor with the funny name"—she nodded to Cecilia, who grinned from ear to ear—"spoke to me about a very serious matter."

"What kind?" Elsbeth asked.

"Well . . ." Madlen tried to formulate her answer so that the children wouldn't understand but the adults would know what she meant. "There are many women here in Heidelberg who call the doctor over and over again because they are suffering from misfortunes inflicted upon them by their husbands." She let her words soak in as she looked each adult in the eyes. "Often, the violence inflicted upon these woman is so bad that they end up dying immediately or perishing later from internal injuries."

"Those bastards should be hung up by their family jewels!" Peter yelled, his mouth full.

"Peter! The children!" Elsbeth scolded.

"What kind of family jewels do these men have?" Cecilia asked with great curiosity.

"Well, it depends," Madlen said evasively. "Some have diamonds and some have rubies."

Cecilia nodded.

The innkeeper's daughter came to the table to ask whether anyone wanted anything else. The way Peter stared at the young woman didn't escape Elsbeth's notice. She spooned some porridge into her mouth, lowered her head, and did her best to suppress her tears.

"To make a long story short: the doctor asked me to speak with a woman who is in that situation, in an effort to bolster her courage," Madlen continued after the innkeeper's daughter had left. "There may be other women who need my help, too."

"Why?" Agathe asked suspiciously.

"The sheriff needs her to file a formal complaint in order to press charges."

"Have you lost your mind? That has nothing to do with you; you don't have the right to interfere."

"I agree with Agathe," Peter said after swallowing another mouthful of porridge. "This is a matter between a husband and his wife."

"Aren't you oversimplifying this a little?" Madlen asked. "What would you have women like this one do? Their marriages were arranged by their fathers, and they are totally dependent on their husbands."

"And you think things will be better for them if they report their husbands?" Elsbeth said. "Forgive me, but I don't believe it. It will be quite the opposite—being exposed like that will only serve to further provoke their husbands' rage."

"So it's just to let these men have their way?"

"Mother?" Veit said. "I'm finished. Can I go up to our bedchamber now?"

"Of course. I'll take you up."

"Then I'm coming, too," Cecilia said.

Madlen stood, excused herself, and accompanied the children up to their bedchamber. Veit and Cecilia jumped onto the bed and began to play. Madlen went back downstairs and sat down.

"We've talked it over while you were gone," Agathe declared. "The only thing you will achieve by doing this is that the women will be punished all the more severely by their husbands, and you will become the object of the men's scorn." She looked at Madlen gravely. "Do you want them to do the same thing to you as they've done to their wives?"

Goose bumps broke out on Madlen's skin. She hadn't really thought about that. What would happen if their anger were diverted from their wives onto her? She dropped her head. "No, I don't want that."

"Good," Agathe pronounced. "I'm glad that's cleared up."

Madlen nodded, but in a flash her resignation turned to rage as she remembered the suffering she knew befell these women. "But who will help those who cannot help themselves?"

"Hopefully not you," Elsbeth said sternly. "It's not your job."

"Hyronimus Auerbach told me a story. One that unfortunately is all too true." Madlen told the others what he had confided to her about his niece. Just recounting the story choked her up, and she had to work to suppress the nausea rising up inside her.

There was an embarrassed silence. Madlen looked at the others and waited for them to speak, but nobody said a word.

"Let's say the same thing happened to me," Madlen persisted. "Would you still say that it was my fault, that I let my husband do that to me?"

Peter was the first to rouse himself from the group's silence. "Your powers of persuasion are quite impressive."

"This isn't about me. It's just that I find suffering and injustice simply intolerable."

"It's intolerable to us, too," Elsbeth agreed.

Agathe laid her hands on Madlen's. "You've become a very strong woman."

"I'm incredibly grateful for my happy marriage, and healing and helping people drives me. If we saw a sick or injured person lying in the mud in the middle of the street, there would be no question that we would help him as much as we could. But what happens to the women who aren't lying in the street but who are subject to violence and degradation each and every day? Do we have the right to simply pass them by on the grounds that it's none of our business?"

Peter smiled.

"Have I amused you in some way?" Madlen said irritably.

"Not at all. I was just thinking what a good match you and my son are. You speak in the same way, and you are both driven to defend the rights of all individuals."

"Are you teasing?" Agathe asked.

Peter shook his head. "I only wonder why we thought we could dissuade such a strong-willed woman from doing what she knows is right." He glanced at Madlen. "But there it is. You've already made your decision, haven't you? I can see it in your eyes. It's the same look my son has when he's made up his mind. It's almost as if it's ordained by God."

"I'm surely no attorney like Johannes," Madlen argued.

Peter cocked his head. "Well, I don't see much difference. You witness suffering or injustice and you feel called to do everything in your power to alleviate or eliminate it." He looked at Elsbeth and Agathe. "We have to accept the fact that it's not in our power to dissuade her from her mission."

"But—" Agathe started but fell silent when Peter shook his head. "Are you truly satisfied that you're making the right decision?" she asked.

Madlen tried to smile. "I'm afraid Peter's right. Even if it wasn't totally clear to me until this very moment."

"We should never have come here," Elsbeth moaned. "And we even encouraged you to make this trip! Johannes will never forgive us for this."

"If Johannes were here, he would have taken charge of this issue himself," Madlen shot back.

"Because, as the archbishop's legal counsel, he would have been appointed to it. But you're just a woman, a wife like all the others," Agathe said, trying one last time to persuade her niece.

"What if this is why I went through so much suffering and injustice myself—so that I would be better able to help others?"

Agathe looked helplessly at Elsbeth and Peter. "You are the most obstinate person I've ever met, Madlen Goldmann."

"I'm sorry to be a disappointment to you."

"And the bravest," Agathe added.

"So you're not angry with me?"

"How could I be? You put us all to shame. We who sit here and nag and hesitate to do the right thing out of fear."

Madlen smiled. "I'm going to say farewell to the children and then go to the university." She stood.

"Compared to my daughter-in-law, I'm just a pitiful coward. So much courage and determination!" Peter shook his head wistfully. "Let us know if there's anything we can do to help. I might even become a good person after all." He rose to his feet.

"Where are you going?" Elsbeth asked.

"I'm going to stretch my legs a bit."

"Wait a moment; I'll accompany you."

"No, no. Don't bother." Peter patted his wife on the shoulder as he moved past her. "I won't be gone long." Without waiting for her response, he said good-bye and went outside.

"Everything all right?" Madlen asked her mother-in-law.

"Of course," she said quickly. "And you better go before it's too late."

Madlen nodded, turned, and went upstairs. She said good-bye to the children and told them that Agathe and Elsbeth would be coming up soon. Before she left the inn, she waved at Elsbeth and Agathe, then hurried out. As she walked, anxiety about Peter came over her. She'd noticed the strain between her in-laws—blessedly absent for a few days—had returned. But then she thought of the abused women and the important task of helping them. Yes, that was what she wanted to do. She'd never felt more powerful in her whole life.

❖ ❖ ❖

Madlen was unable to concentrate during the lecture, barely following Franz von Beyenburg's instruction.

The doctor seemed to notice that her mind was elsewhere because after the lecture he asked her to stay. "Is everything all right?"

"Of course. Thank you."

"I only ask because you seem so distracted. Are you worried about something? Perhaps someone reprimanded you because we've allowed you to listen to the lectures here?"

"No, that's not it. Really, thank you so much," she said evasively.

"Well, then"—he opened his hands—"let me know if I can help you in any way."

"I will," she promised. She bade him farewell and hurried out. She was relieved to see Dr. Auerbach sitting on the low wall where they had spoken earlier. She waved and walked over to him.

He stood. "God be with you, Madlen."

"God be with you, Doctor. I'm happy to see you."

He seemed surprised. "Really?"

"Yes. Why are you so shocked?"

"Well, I figured you would greet me a bit more reluctantly. I thought you'd tell me that after thinking about it, you must regretfully reject my proposal."

"Oh, really?"

"Yes. Yesterday, I went to the sheriff's office and outlined the proposal we'd discussed. He suggested that your heart was no doubt in the right place but that you'd have to be out of your mind to help us."

"Well, I hope I won't disappoint you and the sheriff too much by informing you that your assessment is utterly mistaken."

"Really? Does that mean you'll speak with the woman?"

"With her and all the others who are in the same position."

"Madlen, that is fantastic!" He grasped her hands. "I don't know how to thank you."

"When can we see this woman?"

The doctor thought about it. "I would like for us to speak to the sheriff. What do you think? Would it be possible for you to come to the sheriff's office this afternoon? Then we'll be able to discuss things without anyone else getting wind of it."

"Yes, that suits me very well. In that case, let me hurry back so that my children can have a little time with their mother."

"Madlen, you are a remarkable woman!"

"I just hope I can help."

"Of that I'm quite sure. I'll accompany you to your accommodations."

"I can find my way alone. Thank you anyway."

"Yes." He smiled. "Indeed, a woman like you requires no escort."

She returned his warm smile. Then she hurried to the Golden Rooster.

Agathe and Elsbeth had just returned from the market with the children, who enthusiastically described all the things they had seen and experienced. Madlen listened cheerfully, squeezing in a question here and there. But her attention wasn't fully with them. She'd been excited about the prospect of helping the sheriff and the doctor, but she was starting to feel nervous about meeting the woman so soon. She felt insecure. Would she actually be able to help? Did she have the necessary skills? Would simply being a woman who had suffered grave injustices be enough? Madlen pushed her doubts aside. This habitual brooding wasn't healthy.

". . . and then the lady told me she was going to give me an apple because I had such beautiful eyes and that my hair would grow again very soon. I had so much fun." Cecilia beamed at her mother.

"That's wonderful, little one."

"First you must eat something," Elsbeth urged her, after Madlen explained she'd be leaving again soon to accompany the sheriff to the abused woman's home. "You've been walking here and there the whole day."

"I'm not hungry, but thanks anyway."

"Are you all right?" her mother-in-law asked.

"Of course. I learned a lot today, and it seems the lecture had a lasting effect on me," Madlen fibbed.

"This makes you really happy, doesn't it?"

Madlen nodded. "I have to go. Would it be too much to ask you to watch the children again? I'd rather not take them with me to this meeting."

"You're always doing things without us," Veit complained.

"I'll be back very soon," Madlen said, trying to pacify him.

"Where are you going, Mother?" Cecilia asked.

"I'm going to see a woman who needs my help."

"And it's really not going to take long?" Cecilia asked.

"Not long at all. I promise."

"It's all right by me as long as you stay with us afterward," Cecilia said.

"Yes, sweetheart. Then I'll stay with you." She hugged her children, though she was unable to rid herself of her guilt about leaving them.

"Where is Peter?" Madlen asked.

Elsbeth kneaded her hands nervously. "He hasn't come back yet." She tried to smile. "He'll surely return any moment now. You go ahead and help those women. Agathe and I will take care of everything here."

"Is everything all right between you and Peter?"

"Of course," Elsbeth answered a little too quickly.

Agathe touched Madlen's shoulder. "Elsbeth is right. Go now. We'll stay here."

"All right." Madlen kissed her children good-bye and got underway. Something didn't feel quite right, and that uneasy feeling remained as she headed toward the sheriff's office.

❖ ❖ ❖

A deputy announced her arrival, and immediately the sheriff ordered him to bring her in. Once she was inside, he stood and greeted her warmly. "Madlen, I can't begin to tell you how pleased I am to see you. Please come in and take a seat."

She took a deep breath, straightened her spine, and smiled. "God bless you, Sheriff."

Dr. Auerbach was already there. He rose from his seat and greeted Madlen with a bow. "Thank you for coming, Madlen."

She sat down, and the sheriff and the doctor reoccupied their places.

"The doctor and I have been speaking about the women whose lives we fear for the most," the sheriff said. "I can't tell you how thankful we are for your support."

"I'm delighted to help. But I can't promise that I'll be able to convince them." Madlen looked from the sheriff to the doctor. "Tell me, aren't you afraid that it will only make matters worse for these women, once they report their husbands' misdeeds?"

"We've already talked about that," the sheriff answered. "That's why we want to have six specially selected members of the council present when the abuser is informed of his wife's report. After that, if he touches a hair on his wife's head, the husband will be arrested and incarcerated, whether he's hurt her or she claims to have accidentally hurt herself. Besides"—he raised his eyebrows—"I wouldn't believe the latter anyway. This is how we will stop the abusers from here on out. In Heidelberg, we will enforce the laws as set forth in the Saxon Mirror, and these men can't do anything about it."

"And what about helping the women find a place where they are safe from their husbands?"

"That would be difficult. Husbands have the right to determine where their wives reside. That's the law. But I have decided to introduce a decree that will mandate, in such cases, that the wife's custody will transfer to me or to Klaus, the prior of the Augustinian monastery."

Madlen sighed. "I fear even that measure wouldn't stop these men from taking revenge on their wives."

"That's why we must impose harsh penalties, in the hopes that we can make a potential abuser think twice before raising his hand against his wife. Even though other cities in our land might overlook these abuses, I won't tolerate them here in Heidelberg. The Saxon Mirror is unambiguous, and I will act accordingly."

"It's insane that we have to go to such extremes to protect these women," Madlen said.

"That's true. I'm sure it reminds you of Matthias Trauenstein," the sheriff stated. "At first he only *slapped*"—he stressed the last word contemptuously—"his poor wife around. Just a slap or two, then three or four more, then he started punching her with his fists. He always found a reason to abuse her, whether it was a bad business day or he just wanted to make sure she knew who was boss. Then the violence escalated to brutal rapes, more beatings, further atrocities. That swine actually enjoyed what he did to her, and nobody intervened. Until at last, he killed his unborn baby and later his wife. Then he murdered the maid so that he could blame the whole thing on you. Men like him won't quit their abusive behaviors if nobody stops them."

"That's the very reason we have to do something," the old doctor confirmed. "If we don't do it, nobody else will. And I don't want to see any more wounds for which I can only offer superficial treatment. I can't bear to hear any more bald-faced lies about accidental falls down the stairs. What's worse is when these women refuse to talk at all."

"Who will I be speaking to?" Madlen asked.

"Trude von Fahrenholz and Magdalena Grossherr," the sheriff answered. "Their situations are so bad that there's a very real danger they won't survive the next few months."

"Each time I see them, their injuries are more severe than the time before," the doctor said. "With their bodies in such a weakened state, they won't be able to take much more." The doctor shook his head.

"Even scoundrels who are made to confess under torture are treated better than these women."

"When are we going to see them?"

"Today," the sheriff responded. "If we want to help them, we don't have any time to lose."

"I'm ready," Madlen declared.

The sheriff nodded. When he got up, Madlen and the doctor did, too. "I'll come along," the doctor said. "The women know and trust me."

"I don't think that's such a good idea," the sheriff said. "If your involvement becomes known, these honorable gentlemen will undoubtedly stop sending for you, even if their wives are badly injured. It's my job as sheriff to investigate violations of the laws of our city. And Madlen has nothing to fear because she'll be going back to Cologne soon. Since Madlen and her husband are such notable citizens, they will come to no harm."

The doctor deliberated for a moment then nodded. "You're probably right. Can I wait here until you return so I can find out what occurred?"

"Certainly. I'll let you know."

"I will do my best," Madlen assured the doctor.

"I have no doubt about that," he answered. He pensively watched Madlen and the sheriff as they left the office.

Chapter Twenty

"Where am I?" Johannes tried to lift his head, which felt as though it were made of lead.

"In a room in the archbishop's palace, my lord." Linhardt appeared at his bedside.

"What happened?"

Linhardt shrugged. "We were hoping to find that out from you. I'm not supposed to speak to you, and I've been ordered to report when you wake up."

"You're not allowed to speak to me and have to report when I wake up," Johannes repeated in astonishment. "Why?"

"I . . . I'm really not allowed to say any more. Please, forgive me. And don't leave this room. There are two guards standing outside the door. And also out there"—he pointed to the crown glass window—"so I wouldn't try it."

"What are you talking about?"

"It's about the murder, my lord." He didn't elaborate but went right to the door and hurriedly left the room.

Johannes was utterly confused. The last thing he remembered was being with Wentzel in an alleyway near his house. They were on their way to find the fellow who had killed Duretta's impostor. But then what happened? He couldn't remember.

In a few minutes, Linhardt returned, accompanied by the vicar general.

"You're awake! Thank God!" The vicar general raised his hands toward the heavens in gratitude. "Now you can finally explain what happened. What's been claimed is sheer madness," he said indignantly.

The vicar general came over and sat down on the edge of the bed as if he were a trusted confidant. "I'm on your side, Counselor. Don't worry. We'll get this all cleared up."

"Forgive me, Monsignor, but I have no idea what you're talking about."

"You haven't told him?" He turned around and scowled at Linhardt.

The guard shrugged and raised his hands. "I was forbidden to do so, as you know."

The vicar general waved him off dismissively. "Oh, let the sheriff of Cologne talk. The attorney is in the service of the archbishop; he possesses his trust and full authority. And we are here in the archbishop's palace." He turned to Johannes again. "You've been accused of murdering that fellow you were with. But that's out of the question, complete nonsense. So, stay calm."

"Wentzel is dead?"

"If that's his name."

"Yes, his name is Wentzel. How was he killed?"

"With a knife. First he was stabbed in the stomach, and then his throat was cut from ear to ear." The vicar general shook his head. "Barbaric. I never believed for a moment that it was you."

"Why would I have anything to do with it? I got hit on the head and don't know what happened after that."

"Well, there is a witness. And to hear it from him, it was exactly the other way around. He claims to have observed the crime and says that it was you who knocked the poor man down in order to help the man who wielded the dagger."

"I demand to speak to this so-called witness immediately," Johannes hissed. "If he maintains such a thing, it's because he himself committed the crime. I didn't stab anybody with a knife. Why would I? Wentzel was an important witness for me."

"A witness to what?" the vicar general asked.

"He knows who killed the woman."

"Which one? Bernhard von Harvehorst's housekeeper?"

"No, the other one. The one who pretended to be her." Johannes noticed the confused expression on the vicar general's face. "It's a long story."

"Be that as it may," the vicar general said, "you should be aware of the following: the sheriff wanted to take you to jail, but we knew that we had to prevent that." He nodded to Linhardt. Johannes understood that he probably went to a lot of trouble to keep him at the palace instead. The guard returned the clergyman's nod.

"It's of the utmost importance that we prevent you from being taken away from the palace," the vicar general continued. "You have the full authority of the archbishop; therefore, you have preeminent rights. But I'm afraid that beyond these walls, there isn't much we can do for you. That's why I immediately sent for the doctor when Linhardt reported that you were awake. He will certify that you are not in any condition to be brought to the dungeon. They will honor the doctor's recommendations."

"I understand," Johannes said.

"I've sent out our people. They'll try to find more witnesses."

"This is insane!" Johannes yelled. "What reason would I have to kill Wentzel? I needed him alive."

"The sheriff insists all the same. He believes there is a conspiracy because, from the start, the palace, the office of the archbishop, tried to keep him out of the investigation into Bartholomäus's and Bernhard von Harvehorst's deaths."

"I believe there's a conspiracy, too," Johannes murmured. "But not one involving the sheriff."

The vicar general didn't know what to do with this remark, so he simply continued with his explanation. "The sheriff didn't take it too well when the archbishop appointed you to the investigation instead of him. It damaged his reputation in Cologne. He's having a field day now that he has a reason to cause you trouble."

"I have no desire to be pulled into this power play," Johannes said. "This so-called witness, the one you mentioned earlier—who is this man?"

The vicar general shrugged. "Unfortunately, I really don't know. The sheriff said that he didn't want to disclose his identity so as not to put him in danger."

"The man is delusional!"

"Possibly, but that doesn't change the facts. As long as the archbishop is out of the country, the sheriff doesn't trust me to have an unbiased view of you. He wants to get an audience with the king so that he can request a trial."

"He wants to curtail the archbishop's power?"

"Better to curtail his power than to be his employee." He leaned forward again. "I can't trust anybody anymore. There are two guards out there—the sheriff's men, not the palace's. Linhardt insisted on staying with you here, inside the palace." He sat down again, speaking loudly enough so that Linhardt could hear him clearly. "For which he deserves my undying gratitude." Then he continued in a whisper, "My suspicion is that something more sinister is afoot. It seems as though the leading city officials under our imperial rulers want to wrest away the archbishop's power, or at least curtail it. There is a conspiracy brewing, but it's not to the palace's benefit."

"What do you propose we do?"

"Do not leave this bed under any circumstances. Linhardt will stay with you. Upon the changing of the guard, choose somebody you can trust."

"I don't need a replacement," Linhardt pronounced. "I'll guard you with my life."

Johannes threw him a grateful look and then faced the vicar general again. "Do you really think my life is in danger?"

"Frankly, I'm not sure. But think about this scenario: the sheriff's men guarding the door declared that if you tried to escape, they would kill you, and you've been accused of a premeditated, cold-blooded murder. What would people deduce? That the archbishop's fully authorized agent was the leader of a conspiracy to kill an innocent man? That he had been contracted by the archbishop to do this, or that our imperial monarch is such a poor judge of character that he granted full power to someone who then arbitrarily killed a citizen of Cologne?" He exhaled noisily. "Do you understand what I mean?"

"Yes, I understand. Tell me, do you think it's possible that we'll find the person responsible for the murders of Bartholomäus, Christopeit, Duretta, and Bernhard von Harvehorst among these people?"

The vicar general thought about it. "What did you say a few days ago? The murders might have been committed to weaken the position of our beloved archbishop. What if you are looking in the wrong place for the murderer?"

"I hadn't really thought about that," Johannes admitted. There was a loud knock on the door.

"Open the door immediately!"

Linhardt looked at Johannes, who nodded. The guard moved the chair, which had been jammed underneath the doorknob, aside and opened the door.

"Why in the world did you block the door?" the sheriff of Cologne snapped at Linhardt after entering.

"He was acting on my orders," the vicar general said. "We are in the archbishop's palace. And I don't believe we have to have a long discussion about whether your people or mine rank higher here."

"Which is why I will now take the prisoner and *welcome* him to the accommodations we've gladly provided for him," the sheriff responded smugly.

"Not so fast, Sheriff! We're waiting for the doctor to make his examination. He'll be the judge of whether the attorney is healthy enough to leave his bed."

"What do you think, Counselor? Are you strong enough? After all, you merely got hit on the head. As far as I can tell, you're healthy enough to come with me."

"Oh, have you been trained as a doctor?" Johannes asked, his voice oozing sarcasm. "Besides, I would really like to know why I should go with you. I was knocked unconscious, and I certainly didn't attack anyone. You can take my statement right here and now."

"Unfortunately for you, I have a witness who says otherwise."

"Really?"

"You don't know about that yet?" The sheriff sneered. "I can hardly believe the honorable lord vicar general hasn't yet informed you."

"Believe whatever you want." Johannes smiled.

"You know it and I know it. You are guilty of murder! You are a dangerous man, Counselor, and it is my job to protect the fine citizens of Cologne from people like you."

Johannes shook his head. "I think we both know that's a lie, Sheriff. I'm no danger to anyone except those who are themselves criminals."

"Like you?"

"How dare you address me in that tone, Sheriff. I've been patient with you so far, but enough is enough! As you well know, I've been assigned by Archbishop Friedrich to solve the murders. And obviously now someone is doing their best to hinder my investigation."

"Come with me and I promise to give you a fair trial."

"I prefer to stay here at the palace."

"Only if the doctor swears under oath that this is absolutely essential."

"Wrong. I haven't just been assigned to investigate the murders. I have been given full authority to take over administration of all of the archbishop's affairs during his absence. I have been anointed with full power in Friedrich's stead. You see, Sheriff, it wasn't necessary for the vicar general to assert his supremacy in this jurisdiction. I"—he tapped himself on the chest—"have the highest rank here. I even have house rights, which means I can forbid entry or eject anyone from these premises at any time. And you can't do a single thing about it."

"Where is this note of authorization? I would like to see it."

"A copy is in the scribe's study here in the palace. I can submit it to you immediately. And another copy is kept at a secure place known only to me. Oh, yes, and the archbishop himself also has a copy of the document. So you see, there are several ways to verify my rights."

"That may apply here inside the palace, but as soon as you step one foot onto the streets of Cologne, it will be a different story altogether."

Johannes shook his head. "As a lawyer, I can tell you that your claim is not quite accurate. But I don't want to question the king's rights, even though he is subject to the directives of the imperial monarch, the position that Friedrich holds. But oh, well." He raised his hand and gestured affably. "If we are in agreement about the fact that you have no business here unless I explicitly summon you, then we've made a good bit of headway. So you may go now, Sheriff. If I need to speak to you, I will send a messenger."

The sheriff snorted with rage. "If you put one foot on the streets of Cologne—"

Johannes raised his hand to silence him. "When I decide to do so, I'll notify you, of course."

The sheriff glared at him. "I'll convict you of those murders even if I have to go to the king to do so."

"Then have a good journey, Sheriff. And don't forget to take the guards standing outside my door with you. I'm afraid that at this time, they are no longer welcome on my property."

"We'll see each other again."

"I can hardly wait."

"Let me through! I'm the doctor!" someone yelled outside the door. Linhardt opened it to find the sheriff's men blocking the doctor's way.

"Let him enter," the sheriff called out, and the guards stepped aside.

The doctor smoothed his clothing. "Ruffians!" he cried then scowled at the guards. "I came as quickly as possible. Step aside. Everyone must step aside and leave me alone with the patient. I will determine whether he's well enough to leave his bed."

"That will not be necessary," Johannes declared. "I'm feeling very well indeed, Doctor. Thank you."

The doctor looked at the vicar general uncertainly.

"And the good sheriff of Cologne was just leaving," Johannes added. "Have a nice day, Sheriff."

Johannes could see the sheriff bristle. He glared, then departed without saying good-bye and ordered his guards to follow him.

"I thought I was coming to prevent your arrest," the doctor said, obviously confused. "At least that's what the guard you sent relayed to me."

"Our legal counsel here found another way to expel the sheriff from the palace." The vicar general couldn't suppress his mirth. "I'm amazed that you were able to act so judiciously in such a difficult situation," he said to Johannes. "Still, you shouldn't leave the palace. The sheriff will be ready and waiting."

"Where are my clothes?" Johannes asked.

"I burned them."

"Why?"

"They were completely soaked in blood. If the sheriff had seen them, he would have used them as further evidence of your guilt."

"Thanks for handling that with such foresight."

"Is there anything else for me to do now?" the doctor asked. "If not, I will take my leave."

"No. I'm doing fine," Johannes assured him again. "My head hurts, but that will diminish over time."

"With your permission, I would like to examine your wounds before I go."

"Of course."

The doctor walked around the bed and gestured for Johannes to sit up so that he could examine his skull. "You're getting a nice bump there, I can already feel it. Do you feel nauseous? Can you see clearly?"

"Just a throbbing pain, that's all."

"Good. You can lie back again. Stay in bed and enjoy some peace and quiet. You'll be your old self in a few days."

"In that case, I would love to take a nap now," Johannes said. He in fact did feel nauseous but didn't want to admit it to the doctor just yet.

"A good idea," the doctor proclaimed. "Come on. Let the man sleep."

The vicar general nodded. "I'll check up on you a little later."

The vicar general and the doctor went to the door, which Linhardt had closed after the sheriff's departure. The guard opened it.

"Come on, Linhardt. You can give up your post here," the vicar general said.

"I'll stay," he said firmly, looking to Johannes to confirm his decision.

"Thank you, Linhardt. I feel quite secure having you here."

"As you wish," the vicar general said. The doctor and the vicar general said their farewells and left together.

Linhardt closed the door behind them then immediately grabbed a chair and wedged it under the doorknob. "You can sleep easy, my lord. I'm here."

"Come closer," Johannes said.

The guard approached Johannes's bed. The attorney signaled him to lean in close.

"I don't know who to trust anymore," Johannes whispered, "and something tells me that these walls have ears."

"I get the same feeling," Linhardt said.

"Please, tell me how I was found."

"From what I understand, a man—perhaps the one who claims to be a witness against you—got ahold of the police. Richard, one of the archbishop's guards, had just brought in a drunk who'd been hanging around, vomiting in front of the palace. He wanted to put him in jail to sleep it off away from the palace. I've known Richard for many years, and he knows I've been in your personal service for a little while. So he contacted me when he heard the witness's story at the jail. He took over my job of guarding Benedict. I ran to the place this witness had described to the police; they'd just spoken to him. You and the other man—this Wentzel, as you called him—were sprawled on the ground. It was obvious that there was nothing that could be done for the young man. You were unconscious, lying face-down over him. You'd been hit from behind and had pitched forward onto him."

"Did what you saw match what the witness reported?"

"Yes. The police wanted to take you with them, but I told them that you were in the service of the archbishop and that you needed medical attention. I said that they should help me bring you to the palace. Good thing that the sheriff hadn't arrived yet. The police helped me bring you here. Then I notified the vicar general, and you already know the rest."

"I understand." Johannes stroked his chin. "What was your impression?"

"My impression, my lord?"

"When you saw me lying there semiconscious on the dead Wentzel, what did you think?"

"May I speak frankly, my lord?"

240

"I order you to do so, Linhardt."

"What I saw seemed to match what the witness said. He claimed to have seen two men arguing, but he didn't attach any importance to it. Then the fight got louder, and you pulled out a knife, stabbed the young man in the belly twice, and, finally, cut his throat. When that happened, the witness ran over to you and hit you on the back of the head with a piece of wood."

"What is this man's trade?"

"Who? The witness?"

Johannes nodded.

"I don't know, my lord."

"Well, if he's not a carpenter, I ask myself, why would he be carrying around a piece of wood that was big enough to strike me down?"

"A good point."

"We're not in court and I'm not trying to convince you," Johannes stated firmly, "but I have questions and you are a good observer. The last thing I remember is both Wentzel and I getting hit on the back of the head. There was a man in a monk's habit. Wentzel fell to the ground and I did, too. I can't remember anything after that." Johannes shoved the blanket aside and swung his legs off the bed. He was wearing only a linen shirt; he felt ill at ease that Linhardt had to see him like that.

"You shouldn't be getting up yet."

"I just want to try something." Johannes put his feet on the ground, swaying as he stood. Linhardt grabbed him to prevent him from collapsing. Johannes took a deep breath, taking a moment to find his balance. "I'm all right now."

Linhardt let go of him but stayed close by should Johannes overestimate his state of well-being. But the attorney seemed to have gotten ahold of himself.

"Stand in front of me," he ordered, and Linhardt complied. "Wentzel was smaller than me and even smaller than you."

"Should I get on my knees?"

"That won't be necessary for what I'm about to demonstrate." Johannes held out his hand as if wielding a knife. "I stab you"—he thrust his hand forward—"twice. What do you do?"

"I clamp my hands over my stomach and bend over."

"Do it."

Linhardt clenched his stomach then bent over.

"Now, I'm going to cut your throat," Johannes said and held out his hand.

"You won't be able to get to my throat."

"Exactly. In order to cut your throat, I would have to stand next to you, like so." He stepped to Linhardt's side, grabbed him, and moved his finger across his throat. "I cut your throat from ear to ear. I get a blow on the back of my head."

Linhardt stood upright again. "Now I understand. We would have both pitched forward. Wentzel wouldn't have fallen on his back, and you wouldn't have fallen on top of him. It wouldn't have been possible to slit his throat the way the witness described."

"Precisely." Johannes got back in bed and pulled the blanket up. The little demonstration had sapped his strength.

"You don't have to prove to me that you didn't do it. I already believed you."

"I don't want you to just believe me. I want you to really know."

"That means a lot to me. Thank you."

"I'm grateful that you acted so quickly in bringing me here. I probably wouldn't have survived if you'd let them haul me off to the sheriff's jail."

"Why is all this happening?"

"You mean, why does someone want to frame me for murder?"

"Exactly."

"I don't know. I believe that having Wentzel as a witness was too close for someone's comfort. And this someone will do everything in his power to ensure I can't complete my investigation. And he's already attained quite a bit of success in that regard."

"How?"

"I have to stay here in the palace, so I can't go out to perform my interrogations."

"But I can." Linhardt grinned.

"Exactly. You will have to be my eyes and ears."

"I will, my lord. I thank you for your trust."

"We need more men. I don't know how long it will take for the sheriff to find a way to take me from the palace. It's essential that we solve the murders before then."

"Let's not forget the murder charge against you," Linhardt reminded him.

"I'll get to the bottom of that," Johannes said more confidently than he felt. "Which of the men are above reproach?"

"I would entrust any of the men who were present at the meeting in your home with my life."

"I'm inclined to agree with you. Please fetch Anderlin, Georg, Niclaus, Wolfker, and Wilhelm so we can devise a plan."

"Yes, my lord." Linhardt turned to go but spun around again to face Johannes. "As soon as I leave, can you wedge the chair under the doorknob? It would give me peace of mind."

Johannes smiled, impressed with the guard's concern. He slung the blanket aside and got up. Unsteady on his feet, he briefly leaned against the bed for support. Then he walked to the door.

Linhardt pushed the chair aside. "I'll hurry, my lord."

"It's good to know someone like you is on my side."

Linhardt nodded, went out, and pulled the door shut.

Even the simple act of moving the chair under the doorknob wore Johannes out. With a great deal of effort, he dragged himself back to bed then collapsed onto the mattress and closed his eyes. He was dizzy again; he felt as though he had a terrible hangover. He intended to simply rest for a moment to gather his strength, but instead he fell into a deep sleep. He awoke when Linhardt drummed his fingers against the door, calling out his name.

"I'm coming," he said groggily then stood up.

"Is everything all right, my lord?"

"Yes, everything's fine."

Johannes reached the door and pushed the chair aside. As soon as the door opened, six guards entered, one after the other. Linhardt closed the door once they were all inside.

"You don't look very well, my lord." Linhardt caught Johannes's arm and guided him back to bed. "I'm sending for the doctor."

"I'm all right."

"No, I think the doctor should come." Linhardt looked over at the others. "Niclaus, can you fetch him?"

"Yes. I'll hurry."

"You need to rest." The guard spread the blanket carefully over Johannes. "We're here now, and we'll do all we can to help you," Linhardt said, his face lined with worry.

Chapter Twenty-One

Magdalena Grossherr's servant had told her that the sheriff and an unknown woman urgently wished to speak to her and would not take no for an answer. Her whole body trembled as she walked to her front door. "What do you want from me?"

"We want to help you," the sheriff said. "Can we speak with you?"

Magdalena Grossherr's face went white as chalk. "My husband is not home. He would undoubtedly think this improper. Come back in a few days and talk to him."

"I know he's away. This is our golden opportunity to speak with you without your husband. May we?" the sheriff asked, tilting his head and bowing slightly.

She hesitated, looking from the sheriff to Madlen. "I'm not feeling well right now."

"I can help you with that," Madlen offered. "I could prepare a medicinal brew for you, if you happen to have some herbs nearby. Would you allow me?" She smiled, and after a brief hesitation the noblewoman stepped aside to let them in.

Magdalena led them to the dining room. She offered them a seat and something to drink.

"No, thank you," Madlen said cheerfully.

"It's about your husband," the sheriff said. Madlen touched his forearm as a signal for him not to proceed too quickly.

"But first, how are you?" Madlen asked.

"Why are you asking me that?"

"You said before that you didn't feel well. May I prepare a brew for you?"

"No, it's all right. Why do you want to talk to me? Did something happen to my husband?"

"No, nothing happened to him," the sheriff said.

"Well, what do you want, then?"

"There are people who are worried about you," Madlen said.

"About me?" Magdalena smiled joylessly. "I doubt it. Nobody worries about me."

"If that were true, we wouldn't be here."

Magdalena looked to the sheriff for an explanation.

"Have you been treated well?" Madlen asked.

"Why are you asking me that?"

"Because we believe you haven't."

Magdalena looked down at her hands in embarrassment.

Madlen continued, "Lady Grossherr, your husband beats you. And often quite badly, right?"

Magdalena kept her head down and didn't answer.

"Nobody should have to endure what you've been through. Let us help."

"I don't know what you're talking about." She didn't dare look either of them in the eyes.

"Are you cold, Lady Grossherr?" Madlen asked.

The noblewoman nodded. "A little."

"Or is there another reason you've laced up your collar so high on your neck? It's to hide your bruises, isn't that true?"

Magdalena looked at Madlen. "I have no bruises," she said listlessly.

"I think you do. But that is your affair and not ours. If you don't want to show us, that's your decision."

"I don't understand what you want from me." Magdalena's voice quivered.

"We want to prevent your husband from abusing you again," the sheriff said.

Magdalena turned her gaze to the sheriff. "Nobody can prevent Albert from doing what he wants, not even you."

"That's not true," Madlen said gently. "What he does is against the law."

"But he does it anyway. And nobody can stop him."

"I can. If you report him," the sheriff said.

Her eyes welled up with tears. "He'd kill me."

The sheriff shook his head. "Then he'd risk being sentenced to death."

She looked at him skeptically. "No man has ever been brought before the court for that."

"That's not true," Madlen argued. "My husband is a lawyer in service to the archbishop of Cologne. He took on such a case and won a conviction." Although she wasn't telling the whole truth, Madlen felt that telling this little white lie would be worth the reassurance it could offer Magdalena.

"Really?"

"It would go like this," the sheriff explained. "I would find a pretext to call your husband to the courthouse. Once there, he would await six councilmen, and only when they arrived would he find out why he was really there—to be charged with the assault and torture of his wife."

Magdalena's face turned red.

"At that point, we would tell your husband that the charges would be dropped, provided nothing else happened to you and your health improved. To ensure this, every three days, a policeman would come to your home to check in. A woman, a female advocate, would accompany him to see whether you had bruises on your body and, if you allowed it, she would examine you for any other signs of violence."

Magdalena's face turned an even brighter shade of crimson.

"If the police officer or the advocate found any signs of abuse, your husband would be arrested on the spot and put on trial."

"He would never forgive me for such an indignity."

"His forgiveness for this indignity, as you call it, wouldn't matter, because he would never be able to return home."

The woman's expression changed instantly. "But if he was arrested, who would take care of me?"

The sheriff fell silent.

Madlen felt compelled to intervene, to prevent them from being asked to leave in short order. "Did you love your husband when you married him?"

Magdalena looked at her. "I, I don't know. He was good-looking, and he's descended from good stock. My parents paid him a decent dowry. I've never lacked for anything."

"Except he beats you, killing a little piece of you every time he does," the sheriff said bitterly.

"That's how it is." She sounded resigned to her fate.

"It doesn't have to be this way," Madlen said. "I know that is easy for me to say—my husband has never raised a hand to me. We have two children. Do you have any children?"

Magdalena shook her head and looked at the floor. "God has chosen not to send us any. It's my fault. My womb is not fertile."

"Have you ever been pregnant?"

"Yes, many times. But the babies haven't survived because my womb is bad."

"Is that what your husband told you?"

She nodded.

"If you were pregnant, then your womb is fertile," Madlen declared. "But your husband beat you during your pregnancies, isn't that right?"

Magdalena nodded again.

"And he raped you?"

Another nod.

"Don't you see—that's the reason you were unable to carry the babies to birth."

Magdalena looked up. "I would have been able to have children if he hadn't beaten me?"

"Yes. Your husband was the one who killed the babies in your womb."

Magdalena was obviously shaken. "I didn't know that." She placed the flat of her hand on her chest and choked back her tears. "It was especially bad every time I lost a baby. He told me that I was being punished, that the fetus couldn't grow in my loathsome body." She sobbed. "But it was his fault all along?"

"Yes, it was," Madlen said emphatically.

Magdalena cried softly, wiping the tears from her cheeks. Madlen and the sheriff remained silent, giving her time to grieve. Then she sat up straight, as though a jolt had gone through her body. "And yet, I can't report him."

"I can understand that," Madlen said. "Tell me, what do you do with your days?"

The noblewoman looked at Madlen with a puzzled expression.

"I mean, is there anything that you like to do?"

"No, I, I don't do anything."

"And before? Before you were married?"

A smile lit up Magdalena's face. "I sewed. I used to sew—all of my clothes and my mother's and sister's, too."

"Really? Me, too!"

"Truly?"

"Yes. I used to sew primarily for myself and also for my brother and father. Later, when I left Heidelberg, I lived with my aunt in Worms, and together we sewed clothes for rich ladies."

"You're from Heidelberg?"

"I am. I lived here until about eight years ago." Madlen took a deep breath. "I was forced to flee because I was unjustly accused of killing a baby and its mother. Does the name Matthias Trauenstein mean anything to you?"

After a moment, recognition dawned in Magdalena's eyes. "I know you," she said. "At least, I've heard of you."

"Probably everyone here has," Madlen responded lightheartedly, though she felt anything but. "It was a difficult time, and I was hesitant to take up the fight against Matthias Trauenstein. The only difference between you and me is that you have the option of making a decision while I had no other choice." Madlen pointed at the sheriff. "He was the one who arrested me at that time, because he is the arm of the law and the law had spoken. And I'm sitting in front of you today because Matthias Trauenstein was convicted. He lost his life, while I'm happily married, with two healthy, wonderful children. I'm here in Heidelberg as a guest at the university, invited to listen to medical lectures because a doctor recognized my passion for healing and wanted to help me develop it further." She smiled at the noblewoman. "Imagine a life in which you would never have to fear being beaten or having to give yourself to your husband, unless you yourself so desired it. And you can sew. You can sew clothes and perhaps even sell them. Wouldn't that be wonderful?"

"I can't guarantee that last part," the sheriff said, "but I can the former."

"Let us help you, Lady Grossherr. I'm begging you. No woman should have to suffer as you have."

"If I agreed to this, what would I have to do?"

"When does your husband come back from his business trip?" the sheriff asked.

"In a few days, I think."

"Good. Then come to my office first thing tomorrow morning. It's important that you come to me of your own free will so that I can present your case to the councilmen. And it would be best if you could name a servant or a maid who could testify to having heard your screams or seen acts of violence committed against you. Then I'll have a scribe come to take your report. After that, I'll discuss it with six elected men of the council."

"Which ones? My husband has friends on the council."

"We'll go through the names together ahead of time. Does that suit you?"

"You would consult with me on such an important matter?" Magdalena asked incredulously.

"Of course. You deserve to be treated with dignity and respect. And you're an intelligent woman whose viewpoint I trust." The sheriff smiled at her. "From this point on, you shouldn't be content with anything less."

"Trust this man, Lady Grossherr," Madlen urged her. "All those years ago, it was his job to convict me, and he would have done so had I been guilty. But he uncovered the facts and did everything he could to make sure the truth would see the light of day. I trusted him and you should, too."

Magdalena lifted her head. "Tomorrow before noon, I will come to the sheriff's office."

"It will be my pleasure to welcome you." The sheriff started to stand.

"You've made the right decision," Madlen said and stood up as well, whereupon Magdalena rose, too.

"Even though I'm frightened, I'm also relieved." Magdalena walked them to the door, and the sheriff hurried ahead to open it. The servant who had received them earlier was nowhere to be found.

"Thank you for your visit," Magdalena said.

The sheriff stepped outside. "May God protect you."

Madlen stopped in front of Magdalena and opened her arms wide. "May I?"

Magdalena seemed unsure but nevertheless let Madlen gently embrace her.

"You are a beautiful, brave woman. Don't let anyone ever tell you anything different."

"God protect you!" Magdalena said as they released their embrace. "God protect both of you!"

◆　◆　◆

Their meeting with Magdalena Grossherr had lasted longer than they'd planned. Madlen and the sheriff were both exhausted, but their tension had waned when Magdalena agreed to file a report. They decided not to pay a visit to Trude von Fahrenholz, because her husband had likely already returned home from his office, making a private meeting with her today impossible.

Instead, the sheriff accompanied Madlen to the Golden Rooster. He had said good-bye and was starting to leave when a man approached him at the door.

"What luck to find you here, Sheriff! Now I can save myself a trip to the station. My lord just sent me to fetch the police. There's a quarrel inside—a guest is refusing to pay."

The sheriff was annoyed to be bothered with such a tiresome matter. He was particularly concerned about getting back as soon as possible to the doctor, who was awaiting him at his office. "I'll follow you inside, Madlen," he said, holding the door open for her.

"Ah, Sheriff. You're here! Thank goodness. That fellow over there in the back was serviced by one of my girls but now refuses to pay."

Madlen was hoping to squeeze past the crude fellow and go upstairs to her bedchamber, to avoid having anything to do with this situation. But then she heard a familiar voice.

"I did pay. But how much this whore demanded is an effrontery."

Madlen winced. Then she looked toward the back, where she saw her father-in-law being held by a man and yelling at the top of his lungs.

"Peter?"

Peter knew he had been caught red-handed and paused, looking down at the ground. Then his attitude changed. Though still embarrassed, he glared at her. "There! She can pay for me," he snapped at his accuser.

"Madlen, do you know this man?" the sheriff asked.

Madlen felt sick. "He . . . ," she stammered, "he's my husband's father."

"Good. Then give me the money he owes." The stranger stretched out his palm toward Madlen.

"I don't have any money here." She glared at Peter, who'd assumed a bored expression. Madlen could hardly believe that this drunken old man was the same person who'd so recently become her confidant.

"You'll get your money, Dietz," the sheriff intervened. "I'll take care of it myself."

"All right, then." The whorehouse proprietor looked at the sheriff. "But no later than tomorrow. After all, my ladies need to eat."

"You're right," the sheriff answered and watched the man as he headed for the door. "And you should go to your room and sleep it off," he advised Peter.

"I want another schnapps first," Peter said, slurring so loudly that everyone who had been watching the brothel owner leave turned their heads in the older man's direction.

"Peter!" Madlen hissed. "What is happening to you?"

"Oh, shut your trap, you dirty slut. Everyone shut the hell up!"

"That's enough!" The sheriff stepped forward, grabbed him by the arm, and yanked him up. "You're going upstairs to sleep it off right now. And don't let me catch you going to a whorehouse ever again! I'm letting you go now only because I don't want to tarnish your daughter-in-law's reputation."

"Let me go, you miserable cur!"

The sheriff tightened his grip and hissed into Peter's ear, "Shut your mouth before I put my fist in it." Then he dragged Peter up to the second floor.

Madlen followed, deeply ashamed. She couldn't imagine how Elsbeth was going react.

"Which room is it?" the sheriff called to her over his shoulder.

"The second one over there." Madlen pointed to the door.

The sheriff kept one hand on Peter's arm and knocked on the door with the other. "Open up!"

A moment later, the latch was pushed aside and Elsbeth opened the door. "What happened?" she cried.

"I believe this man belongs to you," the sheriff said, then he shoved Peter forward. The drunk old man stumbled into the room. Elsbeth's chin trembled, and she gave her daughter-in-law a pleading look.

"Thank you, Sheriff. I'll bring the money tomorrow," Madlen said.

"All right," the sheriff replied. With a gesture, he bade farewell to the women and then went downstairs.

Startled by the noise, Agathe came over from her room next door, where she had been watching the children. Cecilia trotted past her excitedly.

"Mother! Agatha sewed a bonnet for me from a lovely colorful fabric I found at the market. And Veit got a wooden soldier. Do you want to see?"

"Of course." Madlen glanced at Elsbeth, who was still standing at the door, her face ashen.

Agathe guessed that something had happened by the expression on Madlen's face. "Go be with your children. I'll stay here with Elsbeth for a while."

Elsbeth shook her head. "No, thank you, Agathe. I need to take care of Peter."

"As you wish." Agathe looked at Elsbeth sympathetically. "Tomorrow is a new day. Everything will be completely different by then."

Elsbeth pressed her lips together, trying her best to suppress her tears. She nodded, walked back inside the room she shared with Peter, and closed the door without saying another word.

"Come on, Mother," Cecilia ordered as she grabbed her mother's hand. Madlen let her daughter pull her away. Agathe locked the door to their room after they were all inside.

Madlen felt confused and desperate. She couldn't believe what had happened downstairs. Why had Peter done that? But she didn't want to say anything in front of the children. Instead, she went over to her son, who was sitting on the bed and playing with a little toy. "What do you have there?"

"A wooden soldier. Agathe bought it for me."

"That must have been expensive. I will pay you back immediately, Agathe."

"Oh, no." Agathe waved her hand dismissively. "It's not even worth talking about. Veit liked it so much."

"You are very generous, Agathe. Thank you."

Agathe wanted to ask Madlen for an explanation of what had just occurred, but she decided against it for the same reason Madlen had—because of the children. Instead, she changed the subject, asking about the rest of Madlen's day. "Were you successful?"

Madlen nodded. "Yes. And I'm quite relieved."

"Good. You're doing the right thing."

"But I'm here now and just want to be with my children," Madlen added. She didn't want to waste one more minute thinking about the embarrassing scene Peter had just made. She turned to her son. "What would you like to do this evening?"

"We can't go out," Veit said glumly. "It's going to be dark soon."

Madlen frowned.

"Veit, that's enough," Agathe said, hoping to prevent a fight. She could imagine how Madlen must have felt, dealing with the trouble Peter had caused and guilt over being too late to do anything meaningful with her children before their bedtime.

"But it's true."

"You're being unfair. Your mother had to take care of something very important. She was helping someone lead a better life. And Elsbeth and I took you all over town—we had so much fun today! It's not right for you to act like this, and you know it. Other children your age have to slave away the whole day in a carpenter's shop or in their parents' tavern while you get to see beautiful things at the market. You even have a new wooden soldier. If that doesn't make you happy, I won't bother buying you toys in the future."

Usually Agathe was especially nice to Veit; to hear her speak like this was quite a shock.

"Please forgive me, Mother. And you, too, Aunt Agathe. I just want to spend more time with my mother, like we did in Cologne. And I miss my father, too." He was on the brink of tears. "When do we get to go home?"

Madlen crouched in front of him and stroked his arm. "I know everything is different here, but it will only be a few more weeks until we're back home in Cologne. And this is important to me. Can you understand that and be just a little bit happy about what I've done here?"

"But you do lots of things at home, too," Veit argued.

"It won't take much longer."

"You've said that several times already."

"Because it's true," Madlen said. She was starting to tire of her son's selfish behavior, his always having to have his way no matter what. Madlen wondered whether it had been a good idea to work so hard to give him everything she'd missed during her own childhood.

Veit didn't say anything but made his displeasure known by making a long, sulky face.

With that, Madlen had had enough. "Veit, Agathe is right. You're not behaving yourself, and I expect that to change immediately. There are other people besides you in this world, and they are just as important as you are. I understand that you'd like to be in Cologne again. I miss your father, too, more than I can say. But I have obligations here that I must fulfill now. I am your mother, and I expect you to support me and respect my wishes."

"Yes, Mother." Veit knew he'd gone too far.

"Good. Now Agathe and I will go downstairs and get a bite to eat. Anyone who cares to join us may do so. But anyone who prefers to sulk can just stay right here." She stood up from her squat.

"I'm coming," Cecilia exclaimed.

"Me, too," Veit said meekly. "I'm sorry, Mother."

"It's all right. Let's forget about it now. But I do expect you to change your behavior."

"Yes, Mother."

"I need to wait here until Ursel returns. Who knows where she is and when she'll be back?" Agathe said. She had her suspicions about where the housekeeper was. Several times, she'd noticed Ursel and Gerald leaving the inn one right after the other. They'd be gone for several hours, then return around the same time or in quick succession. Upon her return, Ursel always had a penitent look on her face. Though curious, Agathe didn't ask her about it. She wondered whether she should tell Madlen, who was their employer after all, about what had been happening.

When Madlen opened Agathe's bedchamber door, she was surprised to find Ursel standing right behind it. They greeted each other briefly, then Agathe, Madlen, and the children went downstairs for their evening meal.

Madlen wondered whether she should ask Elsbeth to accompany them. But she thought better of it. Of course Elsbeth wouldn't want to join them downstairs for supper after what had happened. Madlen sighed. Although she had gotten through to Magdalena Grossherr, she continued to fret. Mostly because of the embarrassing incident with Peter, but also because she knew that Magdalena had a very tough road ahead of her. Madlen wouldn't want to trade places with her. Though it had been right to convince her to file charges, Madlen also felt guilty for making it seem like the future would be so rosy. It wouldn't be—of that Madlen was quite sure. But it was a matter of helping this frightened woman, who had been abused for so many years, to have the courage to stand up for her rights and put an end to her anguish. So, Madlen wasn't totally relieved, not yet anyway. She hoped that she could find some peace of mind when she returned to Cologne and could get back into her old routine.

Downstairs, their hostess served up an ample meal, and everybody ate heartily, including Madlen. The warm spiced wine was making her sleepy. She spoke softly so that the other tavern guests wouldn't hear them discussing what had happened at the nobleman's house, choosing her words very carefully so as not to upset the children.

"If she keeps her word, and I think she will, she'll show up at the sheriff's office tomorrow and file a formal complaint," Madlen said. With that, she was disinclined to speak any more about it.

"Mother?"

"Yes, Veit."

"The man beat his wife, right?"

"Yes, my son."

"Has Father ever hit you?"

"Of course not." Madlen stroked his head. "Your father would never do something like that."

"Good. I think that a big man, even bigger than Father, should go to that woman's husband and beat him up exactly as he beat her. He should get back every punch just as hard as he gave it."

"Yes, I think so, too," Cecilia agreed.

"I think," Madlen said, chuckling, "that if this man is foolish enough to challenge the sheriff, that's exactly what will end up happening."

"And he would deserve nothing less." Veit looked at his mother then Agathe with a seriousness that belied his youth. "When I grow up, I'm going to be a sheriff. And then I'll beat up anybody who beats up women."

"A very good idea," Agathe said. "You should eat something so that you will grow up to be big and strong."

Veit took up the challenge, sinking his teeth into a piece of ham. Madlen's heart filled with pride at her son's inherent sense of justice at such a young age. When everybody finished, Cecilia asked to go upstairs.

"Yes. I'll come with you," Madlen said. "I can hardly keep my eyes open." She stood up, and the children slid off their chairs.

Veit grabbed another piece of ham. "I'll eat this later tonight. And when I wake up in the morning, I'll surely have grown a bit."

"Madlen," Agathe said.

"Yes?" She turned around to face her aunt.

"You should be proud of yourself. You're doing what so few have the courage to do."

"Thank you, Agathe." As they went upstairs together to their respective rooms. Agathe's words echoed in Madlen's mind. She was starting to feel really good about herself.

Chapter Twenty-Two

"He's burning up with fever," the doctor said. "It's a good thing you called me. One of you, get some cold water and some linen cloths."

"I'll do it," Wilhelm said and left the room.

"He was dizzy and had difficulty standing," Linhardt said to the doctor.

"That's what I was afraid of," the doctor said. "Perhaps he was hit on the head harder than we thought. The first thing to do now is lower his temperature. He's a strong fellow. If he can get enough peace and quiet and some sleep, he'll be back on his feet in no time. But just in case, I'll fetch some herbs and cook up a nice medicinal brew."

"I already offered that to him, but he told me he doesn't tolerate herbs very well," Linhardt lied. Unsettling recent events had made him too skittish to trust even the doctor or what he might give Johannes.

"Then I'll refrain from making him an herbal concoction," the doctor said. "After all, we don't want to make matters worse by poisoning him." He'd meant it as a joke, but the five guards looked at him stone-faced.

The Master of Medicine

"That was an inappropriate remark, considering what happened to Vicar Bartholomäus," the doctor admitted. He was relieved to see Wilhelm return with a bowl of cold water and linen cloths.

"Very good. Put it there. I'll show you how to make a cold compress. You'll have to change it every hour."

"That's not our job," Wolfker said. "We're guards, not nurses."

"Nurses or not, you're here. And I don't see anybody else around, and I can't stay here myself. So, you'll have to do exactly what I'm going to show you to do."

The doctor dunked a linen cloth in the water, wrung it out, and, after pushing the blanket aside, wrapped it around Johannes's lower leg. Then he wrapped several dry cloths over it. He did the same thing on the other leg and then covered the injured man with the blanket. "So, you see, it's very simple."

"We'll take care of it," Linhardt assured him.

"And if something changes, come fetch me. Even if it's in the middle of the night."

"Thank you."

"I've been here quite a bit lately, not just for this patient but also to examine the dead. I hope the palace can pay me one of these days."

"Before you go, there's something else that occurs to me," Linhardt said. "Tell me, have you taken a look at the man the attorney supposedly murdered?"

"As a matter of fact, the sheriff asked me to examine the body. Why do you ask?"

"How was the man killed?"

"Somebody cut his throat from ear to ear."

"Was there a bump on his head? Like the one the attorney has?"

"Now that you mention it, I really don't know. I didn't check his head. It was plain to see that his neck had been slit."

"Could you examine him one more time before he's buried?"

"I believe that would be possible. But why? Even if he did have a bump on his head, it wouldn't have been bad enough to eclipse the mortal wound on his neck."

"It's not about that. Please, Doctor, please look at him and let us know."

"Who is 'us'?" the doctor asked. "Who will pay for this?"

"The attorney will pay. I can assure you of that."

"Well, then, you've all heard it. Not that you have the authority to use his name."

"You'll get your money, maybe even more than you require."

"Then I'll go to the sheriff first thing in the morning."

"And could you do something else?"

"Of course."

"If the corpse has a bump on its head, please call the sheriff and show it to him."

"Why?"

"Because it's important that he sees it with his own eyes."

"Well, all right, if it's so important."

"Thank you, Doctor."

"I wish all of you well," the doctor said in parting. The guards returned his farewell as he left.

"What's all this talk of a bump?" Wilhelm asked.

"The attorney claims the last thing he remembers was a man in a monk's robe hitting the young scoundrel Wentzel on the back of the head," Linhardt explained. "After that, he himself got hit on the head then collapsed. That's his account. But a so-called witness claims to have seen the attorney kill Wentzel by stabbing him twice in the belly and then cutting his throat from ear to ear. The attorney and I reconstructed the scene earlier, and it couldn't have happened like that." Linhardt asked Wilhelm to take the role of Wentzel then demonstrated what Johannes had shown him. The other guards immediately understood what he meant.

"It couldn't have been the way the witness described," Anderlin confirmed.

"Correct. And one more thing: even if what the witness claimed was partially true, the deceased wouldn't have an injury on the back of his skull, because allegedly only the lawyer got hit on the head."

"Very well thought out," Georg said. "But what can we do to prove the attorney is innocent?"

"He told me it's more important to solve the other murders. He got too close to the real perpetrator, who now wants to get him out of the way by putting the blame for Wentzel's murder on him. Now that we know what we're up against, we have to stop it."

"So how do we proceed?"

"Two of us must speak to the witness who identified Benedict, Lord Tillich, and ask him to repeat his statement, just to be sure we have the facts straight. Next, we'll go to the jail to see Benedict and find out what he said to the attorney. We just might be able to come up with something. Too bad we can't get anything out of Wentzel anymore. If only the lawyer could remember where he and Wentzel were going. Then we could really make some headway."

"Wilhelm and I will go talk to Dietrich Tillich," Anderlin volunteered.

"Niclaus, Wolfker, will you interrogate Benedict again?"

"Sure, Linhardt," Niclaus said. Wolfker agreed with a nod.

"Georg and I will stay here and stand watch over the attorney," Linhardt declared. "As soon as he wakes up, we'll ask him what this Wentzel said to him. As soon as you all are done, meet back here."

◆ ◆ ◆

Niclaus and Wolfker's interrogation of Benedict didn't take as long as expected, and they didn't find out anything new. Benedict didn't tell them anything he hadn't already told the lawyer.

"We will see what Wilhelm and Anderlin learned from the witness, this Lord Dietrich Tillich who identified Benedict. Either he is wrong, and Benedict is the victim of mistaken identity, or one of them is lying," Niclaus said. "In my opinion, only one of them has a reason to do that."

"How's he doing?" Wolfker cocked his head toward Johannes's bed. "Did he wake up at all?"

Linhardt shook his head. "Not even when we changed his compresses. But I do believe he's not as hot as he was before."

"We have to find out what Wentzel told him," Georg said anxiously. "What if he doesn't wake up? That would mean that Wentzel took what he knew to the grave. And it must have been something important, otherwise the attorney wouldn't have taken him out of jail."

"It would help if we at least knew where they'd intended to go." Linhardt rubbed his chin. He paused when he noticed Johannes stirring. A wave of relief flowed through his body when the attorney opened his eyes. Linhardt hurried over to the bedside. "Counselor, thank God! How do you feel?"

"I'm thirsty."

Linhardt picked up the water jug and filled a mug. "Here. Wait a second, I'll help you." He handed Johannes the mug. The man took it in trembling hands, and Linhardt helped him sit up.

"My thanks, Linhardt." Johannes gulped down the water, though his throat was so dry that at first he had difficulty swallowing. Soon he felt the soothing effects of the water, and after a moment he was finally able to quench his thirst. "What happened to me?"

"You had a very high fever, my lord. The doctor came here again. Evidently, the blow to your head was more serious than we initially thought. You now have cold compresses on your legs, so don't be surprised if you can't move very well." Linhardt hesitated. "The doctor wanted to prepare an herbal brew for your fever, but I claimed that you can't tolerate certain herbs."

"You don't trust anyone anymore, do you?" Johannes tried to smile. "I don't, either."

Georg cleared his throat. "Without pushing you too hard, my lord, we must find out what this Wentzel told you. Please, forgive us, but when you didn't wake up, we thought that . . ."

"That I might never wake up at all? I understand. And I thank you for your help in solving the murders."

Georg acknowledged Johannes's praise with a nod.

Johannes took another gulp and handed the mug back to Linhardt, who put the vessel on the small bedside table. The lawyer made an effort to sit all the way up.

"Wait." Linhardt walked over to a chest and took out two pillows, which he stuffed behind Johannes so that he could lean back but stay upright.

"Thank you, Linhardt."

The guard nodded. Then he placed four chairs around the attorney's sick bed.

"Well, this young fellow Wentzel was sent to follow me by someone whose face he'd never seen," Johannes began. He told them the whole story: the secret meeting in St. Alban's Church, their walk to his house, the place where Wentzel had hidden himself day after day and from where he'd observed the impostor Duretta's murder. He finally described how they both had been attacked and beaten to the ground.

"I know that Wentzel flinched a moment before I was hit. He must have seen something or, rather, someone. Then I felt a powerful blow on the back of my head. Before I lost consciousness, I saw a man in a monk's habit behind Wentzel. That man struck him down, too. I don't remember anything after that until I woke up here."

"A man in a monk's robe," repeated Georg thoughtfully. "Exactly like the man Wentzel told you he met at St. Alban's, correct?"

"Right."

"And Wentzel never told you who'd hired him?" Niclaus asked.

"Indeed," Johannes said. "He said that the monk told him he'd been hired to keep an eye on me by the order of the archbishop."

Georg hissed through his teeth. "A rather bold claim for this monk to make."

Someone knocked lightly on the door, and Georg asked who it was.

"Wilhelm and Anderlin."

Georg stood up and went over to the door, took the chair away, and let them in. Then he shoved the back of the chair under the doorknob again.

"Well?" Linhardt asked.

"I believe Benedict might be telling the truth," Wilhelm answered.

"Why do you say that? What did the witness say?"

"Absolutely nothing." Wilhelm and Anderlin moved two more chairs and sat next to the others near Johannes's bedside. "It's nice to see you awake, my lord."

"Thank you, Wilhelm."

"Well, tell us. What did you find out?" Linhardt asked.

Anderlin and Wilhelm exchanged looks. Then Anderlin began to speak. "My lord, how did you find this witness, Lord Tillich?"

Johannes was surprised. "Why are you asking me that?"

"We were there at the house adjacent to the vicar's just a short while ago."

"And?"

"Nobody lives there."

"What are you saying? The witness is gone?"

Anderlin shook his head. "It seems as if this *so-called* witness never existed."

"But I've talked with him several times. And you saw him, too."

"We saw a man who told you something, yes. But he never lived there. We spoke with people who lived on the same street. The house that you met the man in has been unoccupied for over three years, and none of the neighbors have ever heard of a man named Dietrich Tillich."

Johannes was so surprised that his jaw dropped. After taking a moment to collect his thoughts, he said, "The man approached me—he was the one who implied Christopeit's involvement in Vicar Bartholomäus's murder. He told me that Christopeit had been led away by two men. He described someone who fit Benedict's description, and he claimed that he couldn't remember the other ones. He also claimed to live in that house, where he'd been able to observe it."

"Somebody went to a lot of trouble to mislead you, my lord," Georg noted.

"The neighbors said that recently they'd noticed signs of life in the supposedly unoccupied house. But they didn't think anything of it, concluding that perhaps some new tenants were moving in. But the man who called himself Dietrich Tillich actually never lived there. It was a deception, my lord."

Johannes was confused. Which of his discoveries were real, and which were fabrications?

"Suspicion was steered toward Benedict," Linhardt thought aloud. "Why? Why would someone want Benedict to be accused, and how did the witness know about him?"

"His hair," Johannes said. "It's light and easy to describe. I don't believe that it's anything personal. Someone wanted us to suspect one of the archbishop's guards, a man from our own ranks. That's the whole point."

"Benedict ended up being the scapegoat because he's the most conspicuous," Georg surmised.

"It seems so."

"We found something else out," Anderlin announced. "Bernhard von Harvehorst was the vicar's guest on the day of the murder. A woman who lives nearby is quite sure of that. She recognized von Harvehorst and even greeted him outside the vicar's that afternoon."

"And we're just finding that out now?" Johannes fumed.

"No one interviewed her after the vicar's murder. So she probably didn't know how important her observations were," Anderlin reported.

Johannes balled his hand into a fist. "That was my failure," he admitted, and then looked at the guards, one after the other. "I was 'coincidentally' approached by this witness, and then, like a fool, I believed every word he said. Afterward, I didn't make the effort to go house to house like you men did. That was very sloppy work on my part."

"We would have believed the witness, too," Wilhelm said, trying to assuage the lawyer's guilt. "Don't worry about it."

Johannes was grateful for his comment, but he wasn't going to let himself off that easy. He'd been deceived, and he'd put all his energy into investigating the wrong leads. At least now he knew better. He closed his eyes to concentrate. "An alleged witness gives me a tip about a guard," he said, opening his eyes. "A guard who's in the service of the archbishop. An alleged housekeeper, actually an impostor, informs me that Bernhard von Harvehorst never planned to accompany Friedrich on his journey because they were feuding, although this dispute—which you, Niclaus and Wolfker, reportedly knew about—had been settled weeks before. A young man was allegedly asked by someone who claimed to be working for the archbishop to tail me. Christopeit and Duretta probably knew something about their masters' murders and that's why they were killed. And now we just found out that Bartholomäus and Bernhard von Harvehorst had some kind of a meeting shortly before they were murdered. What do all these things tell us?"

"Not to mention," Wilhelm added, "that somebody tried to accuse you of a murder you didn't commit."

"Correct," Johannes confirmed. "The vicar and Bernhard von Harvehorst must have uncovered something, and von Harvehorst went to the vicar's residence so that they could discuss what they'd found before informing the archbishop. And that's when the perpetrator decided to take action. Now he's doing what he can to discredit the archbishop and make it look as though everything happened on his order." Johannes tried to put the puzzle pieces together. "What about the other servants in Bernhard von Harvehorst's household?"

"He had a manservant, as far as I know," Wilhelm answered.

"Where is he now?"

"The archbishop took him in to tend to the stables after von Harvehorst's death."

"We must speak to this man." Johannes felt excitement pulsing through his veins.

"I doubt that von Harvehorst would trust his servant with any secrets."

"Probably not. But if he was taking care of von Harvehorst's horse, he would know when and where his master went on the day before his death. He'd likely know who visited von Harvehorst, and when, as well. We have to talk to him."

"But not today." Linhardt pointed to the crown glass window. "It's already dark, my lord. We should all try to get a little sleep, and we'll speak with the servant first thing in the morning."

Johannes nodded. "I've already put a lot of demands on you men. Go home and get some rest. We'll meet here tomorrow."

The guards exchanged a look. "If it's all the same to you, my lord, we would prefer to stay here and sleep on the floor. There's enough space for all of us. As long as we're not sure who's behind all this, we'd rather not leave you, especially in your current condition."

"In that case, at least find some pillows and blankets that you can lie down on. I'm truly thankful for what you're doing."

"Yes, my lord."

Suddenly, they heard yelling and the pounding of footsteps outside the door.

"Who goes there?" Georg yelled, and the others stood. Niclaus flung the chair that had been blocking the door aside while they pulled out their swords. Niclaus ripped the door open with a jerk. Much to their surprise, there was no one outside the room—the noise had come from farther away.

"Niclaus, Wolfker, you stay here!" Anderlin ordered. The other three men rushed out.

"What happened?" one of them called out to a guard as he ran by.

"A thief! The others went after him, but this fellow is fast on his feet."

"What did he steal?"

"We first saw him coming out of the scribe's office. From what I could see, he had a scroll in his hand."

Johannes heard the words through the open door. He immediately threw his blankets aside, swung his legs off the bed, and stood. Niclaus and Wolfker followed him. After a few feet he stopped, and Wolfker grabbed his elbow. "You have to lie down, my lord."

"No." Johannes closed his eyes then opened them again. "I'm all right." He started moving again, stepping quickly down one hall then another, heading upstairs to the scribe's study. The six guards who had been in his chamber followed hard on his heels. "Damn!" he shouted when he arrived at the scribe's room and saw the mess inside. The scrolls, which were usually organized neatly on the shelves, were now in a state of utter chaos. Those that had been in the first four compartments lay unrolled on the floor, making it virtually impossible to enter without stepping on them.

"I know what the thief was looking for," Johannes said. "I told the sheriff that the parchment granting me Friedrich's full authority was kept in the scribe's office."

"What a cursed scoundrel!" Georg snarled.

"What's going on here?" The scribe pushed past the guards. "Oh, no," he said in anguish. "What is this? Who did this? It will take me days to straighten all this out."

"We have to see whether he found what he was looking for." Johannes stepped gingerly into the room so as not to tread on the scrolls.

"What happened here?" The vicar general entered the room, his face red with rage.

"A theft, my lord," Linhardt said. "It looks like one of the sheriff's henchmen seized a document, signed by the archbishop, which had bestowed full authority to the lawyer."

"I'll speak to the sheriff immediately. And you, Counselor, belong in bed. Come on. The scribe can do this."

"I prefer to stay here to check things out for myself."

"Counselor, you will do no such thing. I implore you to take my advice."

"How were the scrolls organized?" Johannes asked, turning away from the vicar general.

The scribe shook his head in exasperation. Johannes thought he noticed tears welling up in his eyes.

"In front here were mostly the scrolls prepared for upcoming court dates. Besides that, there were recent treatises and authorizations for power of attorney."

"Including mine?"

"Yes, my lord."

"Let's take a look. The thief might not have found it, or he may have taken the wrong one."

"But, Counselor!" The vicar general put his hands on his hips. "Must I fetch the doctor and tell the guards to drag you back into bed? Listen to reason!"

"I'm staying," Johannes snarled.

"But you're wearing only a nightshirt! Do you want to get consumption in addition to your head injury?"

Johannes ignored the clergyman's pleas. He picked up the first document, skimmed it, and handed it to the scribe. "Here. Put this back where it belongs."

"I can read, too, my lord," Linhardt said. "May I help?"

"Yes. Look for a document that has my name on it."

"This is ridiculous," the vicar general snapped. "These are confidential documents! They are not suited for the eyes of a guard!"

"I can't read, but if you write out your name, I can search for it in the documents," Georg said, over the vicar general's objections.

"A good idea," Johannes said. "Scribe, pick up a quill and write my name on parchment."

The scribe obeyed Johannes's order. After studying it one after another, the guards began to check the documents for the attorney's name.

The vicar general continued to admonish Johannes, but after a while he gave up and fell silent. The attorney and his men picked up scroll after scroll, reading them or checking them for Johannes's name. If a guard was unsure, he handed the parchment to Johannes or the scribe. The last one to handle the document rolled it up and gave it to the scribe to put in its correct place. Soon the shelves were filled with scrolls again.

Johannes picked up another document, read it, and stopped short. He'd become dizzy, and he leaned back against the wall so as not to lose his balance.

"Scribe, what kind of document is this?"

The scribe took the parchment and read it. "That's a quitclaim deed. A fief's ownership has fallen back to the principality."

"And it will be given away again?"

"Correct. Three fiefs in all will be awarded at the next court hearing."

"But it's a fief in the Duchy of Cleves under the rule of the House of von der Marck."

"Just like the other ones. The claims would be introduced and granted as alleged in the document. At the court hearing, it will be officially declared and with that the lordship designated."

"But this violates the treaties we have with the von der Marcks," Johannes murmured. "Where are the other documents of this kind?"

The scribe pointed grumpily at the scrolls on the floor. "In there somewhere. But I think I just had one in my hand." He searched around on the shelves, picked up two scrolls, and then pulled out the document in question. "Here, my lord. I have it right here." He unrolled it. "See?"

Johannes scanned the parchment then looked up at the scribe. "Do you know the names of the future feudal lords?"

The scribe shook his head. "No. Do you need them?"

Johannes didn't answer. "And I assume these deeds were all signed by the same official, correct?"

"Yes, my lord." The scribe bent over. "Ah, here we have one of the four." He handed a document to Johannes, who scanned it quickly. Now he understood. He understood everything. "Where is the vicar general?" he asked, his voice cold as ice. The guards looked at the place where the clergyman had just been standing.

"I don't know, my lord. He must have gone," Linhardt said.

"Get him! Arrest the vicar general! Don't let him escape!"

There was a split-second pause, as the guards processed what they had just been ordered to do. Then they started running.

"I still have one last question, Scribe," Johannes said.

"Yes, my lord," the scribe said nervously, obviously shocked by what had just occurred.

"Bernhard von Harvehorst. Was he also aware of these documents?"

"Yes, my lord. It was a few days before his death. I believe there had been a dispute between him and the archbishop. To prove his position, he asked me to select some pertinent documents. By mistake, I gave him the one you're holding in your hands. After reading it, he got very upset."

"Did he tell you why?"

"No, my lord. But from that moment on, he was no longer interested in the other documents he'd originally wanted."

Ellin Carsta

"Did he say anything at all?"

"Just that I shouldn't speak about it to anyone. And I kept my promise. But now . . ." He shrugged. "I don't think it makes a difference now."

"Can you tell me the exact date of that exchange, Scribe?"

"Well, I'm not sure. I know that it was shortly before noon, because I was planning to eat something when he came in. But I can't remember the exact day."

"Could it have been the same day that the vicar was murdered?"

"That's right!" the scribe said excitedly. "Of course it was. Everybody at the palace was talking about the vicar's death that night and for days after. Terrible, just terrible."

"Now everything is starting to add up." Johannes exhaled loudly. "One more question, Scribe. Did Bernhard von Harvehorst show his face here after that day? Did he come here at all?"

"No, my lord. If memory serves, I saw him alive for the last time when he stormed out of here. In fact, that was my last encounter with him."

Johannes patted the scribe's shoulder. "You've helped me quite a bit, Scribe." Johannes stepped over the documents that were still scattered on the floor and went to the door.

"But your document about your full power of attorney, my lord? We haven't found it yet."

"That's not important anymore. Besides, I have a copy." With that, he left the scribe's office.

Chapter Twenty-Three

Madlen spent the next two days attending lectures at the university, walking back to the inn, spending time with her children, then going out again to her see her brother at his workshop. He wasn't in very good shape—he was getting drunk in the middle of the day, and he was sluggish and barely able to keep up with his carpentry work. Madlen didn't want the children to come with her because she didn't want them to see their uncle's reprehensible behavior. The second day, upon taking her leave, she gave Kilian a stern look and told him in no uncertain terms that they needed to talk. Then she left.

And then something else happened. Peter went missing. He and Elsbeth had had a dreadful quarrel, after which Peter had packed his bags, mounted his horse, and ridden away. Nobody had seen him since. Elsbeth thought that he might have ridden back to Worms. She was concerned about his welfare, but she was also furious—not only had he patronized a Heidelberg whorehouse, he'd also taken all their money, which they didn't discover until after he'd left. Fortunately, Madlen had sufficient means to pay for their accommodations.

The morning after Peter's departure, her old friend the sheriff of Heidelberg intercepted Madlen as she was about to leave for the university. "Madlen, God bless you!"

"God bless you, too, Sheriff."

"I know you're in a hurry so I'll make it quick. After the lecture, would you have time to accompany me to Trude von Fahrenholz's home? Her husband will be away at his office closing a big commercial transaction."

"How did you find that out?"

"Well, let's just say that the customer he's expecting might not be unknown to me." The sheriff grinned.

"You're a real character." Madlen laughed. "I'll meet you at your office after the lecture."

"Thank you. I wish you a very pleasant hour. God protect you!" With that he left, and Madlen rushed back into the inn to tell Agathe that she wouldn't be returning right after the lecture, that she and the sheriff would be paying a visit to another battered woman. Then she ran back to the university, arriving just in time for the lecture.

"In a hurry again?" Thomas asked.

"That's just the way it is when you have children," Madlen fibbed.

Thankfully, the doctor commenced his lecture, sparing her from further explanation.

"In the last few days, you've heard a lot about the teachings of Constantinus Africanus. What did you learn that would be effective in treating the ill?" Franz von Beyenburg clasped his hands behind his back and paced the length of the classroom. "Who among you has ever actually assisted the sick?" He looked at his students. Only Madlen hesitantly held up her hand.

"More courage, my dear. Hold up your hand confidently, with pride and decisiveness." He looked around one more time as if waiting to see a further show of hands. "You can lower your hand, Madlen.

What do you expect it will be like when you are a doctor and you approach a patient? What do you think you'll feel?"

"I'll feel good," said Maximilian, one of the students. "After all, I'll know that the patient will start to feel better soon."

"Do you really believe that?" The doctor seemed meditative. "Madlen, tell us, please, how would you describe your feelings when you arrive to care for a patient?"

Madlen was uncomfortable being the center of attention. She cleared her throat. "Worried, but also hopeful about being able to help. Doubt, fear. I don't know. I'm not a doctor."

"But you have helped more people than anyone else here in the lecture hall. Well, besides me, of course," he added, smiling. "I want to tell you why I asked this question. The medical profession is prestigious and often financially rewarding. So, are you sitting here in this lecture hall because of money and prestige, or do you really want to help?"

"What if it's both?" Hubertus von Megenberg asked. "Would that make me a bad doctor?" It sounded almost aggressive, like a challenge.

"Certainly not," Franz answered. "I would say that is an honest answer, though perhaps not so admirable. I ask you this question for one simple reason: to push you to think about why you are here."

"He seems rather contemplative today," Thomas whispered to Madlen.

"Money and healing are closely related," the doctor continued. "Without money, a sick patient would have a difficult time finding a doctor that could heal him. And without the patients' successful healing, the doctor wouldn't be able to earn any money, much less accumulate any substantial amount of wealth. Of course, he could demand payment before beginning his treatment. But soon word would get out that he took money from those he wasn't able to heal." He sighed. "But what am I talking about? Let's move on to medicinal herbs you're already familiar with and those you'll need to get acquainted with. In the interest of fairness, I ask you, Madlen, to contribute only if no one else knows the answer. Because unquestionably, when it comes to herbal remedies, you are the most knowledgeable of anyone here; you probably know even more than I do."

"Of course," Madlen said. Something didn't seem quite right with the doctor, so she decided to inquire about his well-being after the lecture.

The doctor quizzed the students on the more common medicinal herbs, which most were already familiar with. But when the doctor began to ask about more exotic herbs and their medicinal properties, the class fell silent. When no one responded, Franz asked Madlen for her answer.

◆　◆　◆

"That's all for today," he announced at the end of the lecture. "Madlen, thank you for sharing your extensive knowledge with us. God protect you all."

"Dr. Franz?" She approached the doctor as the other students left the hall.

"Yes, Madlen?"

"Do you have a moment?"

"Of course."

Thomas waved good-bye and Madlen waved back. Then she directed her attention to the doctor.

"Forgive me. I hope you won't think me too bold, but I would like to ask you if you're feeling all right. You seem very pensive today."

"You're quite the keen observer." He sighed. "This morning I had a meeting with the dean. Apparently, there have been some complaints about you being my guest, while other students have to pay tuition, and some of their families have also donated generously to the university."

Madlen smiled. "But, Doctor, why does it make you sad? We knew this day would come. And not only because of the money. I'd have had to go back to Cologne soon anyway."

"You're not disappointed?"

"No, not at all."

"Well, I am. Your presence enhances the lecture. Your knowledge is rich, and you are humble. How many of these students can say the same about themselves?" He sighed once again. "But you're right, we knew this day would come."

"I would like to thank you for everything you've done for me, Doctor, and for everything I have learned. I will never forget this experience."

"May I?" He opened his arms wide.

Madlen nodded and took a step closer to him.

He embraced her. "I wish you a life full of joy and happiness. You are a special woman, and it was my honor to share this time with you."

After a moment, Madlen stepped out of his embrace. "Nothing but the best for you, Doctor. I give you my eternal thanks. Farewell." She smiled even though she, too, was sad. Madlen touched his arm, turned around, and walked away. Her steps became faster and faster until finally she was running. She ran down the corridor, outside along the promenade and through the gardens, and quickly reached the edge of the university campus, tears running down her cheeks. She slowed. At the low wall where she'd eaten with Hyronimus Auerbach, she sat down. She took a deep breath and wiped away her tears. She'd known all too well this moment would come but had dreaded it nevertheless. Her time in Heidelberg had gone so fast, and now it was at an end.

Madlen thought of her children and husband. Veit would be so very happy to be going home. And Johannes—she would see him again soon. Everything was all right as it was. She wiped away the last of her tears and forbade herself to sink into a depression. Then she stood up, smoothed her dress, and made her way to the Golden Rooster.

She had almost reached the inn when she remembered her appointment with the sheriff. She immediately turned around and started back the way she'd come, angry and ashamed to have been so caught up in her own disappointment that she'd forgotten about Trude von Fahrenholz's plight. She was relieved when the sheriff cheerfully welcomed her and suggested that they immediately set out for Trude von Fahrenholz's residence.

◆ ◆ ◆

Like Magdalena Grossherr, Trude von Fahrenholz apologized and declined to receive them. It required substantial persuasion to convince her to let them in.

In contrast to Magdalena Grossherr's, Trude von Fahrenholz's injuries were obvious. Her right eye was bloodshot, her lips had a dark-red scab, and her throat was black and blue. And those were only the injuries that could be seen at a glance.

Their conversation didn't last long. She was quite subservient toward her husband, and she made it clear that she had absolutely no desire to file a report or take action of any kind against him. After a while, Madlen and the sheriff had to admit that she was a lost cause, that they hadn't made even the slightest impression on her. So after saying their farewells, they told her she could contact them any time if she changed her mind.

The sheriff walked Madlen to the Golden Rooster. She still hadn't told him about her time at the university coming to an end.

"Sheriff, I would like to share something with you," she began. "Today was my last day at the university. I'll be returning to Cologne soon."

"But . . ." The sheriff was taken aback. "But, I mean, so soon? There's still so much to do. So many women."

"I understand. But now that's your battle, Sheriff, not mine."

"Tomorrow is Albert Grossherr's hearing. Couldn't you at least wait until then? I imagine that Magdalena would greatly appreciate your support."

"There's no reason to rush our departure," Madlen said. "I'll stay until the hearing is over. We'll see what I can do for Magdalena."

"You're a truly great woman, Madlen. When we first encountered each other, the circumstances were quite difficult. You were but a young girl. But now things are different. Your husband is an extremely lucky man."

Madlen looked at the ground modestly. "I have to go now. God be with you, Sheriff."

"God be with you, Madlen Goldmann."

Madlen, deep in thought, entered the inn and climbed the stairs to her room. She was back earlier than she'd expected to be and therefore wasn't surprised that her family wasn't around. She fell into bed, clasped her hands behind her head, and gazed at the ceiling. She was sad but also relieved. She would be resuming her normal life soon. She would soon be able to stand by Johannes and . . . and what? Take care of the children, listen to Johannes talk about his exciting legal cases? Would that be enough? Was that all there was? She rolled onto her side and curled up in the fetal position. Why couldn't she be like other women, content with what she had? What was wrong with her? She turned onto her other side. There were women who were happy just to not get hit for a couple of days. And here she was, feeling bad because she had to go back to her big house and take care of her children. She felt like she should be ashamed of herself for such self-indulgent thoughts. But she wasn't.

She rolled onto her back and again clasped her hands behind her head. What had this short time in Heidelberg done to her? These musings couldn't continue. She'd known from the start that she had to enjoy every single minute and soak in every bit of knowledge because this was a once-in-a-lifetime opportunity. But she wanted more. Everything seemed so unjust, so incredibly wrong. She wondered how she could go on living without her studies. She sighed in frustration. It had been wrong to accept the doctor's offer to come to Heidelberg in the first place. Before, she'd been happy. She'd loved her life. Or had she? She simply didn't know what to think anymore.

The door opened with a jerk, giving Madlen such a start that she cried out. Cecilia laughed. "Mother! You're back!" She ran over, climbed up onto the bed, and cuddled up to her mother. Veit appeared at the door then ran over to his mother, too. "We didn't know you'd be here so soon."

"I've been waiting for you. Where did you go?"

"We went to the castle with Grandmother and Aunt Agathe. Grandmother told us lots of stories. Mother, I know exactly what I want to be when I grow up. I want to be a knight!"

"A knight?" Her children's cheerful chatter did her heart good. She was ashamed of the gloomy thoughts she'd just had. She sat up on the edge of the bed. "Oh, my sweethearts, I'm so happy to have you. And do you know what?"

"No, what?" Veit asked.

"We're going home the day after tomorrow."

"Really?" Veit opened his eyes wide then hugged his mother so enthusiastically that she fell back onto the bed again.

"What did you say?"

Madlen didn't know how long Agathe had been standing at the door. "Yes, Agathe, we're going home. We're going home at long last."

◆ ◆ ◆

At supper, Madlen explained to Elsbeth, Agathe, the children, and the servants that her time at the university was over and that they would start for home in two days. She instructed Ansgar to prepare their horses, then told Ursel and Gerald to prepare their belongings for the journey, and they promised to do so. Madlen vacillated between being excited to see Johannes again and being melancholy about leaving Heidelberg and the university behind.

"But you'll still spend a few days in Worms, right?" Agathe asked.

"Just a day or two, that's all. I'm sure Johannes would like to know what Leopold has accomplished with his father's business."

"I'm also anxious to see what's happened," Elsbeth said, a certain uneasiness evident in her voice.

"Why so sullen, Elsbeth?" Madlen put her hand on her mother-in-law's.

"Oh, I'm just a little nervous about what to expect when we get to Worms. Will Peter be there? And what will become of us if Leopold hasn't been able to resolve our business issues?"

Suddenly the inn's door crashed open and a sheriff's deputy raced in and began to frantically look around. He saw Madlen in the dining area and hurried over. "The sheriff sent me. You need to come with me right away!"

"Why?"

He looked around. All eyes were on him. "I can't tell you right now. Come on!"

Madlen and Agathe exchanged looks. "We'll stay with the children," Agathe assured her.

Madlen followed the deputy out. He ran ahead of her, and she gathered her skirts, making quite an effort to match his pace. "Where are you taking me?"

"To a patient. The sheriff is already there."

Questions whirled around in Madlen's head as she kept up with the deputy, running as fast as she could. Soon the streets became more and more familiar, and she realized that she'd walked through them with the sheriff earlier that day. When they finally arrived at Trude von Fahrenholz's house, Madlen felt a lump in her throat.

The door was open. In the entryway, two deputies stood to the right and two stood to the left of a man sitting on a chair, slumped over and cursing under his breath.

"Come upstairs," the deputy said. Madlen gathered her skirts and ran upstairs. When she got to the bedchamber, she found the sheriff standing over a body lying on the floor.

She let out a cry. "Hyronimus! Dr. Auerbach!" She dropped to her knees. His jacket was soaked with blood. "What happened?"

"That bastard stabbed him. Do something!"

"We must get his jacket off. Cut it off if you have to. I need clean cloths!" To the deputy she said, "Send two of your men to the university campus. Tell them to fetch the Master of Medicine, Dr. Franz von Beyenburg. Run! Run!"

Dr. Auerbach was unconscious, but Madlen could feel his faint heartbeat. The sheriff knelt down and cut off the doctor's jacket then tore open his shirt to expose his chest.

"My God!" Madlen gasped. She could see at first glance that he was bleeding from at least four stab wounds. One of the guards brought the cloths she'd demanded, and Madlen instructed him to get water. She rolled up a linen cloth as tightly as she could. "Press down firmly on the wound to keep him from losing any more blood."

The sheriff did so as Madlen rolled up more cloths and pressed them to the other wounds. The guard came back, carrying a bowl of water. Madlen took the bowl and dipped a rolled-up cloth in the water. "We need some distilled spirits and St. John's wort, if you have it."

The guard nodded and hurried out again. Madlen wrung out the cloth. "Now take the dry cloth off," she ordered the sheriff. He took off the bloodied cloth and applied the fresh moist one. "He's losing too much blood." Madlen could not contain her fear.

"Do something!" the sheriff demanded.

"I've never tended such serious wounds." She carefully lifted the cloth she'd been pressing to the doctor's chest. Was she mistaken, or was there a little less blood on it? When she realized that diminished blood loss could also mean something else, cold chills ran up and down her spine. "Can you feel his heartbeat?" she asked anxiously.

The sheriff faltered at first then put his head on the doctor's chest and listened with great concentration. He slowly lifted his head and shook it, gazing down at the lifeless body. Right then, Dr. von Beyenburg arrived. "Get back!" he yelled, pushing the sheriff aside.

"His heart stopped beating," Madlen said quietly.

Franz felt his colleague's neck for a pulse. Then he removed the cloths Madlen had used to compress the wounds and examined the doctor's injuries. "There's nothing anybody can do for him now." Franz searched Madlen's face. "I'm so sorry."

Madlen, tears running down her cheeks, looked at the sheriff, who was choking back his own tears. "He was such a fine man."

"That pig von Fahrenholz will pay with his pitiful life for what he's done!"

"How did this happen?" Franz asked.

The sheriff pressed his thumb and finger to the inner corners of his eyes to stop the tears from falling. "When I got here, he was still alive. Von Fahrenholz's servant fetched the police, who then alerted me of the situation. The doctor had visited Trude von Fahrenholz to try to convince her to file a complaint against her husband. During the visit, the bastard came home and tried to throw the doctor out. They got in a heated argument. When Trude von Fahrenholz implored her husband to leave the doctor be, he gave her such a violent blow that her head struck that table over there." He pointed, and for the first time Madlen and Franz noticed the woman's lifeless body lying on the floor in the corner of the bedchamber. Franz rose and started toward the body, but the sheriff held him back. "She's dead. She was already dead when I arrived. The doctor told me that von Fahrenholz pulled out a knife and stabbed him when he realized his wife was dead. Those were the last words the doctor said to me."

Madlen continued to gaze at the dead doctor.

"Come on, Madlen," Franz said, holding out his hand to her.

The sheriff looked at Hyronimus Auerbach. His grief made him look pale and drawn. He took a step over to the body, bent down, and gently touched the dead man's cheek. "Adieu, my friend. The memory of your righteousness and courage will remind me to do the right thing. Fare thee well."

Madlen was blinded by a torrent of tears. Franz pulled her into his arms and held her close.

The sheriff stepped past them. "Put that swine into the dungeon," he snapped, looking down at Trude von Fahrenholz's husband.

"I was just defending myself," the man mumbled, but the sheriff had already walked past him.

"Get him out of here! Get that bastard out of my sight, or he won't be needing a judge."

Madlen and Franz released their embrace, and Madlen gazed at the dead Dr. Auerbach one last time. His face seemed relaxed now, even peaceful. "Adieu, Doctor. May God grant your soul peace." She kissed her fingertips and touched them to his forehead. Then she and Franz von Beyenburg left the room.

◆ ◆ ◆

That night, whenever she closed her eyes she saw an image of the dead doctor. Now all she wanted was to get away from Heidelberg and go home. She could hardly wait to be back in Johannes's strong arms, to lead a normal life, one without all the disturbances of recent days. She asked herself over and over again whether she shared part of the blame for the doctor's death because she had spoken with these women. When morning finally broke, she was relieved, though tired and drained. She wanted to seize the day by first going to the university to say good-bye to Thomas then on to her brother's workshop to say farewell. She set off right after breakfast. She had been waiting on campus for just a few moments when she saw Thomas coming down the street.

"God bless you!" He squinted in the sunlight and kept walking, obviously expecting that she'd be going to the lecture hall, too. When Madlen didn't follow him, he stopped. "What is it?"

"I would like to say good-bye," she said.

"But I don't understand . . ."

"Yesterday was my last day. I'll be leaving Heidelberg tomorrow. But I didn't want to go without saying farewell."

"So that's why the Master of Medicine was acting so peculiar yesterday, wasn't it?"

Madlen nodded. "From the very beginning, you treated me well, and I want to thank you for that. You will undoubtedly become an outstanding doctor, a man who can really help people."

"I'll miss you, Madlen. Who but a lucky few can claim to have studied with a woman?"

"I wish you a long and happy life, Thomas."

"I wish the same to you." He bowed. "May God protect you and yours. Best of luck, Madlen!"

She was tempted to embrace him, but decided instead to simply nod. She turned on her heel and went on her way, tears running down her face. She was dismayed by how close she'd come to breaking down during their farewell.

She wasn't sure if she'd find Kilian in his workshop, and she dreaded the thought of having to go to his cottage and risk facing Irma again. To her amazement, she heard sounds coming from the workshop as she approached. She was quite relieved as she knocked on the door then entered. Her brother was sanding a piece of wood.

"Kilian?"

He flinched, startled. "Madlen?" He put the piece of wood aside and clapped the dust off his hands. "What are you doing here?"

"I wanted to say good-bye. We're leaving tomorrow."

"I heard about that doctor. You knew him well, didn't you?"

"How did you hear about that?"

"What? The fact that he's dead or that you knew him well?"

"That I knew him well."

"Well, listen, this is Heidelberg. Do you really believe that nobody knew what you, the doctor, and the sheriff were up to? What was that all about?"

Madlen was confused. Had the deputies gossiped about the meeting in the sheriff's office? She banished the thought from her mind. It didn't do any good to worry about that now.

"I just wanted to say farewell, Brother."

Kilian took a step closer and took her in his arms. "I've been drinking less. Really. I don't want to turn out like our father."

"I'm happy to hear that. You're a good person, Kilian, with a lot to give. There is still time to turn things around. Please take care of yourself."

"Don't worry, I will. And you take care of yourself, too. Although I certainly don't need to worry about you." He gazed at her, his eyes glowing. "I'm so proud of you, you know that? One of these days, I'll be able to live my dream, too. Who knows?"

"May God be with you, Kilian."

"The Lord protect you, Madlen."

She left the workshop with a vague feeling that things wouldn't end well for her brother. But she also knew that it wasn't in her power to change him. For a split second she considered forcing herself to say good-bye to Irma but decided against it. She didn't need any more traumatic experiences after all she'd just been through. She wanted to be in good spirits when she went on her way. So she left the workshop and cottage behind and strolled back to the inn.

She couldn't put her brother's words out of her mind. Apparently, it was fairly well known that she had been working with the sheriff and the late doctor. She didn't know why, but just the thought that people knew about this worried her. But she was relieved when she reached the inn, and she could hardly wait to leave for Worms. She hoped her last day in Heidelberg would go by quickly.

Chapter Twenty-Four

Johannes still wasn't steady on his feet. His head injury was severe enough to cause his vision to blur from time to time.

As soon as Johannes had discovered how the vicar general had orchestrated the murders, he'd sent Linhardt to the sheriff with an urgent request to come to the palace. The sheriff agreed, suspecting why the lawyer wanted to talk to him. He was rather surprised when Johannes explained that, although he knew the sheriff had arranged the robbery of the scribe's office, it didn't disturb him in the least. Johannes added that the sheriff had actually done him a favor.

"You're . . . grateful?" the sheriff of Cologne said.

"Indeed. Without the robbery, I never would have stumbled upon the documents that finally cleared everything up for me."

Johannes told the sheriff that the vicar general himself had prepared and signed documents that would have granted the fiefs in question to some noblemen living in the Duchy of Cleves. The names of these noblemen had caught Johannes's eye—they were the vicar general's nephews. But in accordance with recent treaty negotiations with the House of von der Marck, the possession of the fiefs had been promised to certain citizens of Cologne. A few days hence, when the official court was back in session, the vicar general would have confirmed these documents Johannes had discovered, making them virtually incontestable.

"So, Bernhard von Harvehorst stumbled upon these papers?"

"Yes. The scribe confirmed that. The clergyman was actually looking for a totally different fief record, one that had nothing to do with this situation."

"And that's when von Harvehorst turned to Vicar Bartholomäus?"

"Correct. And that's when Bartholomäus challenged the vicar general. He might have wanted to give him the opportunity to confess and turn himself in to the archbishop. But the vicar general poisoned Bartholomäus instead."

"Who do you think did the actual poisoning?"

"I'm guessing it was Christopeit. From what I heard, he'd actually been in the service of the vicar general for many years. It wouldn't surprise me to find out that he was loyal to the bitter end."

"But the vicar general still had him killed?"

"He was a witness. Another possibility is that the vicar general poisoned Bartholomäus, making Christopeit an involuntary witness. There's no way to find out what really happened unless the vicar general confesses, which I doubt he will."

"And Bernhard von Harvehorst?" the sheriff asked.

"He was probably killed the same evening as Bartholomäus. The doctor could only confirm that he'd been dead for a while. For exactly how long, he couldn't say."

"And then the vicar general eliminated the housekeeper?"

Johannes nodded. "He eliminated anyone who got in his way." The attorney took a sip of water, trying to alleviate the recurring dizziness. Then he pulled himself together and told the sheriff everything he knew, including the events involving Wentzel.

"Now, let's deal with this alleged witness, the one who supposedly saw me murder Wentzel," Johannes said. "I have no reason to lie to you."

"If you committed the murder and want to escape punishment, you do."

"Did the doctor take another look at Wentzel's body before it was buried?"

"Yes. How did you know?"

"Well? Did the deceased have a bump on the back of his head or not?"

"He did," the sheriff growled. "That fact made me seriously doubt the witness's story, even before you called this meeting."

"Tomorrow I'll send a message to the archbishop to inform him of recent events."

"Are you going to take me to task for the missing document?"

"No, not unless you still plan to arrest me if I leave the palace."

"Try it and we'll see." The sheriff guffawed, then waved his hand dismissively. "I'm joking, Counselor. I believe your story if for no other reason than that it's too absurd to have been dreamed up."

"About the reason I asked you here . . ."

"Yes?"

"I would like to entrust the vicar general to your care. Lock him up and guard him well. He couldn't possibly have committed these crimes all by himself. In fact, I believe he didn't have to so much as lift a finger. Rest assured that the people in his employ will do everything in their power to free him."

"I'm honored to be entrusted with this task. And what will you do?"

"As soon as my message is on its way to Friedrich, I'll pack my bags and leave for Heidelberg to find my family. First, I'll stop in Worms, because they might have already returned to my parents' house."

"You don't know where your family is?"

Johannes smiled. "You don't know my wife. Trust me, it's a long story."

"For as long as I can remember, the city and the church have never been on the same side here in Cologne," the sheriff said. "The archbishop's decision to give you full power in his absence may very well have been a wise one."

"You are a man of action and exactly what Cologne needs. It doesn't matter under whose name you seek justice."

The sheriff stood up. "I've underestimated you, Counselor. Now, you should get some rest because you look like you've seen better days. God protect you on your way to Heidelberg or Worms or wherever your wife may be."

"Farewell, Sheriff. You'd do well to watch the vicar general closely. I'm sure Friedrich will know what to do with that murderous traitor."

"You can count on me." With that, the sheriff left. Johannes's head felt like it was going to explode, and he was glad to be able to finally lie down again. He was also relieved that the murder investigation was finally over.

◆ ◆ ◆

Madlen couldn't wait to find out how Albert Grossherr had reacted to his wife's accusation. It was noon when the sheriff knocked on her chamber door, where Madlen had been waiting with Agathe and the children. She opened the door immediately. She was startled to see the sheriff looking so pale and wan. "Greetings, Sheriff. Please come in."

"God bless you." He bowed then smiled at the children and Agathe. "Madlen, may I ask you to come with me one last time? It won't take long."

"Go ahead, Mother," Veit said cheerfully. He'd been in a good mood since hearing the news that they'd be homeward bound soon.

"Yes, of course I'll come." Madlen kissed Veit and Cecilia and traded looks with Agathe. Then she followed the sheriff out. On the street in front of the Golden Rooster stood a deputy with a woman who might have been a good ten years older than Madlen. They walked over to the sheriff and Madlen.

"Madlen, may I introduce you to Lady Wulfhild? Lady Wulfhild works for the city of Heidelberg. She will go with Deputy Walter every three days to the Grossherr residence to check on Magdalena's well-being."

Madlen was quite relieved. The sheriff had succeeded in convincing the council members to provide protection for abused women. "So happy to meet you, Lady Wulfhild."

"The honor is all mine," the woman answered as she curtsied. "You set a fine example for the women of Heidelberg. It's such a privilege to meet you. And please feel free to call me Katherina. And you, too, Sheriff."

Madlen felt unworthy of such high praise, so she simply acknowledged her with a smile.

"Madlen, would you accompany us to the Grossherr residence to discuss with Magdalena what to expect in the future and to instruct Katherina on how to examine women for injuries?"

"My pleasure, Sheriff."

"Let's go."

The four of them set off, Madlen walking next to the sheriff. "How did Albert Grossherr react?" she whispered.

For the first time that day, the sheriff's face lit up with a big grin. "Not particularly well. At first he denied everything, which was to be expected. But that changed when old Sigmund the spice merchant took the floor."

"What did he say?"

"He said that basically everybody in Heidelberg knows that Albert Grossherr beats his wife black and blue. That it was indisputable, despicable, and that there had been no consequences. You know, Madlen, he spoke in such a casual, almost indifferent, way. He went on to say that, up to this point, nobody had been willing or able to change this type of thing. But times have changed, and Lord Grossherr would have to accept that, like it or not. And then the spice merchant made a brilliant tactical maneuver."

"What was it?"

"Well, we had already told Lord Grossherr that he would be getting a visit every three days to guarantee that the beatings had ceased. But then the spice merchant did one better. He said that if the deputy discovered Magdalena had even the slightest of injuries, Grossherr would not only be immediately arrested but all of his business, goods, and property would be put under the control of the city council, effective immediately, after which he wouldn't have a penny to his name." The sheriff smiled from ear to ear, and Madlen laughed out loud.

"Could that actually happen?"

The sheriff shrugged. "I don't know. I suppose it could, if a resolution were passed, though it undoubtedly wouldn't be so easy. As expected, Albert Grossherr objected adamantly to the merchant's proposed plan, but his complaints fell on deaf ears. And the merchant added that it should be quite easy for a big fellow like Lord Grossherr to keep his wife out of harm's way, therefore he had no reason to fear these or any other consequences. After that, the man was at a loss for words."

Madlen laughed again, first softly, then with greater gusto. "At least we can know that money will always be sacred to these otherwise soulless men."

"I was astonished by how united we all were. I daresay, it gave me some hope again."

"It sounds like this is going to work out," Madlen said, relieved and feeling optimistic about Magdalena's situation.

◆　◆　◆

The little group reached Magdalena's home, where they could hear loud shouting coming from inside. The sheriff pounded on the door. "Open up! The sheriff of Heidelberg demands admittance!"

The voices fell silent. For a moment, nothing more could be heard.

"Open up immediately, or we'll kick down this door."

"I'm coming. Have a little patience!" Albert Grossherr called.

"So, we meet again so soon," the sheriff said after the man had opened the door.

"What can I do for you?"

"Spare me the niceties," the sheriff grumbled. "Step away from the door so we can speak to your wife."

"And may I ask what business you have with her?"

"That's enough." Without warning, the sheriff lunged forward. The door banged against the inside wall, and Albert Grossherr staggered back a step.

"Where is she?"

"How dare you!"

"Not another word." The sheriff grabbed Albert Grossherr's collar. "You can shove your indignation elsewhere. Have you done something to her? If you have, we'll arrest you right now and you can take one last look at your beautiful house before it goes to the highest bidder."

"I'm here," a soft voice emanated from above. The sheriff looked up and saw Magdalena Grossherr standing at the balustrade.

"Has he done something to you?" Madlen called, gazing up at Magdalena. "You can tell us. If he has, he'll be arrested on the spot."

Magdalena shook her head. "Not today. But he did scold me for putting him in this position."

"Shut up, you miserable slut."

The sheriff gave the man a shake. "I almost regret that you didn't beat you wife again. What a pleasure it would be for me to take you to the dungeon to join all the other riffraff. Some of those men might

295

even enjoy you." He glared at the nobleman, and for the first time his words seemed to have achieved their intended effect.

"I've done nothing to her, I swear. Yes, I was furious, and yes, I yelled at her. But I didn't raise one finger against her."

"That's true," Magdalena confirmed.

"Well, good," Madlen said, motioning for Katherina to follow her up the stairs. "Let's go to your bedchamber. But first, allow me to introduce you to Lady Katherina Wulfhild. She'll be dropping by every three days to examine you for injuries." From the landing, she looked down at Magdalena's husband and found her voice. "Please take care that you don't fall from carelessness or hurt yourself in any other way. The city officials' instructions are unambiguous: your husband will be arrested immediately and all his property will be confiscated."

Magdalena lifted her head. Evidently her husband hadn't informed her of these additional penalties he'd incur for abusing her. "He would lose everything if he hit me again?"

"Everything. Gone."

"Then what would become of me?"

"You would be cared for in the manner to which you have become accustomed," Madlen said, although she hadn't discussed this with the sheriff. But she took a kind of perverse pleasure knowing that Albert Grossherr thought he would be thrown in the dungeon while his wife would live in comfort.

"May I ask you a question?"

"Of course."

"What if he hits me again, but it doesn't leave any bruises or the like, so I can't prove it?"

Madlen looked down at the sheriff. "Did you hear that? What happens in that case?"

"Well, we would trust your word, Lady Grossherr. It would be the same as if you'd been bruised."

"So that means she only has to claim that I hit her and I would be arrested?" Albert snorted.

"You're a quick learner. So you see, it's in everybody's interest that you're as nice as possible to your wife." The sheriff bared his teeth then finally let him go. Madlen signaled to Magdalena to go with her and Katherina to the bedchamber. They shut the door behind them.

"Should I undress?" Magdalena asked.

Madlen smiled. "Actually, that won't be necessary. Your word is enough to have him arrested. But I would like to show Katherina what to look for if she suspects you've been abused or violated in any way."

Madlen pointed out numerous older injuries, even those that made Magdalena blush and bow her head bashfully. Katherina seemed to be listening carefully, and she asked pertinent questions.

"Thank you," Katherina said when they had finished. She turned to Madlen. "May I say that I would love to be like you?"

"I believe most women would like to be like her," Magdalena said.

Madlen felt flattered but a little embarrassed, too. "Be brave! I knew a woman who lost everything she loved. Her name was Clara. She once told me that a person who loses her courage abandons all hope. We must never quit, because the Lord will hold our hands and lead us through our darkest hours. We have to endure and hold our ground, and in the end, we'll reign victorious."

"I wish that you weren't going," Katherina said.

"You're going?" Magdalena asked.

"Yes, I have to go back to Cologne."

"But how will I go on without you?" Magdalena asked, a trace of desperation in her voice.

"Katherina will be here for you. And you'll soon come to realize that you do indeed have power." Madlen grasped Magdalena's upper arms, but when she saw her wince—her arms were still tender and bruised—Madlen reduced the pressure and let her hands rest softly on them. "Look me in the eyes, Magdalena, and let me repeat what I just said: the Lord holds our hands as He leads us through our darkest hours. I, too, have experienced dark hours. And those dark hours made me stronger than I would have ever been without them. Now, it's up to you—you have the power. A single word from you would be enough to have your husband arrested. All I ask of you is that you do not abuse this power. You have a big task ahead of you."

"Me? What task?"

"There are many women like you in Heidelberg, women who need help. The sheriff and the brave men of the city council are on your side. They'll support you. You must have faith. You must have courage! Be an inspiration to those who suffer the same violence that you have. Lead them!"

Magdalena gasped. "I can't do that."

"Oh, yes, you can." Madlen let her arms drop. "Both of you can help these women. They have no one but you. And once freed from the clutches of abuse, they will join you to protect and help others. Soon, no husband will dare lift a hand against his wife." Madlen took a deep breath. "I've said everything I wanted to say, so I'll go. But let my words rings in your ears, let them become a song that carries you through your darkest days." She embraced Katherina then Magdalena. "May God protect you!" With that, Madlen left the bedchamber. As she went downstairs and headed out the front door, she heard both of the women call down, "May God protect you!" But she didn't turn around. In that instant, she felt that she'd accomplished something truly extraordinary.

◆ ◆ ◆

Johannes took the fastest horse he could find in Cologne. Linhardt and Georg accompanied him, particularly since Johannes hadn't fully recovered his health, and they insisted on stopping to rest frequently. Johannes wouldn't have stopped had he ridden alone, and he appreciated the good it did him.

He thought about Madlen and the children, his parents, his father's business. Who might he find when he arrived in Worms? Probably Leopold would be the only one there, with his wife, children, and parents still in Heidelberg. Had Madlen received the message he'd sent? Presumably not. He regretted the harsh tone of his dispatch. He knew how passionate Madlen was about helping and healing. It wasn't easy for him, but he'd finally admitted to himself that he'd written the letter out of jealousy. But he couldn't do anything about it now. He just hoped his wife wouldn't be too angry.

He longed for her with a burning desire. To hold her again in his arms at long last would be divine. He missed her sweet smell, the touch of her skin, their tender affections. Since they'd received the news of his father's illness from Agathe, they'd shared only one passionate night together. And he missed that. In all the years since their marriage, he'd never once betrayed her, or even thought about another woman. He hadn't been a ladies' man before they'd met, though he had been involved with a few women here and there, without ever getting close to making any promises. But when he met Madlen, he instantly realized that this was the woman he wanted to spend the rest of his life with. And he'd felt the same way every day since.

He jabbed his heels into his horse's flanks, and Linhardt and Georg urged on their own mounts to keep up. They galloped until their horses began to lather, then stopped for a rest. They decided to find a place at the nearest inn. The next day, they left before dawn for Worms.

◆　◆　◆

"Come here." The sheriff of Heidelberg held out his arms. Madlen took a step forward and embraced him warmly.

"I'll miss you, Sheriff."

"I'll miss you and so will all of Heidelberg. Let's not let years go by until we see each other again."

Madlen was sad at the thought that it would probably turn out exactly like that. "Of course not," she fibbed. She walked over to her horse. "May God protect you and allow your courageous undertaking to flourish!"

"Thank you. I couldn't have done it without your help." He sighed. "In few days, the doctor will be buried."

"His spirit goes on. The doctor will be forever in our hearts."

"Let me go now before I break down completely." The great man's eyes welled up with tears. He helped Madlen mount her horse. "May God protect you and your loved ones, Madlen Goldmann!"

She looked at him one last time with deep affection and admiration. Then she rode off, and the others followed.

After they crossed over the Neckar Bridge, Agathe, with little Cecilia sitting in front of her, rode her horse up to Madlen's. "Kilian didn't come to see you off."

"No. And I didn't expect him to."

"Sad, isn't it?"

"A little. But he leads his life and I lead mine, exactly like Father and you."

"But that's different."

"What do you mean? Did Father and you have a falling-out?"

Agathe thought about it, choosing her words carefully. "The women you helped in Heidelberg . . ."

"Yes?"

"I know how they feel."

Madlen turned her head, eyes wide. "Don't tell me that my father . . ."

"No. Not him. Five of his friends. And he didn't lift a finger to help me," Agathe said dispassionately, as though she was simply telling a tale.

"I had no idea, Agathe. I'm so sorry."

"Nobody knew, not even my husband. I wonder why now I can speak so easily about this tragic incident that happened thirty-five years ago. But I'll never forget it, you know? You can never forget something like that."

"I don't understand something," Cecilia said, who had been following the conversation. "Why didn't your brother help you?"

"It is a heavy burden to carry, little one," Agathe answered as she snuggled up to the little girl.

"What kind of burden?"

"An albatross. Like wearing a giant dead seabird around his neck, day in and day out, an eternal reminder of his transgressions."

"Oh, that wasn't nice of him. But you should forgive him because, after all, he is your brother."

Agathe kissed Cecilia's head, and the women rode on side by side. Madlen would never have guessed that the cause of the rift between the siblings had been so terrible. Five men, their father's friends . . . how Agathe must have suffered! Cecilia's eyelids were fluttering; Madlen waited to pick up the conversation until her daughter was asleep. "Is that why you didn't have any children?"

Agathe pressed her lips together and nodded. "There was too much damage." She looked down at Cecilia.

"She's asleep," Madlen said.

"I wasn't even fifteen years old. They were drunk, and they set a trap for me. I should have known. They'd always stared lustfully at me when they picked up Jerg to go on one of their drinking binges. They were all a bunch of brutes, just like Jerg. They treated me like an animal, and I kept on turning around and kicking them away."

"And my father?"

"He was in the barn. I called out to him but he stayed away, tossing back one beer after another. Shortly before one of them threw me to the ground, our eyes met. At that instant, I knew my brother wasn't going to help me. I also knew that no one would rescue me."

Madlen did her best to choke back her tears. "I'm so sorry for all that you suffered."

Agathe's lip twitched.

"What is it? Why on earth are you smiling?"

"Now this same man has a daughter who has declared war against these vile men, a daughter who helps women fight back." She laughed, just a little at first, then bitterly, then loudly.

Madlen felt sick. Had Agathe lost her mind? She waited until her aunt calmed down.

"Don't you think that's incredible?" Agathe said finally. "You know, I left all of that behind me years ago. And now I can witness what a strong, brave woman his daughter, my niece, has become. I now have the honor to watch her bring these dogs down. The Lord is good to let me live long enough to bear witness."

"Even so, I wish you hadn't suffered so."

"Me, too. But we can't change the past. Madlen, your activities in Heidelberg got me thinking."

"What do you mean?"

"Would it be all right with you if I accompany you to Cologne to discuss something with your husband? He's legal counsel for the archbishop. And who would be more suitable to support such an endeavor?"

"But there are already penalties for rape and other kinds of violence in the home."

"But punishment virtually never comes to pass, because women are too afraid to report the abuse. You've shown me that a woman has to be strong in order to make other women strong. And because of you, I would like to be one of those women."

Madlen looked at her with gratitude. "No one has ever said anything so wonderful to me."

They rode on together without another word. They took only a short break at noon in order to reach Worms before dusk. They had barely entered the city when its gates were closed behind them. Everyone breathed a sigh of relief.

Agathe handed Cecilia over to Elsbeth, and the little girl snuggled up to her grandmother on her horse. Then Agathe bade the group farewell and rode off to her house, and the rest of them rode on to the Goldmann residence. Helene was overjoyed to see her mistress and the others again.

"Is my husband here?" Elsbeth immediately asked when Leopold stepped out of the office.

"You're back. A hearty welcome home. And to answer your question: no. He's not with you?"

Elsbeth shook her head.

"You look rather pleased, Leopold," Madlen said in an attempt to change the subject. She looked between Leopold and Helene.

"You'll undoubtedly be, too," Helene announced. "Would you like to see the office? Leopold has worked wonders."

Madlen noticed that Helene addressed Leopold by his first name. When she noticed the lovesick look on the maid's face, Madlen put it all together.

"I would love to see the office," Elsbeth said. "Please, show me everything." She pushed her fear of what may have happened to her husband aside. Then her fear turned into anger. He'd probably squandered what little money he had left on alcohol or whores.

"I'm going to put the children to bed. They are utterly exhausted," Madlen announced. She picked up Cecilia and took Veit's hand. He padded next to her, half-asleep, up the stairs. She was relieved to be back at her in-laws' house and felt as though a heavy burden had been lifted from her shoulders.

When she came down later, she found Leopold and Elsbeth in the office. Helene was in the kitchen preparing the evening meal.

"I'm never going to let you go back to Cologne," Elsbeth declared. "You are a genius in the art of business administration."

"I'm happy you are satisfied with the numbers. It will of course be my pleasure to stay a while longer to further advance your family's financial conditions. But that's not for me to decide."

"I would like to be quite frank with you. I don't know when or even if my husband will return to Worms. If my son could obtain the archbishop's approval, would you remain here?"

Leopold lifted his hands helplessly. "When the archbishop so orders, I will obey." He smiled. "I say this from the bottom of my heart: I would be delighted to stay."

Madlen smiled; Helene, she theorized, was an important part of Leopold's desire to call Worms his home.

They all ate together that evening. In an unusual gesture, Elsbeth asked Helene, Ursel, Gerald, and the rest of the servants to join them. They accepted the invitation with pleasure, though Ursel and Gerald were the first to excuse themselves from the table. Madlen wondered how long it would be before they revealed their relationship to her. But this didn't really bother her. She was just thankful they'd made it to Worms without incident and hoped their trip two days hence to Cologne would be as uneventful.

◆ ◆ ◆

Johannes was thrilled to set his feet on solid ground. He and the guards had ridden their horses like madmen, and Johannes was bone-tired. Not only did his head feel as if it would explode any second, every single bone in his body ached.

"Excuse me, my lord." A young man rode up. "Is this the Goldmann residence? I have a message from Cologne for a certain Lady Madlen Goldmann."

"Yes, you're in the right place."

"I've come from Heidelberg," the messenger explained. "Someone there told me that I just missed her and that she was on her way to Worms."

"Give me the message. I'm going in right now. I'll make sure my wife gets it."

"Thank you, my lord." The messenger handed him a leather cylinder, which Johannes immediately recognized as the one he'd sent earlier. He smiled in spite of himself.

"Here. This is for you." He pulled out a coin.

"Thank you, my lord! That's quite generous of you."

"You fulfilled your duty well," Johannes said, tucking the leather cylinder into his coat.

"A good day to you, my lord." The messenger bowed, adjusted his saddle, then set off.

"I'll send for the servant," Johannes said to his companions.

Linhardt and Georg nodded. They had withstood the rigors of the hard ride much better than Johannes had, and they didn't seem the least bit tired. The attorney climbed up the front stairs and knocked on the door.

"I'm coming!"

Johannes's heart beat faster upon hearing his wife's voice. Madlen opened the door, and her eyes went wide with surprise. "Johannes!" she cried and lunged at him with such vigor that he almost lost his balance.

"Father!" Veit and Cecilia, who'd come downstairs with their mother, charged toward him and fell into his embrace. Johannes picked up Veit, and Madlen did the same with Cecilia. The little family hugged each other tight.

"At long last, we're together again!" Johannes choked back tears of joy as he held his loved ones close. He kissed Veit and Cecilia on the cheek then gave Madlen a longer kiss on the lips. "Never leave me for such a long time ever again!"

"Never again," Madlen assured him with all her heart, tears of joy running down her face. "Never again."

About the Author

Born in 1970, Ellin Carsta is a successful German author who publishes under various pseudonyms. She is married with three children, ages twenty, eighteen, and sixteen. Although writing books is her passion, she also enjoys sports, especially jogging and cross-training. *The Master of Medicine* is the second book in her Secret Healer series.

About the Translator

Terry Laster is the mother of four grown sons. She's also a musician, singer, and former music teacher who sang, studied, and worked in Germany for many years. Terry is also a writer, currently working on her long-overdue historical novel. She currently lives in Soda Springs, California, with her tiny Chihuahua named Angel, who during the winter season can be seen running alongside Terry as she skis on the dog-friendly trails of the Royal Gorge Cross Country Ski Resort.

Printed in Great Britain
by Amazon